A Curse of Shadows

Wolves of Lunara - Book One

USA TODAY BESTSELLING AUTHOR

Heather Renee

CONTENTS

Cave
Alklo Falls
Selaris
Lu
WOLVES OF
LUNARA

Portal Cave
Lunara Academy
Venaris
The Bridge

CHAPTER ONE

ISLA

I'm quite certain something has possessed me. That must be it, because I can't think of any other reason why I just hiked a mountain...for fun. Not because someone was chasing me up the steep incline, with its plethora of switchbacks that are numbered with a baffling disregard for accuracy, but because I *chose* to.

Yet I can't lie. The panoramic glory unfurling from the top of Multnomah Falls is nothing short of incredible. The cascade of water rushes over the edge with a ferocity that almost looks intriguing—another reason I believe someone's taken control of me—and makes my heart soar.

Looking up, the sky is a bright azure without a cloud in sight, and a steady breeze cools my heated skin. My gaze wanders, following the expansive Columbia River before me, and I see the fishermen out on their boats with the small whitecaps around them, reminding me just how fierce the wind can get around here.

The last thought is enough to have me stepping back from the rail at the trail's end and returning my attention to the water behind me. Going back up the steps, I cross over a few fallen trees and take a seat on a log. The creek that feeds the falls is calm, as if the deadly drop only fifty feet ahead isn't anything to be worried about.

Minutes tick by as I watch the tranquil waters, a surprisingly welcome reprieve from the vibrant mayhem of the big city I've fallen in love with. Living in Portland, Oregon isn't for everyone, but the chaos of the people, the mazes of traffic, the whimsical weather, and everything in between—they've always appealed to me. One thing I've never taken to that most do around here is all the opportunities for outdoor activities we're surrounded by in our city. At least until today.

Waking up before dawn, I sat up in bed and an inexplicable yearning took over, encouraging me to escape the confines of my apartment. Even now that I've accomplished my task, I still don't understand why I came here. A part of me hopes that this doesn't happen again, but I also don't hate that after twenty-five years of city living, I've finally hiked Multnomah Falls.

A smile graces my face as that same urge comes back, this time telling me it's time to head back to my car. Maybe whatever demon possessing me has finally had enough—kidding. Mostly.

Portland has some weird happenings in it, and plenty of supernatural movies have been filmed here, but that's nothing more than fiction.

It's still early, the sun having just begun rising in the sky as I started my hike, which means I'm the only one heading down now. Plenty of others are making their way up, smiles on their faces and seemingly eager for the torment that the sharp ascent promises.

I shake my head as I'm practically forced to jog down the mountain. Never again will I see this trail. I'll light some sage when I get home and everything will go back to normal.

There's a twinge in my chest, one I've been ignoring for weeks now. My life hasn't been *normal* for over a month. Not since my best friend was promoted at work and transferred to Seattle for her new role. She's only a few hours' drive away, and we both promised to visit, but that's yet to happen.

While I love my city life, even being surrounded by a couple million people doesn't take away the pain of living without one's soul sister.

For as long as I can remember, Elodee has been by my side. We both grew up in the foster system, and for a lot of those years, our only saving grace was having each other. Until she moved, we'd never spent more than a few nights apart.

To say living alone and doing everything myself this last month has been an adjustment would be an understatement.

I shake off the negativity. I really am happy for her. So much so that I've been looking at making my own job change—maybe something different from the banking job I've had for the last few years—so we can live in Seattle together, even if that feels a little too codependent. I know Elodee would love to have me there, but I also know that I should be okay on my own. At least, that's what I keep telling myself whenever I fail to apply for new jobs that could be perfect for me.

Thirty minutes later, I walk under the freeway to get to the parking lot that's located right between the north and south lanes of the interstate. Not sure who had that bright idea, but it doesn't much matter. It's time to get home.

Getting to my car, I unlock the driver's door of my white two-door Honda, or Susie, as I like to call her. She was the first big purchase I made as an adult and while she's a bit rusty, I love her all the same. Plus, it's not like I actually drive much. I probably spend more on paying for my parking spot at the apartment complex than she's worth, but I don't care.

Now to navigate my way out of this place. I drive toward the interstate, patting the dashboard. "All right, Susie. I know you don't like to go fast, but let's hurry and get home, okay?"

I swear the engine groans in response, but that doesn't stop me from pressing my foot on the accelerator so that I'm not a total hindrance while merging with the traffic.

"Oh, you've got to be shitting me." Now, it's my turn to groan. I don't know how I read the signs wrong, but I suddenly find myself going east on the interstate when I should be heading west.

A trucker speeds past me, honking and making me jump in my seat. "Yeah, dude. I know she's slow, but she's a city car."

I've never been out this far on the freeway by myself. Even as an adult, I don't like to get lost. My knuckles turn white from gripping the steering wheel so tightly, and my breathing feels too rapid as I try to pay better attention to the exits. I need to find one that will allow me to turn around, but I'm so freaked out that I miss the first couple.

Taking some deep breaths, I take the next offramp, called 'Bridge of the Gods.'

That makes me snort. "So much for thinking there's nothing supernatural out here."

One turn after another, and... "No, no, no. What is wrong with me?"

I'm somehow in a line for a tollbooth to go over that damn bridge instead of getting back on the interstate. This is why I never leave the city. One-way streets and roundabouts are less stressful than this crap.

I get to the window, doing my best not to cry as she says, "Scan your card."

"I'm really sorry," I reply with a sweet smile. "I made a wrong turn and—"

The hasty attendant cuts me off with glowering, brown eyes. "You're blocking traffic, ma'am. Pay the toll. There's no need to be difficult."

"I wasn't trying to be."

Before I can say anything, she shoves the card scanner toward my face.

Maybe I should have just stayed on top of the mountain.

I grab my debit card from my purse and grudgingly pay the stupid toll. She doesn't even thank me, just ushers me along toward the ginormous bridge.

I'm doing okay until the pavement turns into what looks like a steel grate for a road and my car begins to rattle, vibrating my body and making my teeth chatter. "Don't you dare break down on this bridge, Susie. I will send you to the scrapyard."

Hovering over my steering wheel, I pull down my visor to block the rising sun's rays and ignore the frantic beat of my heart. This is just a new adventure. Everything is fine. I'm not going to die. I'm not lost. Life is great.

The glare of the sun grows brighter, and I take my foot off the gas because I can't see a damn thing. If I hit someone right now, I will jump right off this bridge.

Okay, maybe not really, but seriously, I can't handle an accident on top of taking the wrong road twice, getting myself farther from home each time.

The shaking stops as heat fills my car, seeping through my skin, calming my racing heart. Well, that's odd. I blink several times, but the light only grows brighter until there's nothing other than a blinding kaleidoscope of fiery oranges, pinks, and reds surrounding me.

This is getting too weird.

I move my foot, intending to press on the accelerator again, but there's nothing there. One second, I'm sitting in the driver's seat, and the next, I'm in a ball of light, floating within its warmth and inhaling…flowers? Sugar? Something sweet, but that's not the point here.

I've officially lost my mind.

Closing my eyes, I try to pinch myself, but controlling my own movements doesn't seem possible. In fact, I'm not even sure I'm still alive. Holy shit, did I just *die*?

I wasn't even going thirty miles an hour. Did the bridge collapse and I can't remember those last few moments as my car plunged into the Columbia? No freaking way.

"Welcome back to Lunara," a man's kind voice says as I'm still surrounded by light. "Did you have a—" There's a sharp gasp before he adds, "Princess Isobella, you've returned."

My vision clears, and what the hell is this?

I'm in a cave of sorts. The cavernous area is a mix of light and shadows and shimmering rock walls, with a ceiling that seems to disappear into the darkness above. The air is cool and crisp and causes goosebumps to rise on my arms.

When I look down, I'm no longer dressed in the yoga pants and sweatshirt I was wearing two minutes ago. I'm clothed in a floor-length gown made of silk that feels weightless against my body. The dark-blue color clings to my curves but doesn't restrict my movements as I turn around.

There's only darkness behind me, and I notice I'm standing on a platform made of engraved stone and a metal emblem that seems to pulse with some sort of vibrating energy.

I start to kneel, feeling lightheaded, but I catch the stare of the man who greeted me, reminding me that I'm not alone.

The stranger is on one knee, dressed in dark, cotton pants and a matching long-sleeved button-up shirt and holding some sort of silver staff with a blue stone at the top that resembles the color of my dress. His head is bowed, but his light-green eyes keep flickering toward me.

When he finds me watching him, there seem to be a million questions dancing within his stare, but he manages to settle on just one. "Are you in distress, Princess Isobella?"

"Um, I'm not sure. And my name is Isla, not Isobella," I tell him, then that twinge in my chest returns.

His face contorts briefly. "Your face and essence… You must be our lost princess."

I've officially lost my mind, or maybe I'm dreaming. Yes, that must be it. I drank too much wine last night as I pouted over having nothing to do on a Friday night. This is a hangover dream, one I'm ready to be done with.

I start to pinch myself and notice perfectly manicured nails gracing my hands. Not only that, but the scar on my right ring finger that's been there since I was in third grade and cut myself on a can of ravioli is no longer present.

"What the hell is happening to me and why can't I wake up?" I ask myself, but this stranger seems to believe I'm speaking to him.

He's still bowed, and his frown only deepens. "I'm going to alert King Asher."

"I need to wake up. I need to wake up. *I need to wake up!*" I close my eyes and grip the sides of my hair. The tips of my fingers brush over a cool metal, and when I reopen my eyes, my normally blonde hair is…rose gold with white and auburn highlights. This can't be real. It's not possible.

A crown falls off my head, tumbling onto the stone platform I still stand on and rolling until it stops at the man's feet.

He picks up the unwanted accessory with gentleness and finally stands. "Your Highness, I don't know what's happened, but please, come with me. I'm sure King Asher will make sense of this."

My hands shake as I release the foreign strands of what should be my hair. I'm not me, but I still feel like me. I have no clue where I am or what the hell happened to my car. My heart constricts to the point of pain as I blink several times, trying to force any of this to make sense.

The coolness of the cave surrounds me and I close my eyes, inhaling deeply. While I'm understandably freaked out, I'm not frightened. Not in the way that I fear for my life, just more confused than I've ever been.

This must be some vivid dream. Maybe if I play along with whatever this is, I'll be able to wake up. Yes, that has to be the answer here.

Reopening my eyes, I nod toward the unknown man and extend my hand, taking back the offered crown. As its weight settles onto my head, I ignore the swell in my chest and pray that in no time at all, I'll be waking up in my own bed, never having hiked that damn mountain and gotten on the wrong freeway.

CHAPTER TWO

ISLA

What began as a nightmare doesn't seem so bad once I stop fighting against whatever is happening to me. Cain, as he finally introduced himself, leads us out of the cave and we emerge into a utopia plucked from the pages of a storybook.

The air is crisp and invigorating against my skin and the twilight above is a tapestry of dusky blues and deep amethyst. Twin moons shine brightly amongst the darkening sky and an explosion of stars seem to just be coming to life. I'm transfixed by the sight and a serenity, both profound and unfamiliar, settles over me, at least for the moment.

"Right this way, Princess." Cain's gentle prompt nudges me back to the present, his voice a soft echo in the quiet of the night.

I peel my gaze away from the sky and remind myself that I should be paying more attention to what's around me as opposed to what's above.

We walk a smooth, stone pathway that leads over a

grass-covered hill. At the top, I pause once again to appreciate the striking view before me. Rolling hills of greenery continue until they turn to a darkness that seems never-ending. Structures, most with their lights off, appear often enough to resemble a quaint town, but it's the opulent castle that seizes my attention most.

The shimmering silver building, highlighted by the moon's glow, sits on the highest point that I can see. There are several levels to it, giving it a cascading effect. The tallest portion has two turrets—both concealed by the seamless stone with few windows—and a domed area between them made of glass and a steel frame. Beneath that, there's a broader section with smaller windows spaced out and one large set of double wooden doors that stand out, even from this far away.

"Your Highness." Cain clears his throat. "We really shouldn't linger."

"Are you taking me there?" I point toward the architectural marvel, the tightening of my throat betraying a nervousness that I try to swallow away. The chances of waking up back in my bed *should* be higher if I just play along. *Right?*

Cain's green eyes spark under the moonlight as he nods. "Yes, that is where King Asher is and where I'm instructed to bring all unexpected arrivals, Princess Isobella."

"It's—never mind." Isobella, Isla. Doesn't matter, it's not like this is real. Though I can't deny, I've never had a dream this vivid. My senses are on overdrive and I'm not a fan.

Out of nervous habit, my hand reaches up to twist a

section of my hair and I wince when I'm reminded that not even my long strands are as they should be.

"To the castle we go, then," I say with a smile that has tension draining from Cain's shoulders.

He leads the way down the path and as we start to pass modest homes made from smooth stucco in varying shades of tan, I begin to wonder where all those who occupy these houses are.

"How many people live here?" I ask to fill the silence and ease my racing thoughts.

Cain keeps his voice low. "There are around five hundred of us on this island now, Your Highness."

"You know, you can stop calling me that," I tell him kindly. "Even if I'm a princess, there's no need for formalities."

A flush of humility paints his cheeks. "If it's all the same to you, I'd prefer to keep with our customs…Your Highness."

"All right, then." I sigh, hoping this isn't about to get any more awkward when I meet the king and have no clue how I'm supposed to act. "If five hundred people live here, why does it feel as if we're the only two out right now?" I know it's nighttime here, but the sky is hardly dark. It can't be *that* late.

"It's the middle of the night, Your Highness," he says, still keeping a low tone. "Your people are resting before the new day."

Considering this isn't real, I push down my surprise that their night doesn't get as dark as nights back home. Plus, I'm pretty sure he's also trying to politely tell me to be quiet.

The castle grows closer and its stature is magnified by

our proximity. I'm forced to crane my neck back to see the top of the turrets and I wonder how incredible the view will be from up there.

Shaking my head, I clear those thoughts from my mind. I won't be here long enough to find that out because none of this is real.

The path we've been following opens to a wider road that curves left toward our destination. There aren't any other homes in this part of the town. The bigger buildings appear to be shops with interesting names like Bianca's Bountiful Books, Claren's Charming Crowns, and Walker's Wolfish Wears.

Wolfish? Odd descriptor, but it works because if these places were open, that would be the first one I'd check out.

The road begins to incline, and we pass under a stone arch that leads into the lowest level of the castle. Inside the tall, grey brick walls stand two guards wearing the same midnight-colored garb as Cain, but they're also covered in silver armor. Though they hold no weapons. Weird.

The moment they see us, both men drop to a knee and murmur my name. "Princess Isobella."

Well, my dream name.

I don't reply, half because I'm still confused about what's happening and because another set of wooden doors I couldn't see before start to open without anyone touching them.

What kind of drugs is my imagination on?

"Where is she?" a man's deep voice booms, echoing from all directions.

My head turns left, then right, but I don't see anything or anyone.

Cain bends to his knee and I start to do the same, not wanting to offend anyone, but he whispers, "You should bow when King Asher appears, not kneel, Your Highness."

This princess thing is sounding a little better.

I attempt to do as Cain suggests, but my posture remains unyieldingly straight and my hands are clasped before me, a show of strength that I'm not certain I possess. Though it's a position that innately feels appropriate for the situation.

From the lurking shadows, a pair of sapphire eyes start to materialize until a tower of intimidation steps out from the darkness. His shoulders broad and tense, a man I assume to be King Asher appears before us—though, he's younger than I expected, maybe just a few years older than me—clothed in regal blues accented with silver threads.

The moment our gazes clash, my stomach churns, likely reading more into his stare than I should. One that feels like a storm of emotions directed right at me—disdain and annoyance, briefly replaced by something softer I can't identify before going blank.

He stops several paces away, his darkening eyes raking over me and confirming my previous thought.

"Isobella." He says my...name without addressing me as 'princess,' but more importantly with a layer of awe. Except the comfort of his tone doesn't match the unease in his face as he appraises me with a glare, or the fact that his singularly spoken word makes my skin pebble.

Though that doesn't stop me from giving him the same treatment. I take in his impressive height, the smattering of dark hair covering his cheeks and tight jawline along with the disheveled strands atop his head. I drag my stare over his broad chest, down to his thick thighs that are hidden by loose, black pants before I force my eyes back to his face.

"Asher." His name falls easily from my lips as I smirk at his glowering presence.

What is wrong with me?

"It is you." His eyes narrow and he tenses, crossing his arms. "How *nice* of you to return home after all this time."

I tell myself to keep quiet, that commenting on his rudeness will get me nowhere. Yet unsurprisingly, my mouth seems to have other plans.

"How *nice* of you to think you can come charging out here and act as if I've done something wrong when I've never even met you." I stand taller, my chin out, and let my arms fall loose at my sides.

My retort seems to shatter some of his hard edges instead of infuriating him, and I breathe a little easier. After being treated like trash and expected to be grateful for whatever scraps I received throughout my childhood, I made a vow the moment I was able to take charge of my own life. One that meant I wouldn't put up with being spoken to like I'm nothing ever again. Apparently, that's carrying through even in my dreams.

Cain rises from his bowed position. "King Asher, I didn't get a chance to tell you before, but it seems Princess Isobella does not recall her time here."

"Five hundred years is a long time, but that's impossible," he says, staying only slightly calmer than before. "Maybe some sleep will fix her...mind. Cain, take her to her room." He glances at me once more. "I'll speak with you in the morning."

As the imposing—not at all sexy—king casually turns around and walks away, my terror returns.

Did he just say 'five hundred years' and send me to my room like I'm some sort of child?

What the hell is this guy talking about? Not only does he sound crazy, but his gravelly voice makes me envision a prison cell, not a swath of comfort. My hands start to shake and the tension filling my body makes it hard to do anything other than watch the arrogant king disappear into the shadows, even when Cain lightly touches my shoulder.

"I'll show you the way, Princess Isobella," he says as the other two guards go back to their sentries.

I can't move. I'm frozen in place as my mind races. Where the hell am I and why does everyone think they know me, but not a single face is familiar? Worse, why does all of this feel so damn real?

There's pressure in my chest as my mind fights to insist on this being a dream and my head begins to pound the second I ask myself, *What if I was wrong in my assumption before?*

I'd been in my car. There shouldn't have been any way that I went from driving across a bridge to appearing in a cave guarded by a man telling me I'm a lost princess.

Yet with Cain still staring at me, waiting for me to unfreeze from my current position, the world around me is too vivid to deny. The rough texture of the stone wall beside me, the crunch of the pebbles beneath my heeled shoes, the moons shining down on us from above. Hell, even my emotions are heightened, as if I can *feel* everything, including the pulsing of the energy from the earth around me.

The cool night air, the racing of my heart, the warmth of the stranger's comforting touch, the contempt from the king. Each one pierces through my skin, making me question my sanity.

"I want to go home," I say, my voice barely audible.

"You *are* home, Your Highness."

I finally look at Cain again and his green eyes plead with me to understand, but I don't know how I'm supposed to do that.

My head shakes. "Home is in Portland with my empty apartment, my crappy car, and a job that kind of sucks but pays the bills." My hand waves around the castle. "This… grandeur…it has to be a fantasy, a dream."

"Please, follow me to your room, Princess Isobella. Maybe you'll feel better there." Cain's eyes cast toward the two guards before lowering his voice. "And I would advise that we continue this conversation elsewhere."

I drop my shoulders and my chin lands on my chest as long strands of hair cascade around my face in soft waves. Tears burn in my eyes and I want to scream, but instead, I take a deep breath and raise my head, grasping on to that air of confidence I felt in front of the king. Then I nod because I really don't have another choice. "Okay."

Cain takes a step forward, then glances back, waiting for me to follow.

The moment I walk under the arch of the doorway, a shiver runs over me, easing my tension but increasing the rate of my heart. I blink several times as a sense of déjà vu hits me.

There's still nothing familiar about this place, but this

feeling of giving in, that isn't foreign to me. Sure, I gave in plenty to the abuse of foster parents, but this is different, bigger. I don't understand how or why, but maybe Cain will help me figure things out.

With heavy feet, I step forward and head for the shadows of the castle. As we walk, I tell myself that everything is going to be fine. I've overcome worse situations…haven't I?

Even if this is real, I'm a princess, according to the name I've been called. They won't hurt me. At least I'm going to keep telling myself that. Maybe I can convince Cain to take me back to that cave and send me home the way I arrived. I don't care if my car has been towed away, I'll walk back to Portland if I have to. I just want to go home. I want to call Elodee, describe all this to her so she can tell me I must have been smoking something crazy, and then quit my job. It's time for me to move to Seattle with her.

This whole scenario has to be a mental breakdown caused by being without my best friend for these past few weeks. That would make more sense than this being real, but the moment I start to doubt the legitimacy of this place, my tension comes back tenfold.

Maybe I just shouldn't *think* for now.

Cain is about fifteen feet ahead of me, so I do my best not to linger long. Plus, I want to make sure I know where I'm going if I need to find my own way to escape later.

As we walk through the dark corridor, lights begin to illuminate on their own. Creepy, but not abnormal. Motion sensors are a thing. Except when I glance back, expecting the glow from the lamps to spread, everything is back to being dark behind us.

I'm okay. I'm not being led to my death. Everything is *fine*.

Scenic paintings hang on the wall with ornate silver frames around them. Each one appears hand-painted and showcases varying nature settings: flowers, mountains, rolling hills, an ocean with…something scaly and large swimming in it. I stop looking too closely after that for my own sanity.

The walls are made from a white brick and put off a coolness, but I don't shiver, which surprises me because I'm literally always cold unless I'm outside under the sun. I even call blankets my second best friend.

Our soft footfalls echo over the wooden flooring as we continue down the wide hallway. Another hundred or so feet and Cain turns toward a set of stairs. "Your quarters are on the third floor, Your Highness. These stairs are the best way for us to get there."

This is a castle fit for a king and there aren't any elevators? Well, that's mildly disappointing. At least my desire to hike showed up this morning. Well, so long as that drive stays with me.

The steps are made of a blue-hued stone, smooth without cracks. The railing on my right is sleek and silver metal. They seem to favor these two colors and I'm tempted to ask why that is until we get to the next level.

In the open corridor, there's a flag hanging on the back wall. Enormous in size and blue and silver, of course. At the center is a silver wolf, howling into the air, standing on top of what reminds me of the rolling hills I saw when exiting the cave.

Above that are the words, *Polaris, Lunara.* Beneath that, in smaller print is *Pride, Strength, Resilience.*

"Is that the name of this place?" I ask, then I try to sound out the word. "Lun-air-uh?"

Cain pauses and smiles softly as he glances up at the flag. "Lu-narr-uh, Your Highness," he corrects, putting more emphasis on the *R*. "And yes, we reside in Polaris, the largest of the islands that make up Lunara."

"How many, uh, islands are there here?" I ask as we keep moving to the next set of stairs. I'm doing my best not to freak out over the confirmation that I'm surrounded by water, lessening my chances of escape.

"There are four territories, Your Highness," he replies. "Polaris, Venaris, Altaris, and Selaris. We used to be one land, but now the sea separates the four kingdoms. King Asher is very proud of our home. He's spent a large part of his life dedicated to keeping us safe."

He speaks of the king as if he were someone to be worshiped, but that man came storming in and confronting me like the world's biggest asshole. Just my luck.

I stop asking questions because most of them will likely lead back to King Asher and I don't like the way my heart races when his name graces my thoughts. Instead, I mentally keep track of the few turns we take to get the next set of stairs. By the time we reach the third level, I expect to be out of breath, but I haven't even broken a sweat.

I guess new hair, new body? That's at least one thing I don't have to complain about.

"Your room is the second on the left, Your Highness," Cain announces before touching the double set of handles.

Two wooden doors open with his gentle touch and the

lights inside the room begin to illuminate, casting a glow into the hallway. I step forward and peek around but stay beside Cain.

There's a four-poster bed with silver tulle draped from the wooden corners, connecting one to the next. The bed is covered in a thick, blue comforter that looks heavenly to sleep on.

The walls are cream in color with more of the same art gracing the walls that I noticed in the hallway, but they seem solely focused on white, pink, and yellow lilies—my favorite flower—in varying depictions. Not odd at all. Nope.

An open door that appears to lead to a bathroom is opposite of the bed and another one is only five feet beside that but remains closed. A small sitting area is set up next to another set of doors with glass windows that lead to a balcony.

My skin tingles and I close my eyes, breathing in this moment and trying to understand what's happening to me and why I feel as if...I've been here before, yet nothing *looks* familiar.

"Are you ill, Your Highness?" Cain asks quietly.

"I'm something," I mutter before entering the room.

Another cursory glance of the space brings my attention to the bedside table, where a single framed photo sits. Three people, including an older man with his arm wrapped around a woman whose blue eyes are eerily similar to mine, but more than that, they're standing next to...*me.*

The new hair I now have hangs in waves over the shoulders of the woman in the photo, but it's the face staring back at me that captures my attention most. There isn't a single detail that varies from what I saw in the mirror this morning. My light-blue gaze is the same, my wide smile, my round nose—everything is as I've always known it except the rose-gold hair with white and auburn highlights, almost making the strands seem pinkish.

"This is me," I say with reverence. "When was this taken?"

Cain steps closer and looks over my shoulder. "About a month before your disappearance, Your Highness."

I shouldn't ask this next question, but I can't help myself, considering something King Asher said before that I chose to mostly ignore. "How long ago did I disappear?"

He pauses, making me tense for his answer. "Five hundred and four years ago, Your Highness."

My heart sinks. I want this to be some sort of cruel joke, but the longer I stare at this photo, the more I see the faces of the people—no matter how impossible my brain is telling me this is—my heart feels a connection to these strangers. With every rapid beat in my chest, I come closer to accepting that maybe—*just maybe*—this isn't a dream after all.

CHAPTER THREE

ASHER

Isobella Blackwood has returned to Lunara. Six words I didn't think I would ever say again.

For centuries, my soul was entwined in a relentless search, combing through every crevice and shadow for her essence and yearning for my future queen, the woman who completed me. Now, as though conjured by a cruel twist of fate, she returns, claiming to have no memory of who she was, and worse, she doesn't seem to recall who *we* were.

The agony that knowledge causes me replaces the void her disappearance created all those years ago with a throbbing that threatens to shatter my heart all over again. Instead of succumbing to the weakness, I focus on my fury. An easier emotion to grasp after facing the vacant look in her stare when she saw me.

Her gaze, once a beacon of warmth, now cuts through me each time I close my eyes, sharper than the most finely honed blade. Though I didn't miss the way she assessed me with unwitting appreciation, the inferno she used to hold for me doesn't seem to have been completely extinguished. Still, after all this time, she's a stranger to me and I to her. A revelation that proves to be a bitter pill to swallow.

Worse, my father was right. He came to me about a decade after my Isobella had disappeared without a trace and told me that a source he trusted but couldn't reveal had told him that this had been my mate's choice. That my Issie had chosen to leave and her final words to me had been a lie, which is where my ire is currently growing from.

She'd promised me that we would overcome the obstacle of me taking the throne so early together, that everything would be okay because we'd be together. And then she was gone. There'd been no note or message passed on to me. Just a nothingness that I nearly didn't come back from.

The beast within me, my kindred spirit, my wolf, stirs with a restless rumble, echoing my internal turmoil. He, too, has been fragmented by the chasm of her absence, our suffering a shared penance through the relentless years.

After storming through my castle, assuming an imposter was present, only a fragile moment passed before her scent seeped into my consciousness—a fusion of sweet vanilla laced with earthy undertones and a spiciness I've only ever smelled from her.

I wanted to fall at her feet, but my father's previous words haunted me the closer I got to her. I'd never believed them before. Even after he assured me Isobella's departure had been her choice, I still searched for her. It wasn't until nearly a century had passed and my kingdom was at risk that I finally ceased putting everything I had into finding my mate. Though my heart never stopped loving her and hoping with each new wolf pup born in our world that her soul would return to me.

Now, seeing Isobella in perfect health, stating she doesn't know me, I feel I have no choice other than to finally believe the words my father told me all that time ago.

My mate chose to leave me and have her memory stripped of our love.

The words are like acid on my mind, enraging me further yet breathing life back into me unlike anything has since her departure. It doesn't matter that she doesn't remember me. Isobella's soul is still the other half of mine, a siren's call I can't ignore.

My rage pulses within me regardless of this knowledge. I've envisioned our reunion countless times, vivid fantasies that only grew with the passing years. I wasn't prepared for her rejection of my existence, for her to look at me as if I were a stranger to her heart. She's changed in ways I can't yet comprehend, but having seen a glimmer of the fire within her has my lips curving upward.

I inhale deeply and close my eyes, picturing my mate in her room, furious with the world for the predicament she's found herself in. The desire to go to her, to make her listen, is strong, but I couldn't *make* my Isobella do anything before and I don't believe that's changed.

Shedding my hastily thrown-on clothes, I consider

going back to bed, but the notion feels impossible even at this late hour and knowing how close yet out of reach my mate remains.

Five hundred years ago, there was nothing that would keep us apart. She shouldn't have even lived in the castle with me until our souls were properly bound together by the gods, but tradition was no match for the magnitude of our love.

The bond we share—or shared—was crafted in the stars, a destiny created by the very fabric of Lunara. Her laughter was the balm that soothed my aches, her joy the light that guided my every step.

With her absence, I did my best to be the king our people deserve, yet nothing has been the same since I lost her.

Beneath my stoic exterior, the faint embers of hope flicker from my wolf, but I know better. Too much time has passed for me to allow my walls to come down so soon. Not that I don't still love our mate—because I do, more than my own life. It's more that regardless of what I've been told and what I've now seen, I can't ignore that Isobella chose to forget me, to shatter us.

Now, she's here, and according to Cain, believing her name is Isla, requesting to go back to Earth. The only world I didn't search because magic doesn't exist there. Our souls don't belong on that plane of existence, yet as I stand on my balcony, I'm back to wondering if it's truly possible that's where she *chose* to be.

My mate sometimes spoke of running away from our responsibilities so that we could be together, no longer living for our kingdom. Yet when I revealed my father's illness, terrified I'd lose her, I never felt closer to my Issie in those moments. During our last conversation, she made me believe there was nothing we couldn't accomplish together. Now, I'm wondering if I never really knew her at all.

Our lives were intertwined since the moment we took our first breaths. Two new souls, born on the same day, over five hundred years ago. She was supposed to be my forever and, looking back, maybe I took advantage of that knowledge.

My jaw tightens and I take a shuddering breath. I don't want to be angry, but everything about this situation is frustrating. So many unanswered questions, so many things I would have done differently if given the chance. Yet going back in time is one thing that's not possible with magic. I must face whatever this is and find a way to do so without fury clouding my judgment.

A grumble sounds from within me—my wolf letting me know he'd like to run.

I almost ignore him, but maybe he's right. A bit of time in our true form, under the moons, could do me some good.

Not wanting to waste time by traversing back down the stairs, tempting myself by getting too close to Isobella's room, I step over the railing of my balcony and leap from the fourth level of the castle. Energy builds from within my chest, pushing outward and covering my exposed skin as my body hurtles through the night air toward the ground beneath.

Wind whips around me and my stomach churns from the freefall, but halfway down, I call my wolf forward. My human form curls in on itself for the briefest of seconds before exploding with the power of my inner animal. He appears in all his glory, his large form landing on the grass with a barely audible *thud*.

He shakes out his midnight-colored coat and howls toward the moons, a sorrowful sound I haven't heard in years.

Our front paws scratch at the earth before he takes off at full speed for the forest beyond the castle. His strength fills me, but when he comes to an abrupt stop just before the trees, tension seeps deep within.

An invisible tether draws our gaze back to the castle and my wolf's powerful stare captures the most stunning creature.

There she is. The woman who should be my mate stands on her own balcony, watching us. The distance between us might as well be an ocean, but that doesn't lessen the pain lancing through my heart at knowing I can't run to her like I so often did before.

Her bright-blue eyes start to widen as our gazes remain locked. I take a step forward, wondering if maybe she's ready to talk, but her hand covers her mouth as she stumbles back into the darkness of her room.

I can't sense her emotions from this far away, but is it possible that my mate is frightened? The woman I once knew and loved was never afraid of anything.

A rabid storm of questions assaults my mind and their answers are as elusive as the shadows that hang between the trees of the forest, but one thing is crystal clear: I've been granted a second chance. Whatever the truth may be, I won't rest until I know exactly what happened all those years ago. I didn't just get my Issie back only to lose her again, at least not without a fair fight this time.

If Isobella left me on purpose, then she can do so again, but not without explaining herself first.

I'll give her tonight to get settled, but tomorrow, I'll do whatever it takes to find the answers I seek. Even if that means going to find someone whose only wish was to be left alone last time we spoke.

CHAPTER FOUR

ISLA

Sleep eludes me like sand sifting through grasping fingers. The ceiling—a blank, cream expanse—mocks me with its stillness, offering no solace to the storm within. Hours have passed since I stood on the balcony of my room and I've spent every minute after trying to convince myself that the giant wolf racing toward the forest wasn't real. That he didn't stop abruptly, turning around to look right into my soul.

Nor can I admit to myself his glowing, sapphire eyes looked eerily like those of King Asher.

The thought sends a shiver cascading down my spine and my stomach churns as I grab a pillow, smothering my face to drown out the screams of my frustrations, and not for the first time since being left in this room.

How can any of this be real? How did I end up here and how the hell do I get back to the home I know?

In restless defeat, I turn, and my eyes betray me, locking on to the photo by my bedside. A token to a life I've never lived, a happiness I've never known. The family within the frame feels both alien and achingly familiar, and with every accidental glance, I'm further filled with a sense of love and belonging. Two things I've only ever associated with Elodee and the one good foster home we lived in. Though the latter feels like another lifetime ago.

I reach for the picture and sit up in the bed, resting my back against the white, carved headboard. My thumb glides over the cool surface of the glass and I brace myself against the swell of questions I've battled with all night.

If these are truly my parents, how did I grow up as a child back in Portland, especially when Cain mentioned something about this being from five hundred years ago? The past and present clash within me, a torrent of memories as I try to make sense of everything that can't truly be possible no matter which way I look at things.

I remember very vividly being four or five and every year after. I went to school, I had a life—albeit, not the greatest, but still, I lived.

The woman in this photo is identical to me now, at twenty-five years old. If I was once her, then how am I *me*?

I don't know, but I'd very much like to find out. Pretending this isn't real has only gotten me put in this room and freaked out by a wild animal. It's time for me to be proactive, not only for myself, but for Elodee. She's going to be losing her mind soon when she can't reach me. I thought I'd gotten lucky when I found an old, corded house phone still plugged in on the desk in the room, but either I don't know how it works, or it won't call back to…Earth, or it's just broken because nothing happened when I dialed her number.

With a frustrated sigh, I throw the blankets off me,

then set the photo back where it belongs and get out of bed. The ground is farther away than I expected, and I land on the hardwood floor with a heavy *thump*, but I at least don't fall.

Still dressed in the silk gown I somehow arrived in, I tiptoe toward the door, intent on sneaking out. Only the moment I touch the door handle, it starts to turn on its own within my palm.

Swiftly, I take several steps back and in walks Cain, holding a silver tray. His head bows as he says, "Your Highness."

Instinctively, I nod in return, but he smiles and corrects my action. "You should never bow to anyone other than King Asher or one of the other kings and queens within Lunara, Your Highness."

I swallow thickly. "Right. You mentioned there were other islands before."

Cain steps farther into the room and sets the tray on the table, just past the bed. "Yes, Your Highness. There are the four kingdoms of Lunara, created by the divide during the Great War."

Hmm, that sounds like an interesting story, but that's not my biggest concern right now. I want to talk to the people in that photo and get some answers. They seem like a better bet than the king or someone who works for him.

Glancing back at the bedside table, my throat tightens as I prepare to say words I never thought I would. "How do I find the people in that picture with me... My, um, parents?"

I was told as a child I'd been orphaned thanks to a car

accident, so I'd never had any reason to wonder before—something Elodee and I had bonded over.

Cain tenses, his mouth turning into a hard line as he stands awkwardly next to the table, looking everywhere but at me. "I brought you some breakfast to start your day, Your Highness."

I stalk toward him, grab his arm, and force him to face me as I look up at his emotionless face. "Cain, where are they?"

I don't even know these people and I'm not certain I believe they're truly my birth family because this nonsense about five hundred years ago isn't possible, but if the invisible chokehold around my neck is any indication, my emotions don't give a damn about what is or isn't true right now.

"Your Highness…"

My eyes narrow and I practically growl at him. "Tell me, Cain."

"Your mother died some years ago and chose not to return to this life and your father hasn't been seen since your mother departed."

His words are spoken so rapidly, it takes my mind a few extra beats to understand what he's said, but the moment I do, an ache grows within, spreading until every inch of my body hurts.

My knees shake. I release Cain and lean against the bed, helping to keep myself upright. I wasn't sure that life could be any more cruel after having been left without a family growing up, but finding out I might have had one, yet I've missed my chance to know them? Even if this grief doesn't quite feel like my own, the ache is still as real as ever.

My fingertips rub over my chest, trying to ease the throbbing. This is more than cruel, it's villainous.

"I want to go back to Portland, Cain," I tell him sternly after I find a way to compose myself. My hardened gaze focuses only on him. "I'm your princess and you will do as I demand, or I'll find someone who will. Do I make myself clear?"

His throat bobs as he stares at the floor. "Yes, Your Highness. I will make the necessary preparations for your departure."

I point toward the door and without another word, Cain exits my bedroom, closing the door quietly behind him.

Only then do I drop to the floor, bring my knees to my chest, and let myself break. A lifetime of heartache allowed me those few moments of resolve and resilience, but being alone, I can't find the strength to pretend everything is okay.

For a brief few seconds, hope trickled through. A part of me *wanted* to be their lost princess, wanted the family in that photo. Even if I don't understand anything that's happened since I began crossing that bridge, I know grief.

It doesn't matter that I'm in a world that shouldn't be real yet feels familiar, that the people here seem confident they know me. I can't recall any of them, and I've been teased with the idea of parents, only to be told they're unavailable to me. All that and I've been here for maybe four hours.

Until I can figure out how to get back home, the power of who these people think I am feels like my only lifeline. If I have to be Princess Isobella to get the hell out of here, then that's what I'll do because there's nothing more that I want than to go back to my apartment in Portland, pack up my shit, move to Seattle, and never speak of this craziness again. Not even to Elodee.

Too many hours later, I'm still no closer to getting out of here than I was this morning. Yet because I don't understand how this place works, I feel as if I have no choice other than to do just as I have. Though my patience will only last through the daylight hours.

Once the bright, orange sun that I've been watching has finally disappeared and the double moons return, I'll move on to Plan B.

Several times, I've been tempted to walk out of this bedroom and go back to the cave to figure things out for myself, but the more thought I put into this, the less ideal that seems.

While I've only seen four people, each of them has known exactly who I am—or who I once was or whatever —and something tells me that "sneaking" anywhere around this place will be next to impossible during the day.

Cain at least continues to bring me food, most recently dinner, when he comes with his non-update updates about the portal needing the right energy to open on Earth again. I'm not sure I believe him, but at least the food is delicious.

I pick at the toasted bread covered in what I assume is cheese and which came with a pasta creation I don't have a name for, but I don't eat much. Half because I'm still full thanks to the previous two meals and half because every other minute, my gaze shifts toward the door, hoping that the next time it opens will be when I'm able to leave.

My restlessness only intensifies, especially when I can't seem to forget that Asher said he'd speak with me in the morning, yet he never showed. Why I even care, I'm not sure, but it bothers me that I seem to have been forgotten.

I stand from the table, unsure what to do. I search the bedroom and as much as the main door calls to me, I decide to step out onto the balcony again. I haven't been out there since I saw the wild wolf running rampant across the back yard last night, but maybe with the sky not quite dark yet, the view will be less intimidating.

Just as my bare foot touches the concrete landing, the bedroom door behind me opens. Wind whips past me, seeming to swirl through the room before blowing right back toward my still form. My hair tangles in front of my face and I hold on to the chair in front of me.

A warmth builds deep within me, and I close my eyes, taking a deep inhale. An earthy, cedar scent envelops my entire being, assaulting every sense. My vision flickers, my heart thundering loudly in my ears as my stomach swirls with foreign emotions.

"Isobella." The name is spoken with a deep grumble and filled with an authority that can only belong to one person: Asher.

It takes me more time than I like to get my head right. I don't know why my body would betray me like this, but the two of us are going to have a long talk once we get the hell out of here.

As soon as I'm turned around, I nearly lose my shit all over again.

This entire world is out to get me. I'm convinced of that.

Asher stands inside my bedroom, his eyes pinned on me. He's put together and in control—everything I don't feel—dressed in a white, collared shirt. His sleeves are rolled up his thick forearms and the top few buttons are undone, exposing just enough of his chest to distract me.

Oh, hell. Am I really *that* woman? Apparently so because against everything I *want* to feel, I can't deny that this man is sexy. He is the embodiment of control and composure, yet there's an untamed edge to him that sets my heart racing just by his mere presence. Nobody has said as much, but these feelings make me wonder... Who was he to me before? Why does he seem so furious with me?

He rubs the back of his neck with one hand and shoves the other in his pocket, standing there almost as if he has nothing and everything to say all at once.

And because I can't seem to control myself around him, I speak first, barely containing my frustrations. "Are you here to take me to the portal?"

I swear his face pales for the briefest of seconds, but then his eyes pierce right through me as they narrow in my direction. "You truly want to leave after only having just returned?"

"Of course I do," I say with a bravado I don't truly feel. "Why should I stay?"

"For..." He pauses, seeming to choose his words wisely. "For your people."

I glance behind me, out the balcony, and toward the forest before addressing him. "This isn't my home."

"Bullshit!" His outburst has me spinning back around,

but by the time my eyes are on him again, he's returned to being the epitome of calm, both hands now in his pockets. "Just give us a chance." He pauses once more. "Please."

The way he says "us" makes my chest tighten with a tension that I don't understand and don't want to dig further into as I say, "I have a home and family to get back to."

His eyes widen ever so slightly and his jaw tightens. "A family?"

"A sister," I clarify. "She needs me, and I need her."

The darkening of his eyes makes me think he wants to say something more, but he seems to stop himself, lowering his gaze and taking a deep breath.

"I'm not the princess you want me to be," I add, not comfortable with the silence. "Even if there is some possible way that I once was, that woman isn't me anymore. This place has apparently managed just fine without me for the last five hundred years. What does it matter if I go?"

He mutters something that I don't catch before finally meeting my stare again. "What if you had a reason to stay?"

Again, my chest constricts, making my throat feel as if it were closing up. "I guess it would depend on the reason."

What the hell is wrong with me? Why would I say that? Literally nothing could make me stay here and never see Elodee again.

"I found your father." The moment those four words leave his mouth, it's like a bolt of lightning strikes me, leaving me breathless and exposed.

My heart hammers once again as emotions that don't

feel like mine grow. The tendril of hope I felt before also returns and I do my best to ignore it. Though that doesn't work for long.

Does this information change anything for me? The tightening of my chest says yes, but my head is still fighting against the possibility that this place is somewhere I should be.

Yet my father—a complete stranger and likely not *really* mine—he's here. Knowing there's a chance, even the smallest one, that he's my blood family…

Damn it! I close my eyes, turning away from Asher. Why couldn't Elodee be here with me? This would be so much easier with her support.

I have no clue if these people are lying to me or if any of this is possible, but I can't deny that my reactions and emotions are very real.

A warm hand covers my shoulder. "What do you need, Isobella?"

"Quit calling me that. My name is *Isla!*" I snap and while I feel bad for my outburst, I know right now what I'm supposed to do. "And I want to go home."

Even if this man Asher has found the father of the young woman in the photo next to the bed, I am not her. He's not *my* father and I can't replace the one I never knew with him.

Elodee, however, is my family and I need her now more than ever.

Turning back around, I look up at Asher. I expect to find compassion on his face that matches his previous words, but instead, he seems more furious than he was even last night.

"He's your family. That used to mean something to you," Asher says through tightly clenched teeth.

"It still does," I murmur as tears drip slowly down my cheeks, "but he's not *my* family. He doesn't even know me."

"You've left me no choice." He stands and once again leaves me in the wake of his fury.

More confused than ever before, I decide it's time for me to take back control of my life, even in a world I don't understand and don't really want to believe is real. I'm going to get out of here. No more waiting on Cain or anyone else. This has to end right now.

Except before I can decide on the best escape route, my door is reopening.

Asher enters first, practically dragging an older gentleman with him. Asher's fingers grip the underside of the man's frail arm and his hold appears to be the only reason the stranger still stands.

"What do you think you're doing?" I demand, my eyes narrowing on the king.

Except it's not Asher who replies.

"Isobella?" The man says with an air of shock. His light-blue eyes widen and his hand clutches at his chest, bunching up the fabric of his wrinkled, black cotton shirt that seems three sizes too big. "I can't believe…" He looks up at Asher. "I'll take your offer now."

Asher's voice comes out harsh. "That option is no longer available." Then he narrows his gaze on me. "If you want to save this man, *your father*, then you'll stay, honoring the contract you made before to be part of this kingdom. Otherwise, his death will be on you."

His threat and malice wash over me, but they don't

weaken me. Instead, his words light a fire within my core unlike anything I've known before.

"Excuse me?" I snarl, quiet yet deadly. "From the sounds of it, you offered to save his life and now, because you're not getting your way, you want to blame me for *your* choice? I don't think so. I'm done—"

Before I can continue with my tirade, I make the mistake of giving the unnamed man another glance. This time, our gazes lock and a burst of light explodes behind my eyes, much like the one I saw when I was brought here, only it's not as blinding or long lasting.

I blink several times and lick my dry lips, trying to comprehend this sudden...connection. One that feels as if my soul knows the frail man before me even if I've never seen him before. "You're..."

"Oh, my sweet girl." He coughs and blood dribbles from the side of his mouth. "I'm so sorry."

"You have no reason to apologize." My stare moves to Asher. "But *you* do. Save him."

"Swear that you'll stay." His retort is quick and vicious.

This evil bastard. So much for the kind king Cain described him as.

Still, I don't know what to do. This connection to the older gentleman, a man my heart is telling me is somehow my father, makes me want to stay. Yet I can't fathom the thought of never seeing Elodee again.

"Give me one moon cycle," Asher adds, only slightly calmer than before. "When the second moon disappears in four weeks' time, if you still don't know why you should stay, then I'll send you back to where you came from, and I'll save your father if he still wishes."

Four weeks to save a man's life and possibly get

answers to the questions that have been plaguing me since I stumbled into this world? That doesn't sound like the worst choice I could make. And if this man really is my father, I can bring him back with me. I can't do that if I leave now.

"Fine, I'll stay for now," I declare even as part of me screams in protest, "but if you don't honor your word, I *will* find a way out of here myself."

His responding grin feels like a mutual promise. "I'd expect nothing less."

CHAPTER FIVE

ASHER

Turbulence rips through me, a tornado of regret, fear, and incandescent rage. I've long considered myself a just and composed ruler, but now, Isla—as I've now decided to call her after her little outburst—manages to push my buttons just as easily as she could when we were children.

The plan had seemed foolproof: sway her with the feebleness of her father's life, pulling at what should have been an innate draw toward family and duty. But the moment the ruse failed, so did my self-control.

Desperation can sometimes wear an ugly mask.

Using Grayson's life as a bargaining chip is a vile choice and the worst one that I've ever made. Unease coils in my gut, a beast writhing with every pulse, yet what choice did I have? Letting her go without understanding what the hell happened feels impossible, which is where my current ferocity truly lies. The unknown of what should have been, not with Isla.

The enigma of her memory, the fractured link to her

past life, will undoubtedly haunt my every thought until I know why she doesn't remember her family or the life we once shared. Did she truly choose to forget me and everything she'd had here? Or, as my thoughts ventured to last night, did the intricacies of reincarnation fail her, casting her to Earth for all these years? I've gone through a million scenarios and no matter what I've been told or seen, my heart refuses to accept that she would have willingly forsaken our bond.

Our connection was sacred, unquestionable—she was the very essence of my being, and I hers. She wouldn't have left me like that if she had a choice. The depth of our love couldn't have been fabricated.

Grayson is still with me after exiting Isla's room, but his continued coughing reminds me that his life hangs in the balance and if I don't do something, he won't survive the next four weeks.

"What were you thinking, running away to die?" I ask him with disappointment as we enter a guest room just past Isla's.

His brittle body crumbles in on itself as I sit him on a chair. "I had nothing to live for. My mate's heart was broken after losing her two children to the point that not even I was enough for her. Like you, I had hope, but time snuffed that out years ago, just as I knew it would my life." He looks up at me with a suffering gaze that also flickers with a father's recognition. "That's really our girl in there."

I nod with a frown. "She doesn't remember us, but I would recognize her soul anywhere."

His smile widens for the first time in possibly years. "She remembered me. Maybe only for a moment, but I felt the connection. There was something there."

I leave him on the chair and head to the bathroom to grab a cup. His comment makes me think back to the interaction. Was there something I missed as I threatened Grayson's life to get what I want? I wouldn't think so, but nothing has gone as I hope as of late. For the moment, I'll take his word and the flicker of light it casts over the situation. Especially since Isla agreed to stay.

Returning to Grayson, I extend the claws from my left hand and make a small incision over the veins on my wrist. A small amount of blood pours into the glass before I pull back. Not enough to heal him like he deserves, but he'll at least live thanks to these small doses of my alpha power—something only I can share with him as his king.

I plead with him to understand my next words. "I can't yet revert the damage you've done entirely, but I can buy us some time if you really want to keep living."

His shaky hand reaches for me, barely able to grip my elbow. "I'm not saying I agree with what you just did, but I trust you, Asher. You love my daughter, you always have, and if you can bring her back to me, to us, you do whatever you must."

Taking the offering from me, he manages to tip the cup to his lips, drinking the crimson liquid that thanks to our wolf genes will start to undo the damage he did by denying his inner beast the freedom of shifting for years and, from the looks of it, by starving himself.

As he closes his eyes, allowing the energy he's consumed to breathe a sliver of life back into his body, I can't stop myself from asking, "Do you think she'll hate me for this?"

He coughs slightly and laughs before meeting my uneasy gaze. "Maybe, but you can't have hate without love. She'll understand when the time is right. She always did before."

Grayson's words give me a glimmer of hope that I haven't just made things worse, but while Isobella might have understood in the past, this is Isla. We don't know her any longer, but I'm going to do my damnedest to change that.

Right after I get her to forgive me for what I've done.

The audacity of that man, even if he's a king, is unreal. He wields his power as though he owns me, acting as if he can command my fate without a second thought for my feelings or desires. Yes, maybe that's exactly what he's done, but acknowledging it doesn't make it any less infuriating or wrong.

Though in this instance, I'm okay with having agreed to stay. It's only four weeks. I can survive that so long as I can send word back to Elodee that I'm okay. I don't know what I'll tell her, exactly, but I'll think of something.

Explaining that I'm in another world probably won't go over well and as much as I don't want to lie to her, I know the truth of all this craziness needs to be shared in person.

This reluctant acceptance gnaws at me, forcing me to confront a harsh reality: have I truly come to terms with this not being just some elaborate dream?

The vividness of this world, the intensity of my emotions—they anchor me to a truth I can scarcely believe, but even more, cannot deny. The moment I looked into the eyes of the man who claimed to be my father, something profound and undeniable shifted within me. Despite the logical impossibilities, my soul recognizes him, resonating with a familiarity that transcends memory.

That's not something I can abandon, even for my best friend.

Restless, I pace my room but soon decide that if I'm to remain here, I must familiarize myself with my surroundings. Practical needs come to mind—clothes, toiletries. It's time to take inventory of what's available to me here.

Dressed in the sleek, blue gown that's been my sole attire since my arrival, I admire its feel once more—the fabric's softness provides an unexpected comfort, a stark contrast to my usual jeans and tees.

Still, too many hours have passed and it's time for fresh clothes.

Curiosity leads me to a door beside the bathroom that I haven't yet explored. Pushing it open, I'm greeted by a sight that steals my breath.

"Holy shit." The room beyond is a treasure trove of fashion—shoes, hats, purses, and scarves line one wall, while the opposite is draped in an array of clothing that spans from extravagant gowns to casual wear. It's an arsenal of attire for every occasion, each piece more dazzling than the last. Even better, most of it looks similar to fashion from home. Well, high-end stuff I'd never normally wear similar, but still.

I don't understand why all of this is here, but I guess that's something I can either accept or fight against, but the latter would seem rather stupid on my part. Even if I'm not the woman King Asher believes me to be, I'm here and I might as well be comfortable.

As I step farther into this wardrobe wonderland, my eyes catch a spotlight illuminating the back wall. Crowns, necklaces, bracelets, and earrings, all crafted from white gold or platinum, shimmer under the focused light, each piece a statement of royalty and refinement.

"What the hell have I stumbled upon?" I whisper to myself, my voice a mix of awe and disbelief. My reverie is abruptly shattered by Cain's voice.

"Your Highness?" His tone is tentative as he speaks from just beyond the room. "I'm sorry to interrupt, but King Asher requests your presence for dinner tonight if you haven't finished the meal I brought earlier."

Of course, he probably saw that I'd only picked at the food when he was in here, but the fact that he thinks I might want to be in his presence so soon after the threats he just made sparks my irritation all over again. "*King Asher can kiss my ass*," I mutter with a snarl.

Cain clears his throat, staying in the bedroom and almost out of sight. "I'm not sure I should relay that message, Princess Isla."

His use of my name, not Isobella, catches me off guard —a small, unexpected validation of my identity.

I peek out of the closet, offering him a strained smile. "That wasn't meant for you to hear." *In fact, I'm not even sure how he did*, I think, before adding, "Please tell King Asher that I politely decline unless he's changed his mind about holding me hostage for the next four weeks."

Cain's green eyes widen as he looks more at the carpet than at me. "Yes, Your Highness."

He sees himself out and I grin, walking back into the closet. "Now, what to wear," I muse to myself, ignoring the growl of my stomach now that dinner's been mentioned.

With a sweater, jeans, underwear, and socks in hand—all new with paper tags that are branded with WW and attached with thin silver ribbons—I make my way to the bathroom. The tile floors are heated, which surprised me last night, considering the castle doesn't even have an elevator. There's a glass shower with the overhead spout that had my attention the first time I saw it before, even more than the clawfoot porcelain tub next to it.

I set my clothes down on the granite countertop, between the double sinks. Opening the cabinets next to that, I find a fluffy, blue bathrobe and more towels than I'll ever need along with slippers and eye masks.

Maybe I should have explored last night, but then again, I was still hoping none of this was real before.

Grabbing a towel, I hang it on the hook next to the shower before turning the hot water on. It's time to feel like me again.

I want to take my time washing, but every minute that passes makes my stomach growl louder, craving something warm and soothing, not the uneaten food from nearly two hours ago.

Before I know it, I'm shutting off the water, disappointed I couldn't enjoy this luxury properly and drying off.

I expect the clothes to be a little snug or even too big, but each item fits perfectly, including the jean length, which rarely happens for my short frame.

This isn't strange at all. A lie I keep telling myself.

After brushing my hair and tossing it into a bun with the hair tie I found, I brush my teeth with what I assume is a new wooden toothbrush since the toothpaste still had a seal on it.

Once I'm back in the room, the crown from last night lies abandoned on the side table, glinting softly in the ambient light. Am I expected to wear this while I'm here? It seems redundant; everyone knows who I am already. I dismiss the fleeting urge to place it upon my head and instead, I reach for a pair of heeled, brown boots from the closet. The added inches elevate not just my normally five-foot, one-inch frame, but my spirit, boosting my confidence as I approach the door with a newfound determination.

I have no clue where the kitchen might be in this labyrinth of a palace, but I'm certain I'll encounter someone along the way who can direct me. Not that Cain hasn't done his best to make me comfortable, but I just don't want to rely on him. I need to find my own way around, to claim some autonomy in this foreign world.

Stepping into the corridor, I hesitate, my gaze darting left, then right, and left again. To my surprise, the man Asher claims is my father is sitting just outside my door, his posture one of weary resignation. His shoulders are curved in and hands are folded in his lap while his eyes remain closed. For a moment, I begin to wonder if he's even still breathing.

"Um, hello?" My voice echoes slightly in the vast hallway.

His response is slow, his head lifting to reveal a gentle smile that doesn't reach his tired eyes. This time, when our gazes meet, the expected surge of emotion doesn't materialize. Confusion mingles with relief—had I imagined the intensity of our previous connection, or has the stress of this ordeal begun to warp my perceptions? I don't know, but there is still a kindness seeping from this man that I can't ignore.

"Hello, Issie," he says, a note of hesitation in his voice. "Is it okay that I call you that?"

Isobella? Issie? Isla? They all sound close enough and there's something about this man that makes me want to wrap my arms around him and never let him go, so of course he can call me whatever he'd like.

"Sure," I reply, my voice softening. "That or 'Isla' is fine."

"Isla," he repeats, testing the name as if it offers him some comfort. "I like that for you. My name is Grayson."

A pang of something akin to loss tightens within my chest, an ache for a connection that should be there but isn't. I don't know if it's just being here in this place or if I've officially gone crazy and the lack of pull that I feel toward Grayson now is actually painful.

I glance around again, trying to ignore the growing pressure in my chest. "What are you doing out here? Did Asher not help you somewhere more comfortable?"

Grayson shakes his head, a faint smile playing on his lips as he gestures to a door just down the hall. "He gave me the room next to yours. I was waiting for you—I hoped we might have dinner together."

Now, this is a man whose company I'd enjoy for a meal.

"I'd love nothing more," I say, extending my hand to help him up. His fingers are cold in mine, and a fresh wave of resentment toward Asher washes over me. "I'm sorry you're caught in the middle of his threats."

Grayson's chuckle is tinged with sadness. "I'm sorry to laugh and I don't mean to overwhelm you, but..." He looks up at me with pure joy shining through his familiar, blue eyes. "You have no idea how much I've missed you. Even this temperamental version of you that you'd long since grown out of before..."

He stops talking and my entire body tenses. Not one person has talked about what happened to this Isobella woman, just that they insist I'm her. Maybe it's time I learn more about the shadow of who I once might have been.

Gently, I press for more information. "If it's too painful to talk about, you don't have to, but I would love to know what happened to your daughter."

I might not *be* her, but maybe I'm her doppelgänger or something else that I didn't think existed in real life. You know, like portals to other worlds.

Hell, what else might not be fiction?

With a slight shake of my head, I put my focus back on Grayson as he starts to answer me and walks toward the stairs, his gait carrying on with more ease than I expected after first meeting him.

"She disappeared," he says first. "Nobody knows what really happened, but there are theories, none of them all that appealing."

His answer doesn't offer me any solace and the way he avoids looking at me, I decide to ask about something else that's made me slightly curious.

"Why does Asher seem so angry with me?"

This brings a smirk back to his face. "My Issie and

Asher were…close, best friends since the day they were born in fact. When she couldn't be found, it wasn't just my world that unraveled, but also his."

"Maybe she left because he's such an asshole," I say out loud without meaning to, then I cover my mouth and mutter an apology.

Grayson doesn't seem offended; instead, he nods sagely. "You both had your tempers, but together, you were something special."

As we descend the stairs, I'm having trouble breathing from his revelation since I feel like his version of "close" means more than I want to know. Though Grayson saves me from having to ask by changing the subject.

His eyes look down, then up at me again. "I hope you've kept your strength up because I'm going to be counting on you to not let me tumble down three flights of stairs."

My arm wraps around his waist without a second thought. "You won't fall on my watch."

We make it downstairs without issue, the silence stretching between us because asking more questions seems too dangerous after the previous one. The pressure in my chest has now moved to my head and breathing feels like a chore. Still, I put one foot in front of the other, turning when Grayson tells me to and only stopping once we arrive at a dining room.

The area seems much too formal for just two people, especially when two waiters greet us and even pull our chairs out.

I giggle with a layer of nervousness, then whisper to Grayson, "I've never eaten anywhere this fancy before."

My gaze follows his upward, where there are three chandeliers, each dripping with crystals that glimmer between the lights. The ceiling is made from carved woodworkings, creating tiles above us. The table is a sleek, mahogany wood with navy-blue placemats already outfitted with a full set of silverware and glassware.

"At least not that you remember," Grayson says with a grin as I place the silver cloth napkin over my lap.

I tense up and he quickly apologizes.

"I'm sorry, Isla. I'll be better at accepting that you need time for…certain things."

My gaze shifts toward his and I try to smile, but the action turns into a grimace. "I don't think I'll be here long enough to be okay with any of this."

His shaky hand reaches for mine. "Maybe, maybe not. Let's see where the next four weeks bring us."

The two waiters fill the glasses before us, one with water and the other with what I assume is some sort of red wine, but I barely pay attention to them as I hesitate to say the words that are dying to come out.

"What is it?" Grayson says once we're alone again.

I blink, fighting back tears that I don't understand and letting the words tumble out. "When I go back home, you can come with me if you want."

Grayson's eyes mist over, his voice thick with emotion. "I would love nothing more than to be wherever you are, my sweet girl."

The connection I felt to him earlier might not be smacking me in the face anymore, but the warmth that fills my heart from his words is enough to have me relaxing in my padded linen chair.

Everything is going to be okay. Tomorrow, I'll find a way to call Elodee and maybe I'll even tell her the truth. A partial truth, anyway.

CHAPTER SEVEN

ASHER

She denied me. The sting of rejection pierces deeper than I anticipated, leaving me raw and aching. I shouldn't be surprised, yet the hurt lingers, a stark reminder of my irrationalities. I have no right to feel this way, especially after the spectacle I made earlier. I crossed lines that shouldn't have even been approached, let alone breached. I forgot who I am and acted like a bloody idiot.

My hands, trembling with a mix of anger and regret, clutch the short strands of my ebony hair, pulling slightly as if the physical pain might distract from the emotional turmoil churning inside me. I pace the length of my room, each step echoing the tumult in my heart.

Gods, I know better. Centuries of restraint, of reining in my emotions in the face of all challenges, and yet mere minutes with Isla unravels me completely. It's as if her presence resets all I know, all I've disciplined myself to be. Despite this, or perhaps because of it, I know one immutable truth: this woman is the most important thing in all the worlds to me.

Acknowledging this only sharpens the guilt. The instant I confirmed it was truly Isobella standing before me, not some imposter seeking to usurp my throne, I should have enveloped her in the reverence she deserves.

Instead, I let my anger cloud my judgment, and I unleashed it upon her—a royal blunder. Isobella, the woman whose soul now resides in Isla, never tolerated my darker moods. Why would Isla accept them now?

A deep, cleansing breath fills my lungs as I force myself to pause, to reflect, to acknowledge my mistakes. The panoramic window in my bedroom offers a view of the sea turning ink-black under the night sky, its depths mirroring the disorder I feel.

"Tomorrow will be different," I vow to the reflection in the glass. "I will apologize, and whether or not she forgives me, I need to at least try to understand her struggle."

Hell, she doesn't even know who she truly is. Her wolf must be miserable, trapped within that human body. Unless Isla knows what she is and just hasn't revealed her true self to me.

I'm tempted to show her my wolf first, but maybe I should wait until she doesn't hate me nearly as much as she does now.

A soft knock at the door pulls me from my thoughts, and I brace myself as Malimorte, my trusted advisor, enters. His golden eyes meet mine, carrying a weight of unspoken words. His habitual stroke of his auburn goatee signals unease, a prelude to unwelcome news.

"What is it, Mali?" I ask, shoving my hands into the pockets of my slacks as I face him from across the room.

"Princess Isla had dinner with Grayson tonight, Your

Majesty," he reports with a neutral tone, his gaze steady. "And your father awaits outside. He refuses to leave without speaking with you."

My father. The man whom I've always trusted above all others…except I haven't gone to him about Isobella's, I mean Isla's—I've asked others to address her with her new name, yet I can barely manage the task—return to Polaris. He wished for me to take a chosen mate, one who would at least produce an heir for our kingdom, but I never could. Something I know disappointed him.

Now, I expect him to question every aspect of my mate's return, infuriating me—and I'm not ready for that. I need to find my composure again, not be even more riled up.

"And your mother is with him, Your Majesty," Malimorte adds, adjusting the lapels of his royal-blue vest over the white, long-sleeved collared shirt, his choice of attire while on duty.

Though I'm not sure I've ever seen him not working. I know he takes time away from the castle at least once a week. Yet the man is elusive, keeping his thoughts and feelings private and sticking to the shadows. Almost in a meek way, but my wolf senses Mali's strength and that's enough for me, even if others don't always agree.

I know Malimorte would die for those he cares about and after two hundred years as my advisor, I have no doubt that I'm one of those people.

"Send them in," I instruct, turning toward the bar cart to prepare three drinks. Intuition tells me this will be a night for strong spirits.

He disappears back out the door without another word to me and I take the tray of drinks to the sitting area of my master suite. The front area of my living quarters consists of a large, rock fireplace, two couches, a desk for me to work at when I don't feel like being bothered, and a sitting area where I normally have dinner by myself. Also, where I sit now, waiting for my parents to enter.

I position my mother's wine and my father's whiskey on the table, nearest to the two seats across from me before taking a long drink of ice-cold water. Much to my father's dismay, I've never been a fan of his aged whiskeys, or any alcohol, for that matter. The bar cart I keep stocked is merely for guests.

When my parents enter, I rise from my chair and smile at the two people who gave me life. "Mother, Father." I nod, stepping forward as my mother's arms spread out and her light blue eyes fill with love and concern.

I settle into her embrace, the familiar scent of lavender and sage enveloping me, momentarily comforting. "I'm glad to see you're doing well, considering."

"Considering what?" I query, my head tilting in a mix of confusion and apprehension as they exchange a loaded glance.

"Well, there's been talk. Isobella is here to reject you," she says, her voice a soft blow to my already fragile state. The mere suggestion jolts through me like a physical assault, confirming my deepest fears.

Isla doesn't want me and I only have four weeks to salvage the connection that once defined us. My wolf bristles at the thought, a primal reminder of what's at stake. We've weathered her absence before; the notion of enduring it again is unbearable yet unavoidable.

"That's not accurate," I say calmly. "Isobella has been reborn and her name is now Isla. She doesn't recall her time here and, from my understanding of the situation, believes that she is human."

My father's dark-cobalt eyes widen beneath his greying brows. "I know I had my suspicions, but to know that she actually chose to forget you... It's shameful. When does she leave? We must consult the gods about finding you a new mate."

My jaw tightens and fists clench, anger and defiance stiffening my posture. "I've told you too many times to count, I don't want a new mate, Father. Isla is still mine, and she's not leaving."

He starts to protest, but I cut him off. Composure is a luxury I can't afford at the moment. "You heard wrong," I state firmly.

Mother's hand presses gently against my chest, her touch a balm to my simmering fury. "It's okay, Son." She then addresses my father. "Gideon, I warned you."

Now, I understand why my mother is here.

"Don't *Gideon* me, Sosheena." He stands taller, like the king he once was. "We've known for centuries now that Isobella abandoned our son. Why am I the only one who is capable of accepting this and who is ready to move on already?"

I roar, unable to contain the beast of my anger. "She didn't *abandon* me!" I take a step back, distancing myself from my mother's presence. "Just because Isla doesn't remember doesn't mean it was her choice. Something must have gone wrong. Why else wouldn't she have been reborn on Lunara?"

My father shakes his head and lowers his voice. "Not in a millennium have I ever once heard of a reincarnation going 'wrong.' I'm not trying to hurt you, Asher. I'm trying to protect you. Why must you fight me on this after all this time?"

"She is *mine*, Father," I seethe, staying several feet away from him. "And I am hers. I always have been. I don't care what you think you know or what anyone else has told you—my mate didn't choose to leave me. I know that more than anything else in this world."

Now, if only I'd remembered that when she first arrived, this situation wouldn't be as screwed up as it seems to have become.

My father holds his hands up in surrender. "I'm sorry, Son. For all of it. I didn't realize that's how you perceived my opinion of Isobella."

"Call her 'Isla,'" I insist, seeking at least this small concession.

"Isla," he agrees, nodding. "I can do that, but more importantly, I need you to know that I would have loved nothing more than for centuries of happiness between the two of you. You shared a love that was stronger than anything I've ever seen between two wolves so young. Anything I may have ever said was done so out of love and protection for not only you, but our kingdom."

I can't deny the truth in his voice. I know he's always had my best interest at heart. Yet I've allowed myself to believe that's been true with everything other than my mate, considering how many times he's wished for me to replace her, as if that would be an easy feat.

Maybe I owe him an apology as well. There's a reason I've avoided my father since yesterday and realizing that it has nothing to do with him and everything to do with me is almost paralyzing.

I'm so terrified of losing Isla again that the thought of

speaking with anyone who would question our bond, even if for my own benefit… I just couldn't do it.

Instead, I've stood by as rumors have clearly begun to take root and hid away, trying to force everything to be fine when in all honesty, we're so far from fine that it's not even funny.

"I hear you, Dad," I tell him more calmly. "But you need to give Isla time. What's being said isn't true. She just needs time to understand. She's agreed to stay for at least four weeks."

He raises a brow and grins, instantly lightening the mood within the room. "If you hadn't been avoiding me since she arrived, I might not have needed to count on the gossip mill of our staff to learn what's what."

I chuckle despite myself. He's not wrong.

As my mother takes a robust sip of wine and sets the glass down with a determined clink, she declares, "Well, it seems I've done my job and the two of you are going to talk like civilized beings. I'm off, then." Her tone is light, but there's an undercurrent of firmness in it.

Dad's voice rumbles with a mix of jest and real concern. "And where does my mate think she's going?" He's never quite gotten over his old-fashioned belief that she should be within his line of sight at all times.

With a playful flourish, she blows him a kiss. "Wherever she likes, darling. But don't worry, I'll still be within the castle's walls. You might just have to hunt a little harder to find me later." Her voice carries the melody of their lifelong dance, a mix of independence and affection.

I watch her exit, the lightness of her steps contrasting sharply with the heaviness in my chest. I ache for the easy exchanges I once shared with my own mate. I miss Isobella and as much as I'm trying to respect this new version of her by calling her 'Isla,' I don't know how long I'll be able to handle having her so close yet so far away from me.

"Sit with me, Son." Dad settles into the plush couch with his whiskey in hand. I can't bring myself to sit; instead, I find myself tending to the remnants of the evening's fire, poking at the embers that are dying out, much like my hope.

"Tell me everything that's happened since Isla arrived," he begins, seeming to try to bridge the chasm of my reserve. "I heard she appeared quite disoriented at the portal while Cain was present."

Without looking at him, I nod and keep focused on the charred logs. "That's right. Then he brought her to me per my request and I might have let my fury shine more than anything else, sending her to her room and not checking on her until earlier this evening."

I glance at him and I'm surprised to see both of his brows raised. "I see. No wonder people are saying she wants nothing to do with you and that she's demanding to return to Earth. How have you convinced her to stay, as you mentioned earlier?"

My face twists involuntarily at the memory. "I sought out Grayson, hoping he might sway her. But even his presence couldn't deter her desire to leave. In desperation, I..." I hesitate, the words tasting bitter, "I used his lack of wellbeing as leverage to keep her here for a moon cycle."

He gasps, dropping his glass onto the coffee table in front of him. "Asher Josiah Cromwell, you did no such thing."

"I know it was wrong," I tell him, finally meeting his stare properly. "Hell, it's the worst thing I've ever done, but she was going to leave me, Dad. Without answers. After all this time, I was desperate to make her stay no matter the cost."

"And what has it cost *you*?" His voice is tinged with a mix of worry and curiosity.

"She declined dinner with me tonight, so I'm certain she hates me, but I'd rather her be here hating me than back on Earth, pretending I don't exist."

My father gets up and comes to stand at my side. His firm grip clasps my shoulder and he smiles at me. "You love her as fiercely as ever—that much is clear."

"That hasn't changed, nor will it," I affirm, my resolve hardening.

His grin only widens. "Then, no matter what people say or think, we're going to find a way to make her see this is where she belongs. You don't have to be alone in this, Asher. I may have given you the crown early, but I've always been there for you and my health isn't going to get in the way of continuing to do so now."

His health. I snort to myself. He thought he was dying, but his only issues, even all these years later, are a bum knee and a heart that beats a little faster than normal.

I'm certain he was just tired of his reign and I can't blame him. Thankfully, he's right. He's been there, helping me every step of the way, ensuring our kingdom stays strong and united.

"Have you told Noen or Declan yet?" he asks, the question making my tension return.

Noen and Declan, my two closest friends and also royal delegates. They've been away, working on a trade deal with Selaris on my behalf. I've been tempted to send word to them a dozen times. Yet…I haven't forgotten that I once believed Noen had an interest in my mate. I swore I was past that, but now that she's here, I can't help wanting him nowhere near her.

Petty, yes, but if I'm going to turn things around with this situation, I have to at least be honest with myself.

"No, you're the first person I've really spoken to."

Dad loosens his grip and steps away from me. "Well, maybe it's time you changed that. You're going to need support to figure this all out, especially if Isla has no memory of her time with us."

He isn't wrong, even if I'm not quite ready to admit that.

Still, I'll do whatever it takes to get my mate back, to find a way for her to remember, to have the love I've never been able to let go of reciprocated once more.

I once promised Isobella that I would always find her and it's about damn time that I followed through.

CHAPTER EIGHT

ISLA

Dinner with Grayson was incredible. There was something about the food tonight that made me wonder if maybe the chefs have woven some sort of enchantment into their recipe. Or maybe it was just the company. Either way, everything tasted rich with bursts of flavor unlike any meal I've ever had back home. So much so, I opted for dessert, even though I felt as though I was going to explode.

"It's your turn to help me with the stairs," I tease, groaning and rubbing a hand over my stomach as we prepare to go back to our rooms.

Grayson's laughter is deep and comforting, a sound that's become pleasantly familiar over the course of the evening. Although I'm still unsure of our relation, his presence has an undeniable ease to it, soothing yet poignant, especially as he fights to keep his eyes open.

"I'll do my best." He yawns. "Sorry. It's been a long day for me."

Concern flickers within me as I notice his weariness and place a hand over his on the table. "I can't believe Asher won't heal you."

He looks down at his lap, then back up at me with an expression I can't identify, but it's almost tortured. "King Asher is doing what he believes is best and I won't lie to you, Issie. I agree with his choice since it means getting more time with you. I know this is all a lot for you and there are so many things that you don't understand yet, but I hope before you make your final choice to leave that you'll consider all the facts before deciding to go back to Earth."

He speaks as though there could be a single thing to keep me here. As much as I want to save Grayson, I can't and won't choose him over Elodee for more than the promised four weeks, especially when he's agreed to leave with me. I need to go back to her. Outside of that, there isn't anything in this place that makes me want to stay and I can't see that changing.

"You're partly right," I concede, squeezing his hand. "There's a lot I don't understand—like how I could possibly be someone from centuries ago, or why I'm even here. But I know where I belong, and it's not here. Hell, I don't even want to know how any of this is possible. I just want to save you and get back to the family I left behind."

He grimaces. "You have a family?"

Well, this is awkward.

"I have a person," I say. "Elodee. She was my foster sister and has been my best friend and soul sister since I was a toddler. I can't abandon her. Not for any reason."

His previously tired eyes start to brighten and he nods.

"No, you can't and we won't let that happen, I promise you. Now, if you don't have any questions that I can answer for you, then how about we head to our rooms? This old man needs his rest."

As Grayson starts to stand, I move to help him, but he pushes his chair out on his own this time. He at least takes my offered hand and loops an arm through mine. As we ascend the stairs together, I marvel at how naturally our movements synchronize, his steps steady beside mine.

Pausing at his door, Grayson's voice lowers to a whisper. "Issie, I know we've just reconnected, and this may be too much to ask, but..."

The unexpected vulnerability in his voice sends a shiver down my spine. My intuition screams that this connection, however inexplicable, matters deeply.

My hands squeeze his and my skin gets goosebumps. Maybe I *should* start asking questions because there has to be more at play here than me having some sort of doppelgänger from the past. Feeling this connection to this stranger, even if it's not as intense as it was the first time our eyes met, isn't normal.

I've never allowed my walls to come down with anyone so fast, but I can't deny that I want to give Grayson anything he wishes for. Well, as long as it's not staying in this place past the four weeks that I've agreed to.

Which is why I find myself smiling warmly at him and saying, "You can always ask."

He hesitates, emotion warring in his eyes as he looks toward the wall on our left. "I'm sorry. Your moth—my... wife used to say that same thing. I wasn't expecting that."

Without thought, I hug him because regardless of how unreal all this is, my heart breaks for what this man has lost. A daughter, a wife, and who knows what else.

He accepts the embrace, his body tensing before relaxing and pulling back to look at me. "About that favor. Please, keep an open mind and when you're ready to talk, don't be afraid to ask any question that comes to mind. There is nothing you could ask that I won't answer as long as it has nothing to do with King Asher. Any curiosity you might have about him needs to be handled between the two of you."

I scoff before he's even finished speaking. "I assure you, I know all I need to about that man and there will be no reason for questions where he's concerned."

"Sometimes we don't always make the best first impression," Grayson adds, his lips seeming to be fighting a smile. "You might change your mind."

Doubtful.

"Well, goodnight, then," he says, offering me another smile that has deep lines forming around his eyes.

"Sleep well."

He steps into his room and I head the short distance to my door. Inside, my bedroom is quiet and I throw myself onto the mattress, stretching my body out and groaning. Not only because I'm ridiculously full, but because Grayson has made my mind begin to churn.

I don't want to know more about this place. I just want to do my time here and go home, feeling proud that I've helped save a man's life, one my heart tells me deserves at least that.

Our conversation replays through my mind and when

I remember his reaction to me saying, *"You can always ask,"* I sit straight up in bed.

"Holy shit." My head shakes and I struggle to breathe. How could I have been so…stupid, aloof, naïve? None of those feel right, but *oh, my God.*

"These people are centuries old." The words tumble out in a jumble, but that doesn't make them any less real.

I know I've said and heard "five hundred years" several times now, but it's as if my mind had been protecting me from truly understanding what those three words meant to the bigger picture. Unless there's something else that I'm missing…

Grayson says I'm his daughter and he looks about eighty, but Cain said the photo was from five hundred years ago.

How could I not have questioned that then? I mean I was overwhelmed with the surly king, having just been transported to a world that shouldn't exist, and everything else in between, but still.

Five freaking centuries? I can't un-know this now that the information has been highlighted within my thoughts.

This is something I need to ask Grayson about now. Even if I intend to leave this world behind and never think of it again, I know I won't be able to let this go. Plus, Elodee will kill me for not finding this information out once I explain what the hell has happened to me. I might not have wanted to tell her everything before, but this isn't something I can keep to myself any longer.

Before I can get up from my bed, there's a soft knock on my door. Maybe the answers are coming to me instead of me going to them.

I expect to see Grayson on the other side, but when I

twist the handle and open the door, I jump back. There's a regal woman standing in the hallway, smiling sincerely at me as if I should know her. "Hello, Isla."

"Uh, hi. I was, um, just headed to, um, see Grayson." I'm not sure what to do and I probably look like a blubbering idiot, but I don't really care after this latest revelation.

Taking in her appearance, I try to guess her age and can't help but wonder if she's much older than the fifty or so years she appears to be.

Her light-blue, almost-silver eyes are soft with fine wrinkles at the sides that seem to only be there because she's grinning at me still. Her greyish-blonde hair is pinned up on her head with braids and twists. I can't begin to understand how they're even staying in place. She wears a silk gown, much like the one I arrived in, but silver in color, and a diamond heart pendant sits on her chest, glinting under the light from my room.

"I'm Sosheena," she says, then adds, "Asher's mother."

Of course she is.

"May I come in?" she asks politely, glancing behind me.

"Sure, I guess." Apparently, my questions for Grayson will have to wait until after whatever this is.

She enters with the grace of a queen, practically gliding over the floor as she walks past me. Hell, she probably *was* the queen before, considering she's Asher's mother, but maybe the hierarchy here doesn't work like it does in England. Though they have similar accents, so maybe. Another thing to ask about. I should probably start making a list.

Sosheena takes it upon herself to sit at the small table

on the other side of my room and waits patiently for me to take my own seat. Yeah, this is weird.

"I wanted to come by and personally welcome you to Polaris." She smiles again, but this time, the action doesn't quite reach her eyes as she adds, "I was friends with your mother."

Breathing becomes harder and I tense, but I don't know what to say. The woman in the photo next to the bed with Grayson, she isn't *my* mother. Yet I still yearn to know more about her. I shouldn't and I tell myself not to, but given the fragile hold I have on my previous revelations…there's no stopping the words that tumble out of my mouth.

"What was her name? What happened to her? How is it possible for you people to be so damn old, but also not look *that* old?" I suck in a breath, then loosely cover my face as I mutter, "I'm sorry."

She laughs and waves a hand in the air, like everything I just asked is completely normal.

"You don't need to apologize, Isla," Sosheena says comfortingly. "I'm not sure how much my son would appreciate me telling you, but after the bits I've pieced together since your arrival, something tells me that you deserve to know more, even if it's overwhelming for you. No one should make important decisions with only pieces of the truth."

Why does she make so much sense? As much as I don't want to believe any of this can be real and would love to pretend that I'm still dreaming, her offer of information feels too intriguing to deny. Maybe it's the way she's said the words or the fact that I don't feel anything for her—at least not the connection I do to

Grayson or the irritation toward Asher—but I agree with her.

"I didn't think I wanted to know. I'm even pretty sure I suppressed things that were outright spoken to me, but if you can tell me more, I would be very grateful now," I say, still doing my best to breathe properly.

"Well, first let me ask this. How much do you know about reincarnation?"

I gape at her. "What now?"

I thought doppelgängers were weird enough before, but reincarnation? No, that's not possible. Then again, I didn't think being transported to new places and people being multiple centuries old was, either.

There's no way I can sit here and take this information. The need to move is too strong, forcing me to stand up from the chair and walk halfway to the door before turning around. I cross my arms and tap my foot as I stare at the woman before me.

"I know what reincarnation is, but please tell me the panic attack I'm having in my mind right now is for nothing and you're not saying that's what you people are. Reincarnations."

"No, dear." Her words and light chuckle have my shoulders dropping until she adds, "*We* are all reincarnated. You *and* us."

My hands cover my face again and I groan loudly. "That's not possible."

Her laughter increases. Though I don't feel like she's laughing *at* me. I'm sure I seem rather ridiculous right now.

"Oh, it is," she says. "You just didn't know it before, and now you do. As for your questions before, your mother's name was Florence. I could spend hours talking about what happened to her, but the short version, while devastating, is rather simple. She died of a broken heart and chose not to be reborn—a choice we can all make each time we die. We're *so old*, as you say, because of the magic of this world. We age much slower than humans and for my son, as the king, he doesn't age at all while holding his title. I could explain the whys behind those things, but we should probably stick to the basics for tonight, given the paleness of your face."

I've never been much for vulgar language, but... fuck me.

I pinch my arm and while there is a harsh bite of pain from my longer-than-normal nails, I don't wake up from this craziness.

How am I supposed to accept that this is all real? How do I leave here and pretend I don't know these things now? This is why I wasn't going to ask questions. I didn't need to know the answers because they only lead to so many more questions.

Yet Sosheena's earlier words now haunt me.

"No one should make important decisions with only pieces of the truth."

I close my eyes and take a deep inhale. The action is sharp and jagged and burning, like swallowing fiery icicles that are breaking apart as the air is forced down my throat. Still, I take another breath, then another until the action becomes easier to manage.

"There you go, Isla," Sosheena says. "Just breathe and everything will be okay. I promise."

Looking back at her, I shake my head. "Don't make promises you can't keep."

A frown etches deep on her face and she looks away for the first time since appearing at my door. "You're right." Her gaze slowly returns to mine. "I shouldn't make a blanket promise like that, but I *can* promise that whatever you're feeling now, however shocking all this seems, it will get easier. That's not to say it won't get worse first, but your best chance of surviving all of this is knowing the truth."

I really hate that she's most likely right.

"So, reincarnation?" I ask, still standing in the middle of my room, because there isn't a part of me that doesn't agree with her at this point. "That means that I've died before and come back to life. If this is something that all of you do, why is it that people remember me, but I don't remember them?"

"Hm, that's the golden question, isn't it?" she muses. "One I can't answer for you. I wish I could, believe me, but nobody was there with you that we know of when you died that first time. There were no signs of a struggle, no body, no blood, just nothing. You were gone and none of us knew why. Of course we could guess, but no answer was a good one."

Well, that sounds pretty damn terrible.

"I'm sorry," I start to say, but she cuts me off.

"You were once going to be the future queen," she tells me. "You don't need to apologize for anything, Isla. Fate is something we can't control. All we can do is our best to adjust to the situation like we've done throughout the years and I hope you're doing now."

"Future...qu-queen?" I stutter. What the hell is she talking about? I know Grayson said Isobella was close with Asher and I might have assumed that meant they dated, but being his *queen?* Never once did that cross my mind.

Her fingers lightly cover her lips, but the action doesn't hide her grin. "I've said more than I intended. How about something else? Yes, our memories. Typically, when those born in Lunara die and choose to be reborn, they eventually remember everything about their past lives. As their maturity grows, so does their memory. Oh, that gives me an idea. How do you feel about school?"

I lean against my bed now that I'm not losing my mind as much as before. Though I still want to know more about this future queen business. Maybe Grayson will tell me more tomorrow. I don't think I'll go see him after this conversation. My mind is already on overload.

"School?" I finally reply. "I was never the best at it, but I graduated."

"You should join in on some of the classes," she replies animatedly. "Yes, that would be a great idea. You can learn more about Lunara while you're here because it's not just the truth of your heart that you need to know before deciding to leave. You should know where you're from, Isla. Even if you leave, this is important, no matter your choice."

"You should know where you're from, Isla."

I thought I did. I thought that I was born in Salem, Oregon to my parents, Sandy and Blake Jessup. I thought I knew everything that I needed to know, but suddenly, I'm not so sure.

"Can I use a phone to call back…to Earth?" I ask because in this moment, with all these admissions, there's nobody I need more than Elodee.

Sosheena's grimace doesn't give me much hope even

before she answers. "We don't have the technology to do so, but we can send a message to someone if you'd like since you're not able to leave just yet."

Of course I can't. I'm sure even if I promised to come back, to let a guard or someone come with me, that prick of a king still wouldn't let me call Elodee myself. Regardless, a message isn't enough. Hell, not even a phone call is, but it would have been better than nothing.

"What happened to my car and everything in it when I…came here?" I ask next because if she's going to send a message on my behalf, then it needs to come from me, on my phone, and not some stranger. Elodee has probably already filed a missing person's report on me.

"The portal you came through was an ancient one," she says thoughtfully. "I don't have the answer to that question, but I can let you know tomorrow morning, yes?"

My body sags and I just want to crawl into bed. "I guess that will have to work. If you're going to send a message for me, I'd prefer to have something texted from my phone that was left in my car."

She gets up from her seat and stops in front of me where I still rest against my mattress. She grabs both of my hands and her warmth seeps into me, relaxing my muscles. "I'm not sure what a *text* is." She chuckles. "But we will figure this out together and more than that, I will make sure your stay here is as comfortable as possible. If you don't believe anything else, please believe that. Your mother was my dearest friend and I—" Sosheena pauses to clear her throat. "I know she would have done the same for me if our roles had been reversed."

I watch as the former queen leaves my room without

another word. As soon as the door closes behind her, I don't even bother to undress. I push myself the rest of the way onto the bed, wrap myself in the comforter, and pray for sleep because my mind can't take any other thoughts tonight.

Not of reincarnation, magic worlds, ancient portals, or anything else. I just want to shut it all off, even if for a few hours.

CHAPTER NINE

ISLA

The morning sun barely touches the edges of my curtains when a persistent knock pulls me from sleep. I burrow deeper under the covers, determined to ignore the world a little longer, but the voice that follows the knock seeps through the wood.

Asher.

Just thinking his name makes my chest tighten. Of all the people I'm least prepared to face, he tops the list. I muffle my groans with a pillow, hoping to drown him out. Yet he persists, his voice softening into a plea.

"I have something for you, Isla. I won't go until I see you're all right. Just a moment, and then I'll leave you to your day once I do."

That's a change from the domineering man I encountered yesterday. Hell, the man from then probably would have busted down the door and not replaced it out of spite. Still, curiosity piques despite my irritation.

I throw the blankets off, not caring that I'm still in

yesterday's clothes or that my hair is probably a mess. Asher can think whatever he wants about me.

I swing the door open with a brisk pull, and there he stands—less the monarch, more the penitent. In his hands is a bouquet of my favorite flowers, yellow and white lilies, their vibrant blooms placed in a delicate pink crystal vase.

He extends them with a gentle voice. "These are for you, as an apology for my behavior before."

My hand grips the door as I lean casually against it. "For which *before*? When you demanded your servant bring me to this room or when you used a man's life to force me to stay here?"

He at least looks ashamed as his eyes cast down to my feet. "I'm sorry for *both* those things, Isla. There is a lot that you don't know and I'd love to tell you, but I didn't come here to bother you."

I scoff and nod toward the door. "I'd say continually knocking and telling me that you won't leave until I open is the opposite of that statement."

"Yes, I'd have to agree, but I needed to see that you were okay." He glances behind me before meeting my hardened stare again. "Please take these flowers, even if you don't accept my apology."

"Great." I grab the vase from his hands, ignoring the flare of warmth that floods through me when our fingers brush together. "Now, goodbye."

I shut the door in his face and lock it. Of course, he could likely easily get in, but the action makes me feel better as I stomp across the room. There's no way in hell that I'll ever forgive that man for his actions. Flowers or no flowers, he doesn't deserve my mercy.

When I set the massive arrangement on the table, I notice a folded note tucked between the stems.

I cross my arms and shake my head. "Nope, I'm not going to read that."

Heading for the bathroom, I'm intent on getting in the shower and starting my boring day of hanging out in this room, but I practically growl as I hesitate to pull my pajama shirt over my head. "Damn it!"

I go back to the main room and grab the stupid piece of paper.

Isla,

In case you didn't let me say it before, I'm sincerely sorry for the way I've acted since your arrival.

I roll my eyes. Yeah, you should be, buddy.

As you've learned by now, we Lunarians live long lives and your arrival brought me back to a painful time in my life. That's no excuse, but it is the truth. You won't see that version of me again, I promise you that.

These people and their promises… Though his words do remind me that I need to figure out just what the old me's relationship was with this man. Being close to him and being engaged with the intention of becoming a queen are two completely different things.

I shudder. Though I don't know if the action is

because I'm actually freaked out over the potential answer or something else entirely that I will refuse to admit even on my deathbed.

> *Please enjoy these flowers. They were your favorite before and I hope they still are. They also remind me of brighter days. Maybe they can do the same for you.*
>
> *If you feel up for it, I encourage you to explore the castle, or even the town. Ask Cain to go with you if you want an escort. I've requested that he be available to you at all hours should you need him.*
>
> *My invitation to dinner last night, that you rightly declined, stands open for every evening you're here, should you change your mind.*
>
> *I'll see you soon, Isla.*
>
> *Asher*

I crumple the note within my palm and throw it across the room. More out of frustration for myself than the infuriating king.

I certainly don't forgive him and his words shouldn't affect me, yet my mind reels, wondering when he's going to come see me again. Will he show up every morning or does he plan on checking on me multiple times throughout the day?

Well, if I'm not here, then I won't have to see him. Maybe I should take his suggestion and go exploring.

Though not in the castle. This place is where I'm most likely to run into him and I'm not ready for that. Not if he's going to act all nice and apologetic. My body thinks too highly of that man and I need my mind to remain in charge. Distance will be key for that.

Quickly, I shower but don't bother to wash my hair. The sooner I can get out of this room, the better.

Within fifteen minutes, I'm as ready as I'm going to get. I've brushed my hair and put a few curls in because, well, with all these fancy clothes and the fact that people keep calling me a princess, I should probably be a little more put-together than my normal self if I don't want to draw more attention.

I'm dressed in black slacks that feel like air against my legs and opt for silver flats that match my sweater, hoping these clothes are something I'm supposed to wear. I didn't actually ask before, assuming they were for me. *Oh, well.*

As I head to the door, my stomach swirls and I almost don't reach for the doorknob. Maybe staying in is best. Maybe jumping out the window would be even better. Kidding. Mostly.

With an aggravated sigh, I open the door and am surprised to find an empty hallway. I expected someone to be waiting for me. Not sure who, but these people would be right not to trust me. I wouldn't blame them for having me followed. Though I'm grateful to be getting out of this room, even if I'm nervous.

As I walk down the stairs, people pass me without the wide-eyed stares from before. Instead, I receive polite nods and smiles. Everyone's dressed in slightly fancier business-style clothes than mine, but I don't feel out of place.

By the time I get downstairs, I remember that I wanted to chat with Grayson again but decide that I can wait until dinner tonight. That is if I don't join Asher…

Giving my head a solid shake, I head down the hallway that Cain brought me through my first night here. The castle feels brighter this morning. The intimidating aura lurking with the shadows is replaced by the glory of the stone walls, wall sconces, and aged portraits that seem more magnificent than I remembered.

I want to linger to appreciate the beauty of everything, but the farther I get from my room, the harder it is to breathe. I need fresh air urgently.

My stride lengthens and I find myself going out the double doors that once again open on their own. Freaking magic. I want to say I'm surprised any of this is real, but after learning about manifestation from Elodee and seeing how powerful thoughts really can be, I can't deny that anything is possible. Though that's more her expertise than mine.

Outside, Asher's voice reaches my ears. He's not talking to me, and I can't even tell where he is, but I'm not ready to face him again. I dart around a corner, finding a secluded walkway that takes me around the side of the castle, farther from the front gates.

Eventually, I slow down as I reach a vast back yard. Though calling it a *yard* seems inadequate—it's more like a sprawling field of perfectly manicured grass resembling a prestigious golf course. To my left, the open area stretches under clear, blue skies. To my right, another intriguing structure beckons me with its numerous windows. But it's the forest in front of me, dense with towering trees under a sunlit canopy, that captures my full attention.

My shoulders instantly soften the moment I take in the tall, thick trees and I know where I'm going.

As I'm walking across the yard, it almost feels as if I'm moving over water. My steps are light and fluid and sure. Not that I've ever been clumsy, but this new surety within my body is foreign. Though not in a bad way, just new. Confidence isn't something I've had in spades over the years.

I've always known I'm a good person and worthy of good things, but knowing and believing are two different things. Still, I've been trying. Especially with Elodee gone, I needed to be my own hero.

A snort of a laugh escapes me. "And look how that's working out for me."

Getting to the edge of the forest, there's a breeze, blowing the taller grass here ever so slightly and carrying the sound of chirping through the air. The moment I step off the grass onto the dirt ground, a chill runs through me. I close my eyes, surrendering to the overwhelmingness of... I don't know what, but whatever is here, it's as if my soul is yearning for the freedom within the shadows of these trees.

Every footstep forward brings a boost of energy flowing into my body and the desire to lie down, soaking up whatever power is here, nearly consumes me. My skin tingles and itches and my bones, it's like they're craving to be stretched.

"What kind of magic is this?" I whisper to myself, pausing to lean against a tree. I press my palms against the rough bark but suddenly pull back as something pricks me. There's no mark, yet the pain lingers.

As I rub my hands together, they grow uncomfortably warm. Before I can process this odd sensation, a rustling noise comes from behind.

I whip around, my heart racing. Is this place getting darker, or is my mind playing tricks on me?

The leaves crunch louder, and I inch closer to the tree, wishing that I could disappear within its bark as I slink closer to the ground, attempting to make myself less visible.

What the hell was I thinking going into a forest that I know nothing about?

My mouth drops open, and I nearly scream out of frustration. I don't know how I could have forgotten that I saw a large wolf out here my first night in the castle. Though that doesn't mean whatever is nearby could be the same beast. Maybe they're more nocturnal and whatever's getting closer is just a squirrel or raccoon... with rabies that will want to tear my eyes out.

Yeah, that's not helping.

It's time to make a run for it.

Getting back up, I take a step away from the tree and a deep growl stops me cold as the rumble echoes around me, loud and menacing. *You've got to be shitting me.*

"Easy, boy," I say calmly, remembering some random video about bear safety that I watched years ago. Not that I think this is a bear based on the sounds and what I've already seen, but maybe the same rules apply for all savage animals.

"I'm a human. You don't want to hurt me."

More branches break and the growl turns into a snarl. Great, so not a friendly animal. More like a rabid dog.

Golden eyes break through the shadows, leering right into my soul, and I do the next stupid thing I can recall.

My arms go up in the air, making myself as big as possible while screaming like a banshee. "You can bite me, but I won't go down without a fight," I feebly threaten, as if this beast can understand my words.

Holy shit, is this actually working? What I believe to be a wolf creeps back into the shadows and I start to walk backward, but my hope only lasts for so long.

I trip over an exposed root and the moment I'm down, a large shadow flies over me, something new and headed farther into the forest. There's a beat of silence before I hear the clash of teeth and more growls.

Not wasting a moment, I scramble to my feet, smacking my cheek against a branch, and run like hell in the opposite direction. Only, I don't think I'm heading back toward the castle. *Great.* Not even an hour on my own and I've nearly been eaten alive, I'm bleeding, and I'm likely about to get myself lost.

Still, I don't stop running. At least not until I hear my name called.

"Isla!" Asher roars into the dark forest.

I pause, my chest heaving from the exertion, and my legs shaking with adrenaline. My head swivels around and it's not even a minute later that Asher comes skidding to a stop in front of me.

There's a cut on his forearm and his eyes are practically glowing, making me take a step back.

He holds his hands out in front of his body, reaching for me. "It's okay, Isla. You're safe."

I shake my head and point toward his face, then his arm. "You just… How did…?"

Asher comes closer and lowers his head. "There's something we haven't told you yet and we probably should."

Or maybe they shouldn't because I have a feeling that whatever comes out of his mouth next is going to turn my entire world upside down for what feels like the hundredth time since appearing in that cave.

CHAPTER TEN

ASHER

This is not how I envisioned revealing my true self to Isla. My plan was for Isla to gently acclimate to our world, to unveil the magic at a pace she could absorb without losing her mind. Yet here I am, forced into this revelation by circumstances spiraling beyond my control. My mother's preemptive disclosures already pushed the boundaries, and now, I find myself doing exactly what I didn't want.

Though my primary goal remains unchanged: I cannot —and will not—lose Isla again.

"I didn't think you'd venture this far out, but of course, you always defy expectations," I admit with a reluctant grin, trying to inject a lighter tone into the unfolding drama.

"But that wolf and the other… How did you…make them go away?" Her stammering is only going to get worse the longer I wait. I know this, but it doesn't make the words I say next any easier.

"He was a young wolf who thought you were an

intruder," I explain with measured calmness. "Once I set him straight and made sure he knew you weren't to be bothered ever again, I let him go."

Her face drains of color, her eyes widening in disbelief. "You told a wild animal to leave me alone? Are you serious?" The skepticism in her voice isn't to be missed.

"That's not what he is." The weight of my next words feel like a boulder in my throat. "He's one of my wolves, part of my pack."

Confusion etches her features as she takes a hesitant step back. "What are you talking about?"

I steel myself against the surge of emotions threatening to overwhelm my composure. "We're wolf shifters, Isla. Part human, part beast, but far from wild."

Laughter bursts from her, sharp and disbelieving. "That's a joke, right? I'm going back to my room now." She turns to leave, the dismissive gesture a knife to my chest, but now that we've started this conversation, there's no ending it until she understands.

I block her path, urgency bleeding into my voice. "You need to hear this, Isla."

"No." Her denial is flat, resolute. "I *need* to be here for four weeks as promised, take my—Grayson and go. I've already learned too much. I don't need to know more."

I hear the words leaving her mouth, but as I gaze into her eyes, a flicker of curiosity battles the defiance staring back at me. She's intrigued, despite herself. "Please, just listen. We are wolf shifters, and so are you."

Her laughter is a dark melody that fills the space between us. "You've lost your damn mind. I'm not a werewolf. Hell, I'm not even going to admit you are when things like this are supposed to only exist in fiction."

My face scrunches in confusion. "I don't know what you've heard, but we don't *wear* our wolves. We shift into them. They are us. And you can deny this all you want, but I'm telling you the truth."

"I didn't mean…" She pinches the bridge of her nose. "Never mind. Whatever the *truth* is, I'm not *that*."

"You might not remember who you once were, but don't lie to me and tell me that you just *happened* to enter this forest." My tone is firm, unyieldingly seeking the truth only she knows. "You were called to these trees. You might have even felt like running or shifting without realizing it."

She bites her lower lip and looks over my shoulder instead of directly at me. I got something right, at least. Hopefully enough that she's maybe even accepting fragments of the truth I've shared.

Keeping my voice calm, I instinctively reach for her, cupping my palm around her bicep until she flinches, and I let go. "I'm sorry." She glances down at her arm, then back up at me before I add, "Not for that, but for you having to find out this way. I'm not lying to you, Is. This is who we are."

"Reincarnated wolf shifters?" Her words are barely a whisper before she seems to find her strength. "There's no way I wouldn't know if I were a wolf. I'm sure there are… signs."

The grimace that graces her face makes me smile. I don't know what she's imagining, but I would love to. Though she's wrong about one thing.

"You were reborn to Earth," I explain, keeping my

words gentle and clear. "There is no magic there, which means your wolf has been suppressed for—" I'm at a loss for words as I realize that if she's continually been reborn to Earth all this time that her poor wolf has been locked away for five centuries.

Not only does my heart break for her inner animal, but my own howls within my mind. Isla isn't just the other half of my soul—she's his too—and knowing that his mate has been trapped? There are no proper words to describe that grief.

"For what?" Isla asks, encouraging me to finish my sentence and at least seeming more intrigued about what I have to share.

"Since you died the first time," I tell her. Though another thought occurs to me. "Do you ever have vivid dreams about places you've never been to but that seem almost too real?"

She shakes her head and I'm not surprised, but I at least had to try. If she'd dreamt of any of her past lives like the children born here do as they begin to mature, then it might have given us some much-needed answers.

"You're not lying to me, are you?" she asks, rubbing a hand over her chest, her expression mingling confusion and realization. "This is all real, I'm not stuck in the world's longest dream, and..."

Her eyes close and I want to say something to fill the silence, but I wait for her to find her words, to finish what she was going to say.

"I once lived here."

That's not what I was hoping for her to confess, but it's a start.

"Yes, to all of that," I tell her sincerely, noticing that the small cut on her cheek hasn't healed yet. Though the deeper one caused by the young wolf—who was so distracted by Isla's new scent that he didn't realize his alpha was coming for him—on my forearm is barely a pink mark.

Could it be possible that something went wrong with my mate's reincarnation and she's no longer one of us?

That's a question I don't know how to answer, but no matter, she's still *mine*. I feel that in my soul and nobody can tell me otherwise. I'm going to do whatever it takes to make sure she's not only okay with what she's learned, but that she decides to stay for the right reasons, not because I've forced her hand.

Ripping a piece of fabric from the sleeve of my shirt, I hold my hand out. "May I?"

Her fingers press to her cheek, coming back with a spot of blood on the tips. "Oh. Um, sure."

I do my best to hide my surprise that she didn't just take the cloth from me, but I'm sure I have her shock over the information I've revealed to thank for this moment.

With the utmost gentleness, I dab at her cut before applying the slightest pressure. She only winces once and I swear my heart is going to burst out of my chest when she leans into my touch.

"So warm," she mutters with her eyes closed. The words are so quiet that I don't think she intended for me to hear them, but she likely also doesn't know about wolf shifters' advanced hearing.

It's been too long since we've shared this closeness, felt the whispers of our shared connection, too long since I've openly gazed upon my mate.

The sight of her standing before me, seemingly

unguarded for the first time since her return—her long lashes casting shadows on her cheeks, her lips slightly parted in a breathless moment—stirs memories long suppressed. Each detail of her face etches itself deeper into my mind, surpassing every recollection I've had in the passing years.

Braving her wrath, I let my gaze wander while she seems to be otherwise occupied with her own thoughts. Her sweater cloaks her curves, yet my hands remember the silkiness of her skin, the way she used to arch into my touch, whispering my name in the quiet of the dark.

Fuck. I need to stop. She's not ready for this and I know I could quickly lose control with her, if only she'd let me back in, and I'm perilously close to overstepping.

When I pull my touch away, the cut is no longer tinged with red, but just a bright, pink line that should heal fine, even by human standards.

Her eyes flutter open, and she takes a step back, likely realizing just how close we've become. Her voice, barely above a whisper, breaks the intimate spell. "I should probably get back."

Despite the pang of her words, I seize the moment. "Would you first mind if I showed you somewhere else that you might enjoy visiting?"

We're close enough to the cave that we used to call our own that I begin to wonder if her subconscious was taking her there all along.

Her shudder saddens me. Though not half as much as her next words do. "I don't think I'll be leaving my room again."

"I'm so sorry, Isla," I tell her sincerely, staying close. "I should have sent word out to the whole pack about your arrival, but I was trying to keep—I just wasn't thinking. They all know now and I promise that you're perfectly safe going wherever it is that you might want to explore."

She swallows thickly. "How do they know 'now'?"

I tap my head and smile. "A wolf perk. As the Alpha King, I can speak with my people all at once or individually to them. Though they have to be on the island for my words to reach them. It's the same between mates, but just between other pack members."

"So, you're, like, a telepath?"

My head shakes and I chuckle. "No, I'm a wolf shifter with certain abilities thanks to my heritage, passed down from the gods who created us."

Now, she chokes and her cheeks flush once more. "You're a god?"

I should probably stop speaking, but the fact that Isla isn't running away from me encourages me to continue. "Yes and no. I'm a wolf shifter first and foremost, but my spirit was created by the gods and enhanced before my birth, marking me as a future king. So, technically yes, I'm a god, but I don't normally associate that title with myself."

She snorts and rolls her eyes. "Right. I'm sure the younger version of yourself used that to your advantage quite often with the ladies."

This time, I don't hesitate to intrude on her space. If Isla believes nothing else, she needs to know my next words without a doubt in her soul, words that I can no longer keep to myself, even if I know they may be too much and too soon for her to hear.

"There has never been anyone other than you, Isla." My face is only inches from hers as she presses against a tree and I reach to cup my hand around her neck, stroking my thumb over her skin, reveling in the way her flesh pebbles beneath my touch. "You and I were written in the stars, born on the same day, destined for one another from the very beginning. The day you went missing, I lost half of my heart. I thought I would go insane—literally—without you and without knowing what had happened. No one could stop me from searching every crevice of our worlds for you, not for over one hundred years."

My touch presses nearer to her skin as I watch her eyes slowly glaze over, but still, I continue. "You could have remained gone for the rest of my existence and I never would have replaced you as my mate, not for any reason, not for anyone. So, no, I've never used being a god to my advantage. I never had a reason to, not when my heart was already spoken for the moment we were born."

Isla blinks several times and I expect her to do something, even if that's pulling away from me, but she remains in place and just says, "Okay."

I'm not sure if that's a good thing or not, but I do know that no matter what happens next, Isla is going to make me work to earn her love again. Though she better be prepared because there's no holding back anymore.

Not now that she knows who we really are.

CHAPTER ELEVEN

ISLA

I'm not sure what I'm supposed to do right now. I was firmly in the "Asher is a total ass" category, but then he cornered me and said what he said, and oh my God, werewolves or excuse me, wolf shifters are real? And *I* might be one?

My head spins with this information and my body hums with uncertainty that feels like a live wire, ready to unleash itself on the world. Worse—or maybe not—the urge to go to Asher, to let him touch me again, nearly consumes me. Yet a part of me still screams for restraint.

Just this morning, I was dead set against this man, certain he was nothing but a royal ass. But now, his confession about our shared legacy tugs at strings within my heart that I didn't know existed. I can feel my resolve melting, slipping right through my fingers while my body buzzes with coiled tension that craves his nearness.

How can this be my life right now? Believing all this is real is one thing, but suddenly feeling as if I'm supposed to be part of something bigger, to accept that magic exists, but not only that. That me, the woman I am now, is a part of all this? That's a leap of a different magnitude.

Images of Elodee flash through my mind, grounding me with a jolt of guilt. She's my rock, the one constant in my life. How can I think of staying here, entangled in this new, alluring world, when she's back in Seattle, all alone?

My heart hammers with a barrage of *what-ifs*. What if I embraced this bizarre truth? What if I let Asher *show* me everything he's just confessed? What if I actually am a wolf shifter who's been trapped on Earth for centuries?

What freaking if!

As Asher and I navigate through the lush forest, around mountains, and past a soothing river, the fresh, earthy air does little to calm my inner turmoil. I take several deep breaths and even shake out my arms, trying to physically remove the chaotic thoughts running rampant through me.

While the breathing and movements do help, it's the profound sense of belonging that tells me nothing is ever going to be the same again. The soul-deep recognition—just like the first time I saw Grayson—that this is where I'm meant to be.

I don't know if that means forever, but I do know, right now, in this moment, there's no more fighting against what's happened to me. No more not asking questions because the answers might be too intimidating.

If I was born in this world, if I'm not quite as human as I always believed, then there's more to do here. Hiding in my room is no longer an option, especially when nobody seems to know what happened to me.

It's time to start facing my new reality.

"Where are we going?" I ask, feeling only slightly

guilty for ignoring the most romantic confession in history that he gave to me back there. One that still has my heart racing with the intensity of his words and makes me wish I could remember loving him just as fiercely.

Asher glances over at me, slowing his pace so that we're now walking side by side. "There's a cave just ahead that always felt like a secondary home of sorts to us. Even as kids, you and I found solace there."

I can't help but laugh. "We lived in a castle but made a home out of a cave?"

The idea seems absurd until his reply.

"You were never fond of the spotlight," he says whimsically. "All you ever needed was your family and… me. That was enough, but we also had a duty, and you understood that, too. Or so I thought."

The heartbreak that radiates from him as he says those last few words weighs heavily on me, like a boulder I can't outrun.

"What do you mean?" I'm not sure I want the answer to this question, but I have a feeling that in order to understand who I am, I need to know who I was, even if that was a different lifetime.

He stops and faces me, grabbing both of my hands. My first instinct is to pull away, but as the heat from his palms seeps into me, I decide to stop fighting against the fantasy of this world. It's only been three days and my mind is more than overwhelmed, but resisting all this isn't going to help me. It's like trying to stop a derailed train: completely pointless.

"I'm not sure because we don't know all the pieces of information that we should," he says, "but you disappeared right after I shared that my father was stepping down and I was to become king centuries sooner than either of us planned for."

I blink, unsure what to say when I have no memory of this.

He continues. "You promised we'd get through whatever obstacles we were to face together and then, before that same evening's dinner that you planned, you were gone, no trace of you left anywhere that we could find. You took nothing with you and no amount of magic could track you. It makes sense now if you went to Earth, but I still don't understand how you continued to be reborn there."

"Yeah, me, either," I mutter, releasing his hold on my hands, then I begin walking again as I try not to be frustrated that I've been told so much yet still feel like I know nothing at all.

"But you're here now," Asher says with an elation that I don't know how to match. "I know you'd rather be back on Earth and I'm sorry for forcing your hand, but in my defense, I was more desperate to keep you close than I've been in my entire life. I was wrong to go about things the way I did, but I wasn't trying to intentionally hurt you. I just wanted more time to figure things out."

Funny, Asher's earlier romantic confessions made me forget that I was supposed to despise him for using Grayson's life to control my choices. Yet even now, being reminded of what he did, there isn't a part of my heart that still wants to blame him for what he did. Hell, after seeing this new side of him, I no longer believe that Asher would sit by and let Grayson die even if I chose to walk away.

Maybe it's the magic of this world, or that I'm

exhausted and it's not even noon, but I'm okay with not hating him any longer. Asher holds answers that others won't tell me and...even if I didn't want to admit this before, there's been an attraction to this man since the moment I first laid eyes on him.

Whether that's from past me or current me or even both, I don't know, but learning that we once shared such a strong connection makes me no longer care.

But I do have one very important question that can't wait.

"Can humans live here?"

His head cocks to the side and his lips pinch together. "I don't know. Nobody has ever asked that before, at least not that I know of. Are you not sure about whether or not you're a wolf shifter in this life?"

His question is sincere and without judgment, something I appreciate because even if I'm done fighting, I'm still going to need time to come to terms with a lot of these things.

"It's not that," I explain. "My best friend, Elodee, is back on Earth. She's the only family I've ever truly had in my life and if I'm still"—I swallow hard before I can force out these next words—"a wolf shifter, that changes things, but I won't leave her behind. We're all each other has."

There's a pain in my chest at even the possibility of doing so, but also with the thought of leaving Lunara behind before I truly know who I am or what happened to me.

After hearing Asher's agony thanks to my disappearance, I feel like this is something we both need to figure out. Not only because what if there's key information that I'm missing to make me understand why

I never came back or what if someone did something to me and never got caught?

I've watched enough crime and mystery shows back home. People get away with murder every day. If someone took away the life I was supposed to have, they're going to pay for that.

Though it hasn't all been bad. I have Elodee and I wouldn't give her up for anything. Not even for the future I was supposed to have. She deserves better than that from me after all we've been through together.

"As soon as we're back at the castle, I will find out about your friend," Asher promises with a conviction that makes the pressure in my chest lighten. "You came here without the energy you were blessed with at birth. There has to be a way to do the same for Elodee."

My fingers brush over a lower branch of a nearby tree that we walk by, the soft leaves a vibrant green that I've never seen on any plant life back home. "She would love it here." Then I chuckle. "She wouldn't fight to go home like some people."

Asher's elbow bumps me and he grins when I look up at him. "You wouldn't have been *you* if you didn't put up some resistance."

At least that's always been a part of me, a comforting fact as we start to slow.

The trees become sparse and there's a small clearing of grass and wildflowers in front of a rock hill that seems to come out of nowhere. The outside is covered in moss and it's probably at least twenty feet tall. Looking around, I don't see where the cave might be, though.

Asher grabs my hand for the second time and once

again, there's a current of energy that passes between us, nearly taking my breath away.

I stare at our clasped hands, expecting there to be some physical evidence of this connection, but there's not a glow or spark to be seen.

"Here we are." Asher's voice cuts through my reverie.

Glancing up, I finally see the opening, hidden around the corner. It's dark inside, but the moment we pass across the threshold, Asher touches a light that seems to be linked to several others, each spaced about three feet apart through the entry area.

"We added these solar lights about five years after we found this place," he explains. "Year after year, we made changes until this cave became the haven we couldn't find anywhere else on our island." A frown creases his face. "I haven't been here in so long. Without you, it was just a place that made the void in my chest ache all that much more."

I place a hand on his bicep and squeeze. His anguish is so tangible, it's almost as if I'm experiencing his heartbreak, barely capable of remaining upright from its weight.

"I'm sorry, Asher," I tell him sincerely. "If there's a way for me to remember, I'm going to do that. Not only because I want to know what happened to me, but because you deserve the truth as well."

When his gaze meets mine, tears glimmer in his eyes as he looks at me, raw emotion laid bare. The intensity of this moment wraps around me so tightly that I can't decide if I'm going to drown or find the comfort I've been searching for.

I inch forward to wipe away the few tears that fall, but

his movements are quicker than mine. Before I can take my next breath, Asher's hands are holding my face between his palms and his mouth is a hairsbreadth away from mine.

My eyes dart between his lips and his heady stare, unsure of what he's going to do or even what I want him to do.

I'm frozen in place, desperate to know what's coming, but then, just as quickly as he touches me, Asher backs away.

"I'm so sorry, Isla." Asher's hands scrub over his face as his chest rumbles. "This is harder than I realized it would be."

Yeah, tell me about it.

If the wave of disappointment crashing through me right now is any indication, I'm in for one hell of a time figuring out what I want. Though the one thing I know with certainty is that I don't want to lead this man on.

No matter my attraction for him, I haven't loved him for over five hundred years like he has me. Kissing him for me would be like scratching an itch. While that itch might turn into a flaming inferno of passion with just one graze, I have a feeling for Asher, it would mean so much more.

He might have been an ass those first two meetings, but there's no denying the weight of his suffering. If movies and shows have taught me anything, it's that supernaturals love with an intensity that humans rarely understand. While I could be way off the mark with my assumptions, based upon what I've witnessed with Asher, I don't believe so and he deserves better.

"If you want to leave, we don't have to stay here," I

offer with a gentle tone, trying to mask the tightness in my chest. But before I can finish, Asher shakes his head firmly.

"No, you need to see this place," he insists, his voice regaining a bit of strength. "Avoiding the spots that hold your deepest memories won't help you remember."

As we venture deeper into the cave, the amber glow from the lamps cast long shadows against the uneven walls, highlighting patches of tall grass that sprout randomly from the earthy floor. There are no flowers here—only the simple beauty of earth untouched. The path soon widens into a cavernous room that unexpectedly houses what appears to be a…hot tub or some sort of bath.

I thought it was warm in here, but I blamed that on my thick sweater. Now, I'm not so sure. Kneeling, I brush my fingers over the water's surface, disrupting my reflection on its surface. "Is this…"

My words are cut off and I suddenly can't breathe. My balance becomes shaky and before I know what's happening, I go face-first into the pool of hot water.

I gasp for air and my arms flail, trying to grab at the side, but instead, a vivid memory floods my senses.

Shedding my clothes, I jump into the water, giggling without a care in the world. My hair is pinned to the top of my head and a few strands fall around my grinning face. I point a finger at someone I can't see before beckoning them toward me.

"You're not going to leave me here all alone, are you?" I tease, standing waist deep in the hot spring, not hot tub.

"Never," a deep grumble says. "You're mine until the end of time."

It's Asher who comes into view, confidently striding into the water without a stitch of clothes on, his presence as imposing as it is comforting. His arms wrap around my waist, tugging until we're flush together. His lips come down on mine and I swear I can taste his woodsy scent.

"Asher." I breathe out his name, my heart pounding against my ribcage, but instead of skin, my hands find the wet fabric of his shirt.

Reality snaps back harshly. "Gods, Isla." Asher's concerned voice cuts through the haze of my memory. "Are you okay?"

Embarrassment colors my cheeks as I scramble up from the cave floor, muttering incoherently before rushing to grab a towel. When I return, Asher's expression oscillates between concern and disbelief.

"You knew where to get a towel," he observes, astonishment changing his tone from concern to a light, joyous note. "Did you remember something when you fell into the hot spring?"

The intensity of the memory—or was it a mere daydream fueled by that almost-kiss?—leaves me unsettled. How am I to explain this without sounding utterly deluded by desire?

"I, uh, don't know," I say, wiping my face with a towel that's rather stiff, likely from having sat untouched for who-knows-how-long.

His hand, warm and reassuring, cradles the side of my face. "What happened, Isla? There's nothing you can't tell me."

The moment those six words leave his mouth, the weight of their truth settles over me like a warm blanket.

Still, I hesitate to reveal what I saw because it's not like anything was said to pinpoint a time or event. It was just the two of us, getting ready to go at it in the water. Something I suddenly feel like happened quite often before.

"I was in the water, waiting for you," I finally admit. "You joined me and then…I was back to the present. I don't know that I'd call that a memory since I looked like me. There's no way to tell the difference."

"Our clothes," he says. "What were we wearing? Things have changed here, just like they do on Earth."

There's no hiding my blush and Asher proves that I'm right to trust him when he seems to understand what I'm not saying without forcing the words from my mouth.

"It's okay," he promises with a sweet smile. "No matter what happened, this is progress. I was right to bring you here and I think when my mother mentioned having you go to Lunara Academy, she was onto something as well."

Wrapping the towel around my dripping clothes, I ask, "What do you mean?"

"When our souls are reborn, it's not with our full memories," he explains. "We grow and learn and as we mature, more from our past lives comes back to us. You're already grown and mature, but you haven't learned."

If this is the only way to figure out why I disappeared, then I'm in, all in.

"When do I start?" I ask with eagerness.

Asher grabs my hand and starts leading us back out of the cave without attempting to dry himself off. "First things first. We need to find out about getting your friend here. I know you asked my mother about finding your phone and relaying a message, but that's a bit more complicated given the older portal you used. We're not actually sure where your belongings have gone…"

I gape at him. "Are you saying an entire car was just swallowed by the universe, never to be seen again?"

"Were you particularly attached to the vehicle?" His head tilts and eyes pinch at the side. "I can keep trying to locate it if…"

My hand waves, cutting him off. "No, it's just a lot to still process. I don't care about the car. Just Elodee."

He gives my hand a squeeze as we keep walking. "We will find a way to bring her here, I promise. I don't want you to worry about anything that you don't have to if I can help it."

Oh, hell. Can this man get any sweeter? Something tells me the answer is a resounding yes.

CHAPTER TWELVE

ASHER

As we enter through the castle's back entrance, I take Isla up a private set of stairs that leads to a different section of the castle. Fewer of the staff frequent this area and I'd rather they not see us in our wet clothes, coming to their own conclusions about what we were up to.

I steal a glance at Isla. Her eyes, wide with wonder, dart around, absorbing every detail of her unfamiliar surroundings, almost as if none of this is real for her yet. I shouldn't be surprised, given this version of my mate has never been in this section of our home, but a part of me hoped that once we came back here, more memories would begin to appear to her.

"You can use these stairs anytime you'd like," I tell her, placing my palm on her lower back as we exit the dark hallway. "You'll encounter fewer people this way if you'd like to remain unseen."

When Isla looks up at me, her gaze is full of

excitement and curiosity. "Are there secret doors in this place? Hidden hallways or rooms?"

I chuckle because those were always her favorite part and I'm surprised she hasn't found the one in her room, even if by accident. "Yes, I'll show you one right now, actually. In your own room."

She claps her hands excitedly, then tugs animatedly at my arm. "Where? I looked everywhere in there."

My smirk only grows. "Right this way, Princess."

Her eyes roll at my use of the title, and she groans. "I don't feel like a princess."

I wrap an arm around her, pulling her close for a brief moment, reveling in the warmth of her body that reminds me of a love I thought I'd lost for good. "You never did before, either, and there's nothing wrong with that."

"Wait." She freezes in the middle of the hallway, coming to a complete stop just before we get to her room. "If we're both from here and I'm a princess and you're a king, are we…?"

Her hands cover her stomach and she looks like she's going to be sick, but I quickly ease her worries. "We're not related, Isla. Your father was a king in his past life. Since he didn't have any heirs before his death, the crown went to the next wolf blessed by the gods. Still, your family retains its royal bloodlines."

"So, your gods choose who the ruler is? The people have no say?" She doesn't seem very impressed with that information.

"Yes and no," I tell her as we keep walking. "Once before, a king was overthrown and the one who took his place was a vile creation, causing so much mayhem, our entire country went to war. Yet he had the support of more than half our people."

"The Great War that separated the islands?" she asks, opening her door. "Cain mentioned that to me before."

So much for hoping that was just something she remembered.

"That's right," I tell her, stepping inside her bedroom. "When the lands were separated, new rulers were chosen, none of them blessed by the gods. It wasn't until the next wave of leaders was born that the gods resumed their selection process. It was up to us to listen. There are books in the royal library I can show you if you want to learn more before going to Lunara Academy."

She nods, peering intently around her room. "Yeah, that would be good. Now what about this secret passage?"

Taking my time, because I'm enjoying her eagerness, I walk to the left side of her room and start at the corner, placing my hand over the wall, gently gliding it over the surface as I move. "Hm, it's been so long. I'm not sure I actually remember."

She smacks my shoulder playfully and practically growls. "Don't play with me."

Gods, I haven't had this much fun in centuries. For so long, I've been nothing more or less than the stoic king, doing his best for his people. Doing anything that didn't further my kingdom was never on the agenda.

Having Isla here makes me feel like I'm twenty again, carefree and in love. I shouldn't open myself up like this—it's a risk that could ruin me—but even if she still chooses to leave, I might as well die. I won't survive losing her a second time, so there's no point in holding back any longer.

"You were lying, weren't you?" She huffs, standing by closely as I make my way down the wall, lightly touching the surface with my fingertips.

"It's here somewhere," I muse, knowing that as soon as I get past the closet door, I'll find what I'm looking for.

Placed between the closet and bathroom is a small, hidden door, not even two feet wide, that leads to a set of stairs that will eventually end at an exit to the backside of the castle, but they also go to every floor within the castle, ending on the basement level that hasn't been used in eons.

Her foot begins to tap incessantly, so I decide to put her out of her misery. I grab the thick, white moulding, circling the carving for the hidden switch before pressing the disguised button. A quiet click sounds and the small section of the wall pops free.

"Holy shit," Isla mutters, trying to move around me. "Where does this lead?"

I grin and look right into her bright stare. "To my room."

"Oh." She casts her eyes away.

"I'm kidding, Isla." I tap her chin, lifting until she looks at me again. "I mean, you could get there from here, but I'd have to let you in. The only places you can enter without needing doors to be unlocked are the exits for each floor and the basement. Though I don't recommend using this as your means of travel through the castle unless there's an emergency. It's too easy to get lost and trapped in the walls."

She shudders and peeks around me. "It's dark down there and basements freak me out. Secret doors aren't as exciting as the movies make them seem."

"I think you may be right." I tell her and then with regret, I know I need to leave. "I need to have a meeting with my father about Elodee. Oh, and if you have coordinates for her we will use those."

Her brow raises. "Coordinates? Like an address?" She shakes her head and grins as she walks toward the small desk across the room. "Everything here seems so normal until it doesn't."

"I hope that's not a bad thing," I say as she starts to write down what I assume is the information we need.

"Just different." Isla hands me the folded paper and shock exchanges between us when our fingers touch, something she doesn't seem to notice as I do. "This is where she lives. Remember she won't go easily and she's probably freaked out that she hasn't heard from me. You can't hold it against her if she fights back."

"She's going to be okay, I promise." I glance back toward the door, knowing I need to go even though I don't want to. "I don't know how long I'll be, but you can use the phone beside your table to order lunch in and I can take you out for dinner later if you'd like.

She bites the inside of her cheek and seems nervous about something. I want to press, but we've made more progress today than I expected. I don't want to push my luck.

"If you'd rather stay in, that's okay too," I add before reaching to lightly wrap my hand around her neck, closing the space between us to kiss the top of her head. The sweet, vanilla scent of my mate nearly doesn't allow for me to let go, but I force myself to step back.

Her cheeks are flushed and her eyes closed as I head

toward the door. She may not say anything with words, but her physical reactions are more than enough for me, for now.

After this morning, I at least feel more confident about having a chance to get my mate back. Now, I just need to get her friend here and hope she doesn't think we're all insane.

As I exit Isla's room, I glance down the hallway and remember Grayson. There's something equally important that I need to do before I meet with my father.

Using the mental connection I have with all my pack members, I call only to him. *"I'd like to meet with you about something urgent. Can you be in my office in ten minutes?"*

His reply is immediate. *"See you there, Son."*

Going to Grayson's door, I knock before cracking it open so that he doesn't have to get up. "Mind if I come in?"

He coughs and laughs at once. "Do you really need to ask as the king?"

No, I don't, but I always will unless my people give me a reason not to.

I step inside, finding him as frail as he was yesterday. Despite the dose of blood I gave him last night, he shows little improvement. *Damn it.* I hope I'm not too late. Isla will never forgive me if I fail him.

Without asking his opinion, I go to the bathroom and grab another cup. This time when I extend my claws and cut my wrist, I go deeper, allowing the blood to surge into the glass.

Grayson attempts to sit up, his voice raspy with concern. "What are you doing? That's too much."

My head shakes. "Seeing you now, I'm not even sure if it's enough, but you're going to drink every drop I give you until we find out. Isla no longer needs to choose between leaving or saving you. I can't watch you suffer any longer."

He reaches for the cup, his hands trembling. I support him, carefully bringing the drink to his lips. He gulps eagerly, but I moderate his intake to prevent him from choking. "Easy, Grayson. There's no rush."

He wipes his mouth with the back of his hand, his voice breaking. "I almost lost my chance, Asher. I almost gave up and my Flo… She'll never get to see her girls again. They'll never truly know their mother."

The man I've always looked up to begins to sob and I'm unsure what to do, especially when he's making no sense.

"What do you mean by 'they'?" It's been nearly three hundred years since I've heard anyone speak of Isla's sister, Estee. She was the first wolf to abandon her pack, but I never blamed her. Losing Isla was hard on all of us, but most of all me and Estee.

Grayson sits up more on his own and grabs the cup from me, taking another drink before answering. "I know it may seem crazy, which is why I hadn't said anything yet. First, I wanted to speak with Isla more when she returned because she said something to me last night, but I don't think Estee chose to leave us."

My chest tightens at this revelation. Have I failed my mate in more ways than one? I did my best to take care of her family after her disappearance, but Estee leaving ruined any progress I'd made with them. If she'd been forced out and I did nothing to protect her…I'll never forgive myself.

Not as her king or her family.

"What did Isla say?" I ask finally, sitting up straighter on the bed before refilling his cup.

Just like when I told him that his daughter had returned, his eyes grow bright, a mixture of hope and nostalgia flickering across his face "She mentioned Elodee, her friend from Earth, calling her a 'soul sister.' It struck a chord, Asher. It's more than just a feeling."

It's not possible. They couldn't have both been reborn to Earth without any of us knowing. *Right?*

The implications hang heavily between us. "You think Elodee might be Estee." Saying the words out loud sends a shiver through me. "Gods. After all this time." I run a hand through my dark hair. "I was just going to talk to my father about bringing Elodee here so that Isla might feel more comfortable. Assuming she was human, I was hoping an exception could be made, but if you're right…"

"We need to go find her," he pleads, the color already returning to his cheeks as he finishes the cup of my blood.

I clasp his shoulder and nod confidently. "We will, but we need to handle this carefully. Just as Isla doesn't remember her past life, I don't assume Elodee will, either. She's going to wonder why her friend has been missing and not trust us."

"We'll bring Isla with us," he suggests, and while I don't want to force my mate to stay anymore, I don't know that's a good idea. She's only just had her first glimpse of a memory. What if going back to Earth, even for a short period of time, ruins that? Worse, what if we're wrong about Elodee?

I don't want to hurt Isla and, selfishly, I don't want to set back any progress we made today.

"This isn't my favorite choice, but what if we just take Elodee, unconsciously, and have her wake up in Isla's room? Once she reappears in our world, we'll know right away if she's Estee, then we can explain what we've confirmed to Isla and let her handle the rest," I suggest because it seems like the best way to avoid the most drama. Magic may not work on Earth, but not everything we use is made from our unique energy. Our sleeping potions would be enough to knock out a human.

Grayson seems to seriously consider this idea but doesn't readily agree. "What does your father know already?"

"Not enough," I admit. "Come with me. I'm meeting him now."

I give Grayson a third cup of my blood as he nods and carefully gets out of bed. He's still much too thin, but his body doesn't tremble like before. He holds up the glass. "I may need a few more of these before we leave Polaris."

"You can have as many as you need."

We move swiftly through the castle and I'm impressed with how quickly his strength is coming back, considering he looked worse off when I entered his room. Still, I appreciate his urgency because if he's right...

Someone murdered my family.

I don't know how or why, but if both Blackwood sisters had the same fate, what else could it have been?

Even thinking that, I still don't know how it could be possible, but I'm certainly going to find out and when I find the person who took my mate from me... They will be *begging* for a fiery afterlife by the time I've finished punishing them.

My father is already waiting for me, speaking with Malimorte outside my office when we arrive. I barely nod at them as I shove my door open.

With every passing second, knowing that there's a possibility someone purposely stole the lives of these women, my ire becomes more tangible. I can feel the blood rushing to my face and the tensing of my shoulders increasing tenfold. I don't know how I'm supposed to suppress this rage when I want to rip the heads off anyone who could be responsible for this.

"Asher, what's wrong?" my father asks, but I don't answer him first.

"Malimorte!" My voice booms louder than I intend, and he enters behind Grayson, closing the door.

"Yes, Your Majesty?" His eyes meet mine, unafraid of the wrath I'm barely containing.

Good, that should hopefully mean he has nothing to be guilty about.

"I need you to stay here and take notes about everything we speak of on paper, then give them to me," I tell him. I might be furious, but I've been doing this job long enough to know that no matter what's decided in this room right now, we could miss something important with emotions so high.

I'll want to review everything more than once until we know the truth.

Mali comes around to my desk, grabbing what he needs to take notes, then stands at the back of the room before I address my father.

"Grayson believes that Isla's friend from Earth is actually Estee," I state clearly.

My father's jaw tightens and his eyes narrow, glancing between the two of us. "Why would he think that?"

Good, he's as angry as I am.

Grayson answers first. "Isla considers this woman she calls Elodee her family, more especially her *soul sister*. On top of that, I've never understood why Estee would have left us with only a note. It never made sense, but then Flo gave up her life to the grief and I realized that we all needed to process in our own ways, and nothing had to make sense. Except the moment Isla mentioned Elodee, my same suspicions came back, stronger than ever."

Dad nods and drums his fingers over the arms of the chair beneath him. "Well, that's not something we can ignore, can we?" He looks at me. "I assume you already have a plan?"

"I do," I say gruffly, but Grayson cuts me off first.

"I'd like to be the one to go get her," he says. "I'll follow your every order, but I'd like to be part of the retrieval."

He's now finished his third cup of blood and his voice is strong. I'm not sure he's up for the task, but I can't deny a father the opportunity to reclaim his daughter. Not when he's the one who pieced everything together.

With Noen and Declan still off island handling trade deals, it's easy to make my decision since the only other men I trust with my own life are in this room.

"You and Mali will go today," I say. "Find Elodee, give her a sleeping dose, and bring her right back here. No stops anywhere else, no speaking to anyone. Your strength will be dulled on Earth and we can't take any risks."

Especially with Grayson. I really shouldn't let him go, but I don't change my mind.

He slides his cup across my desk. "Then I better get stronger. I'll take another dose."

Cutting open the faint pink line again, I extend my claw and hold my wrist over the glass before looking up at my advisor. "Is this going to be a problem for you, Malimorte?"

My father holds a hand up. "Wait a minute. You honestly think it's a good idea to send a man who was recently close to his deathbed and your assistant, who, from my knowledge, has never seen combat, to retrieve a human whom you think might be one of our princesses?"

Without blinking, I simply say, "Yes."

"Have you lost your mind, Son?" he asks incredulously. "At least let me go as well."

"Absolutely not. Your departure would draw attention, especially without Mom," I tell him. "Mali and Grayson can easily slip out without anyone questioning what they're doing. I refuse to let the person who might have done this learn that we're onto them."

He raises a brow and tilts his head to the side. "You haven't even said what it is you think someone has done. Only that you think this girl might be Isobella's sister."

"Isla," I correct with a growl. "And like you said before, reincarnation hasn't ever just 'gone wrong.' If we find Estee, I firmly believe that someone must have killed them, stolen their lives, and found a way to make sure they didn't return. Whoever that was, I will figure it out and they will pay with blood. Until then, this information stays within the walls of this office."

I asked to meet with my father because I wanted his

advice about bringing a human here, but that's likely not the case any longer. If he doesn't agree with my choices, then that's on him. This is happening and I don't care how long it takes, Isla will remember what happened to her and then I will get my vengeance.

Even if I have to start a war to do so.

CHAPTER THIRTEEN

ISLA

Unease churns in my stomach as I lie on my bed, staring at the ceiling, feeling an inexplicable dread. I haven't felt right since visiting Grayson's room to find it empty. He seemed somewhat better at dinner last night, but now, anxiety gnaws at me—what if his condition has worsened?

I need to speak with Asher, tell him I won't leave before the four weeks, so long as he heals my—Grayson.

My entire body shakes. I almost called him my dad, for the second time. Is that because of what I've been told, or because I'm starting to remember? The unknown blurs, leaving me more eager than ever to figure out a way to trigger more memories besides being in that cave.

I need to remember. I need to understand what happened to me, why I vanished from this world.

More than that, I need Elodee. I hope that whatever is taking Asher so long to return is because he's one step closer to bringing her here.

I sit up in bed, eyes wide. "Shit. They can't just *take* her.

She'll try to kill someone and my bestie is nothing short of a badass."

Elodee is the kind of woman who takes judo classes for fun because she enjoys bringing grown men to their knees. Yet at the same time, she's this ray of sunshine who makes people gravitate toward her. It's easy to assume she's sweet and kind until you mess with her. Then the claws come out.

That thought makes me snort and glance at my own hands. Asher said I was once a wolf shifter. I saw his wolf.

Oh, God. I *saw* his wolf. That ginormous beast was Asher. With all the revelations over the last two days, my mind didn't quite hold on to that fact, but there's no way I can turn into something…so ferocious.

I'd know, right? Like there should have been some sort of sign over the years if I were more than human. I know everyone here said magic doesn't exist on Earth, but still. I shudder from head to toe. Shifting into an animal is possibly the least awesome thing I've learned since coming here.

Getting off the bed, I decide it's time for me to find Cain. Asher said I could use the phone to order lunch, but before he also said Cain would be available to me. As much as I thought I didn't want to leave the room after the forest incident, being in that cave changed everything.

A part of me still doesn't want to believe any of this is possible, but the longer I'm here, the more I learn, plus that flicker of a memory… I can't deny that there's something anchoring me to this place. It wasn't just seeing Grayson and feeling a connection to him. I didn't want to admit it before, but now, there's a rightness here.

I've been without Elodee this whole time and I haven't felt half as lonely as I did in our apartment by myself.

With Asher no longer being an ass, and the prospect of Elodee being able to stay with me, it's easier to accept that maybe this is exactly where I'm supposed to be.

I go to the closet and put on a new pair of shoes. After showering and changing earlier, I hung my wet clothes in the bathroom, but I think I might have ruined the flats when I fell in the hot spring.

Zipping up the boots, I straighten the black, knee-length skirt that I paired with a blue sweater and head for the door. Once in the hallway, I peek left before heading right toward the main staircase.

I get to the next floor of the castle and finally see someone. I smile and wave, still not used to people bowing to me. "Hello," I say. "Do you know where I might find Cain?"

"Princess Isla," she replies, her voice tinged with a deference that still feels foreign. "Cain should be in his office on the first floor. If you follow the stairs one more level down and turn right, he'll be the second door on the left."

"What's your name?" I take in her hazel eyes, tawny complexion, and polite demeanor as I ask her name.

"My name is Desiree, Your Highness." She nods, nearly bowing again as she answers and her feet begin to shift.

"Well, thank you, Desiree," I tell her kindly. "I won't keep you from your work. I just wanted to know whom I was thanking."

She curtsies once more, then continues in the opposite direction I need to go. Resuming my way down the steps,

I only get halfway to the next floor before my name is called.

I turn to find Asher taking the steps three at a time, wearing fresh clothes, looking every bit the king people call him. His navy-blue slacks are pressed with a perfect crease down the front of each leg. His matching suit coat is left open, revealing a white dress shirt layered with a white vest and blue sash, trimmed in silver. Medals are pinned to his left shoulder, at least seven or eight of them of varying colors.

When my gaze gets to his face, I find I'm not the only one staring intently. The urge to go to him, to wrap my arms around his neck, kissing him until I can't feel my toes is nearly too much for me to handle. My legs shake as he stops in front of me and I have to look at the ground, waiting for him to address me.

"I'm headed into a meeting with my advisory council that I forgot about," he says, which likely explains his fancier dress. "I saw you on my way. Is everything okay? I didn't think you'd leave your room."

"Grayson wasn't in his and I got worried," I admit. "I was going to find Cain so that he could help me figure out where he went. Did you learn anything about Elodee? Can we go get her when you're done?"

He reaches for my wrist with one hand and lifts my chin with the other. His thumb strokes over my heated skin as I'm forced to look into sapphire eyes. "Why won't you look at me?"

Even now, my eyes dart left, right, up, and down. This man no longer infuriates me. He makes me feel… unraveled, seen.

"I, uh, I'm just tired." Tried and true excuse. Now, I just have to hope it works.

Asher glances around before stepping another few inches closer to me and lowering his voice. "You're not afraid of me, are you?"

The pain in his voice guts me and I place a hand on his chest, shaking my head. "Far from it. Quite the opposite, in fact."

The moment those words leave my mouth, I realize I've probably overshared, given my earlier thoughts about holding back with this man. Except Asher doesn't seem to care as he trails his fingers up my arm, across my shoulder, not stopping until my face gently rests within his palm.

"Isla, I know we didn't talk much about what it means to be a wolf shifter earlier and while everything you've seen so far may seem very *human* from the outside, we are still part animal," he says, his eyes staring at my mouth as his tongue wets his own lips. "We have desires stronger than most, especially for our mates. Without your wolf being unlocked yet, which we will work on soon, the emotions you feel might seem out of place, but just like we can't control when your memories start to return, we can't control how strong or fast our connection may return."

Mates? So, fiction did get something right and I was right before when I assumed that things were more intense between people here. I'm not sure if I find that comforting or not.

Asher takes a deep inhale, closing his eyes briefly. "I hope you know I will never push you for anything you're not ready for, but I also won't lie to you. I've waited five centuries for you. You are my life, my heart, my reason for breathing. I'm here for you in any capacity you'd like me to be, and I can't apologize enough for treating you as anything less than priceless when you first arrived."

As if his first romantic speech hadn't been enough to be my undoing. Driven by an impulse I can't control, I rise onto the balls of my feet, giving in to the desire to taste the truth of Asher's words on his lips. My fingers, trembling with a mixture of nerves and anticipation, clutch at the lapels of his jacket. He closes the slight distance between us with a step, his intentions as clear as mine.

When our lips meet, it's like a spark igniting into a blaze. My mouth parts, inviting a more profound connection, and our tongues explore in a tender, searching dance. The kiss deepens, fueled by a yearning that has waited centuries to be sated. The scent of cedar, somehow both wild and comforting, envelops me as Asher angles his head, devouring me. His hands find my waist, pulling me closer against him, his body a solid wall of warmth.

A low rumble vibrates from his chest, resonating against my own heart as he presses me gently against the cool, hard surface of the wall. The world narrows down to the space between us, every nerve ending alight with electric *need*. But just as the kiss promises to spiral into something unstoppable, he pulls back abruptly, a storm of emotion swirling in his eyes.

As he turns his face away, the sharp lines of his jaw are tense. "Gods, you have no idea how painful that was to stop," he growls, his chest heaving just as much as mine, "but we shouldn't do this here."

My breath catches, the sudden loss of his warmth leaving me momentarily adrift as I glance around, seeing the shadow of someone running up the stairs. When I look back at Asher wearing his kingly wardrobe, I'm forced to remember that he's not just any man, as much as I might wish otherwise.

"I'm sor—" I start to say, but he kisses me quickly, just once more.

"Don't ever apologize for kissing me," he says, words filled with an air of authority. "I'm not ashamed of loving you in front of the world. I more meant that we shouldn't get too carried away right here."

My fingers lightly touch my lips as I grin because he's right. Not caring where we were, I had no plans of stopping.

"Right," I say, smoothing my hands over his vest and sash. "And you have a meeting to get to."

The rumble in his chest makes me smile wider, especially when he says, "If it didn't have to do with Elodee, then I would cancel it."

"Are you bringing her here?" I ask with unmasked excitement, remembering that he didn't answer me earlier. "And what about Grayson? Is he okay?"

His hands hold me close. "There's much more I need to share with you privately, but right now, all I can say is that Elodee is coming here. We're going to give her a sleeping concoction and bring her back today. She'll wake in your room and after the two of us have spoken, you'll get to be the one to tell her everything else. As for Grayson, he's just fine. I healed him and he's helping bring Elodee back."

The elation that fills me from those words has me

feeling as if I could jump from the roof and fly. "She's coming here now? Like, right now?" I grab his suit coat again and kiss him, just not as thoroughly as a few moments ago. "Thank you, Asher. For that, and for Grayson. You have no idea what this means to me."

He smiles in return, but the gesture doesn't quite light up his face like I expect. "Anything for you, Issie."

I thought Grayson was the only one to call me that, but I don't hate the nickname coming from Asher as well.

"There's more to discuss," he adds. "But I really do need to go. I'll meet you in your room in an hour."

His lips press against the top of my head as he holds me close for only a brief second before he's bounding back up the stairs again.

I stand there, leaning against the wall and grinning like a fool. Three days ago, I thought I'd died or was stuck in some twisted dream. Now, I may have no clue what's going to happen next, but I do know that I'm no longer afraid of what's to come.

CHAPTER FOURTEEN

ASHER

Something deep inside is unraveling. I know Isla is going to be the end of me—a sweet, intoxicating demise, but a demise nonetheless. Our kiss on the stairwell made me briefly forget who and what I'm supposed to be, a lapse that even now sends ripples through the steadfast façade I maintain as king. She's once again, and very quickly, become my core, my singular focus, and while I'm consumed with gratitude that she's back, I'm equally haunted by the constraints of my responsibilities.

The words Grayson uttered have ignited a slow-burning fury within me. I thought I had considered every possibility—her leaving of her own volition, or worse, her being taken from me—but none made sense. There were no demands made, no enemies claiming victory, and an unsettling silence on her whereabouts.

Part of me had reluctantly accepted the possibility that she had simply chosen to walk away without reason. But now, the prospect that she might have been forcibly cursed to Earth changes everything. If this proves to be the case, nothing will stop me from uncovering the truth and exacting a bitter vengeance.

I take a deep breath, trying to calm my heart before stepping into this meeting with my advisory council. I was hoping to avoid this, but that's part of the job as king. I can't ignore everything for days on end without the council being forced to check where my head is at. That is their job, after all.

Pushing open the doors to the meeting room on the fourth floor, I'm greeted with the faces of four of my five council members. Malimorte has already departed for Earth with Grayson. Though no one in this room is aware of that fact.

I should be able to tell them, but I'm not going to. Nobody else needs to know what we're up to until I have more answers. I won't risk Isla's life by sharing too much information.

"Your Majesty," Arthur says, the eldest of my advisory team, having even served under my father. He rises first as I close the doors behind me and bows, casting his dark eyes downward briefly. "Thank you for meeting with us today with all you have going on."

They might have requested the meeting, and I could have denied, but that's not the kind of ruler I've chosen to be. While I don't intend on telling them more than they need to know to feel at peace with the arrival of my mate, they still deserve my presence until I learn otherwise.

"Of course," I say, taking my seat at the head of the table. "I apologize for not sending word sooner."

Henree, sitting on my left, clears his throat. "Yes, Your

Majesty. We were surprised Malimorte didn't report anything to us and that he was unable to join us now."

"He has an urgent family matter that I've encouraged him to deal with," I explain, something Mali and I already discussed in private as his cover for being gone. As my primary advisor, it's not often he's missing from my side for these things like this.

"I see, Sire." Henree adjusts the silver bowtie at his neck as his golden eyes glance across the table. "Isaac, will you get us started, then?"

Isaac, the second oldest member of my council, meets my stare. His dark-hazel eyes narrow ever so slightly before he begins to speak. "The people have voiced concerns about the rumors they've heard of Ms. Blackwood being here to reject you. How should we respond to this, my king?"

My blood boils on the inside from the reminder that I almost lost her a second time and what I was forced to do to prevent that. Still, I keep my expression controlled and I flatten my palms over my thighs beneath the table. "Princess Isla, as she should now be called, is not here for a rejection. We're unsure at this time what happened to her before as her memories are not what they should be, but she is here to stay for now."

"And that is information we're allowed to share, Your Majesty?" Archie, the recorder and history expert of the group, asks. He peeks up at me, his salt-and-pepper hair falling across his gaze.

"Yes," I say tersely. "The people have nothing to worry about where Isla is concerned. She's adjusting and we will update when there's something more to share."

"Will she be the next queen, Sire?" Arthur asks next, a valid question, but unfortunately, one I can't answer yet.

"This is my pack, my land, my people," I say with authority. "I have given my life to them, doing everything needed to keep them well cared for, protected, and everything in between. If anyone wants to know anything more before we're ready to share, perhaps remind them of the many centuries I have spent proving my loyalty and ask for their patience in return."

"Yes, my king," Arthur replies, but he doesn't meet my steady gaze, letting me know my answer isn't enough for them.

I'm not surprised by that, but it's all I can offer at this time. While the people of my territory have always been important to me, I won't hold them above Isla. I'm sure that's exactly what they're concerned with now, but I can keep my mate's privacy secure while also making sure our land is protected from threats.

"What else is on the agenda for the day?" I press, hoping the conversation of Isla is handled for the moment.

Henree speaks up next. "Noen and Declan, they're due back soon. Have you heard how their negotiations are going with Selaris, Your Highness?"

A topic I don't mind discussing.

"I haven't spoken to them myself in a few days, but Malimorte let me know before he left that things are going as expected," I explain. "We should be getting the minerals we need for our crops in exchange for lumber and the families who have requested to move have been approved with new members joining us from their lands as well."

The last part is my least-favorite part of negotiations. Approving members of my pack to leave isn't something I enjoy because typically, it means they're not happy here. Though sometimes, it's as simple as mates finding one another and being from different islands. Someone always has to move, and I've never denied my people their happiness by forcing them to stay.

The biggest downside is bringing in new wolves from other islands. I haven't had a threat made against my crown in over a century, but bringing in those who have been raised under a different leader never fails to make me wonder if one could return.

Our four islands have operated smoothly for years, but everything is surface-level diplomatic. One misstep and any deals we've made for peace could come crashing down around us.

"Speaking of new members…" Arthur says, looking over a piece of paper in front of him.

As I navigate through the rest of the meeting, my thoughts stray, unbidden, to Isla. Her image—the taste of her kiss, the sound of her laughter—invades my senses, a vivid reminder of what I've regained. The meeting drags, each minute an eternity away from her.

Once dismissed, I'm left with the echo of my council's concerns, but none weigh as heavily as the need to protect Isla. I know what I must do. The kingdom can wait. For now, my heart cannot.

CHAPTER FIFTEEN

ISLA

It's been hours since I've returned to my room. Cain brought me lunch and updated me on Asher, stating his meeting is running longer than usual, but that he will be with me soon. Though Cain has nothing to say about the subject I'm most excited about right now.

Elodee.

She could be here tonight. I could have my best friend with me and she can properly freak out with me over the unreal reality that this world, and everything in it, actually exists.

I've spent the afternoon weighing everything I've learned about this strange, enchanting place. Aside from missing Elodee, I find few downsides. Even the daunting prospect of turning into a wolf sparks more curiosity than fear as I lounge in the bath, my mind swirling with *what-ifs*.

Attempting yoga on my bed after bathing, I seek the elusive peace that might connect me to the wolf Asher insists lingers within me, a creature reborn through death and time. The notion feels like a myth, an ancient tale told by a fireside, under the stars.

Still, no new memories have surfaced and I haven't sensed another being hanging inside my head, but I have decided that I want to see Asher's wolf. I'm pretty sure that was him I saw the first night I was on the balcony. He was so far away and it was dark. I think if I'm going to bring my animal spirit to the surface, I need to better understand how all this works.

What does it take to transform from human to beast? Who is in control? How do I change back? What happens to my clothes? So many questions and not enough answers to come by as I sit here alone.

I get up from the bed and head to the small desk to grab pen and paper. My mental list feels as if it has hit capacity. I need to start writing these things down before I forget some of the more important pieces.

After filling up nearly two pages of notes, there's finally a knock at my door. I drop my notes onto the end table and before I take a step away from the bed, Asher is letting himself in.

His sapphire eyes light up the moment they settle on me, causing a warmth to spread throughout my chest. I take a step forward, then hesitate.

I barely know this man. I shouldn't want to wrap my arms around him the second he's within my sights. I shouldn't want to taste him again and wonder how much he was holding back earlier because we were in public.

Yet my skin tingles in anticipation and my muscles bunch, wanting to leap forward into his embrace.

"Isla," he cautions, his voice a low thrum. "As a wolf shifter, my senses are... acute." He steps closer, his gaze intense, predatory as he inhales deeply. "And right now, your thoughts are like a siren to the beast within me."

Oh.

Oh.

Son of a… He can *smell* my thoughts? Or probably more like the reaction my body is having to said thoughts.

I'm in so much trouble.

"I'm sorry." I step back until I'm pressed against the mattress behind me.

He continues to stride forward, not stopping until he's standing in front of me. Close enough to feel the heat rolling off his skin but never actually touching me.

"Never apologize for your desires." His words come out layered with a rumble that lights my inside on fire.

And when he strokes the back of his fingers gently over my cheek, my eyes flutter closed as I grip the comforter behind me, doing my best to stay upright.

Seconds tick by as I lose myself to the velvet of his touch. My previous racing thoughts are nothing but a distant memory until he speaks again.

"You should know, we have Elodee." His words are like ice water over my senses.

My eyes snap back open and stare up at him, still standing close. "Where is she?"

I move to pass him, but he catches my wrist, his grip gentle yet firm. "Before you see her, there's something you must know."

Anxiety clenches my stomach. "If someone hurt her—"

His soft chuckle cuts me off. "Nothing like that. She's in perfect health, sleeping soundly in the next room, even, but you need to understand who she is before you see her again so that you can explain everything to her when she wakes."

I struggle for breath, my hands starting to tremble. "What do you mean?"

Losing Elodee will kill me, so if Asher is about to tell me she can't stay, I don't know what I'll do.

His next words are a cautious whisper. "You once told Grayson she was like your soul sister." I nod in confirmation before he continues. "You were more right than you knew. Issie, she *is* your sister."

"I'm sorry. What?" My eyes feel as if they're going to pop right out of their sockets as I shake my head. "We were foster siblings. What do you mean, she's my sister?"

"Before you vanished, you had a sister named Estee," he explains, his voice gentle. "Nobody has brought her up to you because we didn't want to hurt you while you were still processing so much. We thought that she'd died and chosen not to come back. Now, we believe whatever happened to you, Estee must have figured it out and the same thing happened to her."

The room spins as I absorb his words. This reshapes everything I thought I knew and all I've yet to understand. "Why would anyone want to harm us?" I whisper, the question a weight in my heart.

Asher steps closer, enveloping me in his presence. "We don't know yet. But whatever their motives, they underestimated your strength. We'll find the truth, Issie. I promise."

In that moment, his vow feels like an anchor, grounding me amidst the storm of revelations and giving me a hope that I didn't know I needed. Plus, he's right.

Whoever might have done this to us, they won't go unpunished, even all these years later.

A shudder courses through me at the thought of our tormentors still lurking, possibly planning to strike again. "So, they murdered me, then my sister, and we've been stuck on Earth ever since? Am I understanding what you've pieced together correctly? And what if they get to us again before we figure this out? We will go back to Earth, taking away my memory of these last few days?"

My stomach hollows out. Losing the knowledge of what I've gained since stumbling into this world paints a shadow over my heart.

Asher's grip tightens on me reassuringly. "Nobody is going to take you from me again. I can promise you that," he declares with fierce certainty. "And yes, I believe you were cursed to be reborn on Earth. Though I can't fathom how—since magic supposedly doesn't exist there—your soul managed to leave Lunara and be reformed into another life without the blessing of the Gods."

I lean into his warm touch, seeking comfort. "How is that even possible here?"

"The gods," he explains solemnly. "Every soul born in Lunara has the choice upon death to return to the realm of the gods, where they can stay and rest, or to be reborn, living another life."

"Is their world, like, heaven or something?"

"Or something," he replies, a bit of tension lacing his words. "The gods have long kept to their own world, and we prefer to leave them to it, only seeking their help when we have no other choice. When one of us chooses not to be reborn, there is a place where our souls rest. The gods are very vague on what that means, but they promise peace and nothing more."

Interesting. I guess it makes more sense now that my mother would have taken that option. I may not have ever thought about having children, but I can imagine that losing two of them would be unlike any other pain in the world. Recovering from that doesn't seem possible.

"Grayson." I gasp. "He was close to death. He wanted…"

Asher nods. "You returned just in time. Another few days and he would have been gone."

My mind reels at the thought. He's the only real connection I've felt since coming here. Sure, there's the attraction to Asher and a sense of home in my surroundings, but that split moment when my heart opened to Grayson, when I knew he was family, I can't forget that. I also can't imagine almost never having met him.

"Is Elodee with him now?" I ask because I can't wait any longer to see her. I need her to be with me and I need to be the first face she sees when she wakes up. More than that, I need to wrap my arms around her and have a good cry because, holy shit. I thought what I'd already learned was a lot, but this is another level of unbelievable.

His hand slips down my arm and his fingers entwine with mine. "I'll take you to her and then we can carry her in here. She should only be out another twenty minutes or so."

We exit my room and I move in front of Asher, releasing his hand to rush into Grayson's room. Throwing open the door, I see him standing over the bed, looking like a completely different man than the one I had dinner with last night.

The color is back in his face, his stance is strong and steady, and his shirt doesn't hang as loosely from his frame. Hell, he might even be a couple of inches taller.

As he smiles at me, a profound connection—a burst of familial warmth—floods through me, reinforcing the bond I've only begun to rediscover. It's like the sun's rays piercing through a long, overcast sky.

I close my eyes and another memory flickers within my mind, drawing back to a time I don't ever want to forget again.

"Higher, Daddy!" I giggle, grinning widely at the brunette girl next to me on the swings. She's maybe a few years older than me in this memory, but I would recognize her anywhere.

Elodee.

"Me next, Daddy," she exclaims, kicking her feet wildly.

"I only have two arms, girls," Dad says joyfully. "You can either each get one big push at a time, or small pushes together."

"Big ones!" Elodee and I scream together as I hold on to the chains of the swing with all my might. Though I do wonder... would I be able to fly if only I let go? Even if I couldn't, I'd still be okay because Daddy would catch me.

He always has.

I blink rapidly, coming out of the memory. Asher's arms are around me, keeping me upright as tears stream down my face. "Dad."

The word is barely a whisper on my lips and laden with years of loss, but he seems to have no problem hearing me. "Oh, Issie."

I stumble forward and right into his arms. "I missed you so much."

One hand holds me tightly around my back and the other against my head. "Oh, my girl. You have no idea."

We stand there, crying together, and the more time that passes, the stronger my connection to this man grows. Almost as if there's a tether tying us together, bonding us for all eternity.

Memories come, but they're more like brief flickers of moments in time. Each one with Grayson in them. Sometimes it's just the two of us and sometimes Elodee is there as well, but it's never more than that.

I crave to see my mother, to hear her laugh and see her smile, but her image never comes.

"I don't know how I could have forgotten you," I tell him, wiping at my face with my hands and looking up at his face. "It's undeniable now."

"We're going to figure this out, Issie," he promises, giving my shoulders a squeeze. "I'm just glad to have both my girls back. If only your mother could be here, then everything would be perfect."

A twinge of sadness accompanies his words, but the memories of her are too faint, too intangible for true sorrow. Instead, I find solace in his strength, in the promise of answers and justice.

Elodee makes a noise and I move to get a better look at her, needing to see my best friend, my...sister. I laugh to myself. She's going to love that more than anything.

"El?" I say softly as I take her hand and inspect every inch of her body. Like me, she's changed ever so slightly. The scar on her forehead from when I accidentally hit her with a toy truck when we were little is no longer present.

Her skin glows, a creamy radiance that seems illuminated from within, and her hair, now woven with strands of deep purple, adds an exotic flair to her natural brunette. As she turns restlessly, murmuring in discomfort, I gently cup her cheek, trying to soothe her. "It's okay. I'm here."

Her discomfort is palpable; she shifts again, a groan escaping her lips, but her eyes remain shut. Concern tightens my chest, and I glance anxiously at Asher and Grayson. "What's wrong with her?" My voice is edged with panic.

Nobody answers me and anxiety constricts my chest like a vise. I lean closer, pressing my ear against her chest, listening to the strong, steady beat of her heart. Yet her body betrays signs of distress: her arms twitch, and her torso twists in silent agony.

Impatience and worry sharpen my tone as I shake her gently. "Elodee, wake up!"

"Damn, Isla," she murmurs, her voice thick with grogginess. "Give me a minute. I just had the craziest…" Her words falter as her eyes flutter open, confusion clouding her gaze as she takes in her surroundings. "Holy fuck. Am I still dreaming?" She rubs her temples, squeezing her eyes shut again. "What is wrong with me?"

My hands cover hers, grounding her. "Absolutely nothing is wrong, and you're not dreaming. I thought the same when I got here."

But she's disoriented, shaking her head in denial, unwilling to accept this new reality. "Something is wrong with my head. I'm seeing…"

Asher steps beside me, his voice steady. "She's remembering already. Estee, can you hear me?"

Her response is snappish. "Of course I can, idiot. You're standing right next to me."

Asher raises a brow and I apologize on her behalf. "She's never really been a fun person to wake up." Then my eyes widen and my attention goes back to Elodee. "You didn't correct him when he called you 'Estee.'"

Her eyes finally open and instead of the brown I've always known them to be, they're golden and bright. "Why can't I tell what's real and what's not?"

"Do you know who I am?" Asher asks her and she shakes her head. "That's okay. You're not supposed to remember everything at once." He turns to me. "Why don't the two of you go into your room and you can explain things to her?"

I glance behind me, wondering why Grayson hasn't said anything, and then I realize he's not here. "What happened to—"

Asher cuts me off. "He thought it would be best not to overwhelm her more than she already was. He'll see her soon."

Why doesn't that surprise me?

I smile down at my best friend and now sister. "Think you can walk or am I going to have to carry you?"

"It's about damn time you did some of the lifting between us," she jokes as she pushes herself up, looking around. "Where the hell are we and how did we get here?"

"That's what we're going to chat about," I promise, happier than I've ever been in my life. We might not have all the answers between the two of us, but just having Elodee here is everything to me and I hope she's about to handle this a hell of a lot better than I did.

CHAPTER SIXTEEN

ISLA

As my sister and I enter my room, the weight of anticipation settles heavily between us. I guide Elodee to the table, where she sits, her expression taut with confusion and curiosity. Silence stretches uncomfortably, amplifying my anxiety about explaining our surreal reality. The truth about Lunara and our existence as wolf shifters feels daunting, almost suffocating.

"We're in Lunara," Elodee states, her voice brimming with an inexplicable certainty.

I fidget with my fingers under the table, bewildered. Though also thankful for her confidence. "How do you know that?"

She gives a half-shrug, her gaze darting around the room, not quite settling. "I've been here before. I don't know how, and maybe it sounds insane, but this place feels like… home." When her eyes finally meet mine, they shimmer with an unspoken recognition.

Emotions swirl within me—relief mingled with a sting

of envy. Relief that she's accepting our reality with ease, yet envy because how does she remember and I don't?

This might be more than I can handle on my own, yet I'm not ready to share her with anyone, so I decide to wing things on my own.

"From what I've learned," I begin, "we were born here and died way too many years ago, being reborn on Earth —like reincarnation—and we, um, we're..."

"Wolf shifters," she finishes for me, but she frowns. "I'm remembering bits and pieces, but I don't remember you. If we're both from here, why don't I remember you before these last twenty-something years?"

Her voice cracks, sending ripples of distress through me. "I don't know," I admit, my heart sinking with inadequacy.

Suddenly restless, Elodee stands, pacing near my bed as memories seem to flicker behind her eyes. "I've lived multiple lives, most on Earth and a few here," she says, stopping to face me, tears brimming. "I had parents before. Different ones, with each life. And the last ones, the ones we shared... Gods, Is. They were everything we always dreamed of."

"Our dad is still here," I blurt out, seizing the chance to bridge her fragmented memories with our present. Maybe Asher was wrong. I'm not sure I'm the right person to be having this conversation with my sister, considering she seems to know much more than I do.

She comes back to me, fingers wrapping around my arms and lifting me from the chair. "Where is he?"

I wince. "Easy, El. You're stronger here."

"Elodee," she muses. "That's not actually my name. It's Estee."

"Oh, yeah. Mine was Isobella, but they've been okay with calling me 'Isla,'" I tell her, suddenly feeling nervous for some reason.

She smiles softly and shakes her head. "I think 'Estee' will be just fine."

"Right." Why is none of this going like I imagined?

She tugs at my hair and chuckles. "I like what you've done with the new color. Would have been nice to know before I filed a missing person's report and blasted your picture all over social media, going as far as harassing the FBI until they sent someone to speak with me, but I guess they never would have found you, anyway."

I nearly choke and my eyes widen. "You called the FBI? Why?"

"My best friend was missing," she says, as if that explains everything. "What did you think I was going to do? Moving to Seattle was the stupidest thing I'd ever done. I was already trying to transfer back before you stopped answering your phone and when I didn't hear from you for a full day, I quit the next day and went back to the apartment to raise hell until I found you."

I throw my arms around her and hug her tightly. "I missed you so much, El. I mean Estee." Pulling back, I frown. "That's going to take some getting used to."

She taps my nose and grins. "As long as we're together, it doesn't matter. I was losing my mind before some man showed up. I thought he was a detective and then he jabbed a needle into my arm." She rubs near her right shoulder. "I don't remember anything from that point until waking up in the other room, but the longer I'm standing here, the more I'm remembering other things."

Fascinated, I pull her back to the table, deciding maybe

I can handle this on my own for a little longer. We take our seats again as I ask, "Like what?"

Her growing smirk has me already shaking my head as she replies, "Well, I was a badass, for one. Like a warrior who couldn't be touched and I had this wolf. She was incredible." A shadow falls over her face and she rubs her chest. "But she's not with me now."

"Neither is mine, but I don't remember her," I say, wondering if that's better or worse for me. Though this isn't about me and I want to give her some hope. "Asher thinks that we still have our wolves, even if we can't sense them yet. Well, he said I might, and I assume that's the same for you. Then again, I've only had two flashes of memories, so I don't know. Maybe it's not the same." Why is this so awkward and why am I rambling uncomfortably, unable to stop? "Oh, and he did confirm one thing. We are actually soul sisters. I'm not sure if that's just because—"

The squeal that leaves her makes my ears ring and finally shuts me up. She launches herself out of the chair and hugs me until my ribs ache, nearly bringing us both to the ground. "I might not remember the life here with you, but I've known since the moment I met you that you were important to me. Gods, Isla. If I'd lost you..."

Tears burn in my eyes as I hug her again. "I'm so sorry I couldn't call you. I should have fought sooner to get to you, but me coming here was completely different than your experience so far. I thought you'd never believe me."

She pulls back and takes a seat again, eyes bright with interest. "Tell me everything."

I start with the hike up Multnomah Falls, followed by getting lost and going over the bridge that was actually an ancient portal, and then coming here and meeting the asshole version of Asher.

"He didn't actually send you to your room," she says with an air of shock.

I nod but quickly defend him. "While that wasn't even the worst part of my first day here, I understand why he did it now and you shouldn't be mad at him."

Suddenly, telling Estee about Asher using our father's life to keep me here doesn't seem like the best idea.

"And why not?" She sneers. "He tried to keep you from me."

"He's… We're…" I have no clue how I'm supposed to describe what Asher is to me. Mostly because I barely understand it.

She covers her mouth and sucks in a heavy breath. "Holy shit. You're mates, aren't you? While that makes a little more sense, he still better watch his back. Nobody messes with my sister and gets away with it."

There really is no one else in the world like my best friend. I've always known I was lucky to have her in my life, but even more so now.

Elodee, I mean, Estee regards me with a mix of wonder and apprehension, her voice a whisper of trepidation. "You mentioned Dad earlier. He's really here? And what about Mom?" Her eyes search mine for truths she might not be ready to hear.

The weight of the conversation presses down, heavier than I anticipated. "Yes, Dad's here," I reassure her with a gentle smile, my voice softening to cushion the blow. "He can't wait to see you." I pause, the name 'Mom' catching in my throat, heavy with a grief that constricts my heart. "Mom, however…" My words trail off, heavy with sorrow. "It was too much for her after we vanished. She—"

Estee cuts me off. "She died and chose to stay at rest." Her words are resolute, accepting a fate she seems to understand more than I do.

A rueful chuckle escapes me. "It's a little overwhelming how easy this is for you. Asher's mom said I arrived through some ancient portal that hasn't been used in years. Maybe that's why this is easier for you and I'm still struggling."

I know it's not her fault I had to learn these things by being told, but that doesn't mean I don't suddenly feel like the one on the outside.

She reaches for my hands again and holds them tightly. "It's me and you against the world, just like it's been for the last two decades. I may remember more than you do, but there's still a lot of holes. Most importantly, I don't remember you being my sister in any lifetime before this one, which is an issue if we both died then."

"Asher thinks with time, I might remember my last day here and it could help us figure out what happened," I say, trying to push away any self-pity. "Though that was before we realized the same thing might have happened to you. You disappeared years after I did, leaving a note that said you couldn't handle the grief any longer. Everyone thought you chose to die until Grayson, I mean Dad"— another thing that will take time to remember—"started to piece things together. Asher was already going to try to bring you here, but when Dad guessed who you might really be, I think that expedited things."

"Maybe we'll remember together," she says and I hope like hell that she's right, especially since we might still be in danger. If we don't know who made us disappear or why, then what's to say they won't try again?

It took over five hundred years to bring us back here and I won't lose that much time again. Even if I don't remember my life before, my heart yearns for what it's lost and I'll fight with everything I have to keep what I've found.

Several hours later, Estee has finally passed out from exhaustion in my room and I need some air. I consider sitting out on the balcony so that I'm still in the room when she wakes up, but it's not enough.

I suddenly crave movement, the desire to feel the air on my skin as I run, the light of the moons strengthening my soul, and the earth's energy recharging my body.

Maybe this is one of those moments that Asher mentioned before when he said I should still hold my wolf spirit. Could this be one of those signs? I don't deny its possibility, knowing this urge isn't something I've ever possessed before.

Without taking too much time to reconsider, I exit my room, alone and quiet thanks to the late hour. It doesn't matter that another wolf nearly attacked me earlier. As I bound down the stairs, using the back exit Asher showed me before, I'm no longer afraid. Only frustrated that I can't remember more.

Hearing Estee talk about her lives, having our father confirm the memories available to her, the things they could reminisce over together...

I don't want to be bitter. I just want to remember.

Getting outside, I kick off my shoes and tilt my head toward the starry night. The twin moons greet me, lighting the sky up with their glow. My chest expands as I take a deep breath, inhaling the crisp air. Bending down, I dig my fingers into the ground, feeling the vibrations within the earth that I'd never known existed before.

Hell, not even an hour ago did I think this was possible, but with Elodee—*damn it*—Estee here, I'm trying to stop resisting what I don't understand and just accept what is.

I showed up in Lunara, believing I was dreaming and refusing to consider any of this world could be real. Maybe it's a combination of my stubbornness and my unusual arrival that has messed with my memories.

I don't know, but the bliss that radiated off Estee earlier is something I want. No, I need. I've experienced little snippets of that since arriving, but now, I'm craving more. More answers, more connections, more belonging.

Getting back to my feet, I take another inhale as I stretch, then take off at a sprint across the expansive back yard. Considering it's night, I do at least avoid the forest. Not because I'm fearful of the wolves that might be there, but because I don't want to get lost.

My speed picks up and just as I imagined before, energy feels as if it's being charged within me, pushing me harder, lengthening my stride and driving me forward. I run with no destination in mind, just knowing I want to keep the castle within my sights.

Air rushes past me, blowing my hair around as my muscles stretch, the aches seeming more like relief than anything else.

The sounds of water grow louder and I start to slow,

having no clue where it's coming from. I know Asher said these were islands, but I haven't ventured far enough before this to be curious about the ocean surrounding me.

There's only darkness in front of me and behind, the flicker of lights from the castle smaller than I expected. *Oops.* I ran farther than I realized in such a short time.

Here, under the gaze of the moons and the caress of the wind, I feel closer to the pulse of Lunara. The ground beneath me hums with ancient power, seeping into my bones, promising restoration and revelations. The world fades away, leaving only the rhythmic crash of waves to soothe the tumult within. Here, I could remain forever, lost in the embrace of the land that is slowly claiming me as its own.

"Isla?" Asher's voice, soft and tinged with concern, pulls me back from the edge of the vast, starlit solitude I had wandered into. "Are you okay?"

Sitting up, I try to mask the cascade of emotions with a smile. "Yeah, why?"

"I saw you running from my window," he says, settling beside me on the grass, his presence grounding. "I thought something might have happened."

"Estee fell asleep after dinner with Grayson, and I just needed to breathe, you know?" My voice trails off, apologetic. "Sorry, I should have left a note or something."

He twists a strand of my hair around his finger, his smile gentle. "You're okay—that's all that matters. How were things with Estee and your dad?"

"Fine," I reply, too hastily, the word barely covering the torrent beneath. In fact, with how electric my body feels, I have another thing on my mind.

"Can I see you shift?" I ask, causing his eyebrows to furrow slightly.

"Sure, but may I ask why?" His question is reasonable, but I don't really have an answer for him. At least not one that doesn't sound a little crazy in my mind.

"I'm just...curious." My casual answer doesn't seem to pacify him.

He inches closer, his eyes earnest. "You can tell me anything, Isla. I'm here to listen, not to judge. Especially if you're seeking answers."

I hug myself, feeling the unusual buzz under my skin. "Something feels different tonight. It's like there's this energy I can't quite manage," I confess, the night amplifying my restless spirit.

"Different like you sense your wolf?" he asks animatedly.

My eyes cast down because I know how happy that would make him. "No, but my skin itches and my body feels like it's swarming with energy I don't know what to do with, hence the running that I don't normally partake in."

"Maybe this is just your mind trying to prepare for another memory," he says quizzically, not showing any signs of disappointment. "As long as it won't frighten you, I'm happy to introduce you to my wolf. In fact, I know he'd appreciate some time with you."

Well, that intrigues me. "Can you speak with him?"

Asher shakes his head as he stands up, offering me a hand. "No, but after so long sharing the same mind, it's easy to read emotions from him."

Of course it is.

I rise from the ground, brushing the grass from my

pants as another question comes to mind. "What happens to your clothes or jewelry or anything like that when you shift?" My mind conjures an image of clothes being shredded, strips of fabric flying everywhere.

"Thanks to the magic of the gods, wolves that have sworn their allegiance to an alpha king or queen, they get to keep their clothes and any belongings they have on their person," he answers, then grins. "I'm not sure how much would ever get done around here if everyone was always naked. Then again, if that was all we ever knew, maybe it wouldn't make a difference."

"Right." Well, I guess that's not so bad.

Asher backs up and says, "Don't blink. This happens fast."

My eyes focus on Asher, fixated on his tall, muscular form. Flashes of memories from a few nights ago when I saw his wolf from afar try to distract me, but I push them aside as Asher's chest begins to rumble.

A flicker of white energy radiates from his body and it almost seems as if he's starting to bend in half, but then he disappears for the briefest of seconds that I'm not even sure if he really did or not. Before I can try to understand what I'm seeing, a magnificent beast stands in his place.

His head tilts toward the sky and he howls, long and loud, the sound like chime bells to my ears. I step forward, drawn to his energy, unable to stop myself even if I wanted to.

When I'm only a few feet away, the wolf growls and looks down at me. His eyes are a brighter blue than Asher's but familiar nonetheless. His grumbles don't frighten me as I reach my hand out, desperately needing to touch this animal, feel the warmth of his body, hear the beat of his strong heart.

His head bends lower, making me realize that he's not small by any means. The wolf head is nearly as tall as Asher's with fur as dark as the shadows surrounding us.

My hand rubs between his eyes and the rumble he elicits sends shivers down my spine.

"Hi." I laugh, the situation surreal yet profoundly grounding. He nudges me gently, leaning in as if to embrace me, his massive head resting against my shoulder.

I wrap my arms around his chest, weaving my hand around his back. I snuggle closer, my ear pressed against his soft coat, listening to the steady beat of the wolf's heart.

My eyes close and another tether, just like the one I felt earlier with Grayson, starts to grow within me. I think it's going to tie me to this wolf, but instead, my connection to the energy around me feels as if it explodes with a powerful force.

I release Asher and my back arches inward, pushing my chest out as heat swells within my chest. I wait for another memory to come, but nothing comes. Just the warmth of Polaris and a sense of pride for this land filled with magic I don't yet understand but suddenly feels closer than ever before.

Home.

Just as Estee said earlier.

There was a connection before, but it was something I could have walked away from if it meant keeping my best friend in my life. Now? Now, I can't imagine any other place I'd rather be.

Asher's wolf whines and nudges me with his cold nose.

"I'm sorry," I tell the beast. "I'm okay. My ties to this world seem to have finally snapped into place."

His head turns away from me and I wonder if he expected me to feel that same tie to him. Deep down, I think there's something there, which is why I don't still want to hate Asher, but what he feels for me, I can't say the same. Not yet.

My body starts to feel heavy and I let out a yawn. "Do you think we could lie under the stars for a bit?"

Without answering me, the wolf turns in a circle before lying down on his side, keeping his head up. I settle down in front of him, leaning my head against his stomach as I move to face him.

It's hard to think of this animal as a separate being from Asher, especially when he makes me feel just as safe as his human half. But I don't dwell on those thoughts for long.

In this moment, with the stars as my canopy and Asher's wolf keeping watch, I feel a peace settle over me— a promise of home that's both ancient and newly discovered. Here, with the ocean's distant roar as my lullaby, I let the night embrace me, hoping for dreams that might finally bring my lost memories back into the light.

CHAPTER SEVENTEEN

ASHER

The night under the stars with Isla felt surreal, a cherished memory that won't soon be dismissed. My wolf and I, bonded in the silence of the night, found solace with Isla nestled against his side, her presence a balm to the centuries of waiting.

Before the day's sun can fully rise, I reluctantly wake her so that she can be there when Estee is up. Leaving her bedroom, I head back to my suite to prepare for the day, noting that each time I'm forced to leave Isla's side is harder than the time before. Still, I don't want to rush my mate, nor do I want to risk her regretting anything that has to do with us.

Though as the dawn finishes casting its golden rays through the treetops, I'm already wondering if it's too early to bring her and Estee breakfast.

Yet just as I'm about to call for breakfast, a knock at my door halts me—a knock that brings a challenge I'm not yet ready to face.

It's Noen and Declan. I sense both of them and I've yet to tell them of Isla's return.

Years ago, I hated Noen because of Isla. Well, more like my younger self was jealous of him. They were close, best friends, even, having grown up as neighbors before Isla had moved into the castle with me.

I'd sworn Noen had wanted to take her from me, but after her disappearance, he was there for me. Offering thoughts and ideas of where she could be, always making sure I was doing okay. Sure, his concern seemed most heavily focused on Isla, but there was a comradery I began to feel with him that I'd refused to before.

One that has grown over the centuries and why he's now one of my most trusted friends. Yet I refused to send word to him about Isla's return.

Selfishly, I want to keep her all to myself. I don't want her to remember him before she does me. Yes, she recalled a memory of us in the cave, but it's not the attraction Isla and I share that I'm worried about. I need her to remember our bond, the power of our connection, and how we used to believe there wasn't anyone or anything that could tear us apart.

Now, she's going to have Estee and Noen and I know it sounds pathetic not wanting to share her, even if their presence might help her remember. I just can't help myself.

I'm out of time, though.

"We know you're in there, Ash," Noen calls out as he pounds on the door again. "Open up."

With a heavy sigh, I walk to the door and unlock it before opening up.

"So, he does live," Declan jests. "We thought maybe you'd died since we weren't hearing from you."

"Have you seen anyone else since returning?" I ask, stepping out of the way so they can enter.

The two of them share a look and shake their heads.

Noen runs a hand over his dark-blond hair and narrows his green eyes at me. "I know I'm tired, but is the infamous King Asher nervous about something?"

Declan takes a seat on my couch, kicking his dirty boots on my table before unbuttoning his vest and rubbing two fingers over his beard. "I think he might be." He winks, a spark in his golden eyes. "Now, Asher. Tell us what plagues our dear friend."

Noen takes a seat as well, but I remain standing behind one of the chairs as my stare moves between the two of them. There's never going to be an easy time to say the words, so I just do it.

"Isla has returned."

They look at each other, matching creases between their brows before Declan asks, "Who the hell is Isla?"

Of course.

"Isobella Blackwood." I watch Noen closely as I say her name and his face pales, just as I expected. "She's returned with no memory and now prefers to be called 'Isla.' The name she was born with this lifetime on Earth."

"Earth?" Noen gapes. "How the hell is this possible?"

"We're still sorting that out," I start to explain before Declan cuts in.

"And what of Estee? Did they come back together?"

I raise a brow at him, my suspicions on high alert. "Why would you assume they were together after the note she left?"

He rolls his eyes. "Oh, come on, Ash. Don't tell me you bought that bullshit. Estee went looking for her sister and she didn't want to follow any rules. I assumed that at some point, she got herself into more trouble than she could handle and never found her way back. But if Isobella's been alive this whole time, maybe Estee found her and they decided to stay together, meaning if one is back, then the other could be too."

He makes a good point, one I hadn't considered. Which means there's a chance that Grayson could have been partially wrong before. Allowing myself to jump to the conclusion that someone murdered them may have been preferable to believing my mate chose to leave me, but then again, I always trust my first instinct. Even if this other scenario sounds equally plausible.

"Yes, Estee is back as well," I admit. "We're still trying to piece together what happened. It's only been a few days since Isla—"

Noen is on his feet. "*A few days*? What the hell, Asher? Why didn't you call me back?"

He has every right to be furious with me. I should have sent word to him, but Isla is my mate and sharing her with anyone else was at the bottom of my priority list. Right or wrong, I won't apologize for that.

"Because she doesn't remember you," I tell him, possibly a little too harshly. "She doesn't remember any of this. I'm not going to overwhelm her with too much at once and push her away. She didn't even want to stay when she first arrived. I won't risk losing my mate again, not for any reason."

There's a rumble in his chest as he speaks. "Are you trying to tell me that you're not going to let me see her?

She was my best friend and I know you didn't like me back then, but you've got to be kidding me. Haven't we moved beyond childish jealousy?"

Schooling my features, I won't let him see that he's partially correct. "This has nothing to do with the past and everything to do with the right now. She's only just got her sister back last night and felt her connection to Grayson—"

His eyes widen and his face reddens. "Grayson's returned as well? Fuck, Asher. What else aren't you telling us?"

Noen takes a step toward me, but Declan is quick to move between the two of us. "Let's remember who we are. First, Asher is our Alpha King. If he made the decision not to call us back, then we need to trust he did so for good reason." His stare lands on mine. "But you need to remember that we're not supposed to be just your royal delegates. You've made us believe all these years that we've become more than that. Unless you're ready to tell us that we're nothing more than your ambassadors, I'd consider your next decisions carefully."

It's not often someone questions my judgment as Declan is now. If he were anyone else, I would banish him from the castle, but he's right. He and Noen have become more than two wolves who work for me. They've been by my side for centuries.

"This has been more complicated than I expected," I state. "And as you can imagine, emotions have been high. I needed time to process Isla not knowing who I am to her or where she's from. I believe we've sorted those things out now, but the situation is still fragile."

Noen huffs. "Fragile how?"

"She has only remembered a few small moments from her past," I explain. "Until we know why she disappeared all those years ago, then I'm going to be cautious when it comes to anything to do with my mate."

"She's not just your mate, Asher," Noen points out. "She's her own person, a daughter, and a friend. If you think you can control whom she sees, then you don't remember the past very well. Or maybe this woman isn't who you think she is. Why aren't you calling her 'Isobella'?"

He doesn't trust me with this, just like I didn't trust him when Isobella disappeared. I'd even considered that he could have taken her from me at one point, but when he never left to go after her, I had to dismiss the idea.

"She doesn't want to be known by her previous name, so I'm respecting that and I expect you to do the same. Even if you don't agree," I say pointedly. "Isla needs more time to adjust. I won't keep you from her, but I also won't let you overwhelm her. If she needs space, then she's going to have it."

Noen's shoulders stiffen, and he raises his jaw as if he's going to challenge me further, but then his eyes cast briefly to the side. "I would never do anything to hurt *Isla*."

"I know that, Noen," I tell him. "Still, I need you to respect that she's more than my best friend. She's my mate and I've had to live five centuries with a gaping hole in my heart that her absence left."

Mates have always been a touchy subject for Noen. Whereas Declan prefers his single life, Noen has always wished for someone of his own. He grew up with a father who blamed him for his mother's death, which left a scar time never healed. I feel for him, but he can't fill the role of the mate he has yet to find in this lifetime with just anyone else.

Best friends or not, Isla is mine and only mine.

"Understood," he says, still keeping his gaze averted, a sign of respect and the only reason I say my next words.

"Let's go see if she's still awake and you can see her."

His head snaps up and the anticipation is clear on his face, but he keeps his mouth shut.

Declan nudges me, brows waggling. "Can I come? I'd love to see Estee."

It's no secret the two of them hooked up before. Still, I warn him. "Don't push her, either. While she seems to be remembering more clearly, there are holes. You very well could be one of them."

He scoffs and grins. "Like she could ever forget me."

"I guess we'll find out. She's sleeping in Isla's room for now."

"Cain," I reach out through mind speak. *"Are you back to working the portal or are you still within the castle?"*

"I'll be returning to the portal shortly unless you believe Princess Isla still needs me, my king. Plus, Malimorte said he would take care of anything pressing now that he's back."

Of course he did. That's why he's my top advisor.

"Very well," I reply. *"I'll reach out to him."*

Disconnecting the link to Cain, I mentally call for Mali.

"Yes, Your Majesty?"

"Do you know if Isla and Estee are up?" I don't want to knock on her door and disturb them, when I assume after my evening with Isla that she didn't get much sleep.

"They both are and they're enjoying breakfast on the

balcony as we speak, my king," Mali answers. *"I brought food to them myself so that I could apologize to Princess Estee for stabbing her with a needle. She was not pleased with me before passing out."*

I chuckle to myself. *"No, I don't assume she was. Thank you, Mali."*

Noen and Declan both stare at me expectantly as I cut the link to Mali. They're used to me tuning out and having conversations they can't hear. Still, they get annoyed when they feel as though they're missing out.

"Something to share?" Declan asks first.

"Isla and Estee are both awake." I head for my closet to change my clothes. "We can see them if you're both ready now."

Neither say anything else as I quickly dress in a black button-up and blue slacks. As soon as I step back into the room, Noen is already opening the door. "After you."

I don't comment on his sarcastic tone. Instead, I lead the way to the next floor and then to Isla's room. The three of us remain silent until I knock on the door.

"Do I smell?" Declan whispers. "We haven't even showered after being on that damn ship."

"No more than usual," Noen quips, making me smile. At least things aren't *that* tense because of my decisions.

"You could have showered on the ship," I remind him.

His face scrunches and he holds his stomach. "My wolf already hates being on the water. Showering while the waves are knocking us around makes me nauseous."

Estee answers the door, hand on her hip, and a glare on her face. "I can't even have one meal with her before you return?" She notices we're not alone and sighs. "And you brought friends? Great."

"Hi, Estee," Declan practically purrs.

"And you are...?"

I glance back to see his face fall. "Declan. You couldn't possibly forget me."

The feisty she-wolf shrugs. "Apparently, I can." Then she nods at Noen. "And you would be?"

"Noen," he replies calmly. "I was your neighbor growing up."

"Hm." She taps her chin. "Still nothing, but then again, I don't remember much of anything from my last lifetime here. Just the ones before that and my current one."

Interesting and another reason I'm sticking with my first thought that someone did this to them. She shouldn't be forgetting one life in particular.

"May we come in, Estee?" I ask politely. The few moments I've been around her have already confirmed she seems to be even feistier than she was last time I knew her. For the time being, I intend to avoid pissing her off if I can help it.

"I guess." She moves to the side, then turns to yell behind her. "I hope you didn't stink up the bathroom, sis. We have guests."

"Elodee Jane!" Isla screeches.

Her sister cackles. "That's what you get for still calling me 'Elodee.'"

Gods, these two are going to be a handful together, just like they once were, but worse because they have the excuse of not remembering proper etiquettes.

Isla comes out, wearing only a robe. While the white cotton covers nearly her entire body, it's assuming there is nothing underneath that has my chest growling and me blocking the view of the two behind me.

"Why don't you put on some clothes?" I suggest, reaching for the door. "We'll wait right here."

She mutters something about not expecting guests at the "ass crack of dawn," whatever that means.

I put my back to the door and find that both men are grinning at me. "You're going to need us more than ever, Ash," Declan announces with unreasonable pride.

"How do you figure?"

He and Noen share a look before he responds. "Until that woman officially becomes your mate, you're going to be a grumbling, overprotective mess. You're no good to anyone when you're constantly worried about her, which you should be. Just don't fight the truth. She needs you and you need her. The sooner the both of you admit that, the sooner all this will work itself out."

Declan's insightfulness is one of the reasons I've kept him so close over the years and even now, he makes me wonder: will Isla only get her memories back once she truly accepts who she is? And does that include being my mate?

I don't know, but the thought of the answer being *yes* doesn't make me feel any better. Isla might not be as feisty as her sister, but she still doesn't like to be told what to do and I have no intention of rushing her. Though even my wolf grumbles at the thought of that meaning we'll possibly be waiting years for her to be ours again.

She'll be worth the wait—that much I know for sure.

CHAPTER EIGHTEEN

ISLA

Well, this isn't awkward at all. A lie I tell myself as I get dressed in jeans and the nearest sweater I can reach from the rack inside my closet. Without shoes, I go back into the room and Estee is standing there with a shit-eating grin on her face.

"He's hot," she says, nodding toward the door. "Have you, uh, jumped his bones yet?"

My glare could cut through glass. "*He* can probably hear you and no, we've only kissed."

"Bedrooms are soundproof," she says confidently. "That I do remember from being here before."

"What?" How did I not know this already? "When did you live here? With me?"

She shrugs. "I might have stayed here with you, but I don't remember. And I only visited before, I didn't live here. I don't think."

These multiple lifetimes are going to screw with my head possibly even more than my feelings for Asher already do.

"Right." I glance at the door. "We should probably let them in."

Estee licks her lips. "He's got a cute friend with him. Supposedly, I knew him before and I'm not surprised."

I laugh and shake my head. "Okay, you were wild back on Earth, but this is a whole new side of you, my friend."

She flicks her long, brunette hair back over her shoulder as she sashays toward the door. "Remembering who I am…you'll understand soon. I'll make sure of it." She turns back to me, her face more serious. "But all of this is right, Isla. I know you're confused and maybe even scared, but don't be. We're right where we should have always been. I feel it in my soul."

Little does she know, so do I, which is what scares me.

I can't remember who I was, and I have no clue who I'm supposed to be, but the longer I'm here, the more I connect to this place and these people and now, having Estee here… I can't imagine being anywhere else. There's a peacefulness that overcomes me at the thought of staying forever, yet not understanding why is what still has me hesitating.

Maybe I'm overthinking this. Maybe I just need to embrace all that's around me, including Asher, and let the rest work itself out, but with the way I disappeared—or was murdered—before, I can't seem to allow myself to do so.

Estee opens the door and three men enter. Asher and two I don't recognize. They're dressed more casually than their king in black jeans and blue, collared shirts, but the way they keep their heads held high and shoulders straight, it's as if they're used to being two of the most important people in the room.

The one nearest to Asher with blond hair and hazel eyes stares at me like I mean something to him. His gaze is wide and shimmering with unspoken emotions. When the stranger steps forward, Asher's chest lets out a quiet rumble and the two share a tense look.

Only a second later does the third man speak up. "I'm Declan, a royal ambassador for King Asher here and his best friend." His smile twists with a hint of mischief and the way his blue eyes spark beneath his dark brows makes me believe he's the one Estee hooked up with before. Just her type. "Next to Asher is Noen. We share the same roles, but not the same women."

His smirk and open gaze for my sister has me chuckling, especially as she says, "Well, isn't that great to know. I don't think I would have survived much longer without knowing that."

Openly appraising her, he replies, "I had a feeling."

I leave them to their battle of wits and stares as I look at Asher. He's no longer glaring at his friend, but looking at me. "How are you feeling? If you need rest, we won't stay long."

He's likely asking because of my run last night, but he doesn't need to be worried. As jealous as I was that Estee could remember, I'm happy for her. Maybe her confidence within this world will be what helps me figure things out as well.

"I'll be fine," I tell him with a smile. "Thank you for last night."

"Anytime." He hesitates, then gestures toward his other friend. "Like Declan said, this is Noen. The two of you used to be friends before."

Noen steps around Asher this time and reaches a hand

toward me. "Neighbors first, then best friends. I was a few years older than you, but we hung out near daily for most of our childhoods."

When I go to accept his shake, I catch Asher watching us closely, making me slightly nervous. Am I not supposed to be friends with this guy? I don't know, but I quickly decide that it's going to be my choice, not Asher's, especially after what Noen just said.

"Well, Noen. It's lovely to meet you. Again," I tell him sincerely. "You'll have to be patient with me, as I have no clue who you are, but I'll figure things out eventually."

His smile is friendly and calming. "I'm sure you will."

Asher clears his throat loudly, making me jump a little and release Noen's hand. "Well, we didn't mean to interrupt your morning," he says. "We'll let you get back to your breakfast. My mother should be by in a couple of hours to take you to the Academy."

Oh. Right. The royal school. Not something I'm really looking forward to, but at the same time, if learning is the key to remembering, then I'm not going to argue.

Declan takes Estee's hand and kisses her knuckles. "I hope I'll see you again soon."

"Maybe," she flirts back, but she keeps a couple of feet of space between them.

He grabs onto Noen's shoulder and drags him from the room as I wave goodbye.

"Nice to meet the both of you," I call after them.

"You too, Isla," Noen manages to say before being shoved into the hallway.

Asher still stands close by and he takes another step toward me.

Estee makes an odd noise, then spins toward the

bathroom. "Don't mind me. I'm just going to shower and pretend the two of you aren't sucking face while I'm naked in the next room."

"*Estee*." Asher and I both snarl her name at the same time.

Our situation has gone from pushing each other's buttons to wanting to strangle each other to being restrained and almost too formal, then to making out on the stairs. Now, it seems we're going to go through our awkward phase until we decide if there's going to be more than kissing happening.

Of course there will be, I think and surprise even myself.

Well, I didn't think I'd thought that far ahead, but apparently, my subconscious has and if I'm being honest, I'm not mad about it.

It's not like I've never had sex. I've just never had sex with a king who's also born from the gods and supposed to be my…mate.

Until thinking of him that way doesn't make me uncomfortable, I should probably restrain my libido.

"I'm sorry if we overwhelmed you," Asher says once we're alone. "Noen was upset with me for not telling him you were here sooner. He's been gone on business and I should have told him, but I wasn't ready to share you. I'm still not, but I also know I can't control you, nor do I want to."

His candor is a bit of a shock, but a welcome one, especially when I was thinking some of the same things after his reaction earlier.

"Thank you for telling me," I say earnestly. "And don't worry about overwhelming me. That might be just what I need."

He steps closer. "Does that only apply to meeting new-to-you people or with all things?"

His question makes my skin spark with energy and my breathing heavier. I know the answer I want to say and I almost don't because I also know I'm still confused, but that doesn't mean I stop the words from tumbling out of my mouth.

"*All* things."

"Those two words have never sounded more perfect." His chest rumbles and he grabs my face with both hands, holding me as if I might break, but when his lips crash against mine, there's no holding back.

I hold on to his shirt, pressing against him, as our tongues meet with a renewed vigor. His fingers grip on to my long strands and the pinch of pain has a soft moan rising from within me.

He breaks the kiss and rests his forehead against mine, attempting to catch his breath. "Gods, Isla. You have no idea how much I've missed you."

I really don't, but I've certainly tried to guess.

"I'm sorry I don't remember," I tell him, but he's already shaking his head.

"Don't ever apologize for that," he demands, his voice rough. "We might not know for sure what happened yet, but I know it wasn't your fault. No matter what we find out, nothing will change how I feel."

And I think that's what scares me most. Asher can't truly promise that to me because while his theory makes sense that someone may have murdered me, I have to consider the alternative.

What if I did choose to leave? What if Estee knew and

followed me? What if finding out what really happened changes *everything*?

With how quickly I'm becoming attached, I'm terrified of that scenario and I don't know how I'm supposed to get over that with only brief snippets of memories.

"As much as I'd love to stay right here with you in my arms, Estee is likely listening to every word we speak," he says softly. "Plus, Declan and Noen are waiting for me."

I smooth out the wrinkles I created on his shirt and smile up at him, trying to hide the fears that threaten to strangle me. "Then I guess you better go."

He kisses me again, but not near long enough before he adds, "I'm going to apologize now for however I might act when Noen is around you. He's one of my closest friends and the two of you were best friends before—he wasn't lying about that—but you're still my mate. Being wolf shifters, logic doesn't always make sense to our inner beasts and having another male be so close to you, well, it makes me a little crazy."

While I don't know enough to truly understand what he's saying, I can sense the sincerity of his words and will take them into consideration.

"Thank you for telling me," I say, then I give him a little push toward the door. "I'll come find you after we're done at the school."

He winks as he reaches for the door. "Not if I find you first."

Oh, how I hope he does.

CHAPTER NINETEEN

When I get out into the hallway, only Declan is waiting for me. He's casually leaning against the wall, ankles crossed and pretending to pay attention to his nails more than anything else.

"So, that was fun," he begins, his voice light but the undercurrents of concern unmistakable. He looks up, his expression sobering. "Noen took off."

"Where did he go?" I probe, contemplating reaching out but opting against it, giving him space to digest his encounter with Isla.

"Just said he was going out." Declan pushes away from the wall and we start walking back toward the stairs as he adds, "Speaking as both your oldest friend and your ambassador, you were rather tough on him. Do you really think he'd try to take Isla from you after everything the two of you went through back then when she disappeared?"

"Well, *someone* took her from me." The words leave my mouth before I can truly process them, and once they're out in the open, I can't ignore them. "Maybe he's been keeping me close to make sure I never figure out what he did."

Declan shakes his head. "And maybe seeing your mate after all this time has made you lose your mind. Noen didn't hurt Iso—*Isla* and you know it."

But do I? Doubt gnaws at me, a relentless beast. While I admit to being historically jealous, the possibility that Noen acted out of a twisted sense of protection—keeping her from both me and the throne—nags at me.

I don't know how he would have found out so soon, but it's all plausible.

Declan sighs and frowns. "I don't usually overstep and use our friendship to challenge you, but I want you to consider that you're too close to the situation. I'm not sure where your head is right now because I'm pretty sure you're still keeping something from me about all this, but don't put this on Noen. I may not know what happened all those years ago, but I do know that he had nothing to do with it."

He can't know that for sure, but he's made me consider my actions. Just maybe not in the way he hoped.

If, and no matter how big of an if that might be...Noen had something to do with Isla's disappearance, it will be better for me to keep him close, just as he's done with me, and that's exactly what I intend to do.

"Hey," I say, mind-linking with him, my tone apologetic. *"I'm sorry for overreacting. I shouldn't have treated you that way and I promise to keep my emotions in check."*

Noen doesn't reply right away. *"She's your mate. I'll try to understand too. I'm going back to my room to shower and sleep."*

He breaks our connection and I let him. Until we learn more, I don't really have a choice unless I want to come right out and accuse him of something I have no proof of.

As king, I could, but at what cost?

That's not something I'm willing to risk just yet. I'll just plan on keeping a closer eye on Isla for the time being, reminding her to never be without myself, Grayson, or her sister.

"I apologized to him," I tell Declan before he heads to his room.

He nods and smiles before clasping my shoulder. "I'm impressed. You don't often take blame. You won't regret it."

We will see about that.

As he goes in the opposite direction, my mind goes back to the one thing that did go right this morning: Isla didn't hesitate to kiss me.

In fact, I think she was disappointed when I once again stopped things from escalating, something I don't plan on doing a third time when we find ourselves alone again.

Perhaps I'll get that chance tonight for dinner if I can get Estee to leave her side for a couple of hours. I'm not above asking Declan to help with that, either.

One way or another, I'll have my mate. At least as much of her as she's willing to give me.

CHAPTER TWENTY

ISLA

How is this my life right now? Sitting in a horse-drawn carriage with my actual sister and a former queen, having just left a castle straight out of a fairy tale, and headed to an academy for wolf shifters. My mind is reeling, but I'm also grinning like a fool as I gaze out the window.

The sun is bright, warming my skin even from inside the luxury cart. People stroll through streets, most in groups of two to four. They stare, but everyone smiles and waves as we pass, making me do the same.

"After we're done at the school, can we stop at the shops?" I ask, passing by some of the same places that I saw my first night here. Wolfish Wears now holds a completely different meaning.

"I won't be able to take you," Sosheena says with a kind smile, "but I'm sure the two of you can manage. You have nothing to fear here."

I turn to look out the window again so she can't see my face. Asher said he wasn't telling anyone anything that they didn't need to know until we understood more about what may or may not have happened to me and Estee.

A smart choice, but moments like this with his mother aren't the most comfortable when I know she isn't aware of the truth.

Still, maybe she's right. Maybe I have nothing to fear because I left on my own accord and when I remember… all of this will fall apart.

Knowing that I had this incredible family, a mate who loved me more than his own life, and anything I could have dreamed of, I can't think of a single reason as to why I would have, but the possibility is still there.

As jealous as I am that Estee got her memories back from most of her lives so easily, I wish she would have remembered the most important one.

I reach to scratch my head and then cringe when I remember there's a crown sitting up there. Something Sosheena insisted on. Even if I'm not ready to be mates with Asher, or the queen, I'm still a princess by birth, as is Estee. Apparently, that means it's only proper for the two of us to honor that title when out in public.

Hence, the tiara of diamonds placed atop my head and the pearls around my neck, along with the heels and navy-blue dress I'm now wearing.

Estee's foot nudges me from across the carriage. She's grinning and in her element with all this princess stuff, not seeming the least bit concerned. Our eyes meet and there's a glint in her gaze that has never boded well for me.

"So, Sosheena," she says. "Should we start with the kinder classes?"

I glance at the previous queen and hardly breathe as

her face lights up. "You know, I was going to say the library, but you may be right, Estee." She pauses then nods animatedly. "Actually, a few days with each class level could be just what Isla needs to trigger her memories. I'll speak with the headmaster and see if the teachers wouldn't mind doing a recap day for us to speed up the process." Sosheena looks at me and smiles so widely that I can't help but return the gesture. "Oh, Isla. You have no idea how much I hope this works."

"You and me both," I say sincerely. For more reasons than she can imagine.

We start to slow and I look out the window again. The carriage glides smoothly over a stone path, then starts to turn. There's a large, five-tier fountain at the center of the circular entrance with a howling wolf sitting at the top of it.

To my right, there's a beautiful building with lots of windows, at least four levels, and two grand doors at least twenty feet tall with intricate carvings on them.

I move to exit the carriage, but Sosheena lightly touches my wrist and shakes her head. Another second later, my door opens, and a gentleman greets us.

"Welcome back to Lunara Academy, Queen Mother Sosheena." He then nods politely to me and my sister. "Princess Isla, Princess Estee."

This is so unreal.

We step out of the cart and onto a stone pathway leading up to the massive doors that are already opening.

A man who appears to be in his thirties but could be hundreds of years old around here waltzes toward us, grinning from ear to ear and holding his arms out as he bows. "Your Highnesses. Your Majesty. We're so glad you've come to visit our humble school once again."

"Thank you for accommodating us, Headmaster Keenan." Sosheena glides toward him and the two of them begin walking toward the entrance, but I'm still staring up at the stone siding, stained-glass windows, and the roses that are growing up the sides of the building.

Estee nudges me. "Come on. You can drool over all this later."

"What did you mean by 'kinder' class before?" I finally ask her as we trail behind Sosheena and the headmaster, who are a safe distance ahead, having a private conversation.

"Oh, you'll see." She grins widely and I just shake my head. There's no sense in arguing with her, especially when she adds, "Just keep an open mind and remember that anything is possible. Even in this world, there are no limits to what you can have, Isla. Your mind and your heart are at war even right now. Once you get them in sync, you'll find the answers you're looking for."

There's my optimistic best friend. She's been so hellbent on leaning into her sassy side since last night that I almost forgot she usually does have the best advice.

"It just sucks not remembering," I say, but before she can respond, a bell rings.

Considering this is an academy in an opulent kingdom, I expect to see children on their best behavior, wearing pressed uniforms, but that's not at all what comes rushing out from the hallways around us.

Kids of all ages and sizes yell and laugh and come rushing by us, nearly knocking me over. They all wear matching clothing, but half of their shirts are either unevenly buttoned or left untucked as they run toward, I assume, their next classes.

Some wear little tiaras, others have jeweled pins on their lapels, but all of them radiate joy and nearly as quickly as the tiny tornados of chaos arrive, they disappear.

"That is a sneak peak of what you can expect in class," Estee whispers as we catch up with the others. "Except there are also little ankle biters. Like, *literal* ones unless the rules have changed. I have vivid memories of idiot boys shifting and chasing us girls around the class anytime the teacher would step out."

"Great," I drawl, my shoulders drooping with the weight of how awkward all this feels.

Sosheena turns toward us, still smiling and emanating pure grace. "All right, ladies. I've been given instructions and while Estee had a great idea starting with the kinder class, we're going to need to stick with the library today. How does that sound?"

"Absolutely perfect," I tell her as I notice the headmaster walking away. "How do we get there?"

Inside the school, there are too many hallways to count, three different stairways, wide and swooping, and doors everywhere with silver plaques on them that I can't read without getting closer.

"Right this way," Sosheena says, gesturing toward the center set of stairs.

Estee walks with ease and I try to soak up her confidence. She has this incredible ability to believe that everything is always working out for her. Even more fascinating, things almost always do.

I had a hard time understanding that concept when

she took the job in Seattle, moving away from me, but I'm sure if I said as much to her now, she'd find a way to see the bright side of that as well.

One of the classroom doors has been left open on the second floor. I slow as we walk by and notice teenagers sitting calmly at their desks. Except they're not all wearing the same uniforms like the younger ones running past us were. I see clothing ranging from blues to maroons to charcoal grey to even purple.

"What's with the different colors?" I ask once we're past the door.

Sosheena answers first, eyes bright with pride. "Last century, I convinced the other leaders that it would be good for our children to co-mingle. We might choose to remain as four kingdoms after all these years, but we are still one people, and the children should understand that from an early age."

My heart warms and I nod, unexpectedly wanting to cry for reasons unknown. "That is incredible. Do they live here while in school?"

"We have a limited number of dorms they stay in and we only keep them for eight weeks at a time so that we can bring as many children in as possible," Sosheena answers. "We're the only island with an academy of this magnitude, so the list to get in is quite extensive."

No wonder she seems so proud.

The library is on the third floor and the only thing on this level, it seems. There are multiple doors to get in, each one leading to a different section. Sosheena doesn't stop until we reach one titled "Our Beginnings."

"You may have only been on your first life when you left here before," she explains, "but I think understanding how your home came to be is important. So, we'll find a couple of books here first and then go from there if that works for you."

I nod because there is no way I'm going to disagree with her, but I do mention something Asher said before. "I was told there was a library at the castle as well. How come we didn't start there if I'm not allowed to go in the classes today?"

"You'll do both," Sosheena says. "While we have an extensive library at home, there is nothing quite like the one here and today wasn't about going to classes, anyway. You were supposed to just have a few meetings, but it seems there was a hiccup with communication and they've been moved out a couple weeks."

She frowns and her chest rumbles a bit. I'm beginning to think that it's not often this regal woman doesn't get her way, but I'm more than okay with skipping the meetings for now. Books will hopefully be enough to trigger more memories for me.

"Well, this looks like a wonderful place to start," I tell her with a genuine smile. "Thank you so much for bringing us here today."

Looking around, I notice Estee has slipped away, but before I can go find her, Sosheena grabs my arm and leads me to the right.

"You're going to love this place," she says with glee. "There's so much to absorb in here."

Glancing around, I hope she's right.

The bookshelves are at least fifteen feet tall, each with its own sliding ladder to reach the taller shelves. Every space is filled and there isn't a single book that appears out of place.

Taking a deep breath, I expect a musty scent with how old everything looks, but there's only a fresh, woodsy smell within the building. The ceiling is made up of carved, white flower tiles and there are thin windows placed on the front and back walls, letting natural light in.

Per Sosheena's directions, I take a seat at a wooden desk with a padded bench seat. I barely get comfortable before she's making a stack of books in front of me.

"Look these over," she says as she moves between the shelf next to me and the table. "If the pages of a book don't call to you, set it to the left. When something stands out, place it on the right and those will be what we take home."

"Got it." I peek around again for Estee, but she's still nowhere to be found. Traitor.

Opening the first book, I flip through the pages, one at a time, until Sosheena places a warm hand on my shoulder. "Oh, no, dear. Not like that." She takes the book from me and flips through so quickly that I can't even see the words on the pages. "Trust the energy of the book. It will tell you when to stop."

And here I thought things couldn't get much weirder than learning wolf shifters were real and I'm one of them. Technically.

She chuckles, adding, "We'll be here until dawn otherwise."

Yeah, I'd rather not let that happen.

I look for Estee again, growing annoyed that she's ditched me and I'm supposed to figure out this energy stuff on my own. Yes, I realize Sosheena is here and I could ask her, but that's not the same as having my best friend by my side.

Doing as I've been instructed, I begin flipping through books only about half as quickly as Sosheena is placing them on the table. Before I know it, I can't even see around me, as the stacks are getting so tall, but I do at least hear the hum of a song coming from Sosheena.

Each tome is in pristine condition, the hardback covers sturdy and the binding tight. Even the pages are crisp, but the dates tell the truth of their ages. I've seen books as old as 903 BCE and none newer than the 1500s. After flipping through a few dozen of them, I'm starting to wonder if I can't feel whatever energy I'm supposed to and say as much to Sosheena.

She peeks over the top of the stacks and smiles down at me. "You'll need patience, Isla. There's a reason I'm drowning you in books. Out of the hundreds you touch today, we'll be lucky if three of them speak to you."

Oh. Great.

Another glance around for Estee with no luck and I continue to flip through the books as quickly as I can. It feels like two hours later and my fingertips are red, my backend is numb, and my stomach is beginning to growl.

I also want to murder my sister. How could she have just left me like that?

A little more aggressively than I mean to, I grab the next book and nearly drop it. Feeling guilty, I try to shove down my own annoyances and continue the job I've been tasked with. Though I'm convinced at this point—

My thoughts are cut off when an electric shock rolls through me, forcing my eyes closed as I grip tightly to the book within my hands. I take a deep breath and my shoulders relax for the first time in over an hour.

Except I'm no longer in the library.

I'm in a bedroom, my bedroom. The walls are a seafoam-green color, the bed a soft cream. Paintings of flowers, the ocean, wolves, and... Is that Estee? I also see Asher and Noen depicted in the art. Each one hangs proudly on my walls, all signed with the same initials: IB.

I look down to see my hands are covered in paint and another canvas sits in my lap. My fingers glide over the surface and I smile. The cave.

There are no people in this piece, but I recognize the cave's entrance from having just been there. Wait. There's a flicker of something in the shadows. I lift the painting and peer close, but the harder I stare, the more my head pounds.

Still, I don't relent.

Something is there and I want to know what. What was I painting in the darkness? What answers might I find there?

The bed starts to feel as though I'm sinking into the mattress. I drop the painting, grasping on to the bedding, pillows, and even the bedframe, but my touch never finds purchase.

I'm falling, my speed too fast. There's no light around me any longer and my heart is racing, but I'm not afraid. No matter where I land, I'm going to be okay.

As soon as I accept that, I find myself within the cave. I'm not alone. Asher is here, his hand outstretched, waiting for me.

"Mate," he whispers with a sexy grin.

I take a step toward him, eager to close the distance, then another. With every inch forward, my chest blossoms, heat unfurling from within me.

Mate. Mate. Mate.

This man. He's mine, all mine, for all eternity.

I'm consumed with a love I don't understand, with a sense of security I've never known.

I'm safe and loved and nothing can ever hurt me.

But it did.

I was ripped from life like petals from a flower.

Someone stole this feeling from me. They took away my light, my love, my everything.

Rage replaces the blissfulness that Asher briefly provided and instead of finding myself within the shadows of the cave with him, I'm back in my room at the castle.

Except it's not how I last saw it when I left this morning. No, this is my room from five hundred years ago. I'm on a corded porcelain phone, making dinner plans. I can sense my unease, but underneath that, I have faith. No matter what happens, if I'm to become queen sooner than expected, as long as I have Asher, everything will be fine.

I go to the door. Someone is there, but the image becomes fuzzy. I can't see who's on the other side, but I trust them. I know this without a shadow of a doubt.

At least until a dagger protrudes from my chest and I'm falling to the floor.

I can't move. I can't breathe. No, this can't be happening. We were supposed to have centuries together. I can't leave Asher now. Not yet, not when he needs me most.

My heart slows and I suck in a sharp breath. "Asher."

His name is barely a whisper on my lips. My body is sweating and if I weren't seeing my chest with my own eyes, I'd swear that dagger was still there.

My fingers rub over where the wound once was and tears fall from my eyes.

What the hell just happened?

"Estee, hurry!" Sosheena calls out, but I can't move. I can't do anything. "Isla, dear. Can you hear me? You were trapped in a memory, a strong one. Focus on what you saw. Don't let the thoughts fade away, okay?"

I shake my head. I *want* them to disappear. Not because I don't want to remember, but because this feeling of dying, I don't think it's something I can ever forget, no matter how much I'd love to.

Estee comes into my path of sight, eyes wide and body trembling. She shakes her head, covering her mouth and muffling a sob as she steps farther away from me.

I don't understand. I need her now more than ever. Where is she going?

"I'm sorry, Issie," she mutters, practically tripping over her own feet in her haste. "I'm so, so sorry."

CHAPTER TWENTY-ONE

ASHER

A sense of unease shivers down my spine, echoing through the connection I feel to Isla. Even though we're not bonded, I've felt the draw to her ever since that first night of her return. Now, it trembles, unstable and fleeting, sending a pang of dread through me.

My wolf reacts with a threatening growl, breaking the silence of the ongoing meeting. Rising swiftly, I only manage a brief nod to Malimorte. "Carry on without me," I command, my voice edged with urgency.

Malimorte nods in understanding, seamlessly continuing the discussion about trade terms that Declan and Noen negotiated. But Noen's observant eyes follow me as I exit, his gaze sharp and knowing. He's smart enough to know there's only one reason I would leave so abruptly right now.

"Asher," he calls out, catching up to me with a few long strides. His voice carries a blend of respect and reproach. "You know I respect you as my king, but after all we've been through, I'd appreciate some respect in return."

I don't have time for this, but he's right. Noen has been there for me for years, and I've treated him poorly. Regardless of what I once thought, he deserves to be kept in the loop now. At least as far as I'm letting anyone else in.

"I need to check on Isla," I confess, pressing a hand over my chest, where the bond pulses weakly. "Something's wrong. I can feel it—" Pain clenches my heart, sharp and sudden. "*Fuck.*"

"I'm coming with you," he states and instead of telling him *no*, this time I let him because something is wrong and I'm not sure what I'll find when I get to my mate.

"She went to Lunara Academy with Estee and my mother," I explain as we head toward the stairs. The moment the ache in my chest recedes, we're running through the castle, toward the back exit.

When the high noon sun touches my face, I shift, needing the speed and sense of my wolf to get to our mate faster. Bones break and reform within an instant and then we're running at full speed toward the academy.

Noen is right on our heels, keeping just behind, as is his place. Something he's always respected and I hate that I let my jealousy from all those years ago get the better of me. He didn't deserve for me to keep Isla's return a secret nor did he deserve the way I treated him in my office this morning.

So long as Isla remains comfortable with him, I won't stand in his way of getting to know his friend again. Though as I think that thought, my wolf doesn't seem to agree. There's a rumble in his chest and I'm reminded that I wasn't the only one concerned with their friendship.

Regardless, I'm going to do my best to give Noen the benefit of the doubt until I have a logical reason not to.

Within a few minutes, we arrive at Lunara Academy and I shift back to human form. Noen, however, stays as his mahogany-coated wolf, ready to act at my command.

I turn to Noen, nodding at him as I use mind speak to communicate with him. *"I'm going to go check inside. You do a loop and contact me if you sense anything off."*

"She's going to be fine," he states confidently. I can't tell if he's saying that for me or for himself. *"Let me know when you find her."*

Just as he takes off, I sense Isla's scent wrapping around me. *"Wait,"* I call back to Noen. *"She's coming out."*

He circles back around, eyes on the door just like mine are. Estee runs out first, eyes red and not paying attention to us. I call her name, but she turns sharply, running as quickly as her long strides will take her on two feet.

I'd go after her, but I'm more concerned with Isla and just as my attention goes back to the academy, she's coming through the doors with my mother holding her up. My heart nearly stops when I see how pale my mate is. Her hands shake and I'm not even sure if she's breathing.

Running to her, I take her from my mother. "What happened?"

"I don't know," Mom says. "Isla was stuck in a memory and Estee ran off in tears. Isla hasn't said a word since." She hands me a book. "This is the one that brought the memory on."

Origins of Reincarnation.

Interesting, considering something went wrong with hers.

"I'll get her to the carriage," I say, assuming my mother is going to join us.

"I need to go speak with the headmaster," she says with a frown. "I don't want to bring Isla back here if this is going to be so triggering for her. We'll bring what we can to the castle. The school will just need to be okay with that."

"Thank you, Mom." With Isla in my arms, I nod at Noen before speaking to him. *"Follow us to the castle and keep an eye out for Estee. Someone needs to figure out what happened to them both."*

"I'll go after her as soon as the two of you are behind closed doors," Noen replies, his sense of duty clear in his voice.

I tell the coachman to take us back before I enclose the carriage, keeping Isla tucked into my side. Stroking her cheek, I look down and am relieved to find some of the color coming back to her face.

"What happened, Issie?" My voice is half a plea and half filled with rage. I don't know what memory caused this sort of reaction, but if I can do anything about it, I'm going to.

Her entire body shudders and I hold her tighter as she rubs her fingers over the center of her chest. "So cold."

With a few tugs, I pull my dress shirt over my head with my hand, then turn to cover her with it. "We'll be home soon and I'll start a fire for you to rest in front of."

I want to know what she saw, but I don't push. Instead, I hold her tightly, hoping the warmth of my body and the extra layer of my shirt will make her stop shaking, but even as we pull up in front of the castle, she still trembles.

Lifting her into my arms, I don't bother letting her

walk. I spot Noen's wolf go around back and he lets me know that he's off to find Estee.

People stare as I walk into the castle with Isla in my arms, but I don't say anything to them. They can think what they want for now. My mate is more important than quelling any rumors that may get started from seeing their king walk in shirtless.

"Mali," I call through our mind link. *"I'll be in my room for the remainder of the day and I'm not to be disturbed unless a war is about to start."*

"Yes, Your Majesty," he responds promptly. *"I'll be around should you need anything."*

All I need is for Isla to tell me how I can fix whatever is happening to her.

I go straight to my quarters and settle Isla onto the couch in front of the fireplace before grabbing a few logs and kindling to light. My movements are quick, but even so, when I turn back around, hoping for Isla to appear better, she looks worse.

Her paling face and labored breathing are beginning to chip away at my calm. Being helpless to do anything to make this situation better is going to drive me to insanity.

I grab a blanket from the closet and wrap it around my mate, then I kneel in front of her. "Isla, love. Please talk to me."

She blinks several times, her gaze wide but almost empty at the same time. I reach a hand up to cradle her face and the moment my palm makes contact with her skin, an energy passes between the two of us, lighting up the connection I feel to her.

Isla shudders again, but this one almost seems like it's

a sense of relief. Her eyes flutter closed and she leans into my touch. "I remembered."

"Remembered what?" I plead, trying not to get my hopes too high. I'd actually prefer if she didn't remember us if this is what the memory did to her.

She looks at me again, a longing in her eyes. "My room when I lived with my parents, being at the cave with you, knowing that there was nowhere I'd rather be than with you, and then…the moment someone took that away from me."

I don't speak for several seconds. Words are lost on me and I don't want to frighten her, but she's just confirmed what I perversely hoped for all along, causing rage to build behind my eyes, a storm ready to break.

Someone stole my mate from me. She didn't willingly leave me.

My heart fills with relief unlike I've known in far too many years, yet at the same time, there's a shadow growing within me that desires vengeance and won't settle for anything less than the death of the person who wronged us.

"Who, Isla?" I beg her. "Who hurt you?"

She shakes her head, confusion and sorrow mingling in her expression. "I don't know, but I could tell that I knew them. Whoever was on the other side of that door, they weren't a stranger to me before they stabbed me in the chest."

The words cut through me, sharper than any steel as a growl builds in my chest. "Someone *stabbed* you."

Her nod barely registers with me as she speaks and I try to stay calm for her. "The blade immediately took me down. I don't know how or why, but the memory ended right after I fell to the ground." She grabs my face and holds me gently. "All I could remember was this soul-deep grief of being forced to leave when I knew you needed me most. I'm so sorry, Asher. I never would—"

I kiss the words right off her lips because this woman will never apologize for something she had no control over. There isn't a single part of me that blames Isla for what happened. Yes, I was an asshole when she first returned, but I was confused and overwhelmed. That combined with becoming desperate for answers and to have my mate back made me not handle those things very well. Everything is different now.

She kisses me back, then she starts to shake. At first, I fear she's crying, but then when I pull back she starts to laugh. "You haven't changed at all."

My body tenses, hope threatening to overflow within me. "You remember me, us?"

"Enough," she says with a wink. "Not all the moments, but the connection came to me. It was so strong, like something tangible that I never had to fear would go away." Then she frowns. "I just don't feel it now. The bond, it's not there, but the memory of what once was... No wonder you were so desperate to keep me here before. I never would have left you willingly and I hate that you've had to hurt all these years while I've been ignorant of everything."

"None of that matters now," I tell her because it's true. "We just need to figure out who stabbed you and make sure not only that they don't attempt to do so again, but that the last thing they feel is my hand tearing out their heart."

She closes her eyes briefly and shakes her head. "The

memory was so shrouded in darkness. Even now, it's hard to remember the details."

"My mother is going to bring whatever might help you here," I explain. "You won't need to worry about leaving the castle until you're ready and now that we know you were hurt in your room, I'd prefer if you'd stay in here with me. I can't lose you again, love. I won't survive it a second time. Hell, our entire world wouldn't survive my wrath if someone took you from me again."

She reaches for my hands and squeezes them tightly. "We'll figure this out, but I'm going to need to rest for a day or two before I pick up another book."

"As long as I know you're safe, you can have all the time you need," I promise her. Though it doesn't escape me that she doesn't readily agree to stay with me. If I have to sleep outside her door to know she's safe, then that's what I'll do. Either way, I'm not leaving my mate's side until I know there is no longer a threat lingering in the shadows of this castle.

At least not if I can help it.

CHAPTER TWENTY-TWO

ISLA

It's been eight days since the haunting vision of my death, and each day has been a blend of agony and exhilaration. Memories keep flooding back—tender moments with Asher, laughter with my family, knowledge surfacing without prompting.

All of which is great, except for one thing: Estee. Her absence casts a shadow over my newfound clarity. She hasn't returned after running off from the school, not even for food or clothes, and refuses to speak with anyone other than our father. He's let me know she's physically fine, but she needs time to process a few things of her own before she returns.

I have no clue what could keep her away, and even though I'm not okay with her absence, I'm trying to respect her need for space by keeping myself preoccupied with all things books.

Well, and Asher. Though even that time has been limited.

I gave into his insistence about wanting me to stay in

his room. We've spent every night together in his bed, but nothing has happened. Nothing more than kissing, anyway. Something is holding me back from more. I still feel lost. Whether that's because of Estee's absence or because I still don't sense my wolf, I don't know. Either way, I haven't been in a hurry to rush anything else in my life.

That's not to say that my feelings for Asher haven't grown tenfold as my memories return, but there's something missing and until I figure out what that is... we're continuing as we've been.

My stomach growls and I suddenly have a craving for sausage. I'd always been a bacon person before, but this is how my memory has been working lately. I'll just suddenly know something. For example, one day for dinner I had to have spaghetti and sausage meatballs— maybe there's a theme here—or the other night, on Asher's balcony, my mind conjured an image of a stunning silver wolf shining brightly in the forest beneath the glow of the twin moons. The wolf was me. I knew that without a doubt in my mind, but still, I can't feel her like Asher says I will.

A knock sounds at the door and I put the book I was flipping through onto the mattress before slipping off the bed and heading to the door.

Mali is on the other side when I answer. It's usually him, Cain, or Declan standing guard, each of them just as nice as the other. Though Declan is by far the most entertaining.

"Good morning, Malimorte," I tell him with a smile. "Is Asher done with his meeting?"

He left before I'd barely awoken, stating something

about bickering wolves and that he had to go be diplomatic. He lost me at *bickering*.

Mali tugs at the bottom of his vest and nods. "Yes, Your Highness. His mother has requested the two of you join her for breakfast. May I confirm that you'll be attending?"

This man is always so polite and professional that I wonder what it might take to really piss him off. He seems to handle everything in stride, but Asher assures me that he's a warrior beneath the prim demeanor.

"Yes, I'll grab my shoes and be right there," I confirm, glad for breakfast since I was already craving food a few minutes ago.

I go to the closet that I now share with Asher and slip into silver flats that match the black, wide-leg pants and crisp, white blouse I chose for the day—a combination that feels suitably regal yet comfortable for whatever the day might hold.

When Asher told me that the people here were wolf shifters, I didn't expect as many formalities, but I've grown somewhat used to them over the last week. I can even admit that the upgraded wardrobe has become something I enjoy each day as I pick out my outfits. The only thing I've yet to be fond of is the silly tiara Sosheena says I should wear more often.

It's not like everyone doesn't know who I am in the castle. I don't see the purpose of the glitzy adornment, but I try to play by their rules for most things.

Going back to the door, I find Malimorte still waiting for me, golden eyes focused on the hallway and his fingers lightly stroking his auburn goatee.

"Mali?" I say quietly in case I'm disturbing his

thoughts. "Do you know if my father is already at breakfast?"

He holds up a finger and does the mind speak thing with Asher that I can't do myself. Though I don't consider that a bad thing yet.

"Yes, Your Highness," Mali replies. "He's just arrived."

"And my sister? Estee?" As furious as I am that she's abandoned me, I'm mostly worried about her. Something is wrong and it won't be much longer before I finally charge out into that forest, bringing her back home myself.

Mali's gaze casts down. "No, Your Highness. She is still absent."

Disappointment rolls through me, pressing in on my chest. Still, it doesn't change my plans. "Thank you. Let them know I'll be right there."

"King Asher asks that you please head straight there or..." Mali pauses, likely uncomfortable with being the liaison between mates. "Or he'll resume escorting you where you wish to be."

Escorting me? More like *guarding*, but after the first two days of that overprotectiveness, we've settled on a compromise. Though I doubt I'm ever as alone as I think. It seems there's always a staff member hanging around close enough that I'm not truly by myself even for these short walks through the castle.

I thank Mali again before leaving for breakfast and grin when I see someone dusting the same side paneling near the stairs that was just cleaned yesterday.

Though maybe this time, it wouldn't be bad to have someone with me. I haven't eaten in the dining hall since that time with my father. Paying more attention, I try to recall that evening, at least feeling confident that I need to go down the stairs.

As soon as I reach the first floor, I turn left, watching for anything familiar. I spot a portrait of Asher and his parents and feel rather positive that I'm supposed to turn right at this next corner.

Except as soon as I do, my nose smashes into a hard chest and I stumble back, seconds from falling to the ground before warm hands wrap around my waist.

"Whoa, are you okay?"

I look up to see Noen standing there and freeze for a moment. I haven't seen him since Asher brought him to my room. Not because I've been actively avoiding him, but something felt off with that whole interaction and I wanted more time to try to remember him.

I've been told we were best friends, but Estee is that to me and I wasn't ready for someone else to explain my past life to me. I want to remember it for myself.

"Isla?" A crease forms between Noen's brows. "Are you okay? Did I hurt you?"

I finally shake my head and take a step back before someone sees another man with his hands on me. Probably not a good idea when I'm supposed to be the king's mate...

"I'm fine," I say, forcing myself to smile. "Just didn't expect to, you know, run into anyone. I'm trying to get to breakfast."

"Oh." He holds out a hand for me to take. "Let me show you the way."

I start to move past him, politely declining. "It's okay. I think I've got it."

He chuckles and shakes his head. "By going the wrong

direction?" His hand goes back to his side as he nods toward another hallway. "Come on. The royal dining hall is this way."

Damn it. I was supposed to take another left, not a right at this hallway. Maybe a little help wouldn't be so bad.

As we walk side by side, Noen casts several glances at me before he speaks. "How have you been?"

The words sound forced and I'm a little glad because it seems like I'm not the only one who feels awkward.

"Fine." I shrug, unsure how much Asher has told him. "I've spent a lot of time reading."

He feigns shock. "*You*, reading? I would have never guessed."

I frown. "What do you mean?"

"You never were one for school and books before," he explains with a grin. "You preferred to learn by doing things yourself, instead of having them told to you."

Huh. That doesn't really sound like the person I am now, but I also know how stubborn I can be sometimes, so I'm not terribly surprised by that revelation, either.

"Well, things change," I say with a shrug.

"They sure do." Noen's voice is tinged with a sadness that hits me right in the chest.

I reach for him, lightly touching his forearm. "I know that we used—"

I blink several times, then start to kneel toward the ground. The signs of an incoming memory are getting easier to read and I no longer take them standing up after a few of them have made my legs give out.

I'm in the back yard of my parents' house and fourteen years old. The flowers need watering and that's one of my chores, something I do every day and usually with my mother. She and Dad aren't home today, though, so I'm by myself.

I don't know where Estee is, but I glance to my right at my neighbors' house. That's where Noen lives. He's been my best friend for years and my heart instantly aches. I can hear his dad yelling and I want to go save my friend, but the last time I intervened, things only got worse for him.

Instead, I wait and wait for the yelling to stop. Only then do I go to the fence and peek over.

Noen is leaning against the side of his house, fists clenched, eyes closed, and jaw tight.

"Noen," I whisper, staying in our yard.

He looks up at me and shakes his head. "You heard."

"It's okay," I tell him. "Do you want to come over?"

His head shakes. "I have chores to do over again because apparently, the first time I did them wasn't correct."

I lied. It's not okay. The entire situation with him and his father is terrible and everyone knows it. Yet Asher's dad—the king—does nothing about it. I don't understand why they let Noen be treated like this.

I've tried to bring it up to Asher, but my two best friends don't exactly get along. Though that doesn't change my feelings for either of them.

"I can help you," I tell Noen as he comes to the fence.

He grabs my hands, rubbing his thumbs over my fingers and staring down. "You already do. More than you know." He leans in closer, kisses the top of my head, and releases me. "I'll see you later, Isobella."

I return to the real world, my heart racing and no longer confused why things were awkward with Noen and Asher before. How could I have not seen that for what it was before?

Noen loved me and not just as my best friend. That boy *loved* me.

Blinking up at the man kneeling before me, I try to decide if maybe he still does and that's why Asher hasn't spoken of Noen since the latter returned.

Noen shakes my shoulders when I don't respond. "Issie, talk to me, please."

"I'm fine," I finally say, not missing how he's among the small group of people who still use my childhood nickname.

His arms wrap around me and he squeezes. "Gods, don't do that to me again."

"Am I interrupting something?" Asher's deep voice booms from within the hallway.

You've got to be shitting me right now.

Noen backs up before I have to push him away but still reaches to help me up.

Asher is there in the next second, moving in to assist me.

Yep. I think I've finally pieced this whole situation together. How fun for me. Not.

"Isla," Asher's deep tenor has goosebumps moving over my arms. "Did you have another memory come to you?"

I nod, glancing over his shoulder, wondering if Noen is still waiting here. "One from when I was fourteen. I, uh, remember Noen being my neighbor."

Asher's chest lets out a rumble. "That's why I asked him to stay away. I had a feeling that remembering another strong connection would take you out again. Come on. I'll take you back to the room to rest."

I shake my head and smile up at him. "I need food and

I'd like to see my dad. Also, don't blame Noen. I ran into him, literally. This wasn't his fault."

Asher doesn't seem to believe me, but he does at least turn to the side, revealing that Noen is, in fact, still waiting. "Thank you for watching over her. I've got it from here."

Noen's gaze stays on me a little longer before he finally nods at Asher. "I can see that. Let me know if you need me for anything today. Otherwise, I'll be...out."

We watch in silence as Noen leaves, shoulders tense and movements ridged. When he's out of sight, I turn toward Asher and poke a finger against his chest. "I thought you said you and Noen were now friends."

"We are," he replies as if nothing just happened.

"That's not how you treat *friends*," I tell him. "Noen really was just helping me, and I know what you thought before, but that doesn't change anything for me. Whatever Noen felt for me has nothing to do with us."

"I don't think he ever stopped loving you," Asher admits, pulling me closer. "What do you want me to do? Be okay with that? You're mine and while Noen has been a good friend over the years, that doesn't mean I can pretend him being near you, especially when our bond isn't complete, doesn't make me want to rip his head from his shoulders."

Okay, that's kind of sexy. A little crazy, but sexy nonetheless.

"Can you maybe turn down the murder-y thoughts a few notches and try to focus on the fact that I remembered my friendship with Noen, but I'm still here with you? I didn't chase after him, even though his feelings were clearly hurt. I chose you back then and I'm choosing you now."

Though, and I don't think I should tell Asher this, I am concerned for Noen. If Asher has been his closest friend since I left, how terrible for him to be alone now. More than that, it's wrong.

Asher pulls me into a tight embrace. "I'm sorry, love. I can't control myself when it comes to you—just like when you showed up—but I'll do my best to be better for you."

I tilt my head until I can see his face again. "Not just for me. For yourself and for your friends. You need to figure out how to trust Noen again if he's truly been your friend this whole time I've been gone. There must be a reason for that. Remember that reason and know that nothing between us is going to change because of him. No matter what I remember."

His eyes darken and he holds me tighter. "I promise to try."

I guess that's as much as I should ask for.

Though I do still feel bad for Noen and will secretly do my best to make sure he and Asher remain friends because anything less isn't right.

Asher wraps an arm around my waist. "Come on. The family is waiting for us to eat. I was just coming to find you when you didn't make it to the dining room."

We head in the right direction and when we join our family, I immediately look for Estee, even though Malimorte said she wasn't here. I do at least find my father still present and am glad when he's seated next to what has become my normal placement, on Asher's left.

Even after having spent many hours with Grayson this week, I'm still taken aback by how much he's changed this week. All for the better, but still, watching Asher's blood finally heal him has been everything.

Just ten days ago, my father was on the brink of death, which I've now learned happens when a Lunarian stops shifting and starves themself. He appeared to be in his eighties before and now, he looks like a thriving, handsome fifty-year-old man. It's a good kind of crazy and seeing his smile is something I will never take for granted now that I have him in my life.

"It's nice to see you again, Isla," Asher's dad, Gideon, says from the opposite side of the table. "I thought maybe you were hiding from us."

His smile is friendly, but his words still make me tense for some reason. "Not at all," I reply, returning his friendly demeanor. "There's just so much to read thanks to your wonderful mate's help."

Sosheena brightens next to him. "I'm so glad to hear that. If I can be of any more help, all you have to do is ask."

Dad nudges me with his elbow. "Same here, my girl. I'm all better now and you shouldn't worry about me."

"I'm more concerned with Estee now," I admit with a frown. "Any updates from her?"

He shakes his head and looks away. "Sorry, Issie."

He shouldn't apologize. He's not the one who left without a word.

I love Estee. She's my best friend and now my sister—nothing will ever change that—but I could choke her right about now for doing this. Right after I hug the hell out of her.

"Everyone, please eat," Asher announces. "We have our

monthly pack run tonight and you'll want to make sure you have enough energy."

My sharp gaze immediately goes to Asher's and he's clearly avoiding me, staring more at his plate than anywhere else. I kick him under the table and I catch a flicker of a smile that he seems to be fighting.

Oh, he's up to something and I'm going to figure out what.

Right after I eat some of this delicious food.

CHAPTER TWENTY-THREE

ASHER

While Isla has been busy with her own research, I've been orchestrating plans of my own, in hopes of helping. She still hasn't felt her wolf and the lack of link there, I believe, is crucial, not only for integration back into our world, but also for unlocking the deeper parts of her memories.

At least I hope so.

Hoping to bridge this gap, I've organized a pack run under the twin full moons tonight—a spectacle of unity and primal energy that I've always found rejuvenating. It's a time when the magic of our world becomes palpable, threading through each of us as we run.

Something that I'm eager for Isla to experience, to feel the electrifying pulse of the pack in full sprint, which, if all goes well, should spark something within her.

Until my mate understands who she is as a whole, I don't know that she'll truly be at peace.

I have a visiting elder coming from Selaris who is known for her healing abilities. It's not often that wolf shifters have other gifts, but our older generation, the ones nearing one thousand years of age, have a history of teaching even those who have lived multiple lifetimes a few lessons.

The longest wolf shifter known to live here died at the age of one thousand and eleven. She could barely walk in the end, but I met her a few hundred years ago and her mind was the brightest I'd ever encountered.

I'm hoping for the same from Elyn, the one I've invited here. I've never met her myself, but I've heard the stories from King Theo—a recently crowned alpha and chosen by the Gods since the previous ruler had no heir.

He's been a good addition to Lunara as a whole, something I can't say about all our monarchs. I should have invited him here as well to meet my mate, but that formality will have to wait until things are less complicated.

Leaving breakfast, I expect Isla to go back to the room to continue reading, as she's preferred to do daily since the incident at the Academy. Instead, she starts to follow me.

"We need to talk," she says and I'm instantly on guard.

"Did something else happen in that hallway?"

She rolls her eyes. "No, I already told you everything about that. I'm talking about the way you avoided looking at me earlier and failed to tell me about a pack run tonight. What am I supposed to do while everyone else is out frolicking in the woods?"

She's not wrong about me avoiding her. While I'm eager for Elyn to arrive, I've been uncertain how Isla will receive my plan. She might shut me down and I haven't been ready to accept that possibility, so I've yet to tell her. Now, it seems I'm out of time.

Though I can't deny it's adorable seeing how she's trying to be annoyed with me, but she can't hide the fact that she's jealous, thinking she can't go with us tonight on the run.

"You, my precious mate, will be by my side," I tell her with a smile. "I was waiting until Elyn got here before I told you my plans."

"Who is Elyn and why did you need to wait for her?" Isla asks with evident suspicion as we head toward my office.

"She's an elder wolf and someone well versed in healing."

Her eyes pinch together. "I don't understand. Did someone get hurt?"

I grab her hand, keeping her close to my side. "Healing doesn't only apply to physical wounds. Mental ones are just as important to mend and I think that might help you connect to your inner wolf."

"Oh." Isla pauses, nibbling on her lower lip. "So, what? Is she, like, a therapist or something?"

A chuckle escapes me as I shake my head. "No, at least not from my understanding. From what I've been told, she'll place her hands on you, read your energy, and find the source of whatever is out of balance, helping you to find what you want most. I know that's probably several things right now, but if you're open to it, I think Elyn can help."

As we arrive at my office and I open the door, Isla seems to be considering my plan seriously. My hope rises that I've made the right choice by asking the healer here without talking to Isla first, but then as she stands in front of my desk, a glare deepens on her face.

"This sounds a lot like those energy workers Estee used to talk about." Isla looks away from me, crossing her arms as she mutters, "Damn her for not being here for this."

Isla hasn't said much about Estee's absence, and I've been so focused on the fact that Isla's been remembering the pieces of our past that I haven't considered how her sister refusing to return has affected everything else.

"I'm sorry, Issie," I tell her as I draw her closer. "She hasn't officially rejoined the pack, so I can't mind speak with her, but I can get her back here one way or another."

I'm not above sending a group of shifters to forcefully bring Isla's sister back if that's what she needs. Hell, Declan might even enjoy that particular mission since that she-wolf is all he can talk about.

Isla shakes her head and places her hands over my chest. "No. I might be pissed that Estee left me, but something happened and when she's ready, she'll come back to explain. Though it does make me wonder if I should go back to the Academy library. If we both had breakthroughs that morning, then maybe I'll remember more of the day I was taken by being there instead of staying holed up in our room."

The mention of the Academy sparks a protective instinct in me, but I curb it, respecting her growing independence, while also noting that she called my quarters "our room." Hearing those two words is nearly enough to distract me, but I try to quell my conflicting emotions, circling back to the original topic of discussion.

"First things first," I tell her, my hands rubbing lightly

up and down her arms. "Tell me what you really want to do about Elyn. If this is too much for you right now, then I can send her back. That's on me for not talking to you about it first."

When she smiles back up at me, I swear my feet come off the floor. "I would love to meet her," Isla says. "You're right that there are several things I'm searching for right now, and I don't know that unlocking my wolf will come out on top, but if she can help with either that or even with making the memory of my final day come through clearer, then it's worth trying."

I'd also love if Isla could not only remember our bond, but feel the connection as well, but I'm being as patient as I can be. Though I can't lie. My wish for Isla to have her wolf back isn't just so that she can run with us and be more at peace. I also hope that when her wolf is free that it will allow Isla to understand what I've been fighting for this whole time.

Our love.

"Perfect," I tell her, kissing the top of her head before I take a step away to call for Malimorte. He's not only been helping keep an eye on my mate, but he's overseen Elyn's travel and arrival. I want to make sure everything is as the elder wolf has requested.

Except before I can do that, Isla grabs on to my shirt, pulling me back toward her. "Where do you think you're going?"

"Nowhere," I say because not even checking on Elyn is worth missing out on this moment with my mate.

Isla's touch is gentle as her palms press against my chest, her fingers trailing upward along my shoulders as she rises onto her toes. "I know I've been lost in books lately, and we haven't really dived into discussing 'us,'" she confesses, her eyes locked with mine, "but I want you to know, I'm not going anywhere. Whether or not I regain my wolf or recover all my memories, I'm certain of one thing: this is where I belong."

As I listen to her declaration, a part of me yearns to rejoice, yet deep down, I recognize this is more than just about her deciding to stay in Polaris. Once, centuries ago, our love was a force unmatched, woven from a connection others could scarcely comprehend. The mere echo of that bond now is not sufficient. I need Isla to grasp the fullness of what it means to be my mate, not merely as someone who remembers loving me and thinks that suffices.

What I crave most is to witness the light in her eyes when she looks at me after being apart, to feel again the vibrant energy that flowed effortlessly between us, even though we were never formally bonded. The rhythm of our hearts, the sync of our souls—once perfectly aligned —now feels distant. While I treasure her presence here and now, after centuries apart, I remain unyielding in my resolve to reclaim the profound connection we once shared.

With a tender touch, I brush the rose-gold strands from her face, gently tilting her chin up to meet my gaze. "While I'm relieved you feel at home here, I need you to understand," I start, my voice thick with emotion as my hand rests over her heart, feeling its steady rhythm, a painful reminder of our current disconnect. "There's so much more you're missing. You might remember loving me, but feeling the strength of our love isn't something that a memory can replace. Until we figure out how you can sense our bond again, I'll always be fighting for us."

Her shoulders fall and her gaze begins to drift downward. "I'm sorry, Ash. I'm trying and—"

I lift her chin, ensuring our eyes meet again, my voice firm yet gentle. "You have no reason to apologize. I didn't share this to make you feel guilty. I just want you to know that no matter what you need to do on your own, I don't doubt that you want to be here, but I'm also going to be doing everything I can to fix what was stolen from us."

Compelled by a surge of emotions, I pull her close, pressing my lips to hers, the intensity of my heartbeats demanding I taste her, feel her. Thankfully, Isla responds with equal fervor, holding on to me tightly. Her nails claw at my skin as she presses in closer, matching my intensity without blinking an eye.

Her hands move everywhere all at once as I reach down toward her hips—only, I don't stop there. My fingers grab her right thigh, pulling it upward until her leg is wrapped around my waist. I push her back against my desk, kicking the chairs out of the way as I lay her back.

She moans beneath me, undoubtedly feeling my hard length against her stomach. "Asher." She says my name, almost as if she's warning me, but there's nothing about this woman that I'm afraid of. I want every inch of her that she's offering, even without the bond.

While I'll keep fighting to get back what we had, that doesn't mean I won't enjoy the natural attraction we share now.

It's something I've grown to respect about my mate because even though her soul is the same as it was all those years ago, I've had to remind myself that this woman with me isn't Isobella. She's Isla and while the mate bond might not care about names or rebirth, I respect the difference between who she was and who she is.

My hands slide beneath her shirt, caressing every inch of skin that I touch until I get to the clasp of her bra. With one flick of my fingers, I disconnect the hook between her breasts and grin as she whimpers in response.

I trail kisses down her neck, knowing where my mouth has been dying to be these past couple of weeks. Just as I grip the silk material still covering her chest, ready to rip it away, there's a nudge in my mind from Malimorte.

Ignoring him, I tug at Isla's shirt, but he tries to reach me again. Something he never does unless there is something wrong.

Some days, I really fucking hate my role as Alpha King.

I look up at Isla, taking in her flushed cheeks, perfect lips, and heaving chest. My chest rumbles, annoyance flooding through me for what I'm about to do.

She looks up and her eyes widen. "Why are you stopping?"

"Not because I want to," I practically growl. "I need to answer Malimorte."

"What?" I snap through our mental link, hating that Isla is already sitting up, righting her clothing.

"Elyn has arrived early and says it's urgent that she sees your mate, Your Majesty."

Of course she has.

I want to deny the elder's request, but we need her, not the other way around. I asked for this opportunity and

I'm not going to mess it up because my cock wishes for something else.

Cupping Isla's face gently, I kiss her again before explaining. "Elyn is here early and we need to go meet her."

"Now?" Isla says breathily.

"Unfortunately so." I kiss her again, smoothing down the mussed strands of her hair. "I wouldn't have stopped if this were something I thought we could postpone."

Her lips downturn, creating an adorable pout. "I know, but that doesn't mean this isn't terrible timing."

I reach for her hand, pulling her toward me. "In that, my love, you are very accurate."

The ache in my groin confirms as much, but I've waited half a millennia to have this chance with my mate again. I can wait another day.

CHAPTER TWENTY-FOUR

ISLA

I've never had a blue vagina, but I certainly have one now and it sucks. It wasn't my intention to end up sprawled out on Asher's desk when I followed him back to his office, but I'm also not upset that I ended up there.

Well, besides the fact that we didn't get to finish what we'd started.

I've spent weeks pretending I didn't want to find out what having sex with an actual wolf god would be. Not because I think it would be a bad idea, but there's been this little voice in my head that's made me think that until I understand more about who I am that I shouldn't throw pleasure into the mix.

That little voice is now going to be shoved into a steel box, never to be opened again because she's an idiot.

I haven't felt this alive since arriving in Lunara and I need more of Asher. No, I need all of him.

Except that's going to have to wait until tonight.

Something must be wrong because Asher is rigid and

not really talking to me. Thanks to the little crease between his brows, I think he's doing that mind speak thing and I'm trying not to interrupt, but I also would love to be kept in the loop.

I tap on his shoulder and when he blinks several times before addressing me, I have my confirmation that he's been speaking with someone else.

"What's going on?" I ask as we start to descend the stairs.

"Elyn insists we meet her by the river," he explains, his voice carrying an undertone of urgency that he doesn't elaborate on.

"Okay, but there's something more or"—I reach up, poking at his forehead—"you wouldn't still be talking to someone in here."

His smile doesn't quite reach his eyes, but it still makes my stomach flutter, adding fuel to the still-smoldering inferno within me.

"You're just as perceptive as you always were," he replies, taking my hand in his as we keep walking at a swift speed. "I'm trying to figure out what the urgency is, but Mali doesn't know, either. Elyn arrived by boat and the moment she stepped onto our land, she demanded to see you. I don't like that she's being so insistent, but I've also learned that our elders aren't to be ignored."

Right. Elder wolves. My dad is the oldest wolf I've met here so far at seven hundred eighteen years old. Something that is still hard to accept when he doesn't look a day over fifty, but as my memories return, I've begun to just know things like how wolf shifters age quickest in their first twenty-five years of life, then that slows to a rapid crawl, and how they never appear older than their fifties until about eight or nine hundred years have passed or until they begin to stop shifting.

The energy used when transforming to one's wolf is what makes the aging process of the human form slow to a snail's pace, except for the ruling leader. Whoever is coined the Alpha King or Queen stops aging completely.

Until I remembered that, I realize I should have questioned why Asher still appears to be in his twenties, but I can't really complain. I also try not to think too much about how technically, he's centuries older than me.

Without really getting an answer, we continue to exit the castle. Outside, the crisp air brushes against my heated skin, and we find Noen waiting for us, his gaze seeming to be actively avoiding mine.

"Elyn insisted on the northern part of the river," he says with a grimace, talking to Asher, then nodding in my direction. "It will take you all day to get there if she has to walk."

Asher frowns, then looks down at me. "He's right. I have an idea, but I'm not sure you're going to like it."

"And that would be?" I ask, raising an eyebrow.

"How would you feel riding on my wolf?" He smirks, a playful glint in his eyes. "The two of you already connected before and it's the quickest way to get across the island."

The image of me clinging to Asher's ebony wolf immediately pops into my mind and I start to laugh because I look terrified, but still, I shrug because what other choice do I have?

"Let's do it," I tell him, still chuckling. "Just don't judge me if I scream and don't be worried, either."

That gives Asher pause and he tilts his head as if he's going to question my response, but then he seems to decide otherwise.

"I'll let Malimorte know we're on our way, then," he says, then he addresses Noen again. "Finish the preparations for tonight. We should be back before dusk."

"I'll let you know when the pack is ready."

Noen turns to leave, and my chest is hit with a pang of remorse. I'm not sure what for. Maybe I'm grieving the friendship I only just remembered, or I feel sorry for him, but I can't stop my next words.

"I hope I see you later, Noen."

His shoulders tense and he opens his mouth, but then he keeps walking away from us without replying to me. Well, that didn't go well.

Asher stares at me, his expression blank, as if he's trying to hide how uncomfortable that just made him.

I pat his chest and do my best to explain. "I remembered our friendship. He was so sad before and he doesn't seem much better. Regardless of what he may or may not have felt for me, he was still my friend, Asher. I can't just ignore how he's hurting."

He grabs my waist, pulling on me until we're pressed flush together. "And I can't ignore how jealous that makes me."

I tap his chin and grin. "You're kind of cute when you pout."

"'Cute'?" He frowns. "*Cute* isn't what I'd imagine any respectable alpha wants to be called."

Laughter bubbles up from deep within me. "Were you hoping for *sexy* or *irresistible* or *tantalizing...*"

"Or all of the above," he replies, leaning in to nip at my lower lip. "Now, are you sure about riding my wolf?"

I shake my head as I step back. "But I'm going to give it a try, anyway. Just know if I fall off, I expect a hot bubble bath, a full body massage, and all the chocolate-covered strawberries on this island."

His eyes darken and his chest rumbles. "You can have all of that even if nothing goes wrong."

Hm, yeah, probably not the best direction to take this conversation so soon after nearly ravaging each other in his office.

"You might want to shift now," I tell him, creating more space between us.

"Right." He closes his eyes and takes a deep breath as I do my best to take in every second of the transformation, but once again, the change happens within the blink of an eye.

One second, I see a shimmer of energy around his human form and then in the next, his six-foot-tall wolf stands there, staring at me with an intensity just as strong as his human half.

Stepping forward, I reach out and his head nudges against my palm. "It's good to see you again," I say to the wolf with a sweet smile.

The beast growls softly as I scratch his head, sending vibrations through my body that release any bit of nerves I had about jumping on his back.

It doesn't matter that he's an animal. I know without a doubt he would never let me get hurt.

With that at the forefront of my mind, I move toward his side, never taking my hand away from his fur. "You're going to need to lie down if I'm expected to get up there."

His back is as tall as my shoulders and without anything to use as a step up, I need him to get lower. Thankfully, he doesn't seem to mind and lowers himself for me.

Here goes nothing, I think as I throw my leg over the wolf. I hold on to his thick coat and when he starts to stand, my ankles dig into his sides, but he doesn't make a noise, allowing me to hope that's not uncomfortable for him.

Glancing down, I shudder. Yep. I'm not going to do that again. The ground looks much too far away, but that doesn't matter. This wolf isn't going to let anything happen to me. That's all I need to focus on, or so I tell myself as he starts to trot.

His movements are slow at first until we get closer to the forest. As his speed picks up, I expect to feel every step he takes, but the quicker his pace, the less jostled I am. It's almost as if his paws are barely touching the earth and if the wind weren't whipping past us, I could almost believe we were barely moving.

My eyes close and I leave my cheek pressed against his back, keeping my trust in this powerful animal as I choose to enjoy the ride instead of the scenery. That's something I can check out on the way back, hopefully when I'm running on my own.

I quiet my mind and breathe deeply as a tightening in my chest begins to take root. Not as if I'm scared, but something else I can't seem to identify.

My emotions seem to be at war, feeling safe and content yet also wanting to burst free. Though I can't tell what they want to be free from.

The harder I try to understand, the more my head

begins to pound until I have to stop. Tension riddles my body and I groan, grinding my teeth together.

Asher's wolf starts to slow and I try to tell him I'm fine, but when I open my eyes, I realize we're no longer alone.

Malimorte stands under a weeping willow tree next to a river bend and beside him is a woman I can only assume is Elyn.

Her hair is all silver and fine wrinkles appear around her eyes and mouth as she smiles at me. I try to return the gesture, but with her lavender eyes locked on me, it's almost as if I can't even breathe.

She takes a step forward, her forest-green skirt swishing around her ankles. "It's okay, Isobella. You're safe now."

Hearing the name that I was originally born with sends shivers down my spine that seem to force life back into my body as I start to sit up. My legs feel wobbly, but as Elyn comes closer, I know I have to stand on my own.

She pushes the sleeves of her black blouse up and reaches for me. "You have the strength of the gods within you, child."

I blink, unsure how I'm supposed to respond. Thankfully, she doesn't seem to need me to as she continues. "Come."

For an elder, she's still quite strong, dragging me away from Asher and toward the water. I glance back and Asher is already back on two feet, watching us with concern.

"What are you doing, Elyn?" he demands, following us.

"What you've asked me here to do," she quips without looking at him or stopping.

Asher's chest rumbles and not in the sexy way it did earlier. "You have my respect as an elder, but I won't play games. Tell me what your plans are for my mate."

This has the older woman pausing. She stops and slowly turns her head, one greying eyebrow arched. "I don't care who you are, Asher Josiah Cromwell. At my age, I no longer live by other people's desires. I think that's something I've earned after a thousand years of life. Now, do yourself a favor and go away."

I cover my mouth, trying to hide my laughter because I shouldn't love that she just put Asher in his place, but also knowing that this woman is incredible, and I want to be her when I grow up.

Malimorte joins Asher's side and whispers something to him that I can't hear. When Asher looks at me, there is only defeat on his face. "I'll be right here if you need me."

"She won't," Elyn replies for me before dragging me toward the river again.

I at least wave to Asher and blow him a kiss before following the elder shifter.

I expect her to stop when we get to the bank, but fully clothed, Elyn ushers us into the water until we're waist deep. When she looks at me again, her eyes are glowing, appearing to be a bright purple. "I felt you the moment I got off my ship," she says quietly. "Your soul is screaming so loudly that I don't know how you've been surviving, but we're going to fix everything, Isobella. I can assure you that."

"I actually go by—"

Her head shakes just once. "I don't care who you believe you are right now—your soul is Isobella. If you can't honor her, then you don't honor yourself."

Well, all right, then. I'm just going to keep my mouth shut.

"Good girl."

She places a cold hand on my forehead and within seconds, the center of her palm begins to warm. "You've spent too many years locked away. Even now, there are restraints around your soul that need to be shattered. Do you feel them?"

"Uh, yes?"

She pinches my arm with her other hand. "Do not lie to me. We only have time for the truth. You either feel them or you don't. It's as simple as that."

"I, uh, don't feel them," I say, reaching to rub where she pinched me, but she smacks my hand away.

"Stay still, then." Elyn smirks. "This is going to hurt."

The hand on my forehead lifts away, then slams against my chest so hard, the wind is knocked out of me. I try to breathe, but it's like my lungs are filled with sand. Coughing feels more like choking and heat starts to unfurl within my chest, branding my bruised heart.

"What about now?" she asks, tilting her head. "Do you sense that which binds you?"

My eyes squeeze closed as I try to concentrate. "Something is burning my heart. Is that what you mean?"

"Ah, chains." She clicks her tongue. "Not ideal, but I've dealt with worse. Though you're not going to like me when we're done."

I start to ask what she means, but instead of words leaving my mouth, I choke on water. My arms flail, but again, her strength takes me by surprise as she pushes me further under the water.

Even beneath the surface, I can hear Asher's roar of

objection, but the seconds tick by and I'm still not allowed up.

My lungs start to fill with water and I expect pain, but instead, the grittiness from before is replaced with the soothing sensation provided by the river.

This is not how I imagined drowning to be.

I stop fighting, mostly because I'm running out of air and even if nothing hurts, I know what happens if I stop breathing for too long.

Dots start to appear in my vision and my arms relax, floating toward the surface.

Elyn's fingers dig into my shoulders, and I swear, it's like her voice is in my head as she whispers, "Try not to scream when you come back up."

My head breaks the surface and whatever I thought pain was before is nothing now. My lungs feel as if they're being ripped to shreds and I claw at my chest, desperate to rip my own heart out to stop the agony that grows within me.

"What is happening?" A firestorm is taking over my insides, destroying everything it touches.

"Someone cursed you, child," she says calmly, as if me clawing at my chest were completely normal. "How did you die?"

"A dagger," I screech into the abyss. "Someone stabbed me."

"You're really not going to like me after this." She presses a finger into the center of my chest and it's as if her nail cuts right through my skin. "Very powerful dark magic. No wonder you've been trapped."

"Just fucking fix it," I scream, my head thrown back and fists clenched.

"That's not going to happen by my hand," she says, "but I can do *something* for you."

She shoves me back under the water and this time, I fight her. As the river washes over me, the relief is instant. The burning of my insides ceases, but after a few moments, I know what she means about the chains around my soul.

The weight of them presses in on my heart, tightening with every beat. It's so subtle, but now that I know it's there, I can't deny their existence.

I reach for my chest again, pressing my palm against the heated flesh, but my touch is shoved away as Elyn does whatever it is she thinks will help me.

Once again, my body gets lighter until I start to float back to the surface. The elder wolf keeps one hand on my head and the other on my chest. I sense her energy, but I have no clue what she's doing and I don't care. So long as when I rise to the surface again, there's no more pain.

"I need you to die, Isobella," she whispers to me. "You must die to be reborn and even though you have this new body, your old one still lives. Kill yourself and you will live once again."

What the hell is this crazy woman saying?

"I'm not crazy," she replies, somehow hearing my thoughts. "I'm in your head, connected to your soul. Now, you must die."

I still don't understand, but when she forces my mouth open and I start to swallow water, I begin to realize that she truly means to end my life.

This time, I fight back, punching and kicking, but somehow, she evades every hit. I can hear Asher's roars of wrath, but he never comes for me.

I try to breathe, but there's no air down here and I've taken in too much water. Second by second, my body grows heavier and my heartbeat stops completely.

"You must die to be reborn again," she repeats, and because I don't have any other choice, that's exactly what I do.

CHAPTER TWENTY-FIVE

ISLA

My lungs are burning—a dry, ragged ache unlike anything I've felt before, coupled with a sharp, stabbing pain right at my breastbone. I try to lift my hand to feel for some sort of wound, but my arms are like lead-filled weights.

"I told you she would come back." Elyn's voice filters through from a distance, her tone matter-of-fact.

"I'd keep your fucking mouth shut." Asher's voice is taut with fury, his hands gripping mine with a strength that speaks volumes of his fear and relief.

Well, this sounds like things are going swimmingly.

I hear shuffling and then a deep growl. "I mean it, Elyn. I don't care if you're an elder or that you belong to another pack. You killed my fucking mate and you're not going to get away with that. If I didn't think she needed me right now, you'd already be dead."

Elyn snickers. "Kind of like your mate just was," she taunts, and Asher's subsequent roar makes my skin ice over.

Or maybe it's because he releases me and is probably charging the crazy old lady. I should probably do something about that.

"Ash," I groan between coughs. I throw my arm over my body, forcing myself to turn onto my side, but I end up twisted into a painful position.

"Issie?" The agony that accompanies my name as it falls from his lips nearly rips my chest open, but my body is shaking so badly that I can't concentrate on any one ache in particular.

I open my eyes in time to see Asher drop Elyn to the ground. I'm pretty sure he just had his hands around her neck, but that's not anything I can care about because in the next second, his arms are around me, his body like a shield against the cold and chaos. His warmth seeps into me, battling the chill that has set into my bones, making my teeth chatter.

"You're okay, love," he whispers, his lips pressing a series of kisses to my forehead. "I have you."

I try to talk, but the air is still returning to my lungs and I need a few more moments before I brave more words.

Elyn appears in my line of sight, red marks on her neck, and she stays about twenty feet back while meeting my stare. "Where does it hurt most?"

I start to point to my chest, but Asher turns me away from her. "I told you to stay away from her."

"You might be the king, but you know nothing of what your mate needs right now," she says without an ounce of fear in her voice. "You asked me to come here to help her and I'm going to finish what I started or she'll never find peace, I promise you that."

His chest rumbles, vibrating my whole body as he speaks. "You said you would heal her blocks—you never mentioned anything about killing her. You can't possibly expect me to let you near her after that."

"I not only expect it, but I know you're going to," she says haughtily. "She needs me and, even if you don't want to admit it, you know this to be true, which is why you haven't killed me yet. The bond thrums wildly inside you, searching for its missing half. I can give you that."

Asher looks down at me, his eyes dark and wild. "I'm so sorry, Isla. I never thought you would be hurt like this, or I wouldn't have asked her here."

"I know." My voice is raw and scratchy, but I can't stay quiet any longer. "But I think she's right. I don't remember dying just now, but there's an echo of something inside me that wasn't there before."

"It's your wolf," Elyn says, cutting in. "Once you shift, your pain will be gone and you will know your heart of hearts, but I can't assure that your mind will be fixed. There's a darkness embedded within you that I've never encountered."

Asher's head whips toward her. "You never mentioned that."

"And you never asked," she quips. "You chose to yell and threaten my life instead of considering that I was doing exactly what Isobella needed."

"I told you, her name is Isla," Asher corrects, but based on the smirk on Elyn's face, she already knows that.

"Yes, *her* name is Isla, but she is not the only one who was taking residence within that body," the elder wolf explains. "Your mate was born on Earth and she was carrying three separate souls within her. While Isla and

Isobella are one and the same, their soul was split in half at some point, adding to Isla's confusion and her inability to bond with her wolf's spirit. Now that her soul has been properly forged together by her brief dance with death, she should be able to move forward."

If I weren't so exhausted, I'm pretty sure I'd be questioning everything she's saying, but I can barely keep my head up, let alone process what's being said. Though there's a warmth in my chest that grows with every ragged breath I take as I close my eyes.

A peacefulness amongst the travesty of the wound I can't see but know is there nonetheless. Drawing on that repose, I relax further into Asher's embrace and trust that Elyn is telling the truth.

I have no reason to believe her, but considering Asher almost snuffed the life out of her and she's chosen to stay and finish the job, I also can't ignore her.

I take a jagged breath that feels as though I'm swallowing tiny daggers whose only purpose is to slice at my skin, but when I let that same breath out, the pain leaves my body with the air. Every time I repeat the action, the healing heat within my chest spreads further.

Though that doesn't take away from the void that I can only assume, now that I'm thinking more clearly, is from when I was stabbed, it does provide me with a strength unlike anything I've ever known.

"Isla?" Asher whispers my name, holding me tighter. "Talk to me."

I want to ease his worries, but I can't. Not when I'm so close to…her.

One breath in, one breath out, one step closer to victory.

There's a flicker of a presence within my mind, but that's not where she begins. This being lives in my heart, a beating part of me that I never should have been able to live without yet somehow did.

I wait patiently for her to come forward, knowing she's been locked away for much too long.

Muffled voices sound around me, but all I can focus on is this magnificent beast within me. She's strong and resilient and full of a peace I've only ever wished for.

The closer she comes, the stronger my body becomes, healing from her bright energy that not only relieves my body from the chills, but fills my core with light and love.

Nobody will ever hurt you again, I promise her.

She doesn't speak back to me, but I know she hears me. There's a connection between us that thrums so wildly within me, I don't know how it could have ever been snuffed out to begin with.

Her spirit presses in and around me, forging us together and filling me with an undeniable love that can't be compared to anything in all the worlds.

This wolf is me and I am her, just as I was once Isobella. We are all the same, we are one, and we are finally whole. I may have my own soul and this ferocious animal has hers, but the closer she gets, the more I can feel us merging as one.

She settles within me, a beacon of hope, promising me that no matter what happens next, we will be okay. Together, our joy and success is inevitable, as it always should have been.

Her energy grows, extending from my chest, spreading out through the rest of my body. The vibration of her power rolls through me and I start to shake. My skin heats to an almost uncomfortable temperature and a blinding light appears behind my eyes.

I need to do something, but I don't know what. Everything is bottlenecking within me, overwhelming my senses yet empowering me at the same time.

"Shift, Isla!" Asher shouts, his clamorous demand breaking through my mind.

I can't feel his arms around me any longer, but just as my wolf's strength lives within me, I can sense a longing toward him that begins at my heart and feels never-ending.

Though the intensity of that emotion needs to wait a while longer.

Nobody explained to me how I'm supposed to shift, but the memory of seeing my silver wolf comes back to me and I concentrate on her square snout, her ocean-blue eyes, the perfect tips of her ears, and the steady stance she holds as she remains still, waiting for her chance to run.

You're free, I tell her softly and just like that, my body feels as though it curls in on itself before unfurling with a glory that can't be matched.

A burst of energy explodes from every pore, bones break and shift, but there is nothing painful about this transformation. There is only light and love and peace.

My wolf takes shape and the moment she's in control, her head tilts toward the rising sun and she howls, the sound coming from deep within us, reverberating through the air for endless miles.

Before the sound has faded, she looks at Asher and whimpers. The desire to be with him resonates with both of us, but before we can do so, we have to take care of ourselves first.

Go, I say gently.

In the next second, we're running as if our life depends on every lengthening stride we take. Maybe it does. This time, when my lungs burn, I cling to the pain, knowing there will never be another moment like this in my life.

My wolf is here and I will never let her go again. Her presence hums inside my mind, a steady partner I don't know how I could have forgotten in any lifetime.

She mourns for the years lost but weeps for the time we still have as we race through the forest for no other reason than to bond with one another. There is no destination in mind, just the sense of freedom that only nature can provide us.

As she loops around a fallen tree, she cuts left and starts to slow. Listening, I hear the river once again, but we're nowhere near where we were with Elyn.

There isn't a soul around us, which surprises me. I expected Asher to follow, but I appreciate him giving me this moment with my wolf. One I needed more than anyone could have ever explained to me before.

She stops at the riverbank, her head moving until we can see our reflection on the water's smooth surface. Our chest heaves from the exertion and our eyes seem almost wild, unrestrained, but as her tongue lolls out the side of her mouth, I know neither of us has ever been happier.

Closing my eyes, I settle into the warmth of her spirit. As she drinks from the water, more memories come back to me. None of them standing out brighter than the other, but twenty-plus years of friendship the two of us shared is returned to me.

My first friend, the first being I knew would never hurt me and would show me unconditional love.

As the memories start to fade, our chest starts to pound all over again, but not because of an overwhelming amount of energy we need to expend like before.

No, this time, it beats only for our mate.

It isn't just memories of being one with my wolf before that are returned to me, it's of her and Asher's wolf running together, nipping at each other, knowing there will never be another for either of us.

Suddenly, the drive to get back to him, to feel his skin beneath mine, to mark him and hold on to him for the rest of my long life isn't something I can ignore.

Neither can my wolf.

This time, when we run through the forest, our paws barely touch the ground, eating up the distance we've created.

With every step closer, a tether begins to unfurl within my chest, leading us forward. Asher's woodsy scent envelops me and makes my wolf's body shudder with anticipation so strong that I can't tell who's more desperate for him, me or her.

After too many minutes later, we return to the place we left him, not slowing until he's within our sights. We glance around and notice we're alone. Elyn isn't anywhere close, though her scent still lingers.

Even though logically, I know the elder isn't a threat, a growl grows within my chest as we come to a stop.

Asher holds up his hands. "It's okay. I'm here and you're safe and nobody is going to interfere."

He steps closer, his movements slow, but that isn't working for us.

My wolf pictures my human form and I instantly know what she wants, what *we* want. I need to shift back.

Calling her energy back toward my core is like breathing in the sweetest treat. With every inhale, she comes back to me and the light returns until my body is searing with heat and then, just as quickly as she came to be, I'm back on two legs.

Only I'm missing a thing or two.

None of my clothes have returned with me, but that's the least of my thoughts as soon as my gaze connects with Asher's.

As if the world has been off-kilter every second before this, everything around me steadies. The anchor tying me to this world now extends to the man before me. A man whose love extends beyond reason, whose mind fascinates me in ways I'll never be able to understand but never want to forget.

His breaths give me life. Without him, I do not exist. It has always been him, from the moment I came into this world and not just two weeks ago, but centuries ago.

The colors of the sky and trees and earth are brighter just knowing him and the elation that fills my heart as he reaches for me is more than I deserve, but I take every bit he's offering.

Mate.

My entire essence seems to levitate with the sheer force of the bond we share. He is mine, and I am his—now and always.

CHAPTER TWENTY-SIX

ASHER

My mate is back. Every part of her. Isla stands before me, bare and like the natural beauty I know her to be, and I'm speechless. Every curve is just as I remembered, every freckle and bend, every perfect inch. My other half, my reason for existing, is right here in front of me and the bond we share is alive with energy that can't be contained.

Like two magnets, we're drawn together and I wrap my arms around her, cradling her close. "Fuck, Isla. I don't think I've ever loved you more."

"And I love you," she says between kisses. "More than all the stars and all the moons, in all the worlds."

Her skin is smooth and warm, just like it used to be. I didn't realize how much I missed her heat until now, feeling the erratic beat of her heart beneath my palm.

"I understand what you meant before," she adds. "I may have remembered loving you, but there is nothing that can compare to this charge between us. No words, no pictures, no nothing. It's like a living thing that has to be experienced to be understood."

She's not wrong. As I move, so does she, likely without even realizing it. We balance each other with precision, pulling and pushing with an efficiency that lights my entire world on fire.

"Gods, I've missed you," I whisper against her neck, my hands gliding over her shoulders and down her back.

She pushes against me and I can feel her smile against my cheek. "Show me."

We might be outdoors, but I don't give a damn. That's never stopped us before. I pick her up with ease and carry her toward the nearest tree, laying her on the grass beneath it. "Gladly."

My wolf rumbles from deep within me, the sound echoing from my chest, and I know he wants to come out and play, but his turn is going to have to wait.

Isla's hands tug at my clothes with the same urgency pounding through me. In moments, we're both stripped of everything but the bond pulling us closer. I hover over her, brushing a hand down the center of her chest, memorizing her all over again.

When I kiss her, it's with every pent-up century of longing—fierce, reverent, overwhelmed.

The moment my hands explore her, her breath catches, her back arching toward me. Every sound she makes is soft and sweet, a melody I've replayed in my memories a thousand times but never thought I'd hear again.

She trembles as waves of emotion sweep through her, her fingers gripping my arms. "Asher..."

Her voice breaks on my name, and I hold her, whispering reassurance against her skin as the last of her fear dissolves beneath my touch.

"Love me, Ash," she whispers, voice breaking. "Love me like you never lost me."

And I can't deny her anything—not when she reaches up and touches me with so much reverence, guiding me toward her with trembling fingers.

I brace myself over her, our foreheads brushing, our breaths mingling. As I press forward, sliding into the warmth of her embrace, everything inside me settles into place.

Home.

I move slowly at first, savoring every inch, every gasp, every tightening of her arms around me. She holds my face between her hands, her eyes locked on mine, and the bond between us thrums—bright, powerful, ancient.

Her ankles lock behind my back and she holds my face between her hands, one of her thumbs making a pass over my lower lip. "I love you, Asher Josiah Cromwell. You are mine and I am yours. From the moment we were born and until we take our last breaths, I will never willingly leave your side."

She says the words that are meant to be said for our bonding and the moment they pass between her lips, they pierce right into my heart. Flickers of light appear in my peripheral vision and as much as it shouldn't be possible for us to bond right now, I know I have to give her my vow in return.

"And I love you, Isobella Isla Grace Blackwood. You are mine and I am yours. From the moment we were born and until we take our last breaths, I will never willingly leave your side."

As that last word forms, the tether between us becomes taut and glows with the force of a thousand suns. Spots block my vision, but I don't need to see Isla to know she's mine.

Her essence grows within me, its roots beginning at my heart and extending through every part of my body until I can no longer tell which pieces belong to me and which are hers.

Our movements grow desperate, instinctive, driven by the need to seal what destiny has already carved into existence. The world narrows to Isla—her breath, her heartbeat, her love echoing through me like a sacred vow.

The moment finally breaks over us in a rush of light and sensation. I hold her tightly, kissing her deeply as we fall together, our bodies trembling with the force of our bond locking irrevocably into place.

My heart is close to bursting from my chest and I've never felt more alive than I do in this moment. The sun shines down on us, brighter than I've ever known it to be, and I swear even the birds sing louder from their perches within the trees.

I grin like a lovesick fool down at Isla. *"Mate."*

"I don't know how that happened, but it couldn't have been more perfect."

Hearing her voice within my mind is like the sweetest song to ever play.

"No, it couldn't have been."

I could lie here for hours with her and that's exactly what I intend to do until Isla's eyes pinch at the side and she starts to shake her head.

"What's wrong?" I demand, checking our bond.

Everything is as it should be and I try not to worry until a pain lances through my chest as if I were being stabbed.

I look down and a red mark not only appears right above my heart, but Isla's as well. My eyes dart around us, but there isn't a soul nearby.

"Isla, love," I plead with her. "Tell me what's happening."

She's no longer looking at me. Her eyes are open, but they're glazed over and her mind is somewhere else.

"No," she whimpers. "No, not you. I don't understand."

I want to shake her until she comes back to me, but I have to consider this might be another memory, one we can't risk her not having.

She mutters some more. Most of her words I can't understand, and as tears fall down her cheeks, it takes every ounce of strength within me not to interfere.

It feels like an hour, but it's probably only minutes before she blinks and her awareness starts to come back to me.

Anguish that's nearly as powerful as what I felt when I realized she was gone all those years ago fills me, but the torment isn't mine. These are Isla's emotions and I'm almost afraid to ask what she saw, but I won't let her carry this pain alone.

"I'm right here," I say softly, trying not to rush her. "You're okay. Nobody is going to hurt you again."

Her body trembles as she openly cries, clutching her chest. "Too late."

"What did you see?" I ask, tension riddling my insides.

"I can't...I can't say the words."

"Shh, baby." I bring her closer, kissing the side of her face. "Whatever it is, we can handle it together."

She shakes her head, her sobs growing louder. "Not this. Nothing can fix this." She pulls back, her red eyes wide with fear. "I know who stabbed me."

CHAPTER TWENTY-SEVEN

ISLA

I get off the phone after putting the plans for dinner into motion and feel a wave of gratitude for the staff, whose competence has made this daunting life a bit more bearable. If Asher is to ascend to the throne sooner than anticipated, it will undoubtedly be stressful, but at least we won't be alone—a thought that brings me a layer of comfort.

A knock sounds at my door and I cross the bedroom to answer. "I was hoping to—"

My eyes blink rapidly and air begins to leave my lungs at a rapid pace. I try to process what's happening, but even seeing the sharp blade protruding from my chest doesn't seem real.

I attempt to reach for the black hilt to remove the dagger, but my arms are immobile, failing to respond. My legs give out next, no matter how much I attempt to draw on my wolf's inner strength.

"Help... me..." I croak as I collapse to the floor.

Confusion and fear muddle my thoughts and my vision swims, but I no longer forget who was standing at the door as it closes quietly.

Estee.

Grief unlike I've ever known pulses inside me, eating up every flicker of joy I was just experiencing. Even back then, my sister was my best friend. It doesn't make sense why she would hurt me, let alone kill me.

Yet I know that was her. She stood there, silent and... I blink, focusing harder on the memory. Her eyes. They were dark, almost black instead of their normal blue.

It's hard to breathe, but I force myself to focus and talk to Asher. I need to make this make sense. I need to understand what actually happened.

"Estee stabbed me," I tell him, sitting further up and wiping the tears from my face. "But I need a minute. I need to go back."

His shaking hand reaches for his shirt and he slips it over my head. "I'm right here. You're not alone."

Asher's jaw is so tight that his words are almost garbled, but he gives me the time I ask for, staying quiet as I force my mind back into those final moments.

Estee stands rigid in front of me. I only have seconds before the door closes, but I was right. There's something off with her eyes. She's not herself.

Relief floods through me, but I fight to stay in the memory.

Darkness begins to envelop me and my body becomes cold, no matter how hard I fight to stay conscious. If I could remove the blade, my wolf energy would heal me. Yet none of my extremities will respond to my commands.

I hear the quiet thud of footfalls from inside my room, which further confuses me—yet also brings me hope. A shadow looms over me and I try to see who's there, but my vision is completely gone now. "Help," I manage to whisper again.

"Shh, it's going to be okay," a garbled voice says. "I'm going to fix everything."

I try harder to focus, to conjure the image of whoever has joined me, but I can't force my eyes to see something they never saw before. This isn't the same as when I couldn't see Estee at my door.

My mind reels as I try to identify who's speaking, or even their scent, as the intruder picks my body up, but I'm fading fast and my thoughts are singularly focused.

Asher.

My eyes burn as I come out of the memory, hoping to never return. There's nothing else but sadness for me to find there. All I know is I need to find Estee and *now*. She must have remembered what she'd done and that's why she ran, but there isn't a single part of me that can accept she hurt me willingly.

I don't know how or why any of this happened, but I do know I'm going to figure it out. Whoever that final person in the room with me was holds the answers and I won't stop until I unveil who they were.

"Damn it, Isla." Asher snarls, yet his touch is filled with the utmost gentleness. "Talk to me."

"Use your telepathy thing," I tell him. "I need Grayson right now. I need him to tell me where Estee is."

His teeth grind together as he starts putting his pants back on. "I'm going to fucking kill her myself."

"No, no, no." My head shakes frantically. "There's no way she did this on her own accord." My hand covers my mouth as the amount of pain she's truly been in slams into me. "Oh, God. She's been hiding away, thinking she's... I need to get to her now."

Asher's face pales. "Are you seriously considering consoling the woman who took you from me right now?"

I step into his personal space and poke a finger against his chest. "Let's get a few things straight. Estee is my sister, my best friend, and she is just as much of a victim in all this as I am. You won't make her feel guilty or threaten her or anything in between those two things. I love you, Asher, but you have to trust me on this. I know Estee. She didn't end up with me on Earth because she's guilty."

The bond pulses between us, wrapping around my chest and pushing my inner strength to new heights. I don't expect that since I'm facing off with the man at the other end of that connection, but there's no way I'm going to let him take charge right now.

My sister needs me and Asher is going to respect that.

"Fuck, Is." His hands scrub over his face. "This is a lot."

"This is progress," I tell him, choosing to see this as a good thing. "Maybe she'll know who the shadowed figure in my memory is."

Though I'd think she'd have returned if she did. Estee could out that son of a bitch and relieve herself of the guilt. Either way, it doesn't matter. I just need to get to her now.

A fiery growl echoes around us. "What shadowy figure?"

Oh. Oops. I guess I didn't finish explaining my vision to him. Rectifying that, my words only serve to increase my mate's rage, his emotions so tempestuous that their smokiness fills my insides through our bond.

"Are you sure there's nothing else you remember? That there's nothing else to see from that day?" His words are barely audible thanks to the tension still riddled within his jaw.

"Yes," I tell him confidently. "I wasn't conscious much longer after getting stabbed. I couldn't even tell the gender of the person speaking."

Something that frustrates me still, but my priority isn't there right now. Estee is going to have answers for us. Even if she doesn't have them yet, we need her, and she needs me.

"Where is Grayson?" I ask, knowing I can't wait any longer.

"He's already on his way to find Estee," Asher replies, helping me stand. "We'll go back to the castle, get dressed, and wait for him."

I look down and realize the only thing I'm wearing is Asher's oversized shirt that falls to my mid-thigh. As glad as I am to remember more so that I can get my sister back, this couldn't have come at a worse time.

"I'm sorry, Asher," I tell him through our new mental connection. *"This was our moment and I ruined it."*

His head shakes as he pulls me closer, holding me with love and tenderness. *"You didn't ruin anything. You're here, we're bonded, and you have your wolf. There is nothing that can take away from those things. We might not feel the same about this particular memory, but that doesn't change how much I love you."*

"I love you, too, and thank you for that." I push up onto my toes to kiss him again. *"I'd like to shift again and go find Estee myself, though. Find out where my dad is and tell him we'll meet him there."*

Asher's lips graze over my forehead. *"Of course, Mate."*

My skin tingles and I have to concentrate on staying

upright as he does what I've asked. He might not like my plan, but seeing how quick he is to support me is everything.

I wait patiently, breathing in and out and testing out my new sensations. When I first got here, I was impressed with the way I didn't tire easily while traversing the stairs. Now, it's like I could sprint up and down them a dozen times and still not be out of breath.

My wolf's spirit lingers just beneath the surface, ready for action and waiting for my approval. She's patient and resilient. Hell, she's a warrior.

It seems impossible that I could have ever forgotten her now that I remember and I hate that it took so long, but as she remains close and very much aware of what's happening, I don't sense any resentment.

It wasn't our fault.

The thought is mine, but it's almost as if the words came from her and peace settles over me. We had no control, but we do now and I'm not going to sit by, waiting for things to happen.

We're going to figure out who took our life and who cursed us to Earth and...

"Holy shit," I mutter as I realize what else I've just figured out. I grab Asher's wrist, tugging until I have his full attention. "If I die again, I'm going to end up back on Earth. I didn't just appear there. I've lived dozens of lives there." None of them lasting longer than forty years and each filled with a lonely existence until I found Estee again. Though I don't tell Asher that once I continue. "I was human for the last five hundred years. Whatever happened to me back then, I was cursed."

That kind of dark magic hasn't existed in our world

since before the Great War. I don't know how someone found an object that was capable of doing this to me, but I do know one thing.

They won't get a second chance at taking my life.

There's no way I'm going back and losing Asher again. It doesn't matter if he'd know where I was this time. One way or another, I'm going to figure this out before it's too late.

"I won't let anyone hurt you again," Asher promises, and while the sentiment behind his statement is appreciated, I know this isn't up to him.

This is on me.

"Grayson said we need to head east in the forest," Asher adds, taking my hand. "Estee has been hiding out there."

The eastern part of our island is desolate. The river doesn't extend there, meaning there's very little animal life, and the things that do grow there typically aren't edible.

Damn it, Estee. Why couldn't you have trusted me with what you saw?

"Let's go," I tell Asher, giving him one more kiss before stepping away and calling my wolf forward. Just as the shift starts to happen, I realize I should have taken Asher's shirt off, but it's too late. Well, maybe not. If I'm bonded to Asher, even if done unconventionally, I should be considered part of the pack now, which means his powers are now mine, and I shouldn't lose my clothes when I shift. I guess we'll find out soon.

As I appear on four legs and my wolf gives our body a solid shake, there's no questioning which direction we're supposed to go in. Gods, I really love just knowing these things now.

Another random thought comes to be, unrelated to the situation, but it feels just as important to remember how we came to be.

The twin moons of Lunara exist because the god who created us had twin children. One son and one daughter. He dedicated this world to them, thinking he was giving his children something to play with. Little did he know that his children would give us the ability to be like them so that they would have friends to play with. Though that only lasted so long before they grew bored of us.

There's a deep sense of peace from remembering who I am, where I come from, and what I want. For so long, I've been lost. Centuries of living half-fulfilled lives, never finding love, never having a family of my own.

My lives were spent alone and miserable until this last one. I don't know why the gods chose this life to bring Estee and me back together, and I might not ever know, but I do know I have zero intentions of taking this second chance for granted.

A howl builds within me and as we let the hollowness of the last five hundred years go, I know there is nothing and no one who can hurt me again.

Asher's wolf joins us, his head rubbing against our front flank, eliciting a deep rumble from both wolves. It isn't fair to just get everything we ever hoped for and not be able to bask in the light of our bond for as long as we want, but Asher and I have eternity to spend together.

Estee needs me now.

Together, mine and Asher's wolves run at top speed. Our claws dig into the earth, propelling us forward at an unmatched pace. We run for miles and there is no slowing, not for any reason.

Asher's mind is distracted as he communicates with not only Grayson, but his head advisor, Malimorte. I didn't know Mali before, but I hope to know him better now. I chuckle to myself. He wasn't alive when I was murdered, so I can at least cross him off our suspect list.

Everyone else, though, is fair game.

My mind goes through all possible options, without bias. It doesn't matter how close I was with someone. Besides my parents, Estee, and Asher, it could be anyone.

I hate to think that, but I have to be smart about this. Was it one of the dozens of women who were jealous of me having Asher? Or someone within the pack who wanted to see the royal family shaken?

Worse, I have to consider that Asher's dislike of Noen's and my friendship wasn't unfounded.

I may not have seen it before, but that boy was in love with me. Had he decided that if he couldn't have me himself, nobody could?

With how close he's gotten to Asher over the years, I hate to think so, but I need to find a way to remain impartial to this situation. I can't let emotions cloud the facts.

Someone wanted me gone and once I figure out why, then I'll be one step closer to figuring out who.

"We're here." Asher's voice carries through my mind, disrupting my thoughts.

My wolf takes a deep breath and it doesn't take much effort to scent my sister, or blood.

Without explaining myself, I barrel toward a patch of sparse trees. I don't know what I'm going to find, but I can't hide from this. Not even when Asher pleads with me to let him go first.

I come to an abrupt halt, my heart hammering in my chest, as I finally get eyes on Estee.

Tear tracks stain her cheeks, she's still wearing the same dress I last saw her in over a week ago, and fresh claw marks have crimson dripping down her chest.

My wolf relinquishes control to me and in the next second, I'm running toward where my sister is and joining my dad, who's pressing his hands over the gaping wound on my sister's chest.

"Estee, stay with me," he pleads with her. "I can't lose you again."

"I don't deserve..." Her frail voice fades as I get next to her.

"I'm here," I tell her. "And none of this is your fault. I know what happened. I know you stabbed me, and even if we don't know why, I know you didn't mean to hurt me. We're going to find the asshole responsible. Don't make me do this on my own."

Her eyes flutter open and closed, unable to stay in one position for long. "I hurt...you."

There's no way I'm going to let her suffer like this. As much as I want to strangle her for leaving me, I know I would have done the same if the roles had been reversed. Still, I'm not going to let her go.

I turn around, thankful when I find Asher right behind me. "Your blood."

He's already on it, a cut on his wrist, open and ready. I move over and tilt Estee's head back. "You're going to live and the hurt is going to go away, Estee. Someone did this to us and I need you by my side to make sure they pay."

She doesn't make any other sounds as Asher feeds her his blood that should help heal the wounds she's inflicted upon herself. It looks like she was trying to tear her heart from her chest and I hate that I didn't go find her before. Yes, I was annoyed that she left me, but I should have known better.

Estee has never been selfish. Everything she's done has always been for the betterment of others. She must have thought I would be better off without her, but even before I knew who she was to me, I knew I never wanted to do life without her.

Seeing her holding the dagger that took me out doesn't change that. Not in the slightest.

As the wounds on her chest start to stitch themselves back together, I vow to make sure she knows that first and then I'm going to make her furious with the person who took away our lives, and then...

We're both going to get murderous.

CHAPTER TWENTY-EIGHT

ASHER

No longer having a pack connection to Isla and Estee is something I'm determined to change tonight. Instead of utilizing my alpha command, I find myself shouting at Estee, desperately trying to get her to swallow my blood, hoping her primal instincts will kick in.

Isla remains unnervingly calm, a stark contrast to my growing frustration. She gently pushes me aside once I've given enough blood. "You're going to be okay, Estee. I promise." Her voice is a soothing balm in the chaotic setting.

Sure enough, Isla is right. While I was preoccupied with force-feeding Estee, I didn't notice that she was already beginning to heal. Perhaps she wasn't as close to death's door as she appeared, considering how quickly she's recovering now.

I step back, allowing Isla some space, and it hits me that my mate is hardly dressed. Oddly, my usual possessiveness doesn't flare up. The bond we've forged seems to be steadying my emotions, instilling a deep-seated knowledge that she is unequivocally mine, and I am hers.

It shouldn't be possible, given we didn't have a proper ceremony, but I'll send a request to meet with one of the gods after we get through tonight's full moon run. Not only to confirm the bond with Isla, but to find out what they know about who killed her.

They're not always willing to share information, but their blood runs through my veins and I'll use the power they gave me against them if it means getting the answers I so desperately need.

Isla's continued silence is beginning to unnerve me. She's always been that way when she's most furious. A yelling, loud Isla is the one I prefer. Tranquil Isla is deadly, and I can't stand the thought of her putting herself in danger, but something tells me that I won't have much of a say now that she's starting to piece things together.

Being bonded will help matters, though. I'll at least be able to find her and communicate with her moving forward, no matter where either of us is. That small sliver of peace will have to be enough until we uncover more answers.

A cough breaks my reverie. Estee, tears streaking her face, manages to speak through her sobs. "I'm so sorry, Issie. I don't know why I would have hurt you. Yet I can't make the image of me jamming a dagger in you go away."

Isla shakes her head, cradling her sister's head to her chest. "It's okay. You weren't in your right mind. I could see you, see your eyes. Everything is fine. We're going to figure this out and you're never allowed to leave me again, for any reason."

Estee's sobbing subsides, but the fear and confusion linger. "I wasn't trying to die," she admits with a whimper. "I just wanted to feel a different kind of pain, anything other than thinking I could have possibly betrayed you in any life."

"Shh," Isla says, closing her eyes as a few tears fall down her cheeks as well. "I know and I'm going to make sure you know as well. You never betrayed me and you never will."

Grayson, silent till now, signals me. As we step away from the emotional reunion, his expression is grave. "You're bonded with my daughter."

"Just as I always should have been," I confirm with pride, despite the unconventional circumstances.

"How?" he asks. "How did you do this without...?"

"It wasn't intentional," I explain. "I brought Elyn, an elder shifter from Selaris, here to help Isla remember and it just happened." Gods, having a conversation about having sex with this man's daughter isn't what I thought I was going to do today. "There wasn't even a god present to bless the bond."

He seems to consider this for an extra moment before he says, "At least not that you were aware of. Someone was there, in some form, or your bond wouldn't be strong. It's like the two of you are pulsing with new energy. It's profound."

Interesting. I hadn't noticed, but I'm also not going to complain. The gods don't typically mess with our world any longer unless we call on them first. At least not since Ocules and Aurora grew bored of their *pets*, as they called us, once we'd tried to kill each other off.

If they're choosing to get involved now, then maybe

getting answers from them won't be as difficult as it normally would be.

"Are we certain that it was Estee who stabbed Isla?" Grayson asks, a deep crease between his eyes.

I nod, glancing over at them. They're still huddled together and it seems the tears have finally stopped.

"Isla's memories seem to be mostly back," I tell him. "She said that it was Estee at her door with the dagger, but that her eyes were black, like she wasn't in her right mind. Then the door closes and someone else is in the room with her. Yet she has no clue about their gender or what happened next."

"How can she remember Estee, but not who was already in the room with her?" he asks and I don't have an answer for him. I wish I did, but I'm beginning to wonder if the memory issues both women are having don't have anything to do with their unusual reincarnations.

Thinking more about Estee's darkened eyes that Isla described, there's only one answer I can come up with, but it's still one that's hard to accept. Dark magic hasn't been around in centuries. The older generation of Lunarians, the ones who have lived multiple lives, would know better than to bring that kind of evil back into our world. But if someone stumbled upon a dark object and used it without understanding the ramifications…

"It's the dagger," I tell him, feeling more confident about this theory as the seconds pass. "Isla doesn't remember because she wasn't just stabbed. Someone used dark magic against her."

This has Grayson's face paling. I don't need to explain further to someone who likely not only lived while that kind of power was freely used, but as a previous Alpha

King, he would have also used objects just like that dagger.

"You need to find out the moment that your father stopped sensing Isla as part of the pack," Grayson says with muttered urgency. "He's the only one at the time who had a complete connection to her. I know we both asked him before if he could locate her as the Alpha King and he couldn't, but maybe alerting him to this new information will help to make sense of the past."

Hearing his words and seeing the determination in his strong gaze, which nearly matches my own, makes me more grateful than ever before to have him as part of my family. One of my biggest regrets will forever include letting him suffer alone for so long. I should have fought harder to help him and Isla's mother to heal, just like I fought for our pack.

I was selfish then, but not anymore.

Grayson continues, his thoughts seeming to string together quickly, making me more secure in my own. "You were convinced for so long that she was still alive. Nearly a century passed before your father could talk you into taking your place as king. You weren't officially bonded, but I still believe the two of you shared a connection unlike most mates in our history. It's rare for mates to be born on the same day and I don't think it's a coincidence, either. What if you were right? What if Isla was out there, trapped by dark magic, hidden from us? We never did find her body."

Whoever did this better hope that they're long dead because if my mate spent years ensnared in her own body before she passed on and reincarnated on Earth, they will serve the same fate, but worse. I won't take their memories away. I'll make sure they remember every tortuous second that they'll be spending with me.

"Asher?" Isla's voice echoes within my mind. *"Is everything okay?"*

She's feeling my rage. I'll need to get better at controlling my emotions because I don't want to lie to my mate. Though hiding from her likely isn't much better. But she deserves only good things in this life and I'm going to do my best to give that to her.

"I'll be fine, but we should be getting back," I tell her, turning around to find her eyes on me.

"We're ready," she says out loud, helping Estee back up and giving her a once-over. "You used your claws before. Can you shift now?"

Her sister shakes her head, keeping her stare low. "No, she still hasn't returned."

"That's okay." Isla smiles warmly. "You can ride on my wolf."

I expect to see something from Estee about her sister being able to shift now, but she just shrugs.

"We need to use the back entrance we used before," I explain, knowing that even if my wolf is fine with Isla wearing only my shirt around her family, there isn't a chance in hell that I'm going to allow her to walk through the castle as she is. "Malimorte will be waiting with fresh clothes for the two of you."

At least he will be as soon as I ask him.

Nobody objects and the three of us shift into our animal forms. Grayson's golden wolf flanks Isla on the left and I take the right as Estee climbs on top of her. Once she's situated, I let Isla take the lead, controlling the pace since she's likely never had to run with someone on her back before.

We move through terrain, taking the straightest distance back to the castle. I relay my request to Mali and I also reach out to my father. I need to talk to him about the dark objects. As an heir to the throne, I learned about them during my additional teachings, but I'm hoping between my father and Grayson, they'll have firsthand knowledge that will sort everything out with efficiency.

"I'm going to meet with my father," I tell Isla as the castle comes into view. *"Why don't you take Estee to your old room and get cleaned up?"*

"That was already the plan," she says, and I can hear the grin in her voice. *"Also, who says that's not still* my *room?"*

"I do."

She might be joking, but I leave no room for argument within my tone. I won't sleep alone again for the rest of my life. I don't care how much she used to hate being told what to do—I won't budge on this.

We loop around to the back of the castle. Malimorte and Declan are waiting for us. I haven't shared much with Declan, but he knows something more is going on. It's one of the reasons I've always trusted him. His senses have always been spot on. Yet even knowing that, I've been hesitant to bring more people into this situation than is needed.

Though judging by the look on his face, it doesn't seem as if he's okay with being left in the dark.

"I told him to go, but he insisted on waiting for you, Your Majesty," Malimorte tells me before I've shifted back.

"It's fine. I'll handle him."

Once I'm on two feet again, wearing only the slacks I

had on earlier, I point to the piles of clothes that have been left for the women. "Grayson, once they're dressed in these, will you make sure they get to the room okay?"

"Of course."

Going to Isla's wolf, I run a hand between her ears, sharing a look with the strong animal. Her eyes swirl with barely restrained fury. *"We're going to figure this out and you'll be safe again."*

"Being safe isn't what we're most worried about," Isla replies, her tone rough and tense.

"Just focus on Estee right now," I tell her. *"I'm going to see what I can learn from my father about that dagger. With what you said about Estee's eyes, I think it's a dark object that should have been destroyed before we were ever born."*

"Let me know what you find out," she says, her voice softening ever so slightly. *"And don't worry about me. I'll be fine."*

I step away from her wolf, only because I know meeting with my father is necessary, but as I walk toward the door, I shake my head. *"That's like asking me not to breathe, love. I will always worry about you."*

She doesn't reply as I enter the castle. Mali excuses himself to continue with the paperwork he was reviewing on my behalf from King Aeson of Venaris. Apparently, the insane man wishes to court Queen Sloane of Alcaris. Neither has found their mate and while they're free to choose instead of waiting, this is a complication we've yet to face since the islands were divided.

Bringing two kingdoms together could be an issue, but at the same time, Alcaris has been slowly dying off for decades now. Considering Aeson has never been one of my favorite people, I'm not entirely opposed to Sloane becoming his queen if it means he'll be less of a difficulty when it comes to trade deals.

Though I am surprised. Queen Sloane doesn't seem like the type to be told what to do, which is how she's held her throne for so long on her own. Yet King Aeson is, well, an arrogant prick. Still, as long as there's no risk to Polaris or even Selaris, for that matter, and trade deals are still honored, then I won't stand in their way.

Declan catches up to me and steps in my path. "You know better than anyone else that I respect your role as Alpha King," he begins. "I also know I often speak with humor, but something is wrong, and I want to make sure you know that I'm here to help however you need. I may not agree that Noen has ill intentions with Isla, but you are still my king. More than that, I consider us friends and as your friend, I'd appreciate not being left in the dark on the matters I might be able to help with."

Gods, I don't have time for this. Yet as much as I want to brush him off, Declan has been the one to keep me sane all these years. He came into my life with the right amount of wittiness to help me remember how to live again. Something that not only I needed, but so did our pack.

"I can't talk right now, but I promise to fill you in tonight," I tell him since speaking with my father is at the top of my priority list.

His grin widens. "I'll hold you to that, even if I have to wait for you in your bed."

"Isla's sleeping in that bed now," I tell him with a raised brow. "Do you really want to find out what I'd do to you if she's the one who found you there and not me?"

He sputters a bit and laughs. "Nah, I think I'm good. I'll still find you later—you can count on that."

Yes, I'm sure I can.

Finally free to go speak with my father, I take the stairs three at a time until I get to the suite he shares with my mother.

He's sitting at the couch, legs stretched out, and a whiskey dangling from his fingertips. "Son."

I take in his relaxed position, but there's no missing the tension in his eyes. Something is wrong.

"Father." I walk farther into the room and take a seat in the chair on his left. I can smell the alcohol on him. "Did you have a fight with Mom?"

He frowns, setting his drink on the table in front of him. "Something like that. What do you need?"

"Isla remembered—"

He sits up ramrod straight on the couch. "You bonded with her."

"I did and we'll talk about that, but more importantly, she remembered who killed her."

His eyes darken. "So, why are you here, half-dressed, and not out there, righting the wrong that was done to you?"

"Because it was Estee," I tell him with a sigh, leaning back in the chair.

He lets out a low whistle. "Well, that complicates things. How does your *mate* feel about that?"

"She's convinced that Estee wasn't in control of her own actions and that's why the two of them ended up on Earth together," I explain, adding, "I agree with her, which is why I'm here. Do you remember the dark objects that used to exist?"

Dad's chest rumbles. "Of course I do. One of them took my life."

Shit. How did I forget that? I think it was his second or third one. Either way, it's not something he's ever liked to talk about. Unfortunately, he's going to have to this time.

"Do you know anything about a dagger that would be able to take down a wolf shifter?" I ask, my knee bouncing as I wait for him to answer.

His eyes level on me and he shakes his head. "If you think dark magic had anything to do with Isla's murder, you're going to need to find who did this, Son. They're a danger to all of us and as king, this is your responsibility."

"I know that." I sit up again, wondering if maybe coming to him wasn't the best idea. "What happened between you and Mom?"

If he needs to get this off his chest before he can be helpful, then maybe we can help each other.

"She says I do too much," he replies with a low growl. "That I don't spend enough time with her and the whole point of my giving up the throne was so that I could rest, but she has no idea what I've done for this kingdom, the sacrifices I've made. It's not easy for me to just sit back and do nothing."

It's been almost four hundred years since he officially passed the crown to me, Isla's death having postponed his request by over a century when I refused to stop looking for her. I didn't realize he still felt so at odds with his decision. I knew it was hard for him to admit he had a weakness that could affect our kingdom's reputation, but I was certain he'd moved on from that.

"I'm sorry, Dad," I tell him sincerely. "If you want to do

more, especially in a more official capacity, I will make that happen."

He takes a deep breath and gives his shoulders a shake. "No, I'm sorry. I should be over this by now and it's no wonder your mother is frustrated with me. Plus, you didn't come here to talk about me. You need answers. Though I'm not sure what I can do after all this time. A fragmented memory isn't much to go on."

Settling back into my seat, I hope he's wrong. "Do you think dark magic would have severed your link to Isobella as her alpha back then? You never could confirm if she was dead or not. Maybe this is why."

His brows pinch together and he tilts his head. "It's certainly possible. There's a reason those objects were supposed to be disposed of. That's also why I tried so hard to get you to stop looking for her. I never thought she was dead and then when... Well, never mind that. We need to focus on this memory. Maybe I should speak with Isla and hear for myself what she saw."

"No," I demand, not liking his sudden change of direction with our conversation. "What happened that you're not telling me?"

He swallows thickly and looks away from me. "I should have told you this years ago, but I didn't want to hurt you any further."

"What?" I demand, my voice booming louder than I intend. "I'm sorry. This is just a lot to process. What should you have said before?"

Dad's steady gaze meets mine again and he says the one name I'm not surprised to hear but also don't expect right now.

"Noen."

"What about him?" The pressure in my chest grows heavier by the tick of the clock on the wall beyond me.

"He's the one who told me that Isla left on her own accord," my father admits. "Yet he was also the one to stand by you the most back then. I should have questioned his motives, but at the time, something didn't feel right, and the two of you were friends, so I just let it go. Maybe I shouldn't have. You haven't left her alone with him since she's returned, have you?"

"Do you think Noen killed my mate?" I ask, not because I don't think it's possible, but because at one point, I had wondered if he could have had something to do with it, but everyone made me feel as if my suspicions had only been formed because he was in love with her.

Yet maybe that's exactly why he should have been the person we looked at most.

"I don't know why the boy would have done it, but his father worked for me," Dad says. "He had high-level access to the castle. If he shared any of that information with Noen... Do you know if Edward has returned to Lunara?"

Noen's father died a few years ago. As far as I know, he had no intentions of being reborn. The man had lived several lives, none of them lasting with his mate. He was bitter and tired after losing his mate three consecutive lifetimes and I hadn't tried to talk him out of his chance at peace.

Neither had his son.

Gods, could Noen have really done this out of spite? After centuries of thinking he was my friend, I don't want to believe it's possible, but the moment Isla was back, every instinct in me screamed to keep him away from her.

Was I ignoring what my subconscious already knew all along? I'm not yet sure, but I'm certainly going to find out.

CHAPTER TWENTY-NINE

ISLA

Washing blood off my sister has to be one of the worst things I've ever had to do in all my lives. She cried the entire time, mumbling apology after apology until I finally yelled at her.

Then we laughed.

Laughed so hard that we both cried and then naked-hugged and giggled like schoolgirls as we joked about the two of us together just then being every man's fantasy.

It was cathartic. The whole thing and now, it's time to be fucking furious.

"Someone killed us, Estee," I tell her as I braid her hair.

She's sitting cross-legged in front of me on the bed as her chest rumbles. "I know. It's been a long time since murder was all I could think about, but now, nothing would make me happier than to tear my teeth into someone's neck or to rip their guts from their stomach or to make a million tiny cuts on their body, letting them slowly bleed out or even—"

I grab her shoulder and give it a shake. "I think I've got the picture."

She looks back up at me and raises a brow. "Are you not in the mood to plot the gruesome death of our murderer?"

"I might be if we knew who they were," I say with an aggravated sigh. "But we're skipping a step. This whole time, I've assumed that I would get answers when my memories came back, but they're here now, or well, mostly so, and I know in my heart that there's nothing else to find in my head. We need to get creative and hope that son of a bitch is still alive so we can end his life."

Her fingers drum over her knees. "Do you think it's a man because that's what your gut is telling you or because women aren't capable of murder? You were enemy number one to a lot of our friends once it became public knowledge that you were to be queen one day."

She's not wrong, but it wasn't just our female friends who changed then.

"Noen also wasn't thrilled that day," I say, hating the words more than ever before, but I also know that I can't keep any thoughts to myself. Talking this out is going to be the only way that we find answers.

Well, and possibly using myself as bait.

Before I can tie the braid off, Estee gets up and off the bed. "You think *Noen* could have killed us? But he was like our brother."

I shrug. "A brother whom I think was in love with me and that's why he never did enjoy when I tried to hook the two of you up."

Estee gags. "Gods, those were some awkward months."

She isn't wrong.

"I'm just saying, he's been weird since I've returned," I admit. "That could be because Asher's jealousy came back with a vengeance or because there's something there that we never wanted to see before. Either way, I've only had one very brief encounter with him where we were alone and I think it's time that changed."

The grin on her face is everything I was hoping for, especially when she says, "You want to make yourself a target."

"I do."

"Asher's not going to like this," she says, but I already know, which is why I'm going to need her help.

"Yes, but my sister is going to need me more than ever for the next few days and we won't want to be interrupted."

She shakes a finger at me. "You're an evil genius. I don't know where this is coming from, but I love it. Just remember that you and Asher are somehow mated now, and while that might ease some of his overprotectiveness because he's now more connected to you, that also means he can track you easier."

Shit. I hadn't thought of that. Our mind link and the bond will make this a little harder, but I think I can get away with a few days of doing things he may or may not approve of.

"I'm not asking for permission with this, Estee," I tell her confidently as I get off the bed. "I'll ask for forgiveness later, but we need to do this. It's *our* lives that were ruined by this."

She walks toward me and places a hand on my shoulder. "And Asher was the one left behind, trying to pick up the pieces and keep living. Something not everyone we once knew was able to do."

Damn her being so aware.

"Are you trying to talk me out of using myself as bait?" I ask because if even my sister believes this is a horrible idea, then maybe I'm thinking too emotionally.

She shakes her head and offers me a sweet smile. "Not at all. I think we need to try this at least once and see what happens, but I also want you to consider that we're not the only ones allowed to be pissed or even terrified. Asher lost the love of his life. Our parents lost their children. For too long, I was without my sister, my best friend. I still don't remember how I ended up with the same fate as you, but even I want to be careful. I won't risk losing all of this again. Not you, or our home. This is bigger than us and while I think we need to be doing something about finding out who's responsible, we need to keep the people we love in mind as well."

My sister is the most perfect being in all the world and I can't stop myself from throwing my arms around her neck. "Thank you."

Emotions choke me and those two words are all I can manage. The depth of my love for this woman only continues to grow with every passing day. Knowing that I have someone like her who isn't afraid of being honest and vulnerable, who sees the world through rose-colored glasses, and who has a lack of filter at all the best and worst times…

She's everything to me.

"I love you, too." Estee chuckles, wiping at her cheeks. "Now, can you quit drowning me with love so that we can make a plan for tonight?"

I pull back but still keep a hold on her. "You want to try something tonight?"

Suddenly, I feel completely unprepared and a little shaky.

"Dad said there was a pack run scheduled for this evening," she explains. "Every single wolf shifter within Polaris will be required to be in attendance, even if they don't run. Asher will make a speech to the five hundred and something pack members before starting the run. Most of us will break off into groups, but I have a sneaking suspicion that the fact that I still can't shift is going to throw me into a tailspin of grief and leaving me alone won't be a good idea. I'm going to need my sister and Asher is going to need to lead his pack."

While I have a feeling I know where she's going with this, I still ask about her wolf first. "You had claw marks on your chest when we found you. How did…?"

Her face falls and she shakes her head. "I don't really want to talk about that. Just know, I wasn't trying to kill myself. I may have gone a little insane, thinking I could literally rip the pain from my heart, but it was nothing more than that."

I hug her tighter than ever before. "I'm so sorry, Estee. I hate that you were hurting like that, all alone, and I didn't come for you when I should have."

"It's okay," she promises. "While my last life in Lunara is still fuzzy, I think being on my own was exactly what I needed, even if I lost my mind there at the end. But that's only because I couldn't see myself in the memories like you did. I didn't consider the possibility that I wasn't in control, but the moment you said my eyes weren't normal, the relief was instant."

I pull back before I suffocate her. "Good. You have no reason to blame yourself for what happened to me."

"Oh, don't get me wrong. I still feel guilty." She heads to my closet that's half-empty now since I've been staying in Asher's room. "I should have been smart enough to avoid whatever had control of me, but I at least no longer think that I killed you. So, that's something."

I guess that's acceptable. For now.

I follow her into the closet and watch as she goes to the back wall, opening the drawers that hold my jewels.

When she turns around, a crown hangs from her fingers. "Our plan starts the moment you walk out of this room."

Leaning against the doorway, I return her grin. "Tell me more."

"You're going to play the role of yourself," she says, tossing the crown at me. "You need to be the Queen of Polaris, Is."

I catch the silver-and-diamond adornment, carefully holding it between my hands. "How is that going to help us?"

"Because someone either didn't want you to be mates with Asher or to be queen." She puts her own tiara on. "We're going to rub their failure in their faces tonight. Asher will be forced to announce the fact that you two bonded without the typical ceremony and that you're officially part of the Polaris monarchy. More importantly, you're going to own that role like the fucking queen you were always meant to be."

Oh. *Oh.*

"You think if we enrage our attacker, they'll try to take us out again."

She nods, stopping next at the fancier dresses I didn't bother taking with me to Asher's room. "Play your part and yes. I'll be your weak sister who can't cope with the shitstorm that's been thrown at us and then, when we appear to be at our most vulnerable, we wait."

I join her, grabbing a sleek, navy-blue silk gown from the rack. "They're going to regret the day they messed with the Blackwood sisters."

She nods, a spark of strength in her eyes. "I think that already happened when they were forced to kill me too."

My head tilts. "What do you mean?"

"It was decades later that I died," she says. "We weren't both the original target. I might not remember exactly what happened those years after losing you yet, but I do know that there's no way possible I would have rested until I learned why you were just gone. I still felt you in my heart, and yet you were nowhere to be found. Even if I don't remember, I know I wouldn't have let you go without a fight."

"Wait." I close my eyes, sorting through the knowledge I've begun to have access to. Estee just said that she still felt me in her heart. When we thought we were humans, we still shared a connection so strong that I was certain she was somehow my soul sister. That was before I even knew what that truly meant. I knew because it didn't matter where we were, Estee and I were connected.

Elyn told me in that river that I had to die. That the old me was still alive. Could she have meant exactly what she said? Did I never truly die before?

"Holy shit," I mutter, grabbing onto the shelf as a wave of dizziness overcomes me.

Estee reaches for my arm. "What is it?"

I blink several times before being able to focus on my sister's concerned gaze. "I don't think we died."

Her eyes pinch together. "Uh, yeah, we did. I stabbed you and then someone did something to me. How else would we have ended up on Earth?"

"We were never meant to be on Earth, not by normal standards, anyway," I tell her. "I don't think we were killed. I think we were cursed. Asher mentioned something about the dagger maybe being a dark object. If he's right, this makes sense. Plus, the elder wolf Elyn told me I had to die earlier today. That's when I was finally able to remember more and access my wolf. I couldn't do those things before because I wasn't actually dead, and I don't think you were, either. Except you must have died differently than me because you'd gotten most of your memories back already."

"But not my wolf," she says, rubbing her chest. "She's still not in here. No matter how much I begged for her company while I was gone, she never appeared. It took every ounce of strength I possessed to make my claws appear before I used them against myself."

I grab her hand and head for the door. "Elyn needs to kill you."

Her laughter is strangled. "I'm not sure I like this idea. Maybe we get through tonight first and see what happens."

I nudge her with my shoulder. "Is my sister afraid of the elder wolf?"

"Maybe. Or maybe the risk of dying again and not coming back is more than I'm willing to gamble at the moment."

Grabbing her hand, I squeeze tightly. "I didn't even

think about that. You're right. We can stick with your plan and then circle back to this death theory after we figure out how desperate our murderer might actually be. Plus, if you have your wolf, you won't need me to console you."

"Exactly." Her grin widens. "Now, you just need to make sure you keep Asher blocked from your thoughts before he gets suspicious. We're only going to get one chance at this if we actually draw the attention we're searching for. Let's make sure we don't fuck it up."

She's right and, while the thought of keeping Asher at a distance after I only just got him back makes my stomach churn, it's a temporary discomfort that will hopefully lead to a lifetime of peace.

Asher will understand, or so I'll keep telling myself until tonight is over.

CHAPTER THIRTY

ASHER

Isla and Estee have been sequestered for hours in the bedroom. Despite my numerous attempts to reach Isla through our bond, each of her assurances does little to relieve the uneasiness in my heart. Yet when I've said as much, my mate has merely reminded me that it's been a long, emotional day, and that she's distracted with making sure Estee is okay.

While she's not wrong, every instinct in me is saying to go be with her.

But that's not possible at the moment and I wonder if Isla is taking advantage of that. Five centuries isn't long enough for me to forget that when my mate and her sister are together, trouble has a way of following.

"The sun is setting, Your Majesty." Malimorte's voice breaks through my reverie as he stands at my office door, a subtle reminder of the evening's obligations. "We should be heading out soon."

"Where is my father?" I ask because Isla isn't the only one I'm concerned with. After speaking with him, and also being unable to find my mother, I need to know that they're okay.

I don't know how I've missed that they're struggling, but I know I want to fix this somehow. I know mates aren't meant to get along for all eternity just because the fates deemed them a perfect match. So a fight between them isn't surprising. I just don't want to see either of them suffer if I can help.

I've been so wrapped up in Isla and making sure she's protected that I've ignored many of my responsibilities. Not only to the pack, but to my parents. Now that answers are starting to come to us, hopefully that will all change and things can go back to normal.

Well, the new normal that will include Isla as my queen.

After all these years, the thought still makes my stomach swirl with excitement and anticipation. I never stopped loving that woman and even now, I know how lucky I am to call her mine.

I just need to make sure nobody can take her away from me again and that the pack doesn't question our bonding.

In all the history I've learned, never once have I heard of two mates completing their connection like we did. Yet I know without a doubt in my mind that our bond was blessed by the gods earlier today.

The shared energy between us thrums like a live wire that brightens my mind, fills me with strength, and solidifies my resolve regarding what must be done.

"Gideon and Sosheena have already left for the pack run, my king," Malimorte answers. "They wanted to make sure everything is perfect for your announcement tonight.

Your father insisted that we not only have the standard stage set, but that flowers are brought in, along with the royal banners for the new queen."

Well, that was kind of him. Considering his mood earlier, I didn't expect much from him, but this is how he's been my whole life, showing up when I need him most.

Now, I just need to go find my mate. It's time for us to make our first appearance together as the King and Queen of Polaris.

"I hope the two of you are ready," I tell her through our connection. *"I'll be at Estee's door soon."*

She replies immediately, her tone confident and full of love. *"I'll be waiting."*

Those three words fill me with a trilling sense of urgency. Gods, I love her more than should be possible.

Glancing in the mirror on my closet door one last time, I double-check I haven't forgotten anything. My navy-blue slacks are pressed and the seams of my matching suit coat hang from my broad shoulders perfectly. The white dress shirt beneath is mostly covered by the blue sash I'm required to wear on these occasions. One last look, I confirm everything is as it should be as I press my palm over the medals pinned to my left shoulder, making sure they're all secure.

I turn to Mali, who's also dressed up for the occasion with his medals on display and a silver sash over his chest, marking his role as my head advisor.

Meeting his steady gaze, I nod. "I'm ready."

He opens the door for me, standing aside until I exit my suite first. Together, we make our way through the castle, my steps quicker than usual after having spent the afternoon away from Isla. Having the bond intact helps to relieve the ache distance can cause, but still, I don't think a day will pass that I won't desire to be in her presence for every moment of every day for the rest of our lives.

Knocking on the door, I hold my breath until Isla answers.

As she's revealed to me, my heart races and my fingers twitch to grab on to her hips, pinning her against the wall.

Her rose-gold hair is pinned half up with soft curls framing her face. Her crown rests proudly atop her head and there are diamonds that drape around her neck to match.

Blue silk covers her body but falls so perfectly over each of her curves that she might as well be wearing nothing. With the heels she has on, our height difference isn't as substantial and when I look into her bright, cobalt eyes, I lose myself within them all over again.

"Fuck, Isla," I breathe out, my hands aching to touch her.

She steps just out of reach and smirks. *"Don't forget. We're not alone."*

I don't give a damn who's around. I'll never hide my feelings for this stunning creature.

Not caring that Mali and Estee remain nearby, I close the distance between us and bundle the soft fabric of her dress within my grasp as I press my lips to hers.

The moment she kisses me back, I slip my tongue forward, needing a taste of my mate if I'm expected to get through this evening with few public displays of affection.

Though whether I touch her or not, someone would need to be blind not to see the attraction I hold for this woman.

"All right, lovebirds," Estee says, placing a hand on each of our shoulders. "How about you pick this up later tonight, in the privacy of your own bedroom?"

"Oh, I plan to," I whisper against Isla's mouth before I step back, adjusting my suit. I hold a hand out to my queen and grin. "Shall we?"

"We shall." There's a glow about her that hasn't been there since her return and I want to take all the credit for that after us having bonded, but my mate has always carried her own strength. She was born to be queen. Hell, she could rule this kingdom possibly better than I have.

As I watch her now, owning the role she was destined for, my body relaxes and I stand a little taller.

There may still be a threat out there that we need to deal with, but for tonight, I'm proud to be the mate of Isla Blackwood, the Queen of Polaris.

Estee and Mali walk behind us. When I glance back to check on them, I feel for my advisor, who remains rigid. Estee has her arm looped through his, making it look as if he's her companion for the evening run. Mali, seasoned in the ways of royal etiquette yet always a background figure, looks distinctly uncomfortable with the unexpected attention. Despite his discomfort, this might be good for him, and perhaps for Estee too.

Though Declan will surely be heartbroken when he sees us exit the castle.

"I know I didn't mention this before, but you need to know—you look absolutely stunning tonight," I whisper to Isla as we approach the towering front doors of the castle.

She responds with a playful wink. "I think the fact that

you couldn't keep a safe distance away from me said enough."

"But you deserve to hear the words as well." I give her hand a soft squeeze. "And I will spend the rest of our lives making sure you know how special and perfect you are."

"Keep that up, and we're not going to make the pack run," she replies saucily.

The thought is tempting, but tonight is pivotal. The people of Polaris, and even Lunara as a whole, must recognize her as my queen, a declaration too critical to delay. Should anyone dare to challenge us, they would be wise to think twice. Together, Isla and I make this kingdom stronger than it has been in centuries.

"Tonight will be soon enough, love," I tell her as we walk outside, heading around toward the back of the castle, where I can sense the entire pack waiting for us.

Over five hundred wolves stand united and their collective strength empowers each step forward. My heart beats with unveiled exhilaration, but mostly pride.

Pride for my pack, pride for my mate, and pride for who we are as a people.

As we near, a murmur ripples through the crowd, their senses tuned to the newly forged bond between Isla and me. It's a stirring confusion, one I intend to address directly.

"You'll have answers soon enough, I assure you all," I tell them all at once through the mind link I have to the pack.

As my words register, most of them bow their heads in respect and quiet. The excitement of the pups still sound, but that's nothing we're not used to.

"This feels unreal," Isla says privately. *"I don't think my*

memories could have prepared me for this moment. Seeing them all together like this, it's..."

"*Powerful,*" I finish for her.

"*That's one word, but also, inspiring,*" she says. "*I want to be the best version of myself for no other reason than to be the queen they deserve.*"

And this is why I've always known she was meant for this role, meant to stand by my side.

"*You're already all that and more, Mate.*"

We approach the stage that's been prepared for us at the edge of the forest, facing the castle. Blue and silver banners stand tall with our royal insignia and flowers at the base of each stand.

The pack pushes in, each member eager to be close, all of their lifelines pulsing within my chest. Though none brighter than that of my mate.

"Our moons are full and our pride runs strong," I begin with a booming voice. "Yet I sense your confusion and, while I understand that, I hope by the time I've finished, you'll feel as at peace as I now do."

I pause, waiting for anyone to voice a stronger opinion, then I breathe a little easier when none comes.

Glancing at Isla, who stands tall and strong beside me, I continue. "As I've already shared, Princess Isobella Blackwood, now known as Isla, has returned home. While her memories were missing upon her arrival, causing discord and unease, today an elder wolf from Selaris helped my mate to unlock the knowledge of her past.

"During this time, something unforeseen yet welcome happened. We're not sure how or why, but during Isla's healing, our bond was sealed and blessed by the gods, as I'm sure you can now sense." I place a hand on Isla's back, urging her forward. "Please welcome your queen back home."

"Long live our queen." Only about half the pack murmurs the sentiment and I'm neither surprised nor disappointed. They have every right to question this situation and that's exactly what someone does.

Bernard, a man to whom I've spoken on numerous occasions and who has even worked in the castle, steps forward. "If she has her memories back, will we be informed as to why she left us for so long? And how are we to believe it won't happen again?"

"Thank you for your question, Bernard," I tell him sincerely, then I grin. "It's nothing I didn't expect. Though I won't lie that a part of me hoped you'd merely accept her return and we'd move on."

Laughter moves through the crowd, refueling my determination to be the leader they deserve, while also keeping Isla's safety as my priority.

"My mate was taken from us over five hundred years ago," I state clearly. "While her memories have returned, there are certain aspects that remain unclear. I understand this information is important to you in order to be truly at peace, but I ask you that you also extend grace toward our situation.

"I can confirm there was foul play involved, none of which Isla had any knowledge of. A fact I trust her word on, just as I'm asking you to. If you're unsure if you can take our word, what of the gods? I don't believe that they would have allowed our bond to be complete today if there was anything to be concerned about when it comes to Queen Isla, as she shall now be known as."

Most heads nod, but I can sense there are still others who wish to know the full story.

"All I can say beyond that is that there was a danger to Queen Isla that we weren't aware of before, but we are now. I will do whatever I must to keep her safe, but that doesn't mean I will forsake the pack in order to do so. I have stood as your king even when half my heart was missing and I will continue to do so now. Soon, you'll see an even stronger unity between our people and I assure you, that will be because of my mate."

Someone cheers then another begins to clap until nearly everyone joins in. I try to watch for those who seem too suspicious or possibly nervous, but I also don't want to seem obvious.

"*Your Majesty,*" Malimorte says, interrupting my thoughts. "*Do you see Declan or Noen?*"

Slowly, I move my gaze around the crowd, expecting to find them up front as part of my team, but Mali is correct. Neither is present and that's not acceptable. For many reasons, but most importantly, their absence is a slight to their queen.

After what my father said earlier, I still didn't want to believe that Noen could have been responsible for Isla's disappearance and subsequent death, but I need to think logically.

"*Where are you?*" I demand to Declan through my alpha connection.

Interesting. It's almost as if he's sleeping. I can't get through to his consciousness.

"*Find them both,*" I say to Mali, "*but don't make yourself known. If they see you, make up a reason as to why you're there. Then let me know what they're up to.*"

"Yes, my king."

I catch his nod of respect out of the corner of my eye and put my attention back on the pack waiting for me.

"Please join us, your king and queen, for the pack run," I shout above the cheers. "Let's all embrace our inner animals and let the power of the pack unite us, as it has for centuries."

"You and I will be shifting first," I remind Isla since she's never run with the pack as the queen. *"We need to lead them now and show them that they have nothing to fear."*

She stiffens next to me and nibbles at her lower lip. *"What about Estee? Her wolf hasn't returned. After today, I don't want to leave her alone."*

While I can understand her hesitation, there are some sacrifices that come with our positions that can't be forsaken.

"I'll ask Grayson to stay behind," I tell her. *"I need you by my side for this, Isla."*

She glances at Estee, then me, and nods. *"Always."*

I tighten my hold on her hand before raising our arms into the air. More cheers erupt through the crowd, and just as it always should have been, I turn with Isla and we lead our pack.

CHAPTER THIRTY-ONE

ISLA

So much for having a plan of our own. I only get a few seconds to tell Estee that she'll be waiting with Dad and I'll have to find her later before I have to shift. It's not that I don't want to do this with Asher—I really do—but finding the person who murdered me... Well, that's important too.

Now, I just have to hope that I can find a way to accomplish not only making my mate proud, but showing face to our pack members, and easing their concerns that a mistake has been made by allowing me back as their king's mate.

Only then can I go back to the plan of using myself as bait to draw out whoever might be watching a little too closely tonight.

Even if we only tighten our suspect list, I'll consider the plan a win and hope we get another chance to investigate further.

Wolves begin to appear everywhere. Browns, silvers, greys, blacks, and those with multi-colors stand in the expansive back yard of the castle. Eyes glow under the bright moons and the energy surrounding us is that of strength and honor.

With every beat of my heart, I know this is exactly where I was always meant to be, right here with these people. Seeing them wait for Asher and me to give the signal to start the run, I know this is family. Something I've lived without for far too long.

Never again.

My wolf rumbles low, but the sound is of contentment. She sits next to Asher's wolf, head tall and eyes moving around the pack until we can confirm that each wolf is present.

"I want you to give the signal and take the first step." Asher's voice carries through my mind and I almost snap my wolf's head toward him but manage to refrain.

"What? Why?"

"Because you're their queen and they need to remember that," he says confidently. *"They will follow you, or they can leave. There is no in between. I won't stop them from asking questions—every shifter has that right—but I also won't let you be disrespected and they're going to learn that now."*

Not only does my heart swell, but my wolf's humility is at an all-time low after that little speech. It's almost as if she smirks at the waiting crowd and without waiting to be told twice, she howls into the skies, deep and powerful.

The pack quiets and I begin to worry Asher pushed for too much too soon with them, but then, one by one, yips sound from our people until there is an orchestra of howls that echo far and wide.

We press our head to Asher's flank and then turn to lead the group of nearly five hundred shifters. Our stride lengthens to a steady jaunt. This isn't about racing or staying ahead. Monthly pack runs are meant to create unity and forge bonds.

With every step forward, the beat of the wolves behind us sounds within my mind. I sense each of their spirits, hear the steady thrum of their hearts, feel the vibration of their movements.

Soaking in every second, we lazily run into the forest, moving through the trees as one. Asher remains by my side and each time our gazes meet, the thought of using myself as a target becomes more of a distant memory.

I needed this reminder tonight. For too many years, I've felt on my own. I've had Estee this last lifetime, but there's always been a part of me that was waiting for the other shoe to drop.

Remembering that I come from somewhere that values each person as a whole, never leaving anyone behind… It's everything to confirm what I wasn't seeing before in regard to finding out who my murderer is.

Asher is more than my mate. He's my best friend, my partner, the one person in all the worlds that I should be able to trust most. There's no reason I should have to keep this plan from him.

When we're done here, I'm going to tell him everything Estee and I spoke about. Of course, he isn't going to like using me as bait, but I'll remind him that I could have done this on my own, but I trust him to stand by, making sure nothing goes wrong.

That is how we're going to figure this out, working together to make sure nobody else has to suffer as Estee and I have for so many decades.

"You're the most stunning creature I've ever encountered,"

Asher's gravelly voice whispers through my mind. *"I want to take you to the conservatory tonight."*

Even my wolf's body shivers from the intensity of words, the growl weaved between them, and the thought of what may or may not happen in that glass room.

I didn't remember what the dome section of the castle was when I first arrived, but even then, I was curious. I have to believe that's because somewhere in the deep recesses of my mind, I've always known where I belonged, right here in Polaris.

Staying in the conservatory on a full moons night is something we always talked about. It's the best view of the sky in all the islands and once I was old enough to appreciate sex, I always joked with Asher that one day, we would leave our mark on every surface in that place.

Of course, while Gideon and Sosheena were king and queen, that was never possible. The fact that Asher seems to have remembered that promise made all those years ago further cements my choice not to hurt him by trying to figure any of this out on my own.

"Today is the greatest day I've had in over five centuries," I tell him, wishing I could kiss him, but my wolf seems to compromise by gently nipping at his neck.

Asher's wolf retaliates with a few nibbles of his own and soon, the pack is beginning to spread out, no longer running in formation.

I start to run in the direction of the castle but slow to a stop when Asher calls my name, his tone no longer as warm as it just was. *"I need to handle something before we can be alone for the night. Would you be upset if I asked you to wait with your sister and father for a little while?"*

"Of course not," I reply, pressing my wolf head against his. *"Go be king. Your mate will be just fine."*

"Gods, you have no idea how much I've missed you, Issie." The rumble in his words is mixed with so much love, but also an insurmountable amount of grief.

In some ways, I want to say I had it worse, living without my wolf and my people, but at least I was ignorant to the true reason for my lack of belonging and sense of longing. Asher had to get up each day, missing half of himself and feeling as though he'd failed when he couldn't find me.

He was left without answers, only *what-ifs*, and I'm astounded by his ability to have taken on being Alpha King and not only keeping Polaris safe, but making this place feel more like home than it ever has.

"I love you and I'll see you soon."

"I love you more than all the moons and stars in all the worlds, Isla Blackwood."

We're already close enough back to the castle that I see the treeline and beyond that, the lights that were set up around the stage. Shifters are still gathered there, those who didn't run for whatever reasons they have.

I assume that's where I'll find my father and Estee, so I head in that direction, promising Asher that I'll be fine on my own for the short run back as he heads farther back into the forest.

I should have asked him what was going on, but I'm sure if it were important, then he would have told me.

Following the trees, I trot forward until my wolf spots something off. Our eyes narrow, peering into the shadows. Is that…a wolf pup?

There's a set of paws sticking out from under a tree

branch, but they're not moving and my heart pounds. Please don't let this pup be seriously injured.

Glancing around, I listen for any wolves nearby, but it's just me and the young one. *What the hell?* How could a mother have left her child?

I shift back to my human form, moving quickly as I lift my dress so it doesn't snag on the fallen foliage. I listen for the pup's breathing and it's shallow. Carefully, as not to cause any further pain, I lift the branch, tossing it away with ease.

Interesting. He's on his back, but he still should have been able to wiggle free even if part of the tree fell on him. My fingers stroke his head. "Hey, little buddy. I need you to wake up."

Tomorrow, we need to figure out when I'll be able to mind speak with the pack like Asher does, because this would be much easier if I could talk to the boy's consciousness right now.

Instead, I lift his three-foot-long body up into my arms and cradle him to my chest. A few drops of blood smear along the top of my dress, yet that isn't what makes me tense.

It's the sinister growl coming from the shadows.

"Asher," I call urgently to him through our mind link. *"Get back here now."*

His fear pours into me. *"I'm coming for you, love."*

Branches break as the wolf stalks closer. Before turning around to face my attacker, I carefully set the pup back down, thankful to at least see his chest still moving, even if he is unconscious.

As soon as my hands are free and I've stepped away,

my wolf rushes to the surface, forcing the shift before we've even fully turned around. She comes to life with a vicious roar, teeth bared and claws eager for blood.

It was no longer my intention to make myself bait without Asher in the know, but it seems fate has other plans. A large black wolf with dark eyes and sharp fangs digs into the ground before he launches himself at me.

My wolf ducks and rolls out of the way, but our attacker is quick. He whips around and catches our rear flank with his claws, tearing into our flesh.

Fuck!

Still, there's no giving up. I don't know who this is, but whoever wants me gone again is going to get a hell of a lot more fight from me than they did last time.

We launch ourselves forward, slamming into the other wolf. He bites into our neck, but we do the same to him. Blood splatters everywhere, and I can't tell who's worse off, but my wolf is vicious and relentless.

She pierces his side and then goes for his underbelly, but as she pulls our paw back, his claws rake down our ribs.

"Isla!" Asher's voice booms through my mind just as a shadow launches over us.

Within a second, our attacker is ten feet in the opposite direction and unmoving, while we're left breathing heavily on the ground, crimson leaking from several wounds along our body.

Asher's wolf whimpers and growls when he faces us. He takes a step toward me, but I stop. *"Get whoever that is first. I'll be fine."*

Considering the amount of adrenaline running

through me, I don't feel nearly as bad as I assume I look. Though I'm sure that will change later.

When he turns around, a loud rumble escapes his wolf. *"He's gone."*

"What the hell do you mean?" My wolf lifts her head, but we can't hold it up for long.

"I mean he's fucking gone," Asher snarls. *"This was a setup. I never should have left your side."* He shifts back to two feet, closing the distance between us. *"Fuck, Isla. I'm so sorry."*

"It's okay," I promise him. "I'm *okay.*"

He cuts his wrist and tilts my wolf head back. "Drink."

I don't argue with his harshly spoken word. I know he's not angry with me and the sooner I'm okay, the sooner we can figure out who the hell that was. I assume Asher already knows as the Alpha King, but I don't want to ask until I've healed.

With the way he's trembling and how dark his eyes are, plus the amount of fury that's coursing between the two of us, I can taste how murderous he is. Yet he's here with me.

I can't believe I almost did something this stupid without telling him. How damn selfish that would have been.

Dad and Estee come running into view, both of their faces pale.

"Why did you do this without me?" Estee demands, making Asher's head snap in her direction.

Oh, hell.

I need to shift back right now, or I'm going to have one furious mate on my hands.

Estee's gaze widens as she looks between me and Asher. "We, uh, well, um…"

"Don't be angry," I say to Asher through our bond. *"With Estee's help, I was going to use myself as bait to draw out whoever killed us, but—"*

"How fucking selfish could the two of you be?" His voice roars and even in my wolf form, I can't help shedding a few tears.

"No, Asher," I plead with him. *"That* was *the plan, but during the pack run, I knew it was stupid and decided that I would tell you tonight when we were alone. If you didn't agree to do so together, then I wasn't going to go through with it. I only got caught by this wolf because there was an injured—shit, where's the pup?"*

After a few gulps of Asher's blood, I'm already feeling better. I force myself up, but he places a hand over my wolf's back, keeping us down. "You wait here."

He's still rightly furious, but at least through our bond, I can tell that the emotion is no longer directed right at me.

Estee comes to my side and rubs my head, whispering, "I'm so sorry. I don't know what happened, but we're going to figure this out before it's too late this time."

That, we absolutely would.

Asher comes back with the pup in his arms, handing him off to Grayson. "This is Selene's kid. He's always taking off, so she probably doesn't even realize he was caught up in this. I already gave him some blood, and I don't want to alarm her unnecessarily. He's going to be okay. Take him back to the castle, clean him up, then send someone to get her."

"I'll have someone get Noen or Decl—" Dad starts to say, but Asher's growl cuts him off.

"No, anyone but them."

What the hell? What did I miss?

My wolf finally stands, only minor aches moving through my sides still. Though she won't let me shift back just yet.

Dad stops next to me, bending his head against mine. "The two of you aren't to be left alone again, not even together. I will help Asher lock both of you up if that's what it takes." He pauses, his voice breaking. "If anything happens to either of you again…"

"I'm sorry, Dad," I say, even though he can't hear me. Still, he nods as if he can sense my remorse.

Though it's not like I intentionally let this situation happen. Okay, maybe I put the idea out into the universe, but at least I tried to take it back.

"Estee, go with him," Asher tells her. "I'll be with Isla for the rest of the night."

Under any other circumstance, this would sound divine, but even my sister grimaces as she waves goodbye.

Once we're alone, he faces me and cups my wolf's face. *"Fuck, Isla."*

"I know," I say, full of regret for having let myself be vulnerable, even if it wasn't intentional. *"But you won't have to lock me up. I wasn't trying to put myself in a bad position. I was doing as I promised, heading right to Dad and Estee, but then I found the pup and things spiraled. What happened with Noen and Declan?"*

His head shakes and his jaw tightens until it begins to twitch. *"I don't want to talk about that yet. Just know if you see Declan again, and I'm not with you, run in the opposite direction."* He presses his forehead against my wolf, hands still shaking. *"Can you shift? I really need to touch you right now."*

I have so many questions, but more than I need the answers that go with them, I know my mate needs me. Even though I know it's going to hurt since I'm not fully healed, I pull my wolf energy back and let the change happen.

Searing agony feels as though my ribs are being branded, but thankfully, that's the only part of my body that still hurts.

Asher's frown deepens as I stand on two feet. "Damn it. I didn't realize you were still hurting."

I step into his arms and shake my head. "I'm not now."

He holds me tight, vibrating against my body. His closeness is nearly as good of a balm as his blood.

We stand there in silence for several moments. Howls from the other wolves cut through the quiet night. Some joyful, likely having no clue what's transpired within their pack, and others darker. I wonder how many people know and whom we can even still trust if not Asher's two closest friends.

I knew Noen might have been a suspect and I didn't say anything, something I regret more than anything else as of late.

I nearly tell Asher as much, but he speaks before I can. "If you're up for it, I'd still like to go to the conservatory."

Well, those are the last words I expected to come out of his mouth.

"Yes, but shouldn't we—"

He shakes his head, cutting me off. "I need you, Isla. More than I need to rip someone's fucking head off right now, I. Need. You."

Those three words are punctuated with lancing

torment, and in this moment, I know he's right. Everything else can wait.

As long as we're together, nothing else matters.

At least for tonight.

CHAPTER THIRTY-TWO

ISLA

Asher stays silent the entire way to the conservatory, and with most of the pack still out on the run, there's no one to see us as we move quietly through the castle.

His grip on my hand is beginning to make my fingers numb, but I don't dare attempt to wiggle them. Not when I know he's teetering the line between going feral or breaking down completely.

I'm not far behind him in that aspect now that the adrenaline is starting to wear off. Someone tried to kill me. Again. Worse, I have no clue why.

Estee and I came up with different scenarios earlier, but after five hundred years, I still don't understand why someone would see me as a threat.

Jealousy makes the most sense, as my sister mentioned, but how could that kind of emotion be driving someone *that* insane after all this time?

Walking up the last set of steps on the east side of the

castle, I know that's not an answer I need to worry about now.

My focus returns fully to Asher. Though as we enter the glass-dome room, I do find myself uncontrollably distracted by its beauty.

The clear roof glows a soft silver under the light of the twin moons and the stars feel so close that, as they twinkle, I'm tempted to reach out and grab one.

We step down on to the inset floor. There are multiple telescopes placed throughout the room, each one pointing in a different direction. The black carpet has the silver insignia of Polaris placed at the center of the room and with the door closed behind us, the only sound I hear is the rapid beating of our two hearts.

Asher tugs me closer, holding my face with the utmost care as he stares into my eyes, his gaze shimmering with all the emotions I already sense through our bond. "You're okay."

I grab one of his hands and place it over my chest. "I really am. I'm sorry, Asher. It was a stupid idea to begin with, but I wasn't—"

His mouth claims mine before I can finish, and whatever words I had dissolve under the force of his fear and his love pouring through our bond.

He kisses me like he needs the reassurance to breathe, and I cling to him just as fiercely. My hands slide along his shoulders, grounding him, grounding myself. I unbutton his shirt slowly, deliberately, offering calm where his emotions threaten to break.

He mirrors me, brushing the straps of my dress from my shoulders with a tenderness that makes my throat tighten. We strip away the remnants of fear as much as clothing, until nothing stands between us but the pounding in our chests.

When he finally pulls back, his forehead rests against mine. "I can't lose you, Isla. Not now, not for the next five hundred years. I need the time we lost. I need *you*. Nothing else matters if you're not by my side and in my heart."

His mouth crashes against mine, rendering me speechless for more than one reason. He keeps his one hand pressed over my heart and uses the other to pull me closer, covering the lower part of my back with his palm.

My fingers grip on to his white dress shirt as he devours me not only with his mouth, but his mind and the love pulsing through our bond.

He still shakes with pent-up emotions, so I do the only thing I can think of to calm him. I start to undress him, never allowing my touch to leave his body, no matter where my hands move.

He continues to kiss me, making my skin shiver even before he finally starts to push the straps of my dress down, revealing every piece of me, one slow inch at a time.

Only when we're both stripped free of our clothes does he finally break the kiss. "I can't lose you, Isla. Not now, not within the next five hundred years. I need the time we lost back. I *need* you. Nothing else matters if I don't have you by my side and in my heart."

"I'm not going anywhere," I promise him. "Until we figure this out, you can consider me an extension of yourself. I won't leave you, not for one second."

His forehead presses to mine and he brushes his lips over the tip of my nose. "I'm going to hold you to that."

I wrap my legs around him as he carries me toward the lounge couch near the telescopes. The glass dome lets moonlight spill across us, cool and bright, sinking into my skin like a quiet promise that what happened before will never happen again.

Goosebumps rise along my arms as I breathe in the charged air. The bond between us, the energy of the moons, the strength of my wolf—they fuse into something warm and unshakeable, dissolving the last remnants of fear.

"We're going to be okay," I murmur before kissing him.

He answers not with words but with devotion—soft kisses along my jaw, reverent touches that make my heart twist. His hands move over me with a desperate tenderness that speaks louder than desire: he needs to feel that I'm alive. Here. His.

The world blurs into warmth and moonlight as he worships every part of me, and when my breath catches, he holds me as if he can absorb every tremor of emotion in my body. Our bond hums, tightening, strengthening, filling me with a sense of belonging so fierce it steals my breath.

The intensity of his focus, the way he touches me like I'm something sacred, builds into a wave that crashes over me before I can stop it. My fingers clutch his shoulders as the world breaks open in a rush of light and sensation, my cry echoing through the dome.

When my vision clears, Asher is hovering above me, a rare, gentle smile softening his features. "Thank you," he whispers. "I needed this, but so did my wolf."

"You never have to thank me for letting you love me," I

tell him, holding his cheeks as my thumbs stroke over his stubble. "I need this just as much as you do."

"We're only just getting started." The deep timbre of his voice moves over my body, his words branding me with the promise of a future filled with lifetimes of joy.

He kisses me again—slow, deep, filled with meaning—and guides my hand to his chest. Our bond flares bright and warm, and when he shifts us, rolling onto his back with me straddling him, the movement feels effortless, natural, right.

There's no resistance. There never has been. Asher has always lifted me up, always made me feel like his equal. Not a shadow. Not an ornament. His partner. His queen.

The thought fills me with strength as I settle atop him. I lean down until our breaths mingle, brushing my lips over his. "Me and you."

"Always and forever," he whispers, the words a promise made long before we ever dared say *I love you.*

Our bodies move together, guided by need and emotion rather than urgency. The world narrows to the feel of him beneath me, his hands at my waist, the soft glow of the moons above. When the moment crests again —slow, consuming, powerful—it feels like falling and flying all at once.

Light from the moons once again washes over us. There's a glow within the room that feels like magic. Hell, it probably is, considering how today has gone.

The gods might have stopped interfering in our world, but after allowing me to be cursed to Earth for so many damn years, letting Asher and me bond earlier outside of normal means was the least they could do.

Whoever is watching over us now better keep

sprinkling that magic around us until we figure out how to make sure nobody else will ever tear us apart.

Once I've regained control of my body again, my eyes are on Asher's face. His eyes are burning sapphires and I know he still needs this closeness, but I need a minute to catch my breath. Plus, as much as I know we both needed this physical connection, my mind now needs to be soothed, and I tell him as much.

"I'm surprised you let me wait this long to talk," he says, kissing my neck and holding me tighter.

I angle my head, giving him more space to venture, even though we're supposed to be talking. "You weren't the only one hurting for the other."

He pulls back to look at me. "I know and I'm sorry I yelled at you. It doesn't matter if you'd intentionally put yourself into that situation or not, you deserve better from me. You're your own person and it's never my intention to think I can control your decisions."

"But we're a team," I remind him, cupping his face. "I may have forgotten that when I was furious earlier while talking to Estee, but I know this now and you have no reason to apologize for your reactions. It was too close of a call tonight and now you need to tell me what you know about Noen and Declan. Why should I run if I see them?"

He shakes his head. "Just Declan. We already have Noen. Mali found the two of them once we realized they weren't present for the pack run."

My stomach sinks. "Found them doing what?"

"Noen had a dark magic object, and they were arguing about getting rid of it before I found it because Noen knew I would kill them both without blinking," Asher says, his tone sharp. "They're right. If you hadn't called for me… I was seconds from shredding Noen into pieces."

I know that I suspected Noen, but hearing Asher's words…that slices into my chest a little more than I expect.

"How did Declan get away?" I ask, then to be sure there aren't three people we're worried about, add, "That was him who attacked me, right?"

His grip on my hips tightens. "It was. Mali was waiting for me to get there before making himself known, but Declan mentioned something about needing to go before it was too late. Mali didn't realize that meant he was planning to attack you, which is something my advisor is rather remorseful for not catching."

I'll have to remember to speak with Malimorte myself. If he's the only other person Asher can depend on right now, we need him fully focused, not feeling guilty.

"So, you didn't get to talk to Noen?" I ask, needing any of this to make sense to me.

"I was only there long enough to get my hands around his neck," he says, shaking his head. "He's been trying to get through to me since I found you, but I'm blocking him out. Unless he's going to tell us where Declan went, I have nothing to say to him."

"Maybe I can get the information out of him," I say, and I can see the objection on Asher's face before he even opens his mouth, but I hold my finger over his lips and continue. "With him chained and with you right on the other side of the door, I'd be perfectly safe. But if he truly did this, Asher, we both know why, which means I hold the most power over him."

"You have no idea how much I fucking hate that you're right," he says between clenched teeth.

"I know." I trace my finger over his chest, following the dips and curves of his defined muscles. "And if it weren't the quickest way to find Declan, then I wouldn't suggest it, but I'd rather find him and have this be over and I think you agree."

"Furiously so." He rises quickly, making me squeak as he lifts me into his arms again and rolls us so he's above me, holding me close. "But not tonight. Mali's gathering trackers. Noen's locked down. Declan will be found."

He brushes a kiss to my lips, slow and certain, his forehead resting on mine.

"Tonight is for us," he whispers. "Tomorrow…that battle can wait."

And as he leans in again, the world softens once more into warmth, moonlight, and the steady reassurance of my mate's embrace.

Tomorrow might even be too soon.

CHAPTER THIRTY-THREE

ASHER

The next morning, I wake before Isla and the thought of leaving her even to shower is unacceptable. I knew we needed to be careful until we figured out if there was still a threat to be worried about, but for the attack to happen on the one night when the pack is at its closest? I didn't expect that.

I won't be caught by surprise again.

So, after carrying Isla to the shower in our suite, we wash and get ready for what I imagine is going to be a very long day.

"What should I expect today?" she asks as we leave the room. "I can remember all the basic things about our world, but I was never queen before. I wasn't even trained since you becoming king wasn't supposed to happen so soon. I don't want to do anything wrong."

Holding her hand, I give it a gentle squeeze. "There isn't anything you could do wrong." I tap my head. "Just ask me if you're confused about anything and don't be afraid to walk away if something becomes too much for you. I don't know what Noen is going to say today and Declan is still missing."

A fact that infuriates me to no end. I should have hunted for him myself last night, but I needed Isla. I needed her closeness, her touch, her aura, her everything. My soul shattered the moment she cried out for me when she was being attacked.

The terror wrapped around me like a vise and I knew that being away from Isla, even if I was doing something to avenge her, would only be a distraction for me.

Her presence released the horror of having almost lost her again and I don't intend to let her out of my sight until Declan is captured. That may mean that I can't find the bastard myself, but I know there are other capable trackers on our island and he can't have gotten far.

Isla looks up at me, blinking several times. "Are you going to torture Noen?"

"He hurt you, Isla," I tell her flatly. "I'm going to do whatever I need to so that he can never do so again."

She looks toward the ground as we continue walking, heading for the lower levels of the castle where Noen is being held. "I know and I'm not saying I don't want you to do whatever you have to, but I don't think I can watch that. I knew there was a chance that Noen was involved, but thinking and knowing…it's a little different, especially now that I remember my childhood."

That weasel manipulated her on so many occasions over the years. I know his dad was an asshole, but Noen had choices, and he chose to stay, taking the abuse because that was what kept him closest to my mate. Something that used to drive me insane and that nobody else seemed to see.

Worse, I forgot how much I hated him when he was no longer pissing me off. He'd used that same tactic on me, only pretending to miss Isla as I did as a way to bond with me. Or maybe in his twisted mind, he truly did grieve her.

Either way, I don't know how I fell for that, but it won't happen a second time.

It isn't until we reach the final door to the holding rooms that Isla finally speaks again. "I'm sorry I didn't listen before. Maybe I didn't want to see it, or I really was that naïve, but I know now that Noen cared for me more than he should have. It wasn't appropriate for me to spend so much time with him and maybe if I hadn't been so stubborn, none of this would have happened."

I stop and pin her against the wall, my touch gentle, but my eyes and chest feel as though they're filled with fire. "This was not your fault, Isla. No matter the choices you made, you didn't deserve death just because you were nice to another person. Noen knew what he was doing and this is on him, end of story."

She closes her eyes, letting out a shuddering breath as she nods before looking back up at me. "Okay."

My fingers lightly trail along the side of her face. "Are you sure you want to do this? You don't have to go in there with me."

"I know." She stands a little taller. "But I need to see his face and hear his words. I need this closure because even knowing what Mali heard and saw, I'm having a hard time associating the Noen I thought I knew with a person capable of murder."

That, I can understand because no matter how much I hated that he wanted my mate, I never thought he'd do something like this, not truly.

"Just don't push yourself too far," I tell her. "And don't be angry with me if I pull you out without your permission because I'm not comfortable with how things are going. I'll be honest, letting you in the room with him isn't easy for me."

"And I love you for not trying to control my decisions." She pushes up onto her toes and kisses me briefly. "Now, let's get this over with."

I reach out to Mali. *Is Noen ready for us?*

"Yes, Your Majesty," he replies promptly. *"And there've been no sightings of Declan, but we have a team of thirty wolves searching for him on the island. All of the ships were put on lockdown as well. Unless he decides to swim with the water dragons, he won't get far."*

"Has anyone checked on Cain?" I ask, knowing he's been stationed at the portal again. He'd only stayed in the castle for those first few days because Isla seemed comfortable with him and it was important to me that she have that. Now, I need to make sure our gatekeeper hasn't been taken by surprise by Declan, allowing him to escape.

"Cain is at the portal, dressed in full armor, with his two protégé's on standby, my king. Your father made the request once he heard of Isla's attack."

I'm relieved to hear that even my father has been doing his part to catch Declan. He was out of sorts yesterday and I need to go check on him and my mother to make sure they've found time to discuss their issues in a way that hasn't made anything worse.

Though that's going to have to wait.

"We're coming in," I tell Mali before looking back down at Isla.

"Remember," I say to her, "you're only staying as long as you're comfortable and not at risk."

She nods. "I know. I won't push things too far."

I believe her, but still, my chest tightens and stomach churns with the power of the seas. Letting her into the room with the man who is likely responsible for her death five centuries ago is wrong. Yet she's right. My mate needs this and I'm going to give it to her because no matter how much I hate it, I won't allow Noen to be something that gets between us.

Isla will have her closure and then I'll have his head.

I open the final door that reveals Noen chained to a metal chair. The room is cold and musty and not fit for my queen, but she doesn't even flinch when she sees him restrained.

His head is hanging limply and deep bruises have formed around his eyes and cheeks. There's dried blood on his face, and I'm pretty sure he's pissed himself, but that changes nothing for me.

Mali steps forward from the corner where he's been seated all night. "King Asher, Queen Isla." He bows for each of us. "I'll be right outside if you need anything."

His fists are clenched and his knuckles are bruised, making me grin. I didn't tell him that he *couldn't* touch Noen, so Mali hasn't done anything wrong. I just didn't expect him to react with such violence without being asked.

"Did you learn anything?" I ask, nodding briefly toward his clenched fists.

He shakes his head. "I'm sorry, my king. I know you didn't ask me to do anything, but he threatened our kingdom and that... That wasn't okay with me. All he kept saying was that he didn't do anything, that he was only trying to stop Declan, but if that's what he was trying to do, then why not call for you?"

That's a damn good question and one I plan to ask, but I'm going to let Isla have her moment first because I have a feeling that when I'm done with the bastard, he won't be waking back up anytime soon.

Mali excuses himself and exits the room. Isla can't seem to take her eyes off Noen and I know she wants to be alone with him, in hopes of making him talk, but I don't know that I can leave her.

"Are we just supposed to wait for him to wake?" she asks, her voice devoid of emotion.

"No, I can wake him just as soon as you're ready," I tell her, then I add, "I'll jolt his consciousness with the connection I have to him as his Alpha King."

She nods, still staring at him. "Do that. I'm ready."

I gently grab her chin and force her to meet my gaze. "Are you sure?"

"I am." Her eyes are filled with a determination I haven't seen from her in much too long. "I'm going to do this."

"Yes, you will, love." I lean in to kiss her forehead. "And I'll be right on the other side of that door should you need me, but you'll need to use our bond connection to let me know. The room is soundproof."

This is one of the bigger aspects of this situation that I hate. I won't be able to hear their conversation, but maybe that's for the best. Noen will know this and I trust my mate beyond measure. If there's anything to learn from him, she really is our best option.

She swallows thickly. "I won't put myself at risk."

"I know." My arms wrap around her. "You proved that last night—not that you needed to, but the fact that you called for me instead of trying to handle the fight on your own showed me what I already know."

Isla hugs me back and shudders. "I'm ready for this to be over. I'm ready for us to just be *us*, even if just for a few hours at a time."

"Me too, love. Me too." Lifting her chin again, I kiss her then move toward the door. "Let's get another step closer to that."

"I'm ready," she confirms again, her gaze going back to Noen, and as much as it kills me to do so, I slip out of the room before I change my mind and yell into the mind of the man I currently hate most in this world.

"Wake up, you worthless piece of shit," I snarl. *"Isla is waiting to speak with you. Just know if you even* flinch *in her direction, I don't care if you can help us find Declan or not, I will finish what I started last night and rip your head right from your shoulders."*

"Asher, I didn't—"

I cut the connection off because if I hear his pathetic pleas, I'm going to be tempted to storm back into that room and my mate won't get the closure she seeks.

I won't do that to her unless I'm forced. Though I can't deny a part of me hopes he tries something just so I can watch the life leave his eyes as I end him.

That's the only satisfactory ending I can picture, but it will come in time, that I know for sure.

CHAPTER THIRTY-FOUR

ISLA

Watching Noen become aware again, seeing how his face pinches and the tears that fall down his cheeks, I want to help him, to do something to ease his pain, yet that's likely exactly how we ended up in this situation. I spent our childhood always attempting to heal the emotional and physical wounds his father had inflicted.

I can't do that again. I won't. Not when he could be responsible for taking the last five hundred years from me. No, not could be. He is. Why else would he be speaking with Declan, arguing about a dark object and me?

"Isobella," he mutters, his mouth barely moving.

"It's Isla," I correct with a sneer. "You killed Isobella, stole her life—all because you couldn't have her."

He manages to lift his head up and look me in the eyes. "The only thing I'm guilty of is loving you more than I should have. I never could have hurt you, not then and not now. I mourned you just like Asher did."

Damn it, he's good. There isn't an ounce of insincerity in his tone. Even my wolf remains at the surface, curious about what the truth actually is.

"Then where's Declan?" I ask, crossing my arms and taking another step closer.

"I don't know," he says devastatingly. "Like I told Mali, he misunderstood the argument we were having. I'm not working with Declan. Hell, I didn't even know he had that damn orb until he tried to use it on me."

"He's talking about an orb that Declan had," I tell Asher. *"Should I ask him more about that?"*

"Mali didn't find it," he replies. *"We need to know how they got it and what it was used for."*

Giving Noen my attention again, I struggle to see him as a murderer when he looks so weak lumped over in the chair, barely able to move and openly sharing his anguish like a beacon within the room.

"Where did the orb come from?" I ask, keeping my tone even.

"I don't know," he says pleadingly. "Declan was waiting for me in my room when I returned before heading out to the pack run. I knew something was off with him and at first, I was trying to help him, but then he started rolling the orb between his hands. It was pulsing with dark magic and I could feel the energy trying to latch on to me. I smacked the sphere from his hands and that's when he became uncontrollable."

"How so?" I press, hating that I'm finding his words so easy to believe. Still, I have to admit that's likely only because believing I could have been friends with someone who would do this to me isn't the best feeling.

Noen starts to answer but then coughs until he begins

to choke, fresh blood trickling from the corner of his mouth.

I step forward again, the instinct to help something I can't fight, regardless of what may or may not be true.

My hand lifts, but I stop myself. Touching him would put me at risk. I know this and I won't disrespect Asher's wishes or break my promise.

Thankfully, his coughing ceases, but he's wheezing heavily now. "You know, I used to think the magic within this room was a great tool. I never suspected I would be a victim of it." He struggles to lift his head again, then gives up, continuing to speak without looking at me. "I'm running out of time, Is. My wolf can't heal me in here and even if he could, I know Asher's just waiting for his chance to end me. I don't blame him, but I need you to know the truth."

Gods, I don't know if I can handle that right now.

"I *was* in love with you," he admits. "You were the only light in my life, the only thing that kept me from running away. I knew it was wrong. I knew you belonged with Asher, but I couldn't let you go, even when I should have."

Briefly, his head comes up and he stares right into my soul. "I never could have hurt you. If I were capable of that, I would have tried to steal you from Asher before I would have ever thought to kill you."

"What's happening?" Asher's voice sounds in my mind.

"I'm fine. Give me a minute."

His growl moves through me. *"Then why do you feel so sad?"*

I can't answer him. Hearing Noen out has to come first. I need to feel the truth, to understand what I never did before.

"You need to find Declan before it's too late," he pleads. "I don't expect you to believe me, but if you find him and can figure out what that orb is for, then I know you'll find the answers you need. If I could help you any more, I would." His shoulders tremble as he adds, "I'm not ready to die, Is."

This is so much worse than I could have imagined.

My wolf's spirit settles over me and I've never wished to be able to speak with her more than I do now. Noen being guilty makes sense. He had reason to kill me before and he could have given Declan that orb, using it to send him after me.

So many scenarios and I don't know how to find the facts. Yet the thought of believing Noen, of keeping him alive long enough to find Declan, that brings me peace, makes me feel better about this whole situation.

"We can't let you out of this room," I tell him, just so he doesn't misunderstand what I'm about to say.

"I don't want you to," he replies. "I want there to be no doubt that when something else happens, you know I had nothing to do with this."

"*When* something else happens? What do you mean?" And just like that, I'm back to being uncertain of what is right and wrong.

"Declan tried to kill you last night," he reminds me. "Don't tell me you think he won't try again or that someone else won't? Someone doesn't want you here, someone who has probably hated you this whole time without you ever knowing. Find that person, and soon, because I don't even think Declan did this. At least not on his own."

Please let him be wrong about that. If there is more

than one person out there who wants me dead, I just might try to convince Asher to run away with me. Okay, that's a lie. I'd never walk away from our home and our people, but the idea does have an appeal to it, I can't deny that.

"There's something we're missing," Noen continues, regardless of my continued silence. "Asher knew I was in love with you and that made me an easy suspect. But I'm not the boy you once knew. There's a reason I've stayed away from you since you returned and it's not because I'm guilty. I know better now and as much as I missed my best friend, I found a new one in Asher, and I never wanted to hurt him by getting close to you again. Even if that meant I lost both of you."

He has another coughing fit, but this time, blood splatters everywhere from his mouth, barely missing my shoes. He's bleeding internally. It wasn't a lie when he said he was running out of time.

"You need to come in here and heal him," I tell Asher. *"He's dying."*

"Good fucking riddance," my mate replies harshly.

"We don't have the whole truth," I say, knowing this is hard for Asher to hear because Noen is right. It was so easy for us to believe he could have betrayed us, but I haven't lived an easy life in five centuries. No sense in doing so now. *"If you let him die before we find Declan, I don't know if I'll ever have the closure I need and I don't think you will, either."*

Asher doesn't reply right away and I can't sit here, doing nothing. I go to Noen, lift his head to help clear his airway and rip a piece of his shirt to wipe his mouth with.

"Hang in there," I whisper. "If you're right—though I'm not saying I believe you—I will figure this out."

He groans and starts to say something but then goes completely limp in the chair again.

"Don't die on me yet, Noen," I tell him sternly, then I turn for the door. There's nothing left to learn in this room. Any other answers we need are out there somewhere.

I just hope Asher trusts me enough to help me find them.

There's no handle on the interior side of the door. I raise my hand to knock, but it starts to open before I can.

Asher enters and I'm hit with a wave of fury.

I wince, hating that I've done this to him, but I don't want either of us to have regrets when this is all over.

"If I'm wrong, if Noen is lying, I'll kill him myself," I say, placing my hand on Asher's heaving chest. "Just help him stay alive long enough for us to find out the whole truth."

Slowly, he turns his gaze until his fiery eyes land on mine. "I fucking hate this."

"I know," I say softly. "So do I, but we've already lost enough. Let's make sure we have all of the information before we lose anymore. He meant something to you while I was gone. If he really did this, he isn't going to get away with it, whether he dies now or in a few days. At least if we wait, there will be no questioning if we're making the right choice."

His sharp stare cuts over to where Noen still sits, unmoving. "My only hesitation in killing him right now is for your benefit, not mine."

"Maybe that's true right now, but if we learn Noen

didn't actually do anything, what then?" I press. "Will you still feel nothing toward his death?"

Asher's teeth grind together and his chest rumbles so loudly, the vibrations move through my own body.

"Fucking hell." He stomps toward Noen's battered form and snarls. "You better fucking deserve this."

I watch with pride as my mate makes the right choice. I understand his anger, but this is just one of the reasons why we were meant for each other. To support one another when our own emotions are too heavy for us to see reason.

When Asher comes storming toward me after giving Noen some of his blood, I expect him to blow past me and straight out the door, but instead, he grabs me by the waist and throws me over his shoulder. "You're done in here. For good."

That, I can be okay with. I shouldn't ever have a reason to come in here again. Even though I offered to kill Noen myself if I'm wrong for trusting him, I know Asher would never let me do that. Not even if I begged him to allow me that moment.

Well, maybe then, but still. He's too good to me, either way.

From my position, I see Mali slip back into the room, hopefully to continue keeping watch and nothing more.

Asher remains silent as he marches through the dark stairwell and I want to say something, but I have a feeling giving him some time to process what I've asked of him is necessary.

He exits into the main part of the castle again, and I assume he's going to put me down, but instead, he growls at the nearest group of people and keeps walking once they scatter out of the way.

"Asher Josiah Cromwell, I taught you to behave better than that."

Sosheena's voice sounds from up ahead and oh, how I wish I could see the two of them glaring at each other right now. I try to wiggle out of Asher's grasp, but his fingers dig further into my thighs. I guess I'll stay right here.

"Your office," she demands. "Now. And unless Isla's legs have suddenly stopped working, put her down."

Again, what I expect doesn't happen. He actually listens to her and when I can see his face, it's almost as if he's turned to stone. The tension in his jaw is so tight, I'm surprised it hasn't cracked.

"I'm sorry," I whisper, guilt nearly consuming me.

He looks down at me and while he's still rigid everywhere else, the sorrow shining through his eyes speaks volumes as he says, "No, *I'm* sorry. I just need time and, more importantly, information. You were right and I'm only furious because I thought we were close to being done with all of this, but if Noen didn't do this, and Declan wasn't working alone, I feel ten steps farther behind." He grabs both of my hands. "I can't fail you again."

With every ounce of love and confidence I possess, I say, "You won't. No matter what happens, we can't control our fates. This is going to work out exactly how it's supposed to, and however that is, it will never be your fault."

He shakes his head. "We can't talk about this right now."

What he really means is that he doesn't believe me, but that just tells me that I'm going to have to do my best to make sure we get the happy ending I know we deserve.

"Let's go see what your mother wants, then." I take a step to the side so he can lead the way.

Asher wraps an arm around me, holding me with the utmost care again, all while he still thrums with a vehemence so intense that I'm not surprised I don't see any of the staff moving through the castle like normal.

Gods, I hope Sosheena isn't about to tell us something to make this morning any worse.

CHAPTER THIRTY-FIVE

ASHER

Nothing so far this morning has gone how I expected. Hell, the same applies to pretty much every moment since Isla arrived. I'm trying to control my rage for her sake because I don't want to be angry that she has this incredible heart, and yet I struggle.

Every step I take toward my office to speak with my mother is heavy, as if my boots are filled with lead. My wolf wants to go back and tear Noen to shreds. No longer does learning the truth hold priority for him.

Noen is a risk to my mate. Whether he killed her or not, the fact that someone may have used him as a pawn is enough. At least for my inner beast.

Isla was right, though.

The human part of me, the one I'm barely holding on to right now, would have regrets should we find out that he's telling the truth. That he was blindsided by Declan last night and knows nothing of the attack on my mate.

I wanted so badly to have found the person responsible for ruining my life that it was easy to take the little bit of information that Malimorte overheard and make it fit what I wanted to hear, what I wanted to be true.

So easy to hope that this nightmare is almost over, that Isla will no longer be at risk. At least once we find Declan.

And maybe that can still be the case, but something tells me that whoever did this hasn't been working alone. Plus, Declan doesn't fit the bill. He wasn't on the island the day that Isla disappeared.

Yet there's no denying that it was his wolf I nearly killed to save her last night.

Fuck! I don't know what the truth is, and I haven't been this frustrated since I was scouring every inch of this world looking for my mate, hoping beyond all reason that she was somewhere out there, waiting for me.

Isla's steady grip on my hand keeps me grounded as we walk side by side toward my office. I don't know what my mother wants and if I weren't also worried about her and my father, I wouldn't be giving her a second of my time. Though I have no intention of leaving Isla's side or bringing her with me to search for Declan myself, so I guess, at the moment, I have nothing else to do until new information surfaces.

We enter my office and my mother is already settled in the chair in front of my desk. Isla tries to release my hand, but I hold on tighter, leading her toward my seat. As I take my place, I grab her hips, putting her on my lap.

She arches a brow. "Is this really necessary?"

"Yes." The singular word leaves no room for argument before I put my attention on my mother. "Have you and Dad worked out your issues since yesterday?"

"I'm not here to talk about that," Mom states in a no-

nonsense tone. "But to answer your question, no, I haven't forgiven him for being a stubborn old wolf. He chose to give up the crown and he's regretted that choice for too long now. I've taken his moods lightly over the years, knowing he means well, but after what I learned, it's time for me to step in."

"What did you learn?" I ask, hoping I'm not about to have more problems thrown at me.

"That you have no idea this castle houses dark objects," she says with a huff. "I overheard your father muttering something about them last night with someone. And if you'd been properly informed of their existence, we might have figured this out sooner."

A growl grows within me as my annoyance for my father grows. "Figured what out?"

"That the vault where they're kept has been compromised."

As the words leave her mouth, even Isla tenses above me as she asks, "*The vault?* How many of them are there and how many are missing?"

I don't miss how my mate rubs at her chest and seems to be struggling to breathe. I'd be raging myself if I weren't so concerned with making sure she's okay.

"Yes, the vault has been hidden within the castle since this place was built," Mom explains, hands folded over her lap. "There are at least a hundred various objects. I'm not sure how many are missing, as I don't have access to the room, but Asher should be able to get in as the Alpha King. Though considering Gideon never ended up sharing access, I don't know. I didn't ask when I found out he failed to do so after promising he would. If you don't, at least one person on your advisory council should have access."

My father. Sometimes I love that man and sometimes I want to strangle him. He very rarely does anything that makes sense on the surface and this is another one of those times.

"What do you mean?" I ask, doing my best not to hold too tightly to Isla. "You knew about this before your recent fight?"

"Of course I knew." Her lips flatten as if I've insulted her. "I was the queen. I knew everything that happened in this castle"—she points at me and Isla—"including the way you two used to sneak around. But when Gideon explained that he was worried you'd use those objects to find Isla, I understood why he kept them secret at the time."

"I could have found her with something in that vault centuries ago?" I roar, removing Isla from my lap, then slamming my palms on my desk. "I'll never forgive him for this."

My mate rests her hand over my back, pushing a sense of calmness through me, but there isn't any amount of love that could quell the ire storming within me right now.

We lost so much fucking time. So many years and moments that we'll never get back, not in this lifetime.

I start to go around my desk, intent on finding my father, but Mom gets up from her chair and moves into my path. "He was protecting you, Son. We can't destroy those objects—it's impossible. Locking them away was the only solution. If you'd used them, even with good intentions, your soul would have been tainted in ways you couldn't come back from. Even for your mate, we couldn't let that happen. I just didn't realize he never shared their existence with you once you began to move on."

"I never fucking moved on, Mother," I seethe, my chest pounding and fist clenched so tightly, I can smell the blood from where I'm cutting into my palm. "But I'm also not a child. I wouldn't have risked my soul, and a future with my mate, when I still had hope that after I died, I would find her again. *That* is something the both of you should have known."

She visibly shakes as my voice raises, but her fear has no effect on my rage. There is nothing that can allow me to forgive this betrayal. If I'd known about this vault, I might have understood—

"Where are you?" Grayson's voice cuts through my thoughts.

"My office. What happened?"

"Don't leave. We'll be right there."

I don't want to find out if this day can get any worse, but I have a feeling I don't have a choice in the matter.

I point toward the door and glare at my mother. "Unless you have something useful to share, you need to go and tell my father that I'll deal with him later. He also better be ready to show me that vault and tell me everything that's missing so we figure out what we're up against. Anything less is unacceptable and that's coming from his king, not his son."

She nods respectfully, casting her eyes down. "Of course."

As she slips out of the room, the smallest part of me feels bad for treating her that way, but too much shit has been thrown at me in the last twelve hours. I can't weaken now, not even for my mother.

"Asher." Isla says my name sharply, but when I turn around, she's holding her arms open.

I walk into them without a second thought. "What the fuck is happening around here? I don't know what I'm supposed to do." I shudder within her strong hold. "If I thought you'd forgive me, I'd take you and run away, leaving all this behind, if it meant keeping you safe."

"I know, my love," she says quietly. "But we're not going to do that and one way or another, this is all going to sort itself out. I just need you to be strong a little longer without killing anyone who may not deserve it. Now, tell me why you kicked your mother out?"

"Your father, and I would assume sister since he said 'we,' are headed here." Gods, please don't let what they want to talk about be anything other than something that gets us closer to the end of this mess. "I knew I needed a minute to calm down before they got here. That wasn't going to happen with *her* in the room."

She pushes me back until she can see my face. "Just remember, your mother loves you and you love her. You can deal with your father in your own way, but give your mom some grace. She came to you as soon as she could."

That's easier said than done, but Isla is the only light in my life right now. I have to try harder to believe in her and her newfound faith that everything is going to somehow work out.

I press my forehead against her, soaking up her strength and trying to steady my breathing. Our bond pulses between us, easing my tension ever so slightly. I really would be okay if it were just me and her, for the rest of our lives. There is nothing more I need in this life than to feel her warmth and love, giving me a reason to live.

All too soon, my door crashes open. As soon as Grayson and Estee slip inside, they close the door behind them, and just like that, the sliver of peace I was attempting to grasp on to is ripped away.

"I remember how I died," Estee announces. "I went to Elyn and asked her to kill me like she did Isla—"

My mate cuts her off. "Why didn't you tell me before? Are you okay?"

Estee waves a hand in the air. "There isn't time for that. I remember. I saw *everything*." She trembles with palpable fury. "We need to get to the basement now."

"You know who killed you?" Isla demands before I can.

"Yeah. Declan, but that's another problem to deal with after we're done," she says, reaching for her sister's wrist.

I step between them, my chest letting out a warning growl. "Why? What did you see?"

Grayson pulls her back to his side. "I told you to explain everything before you rushed them. He needs to know."

"And I want to make sure I don't get sent back to Earth," she snips, rolling her eyes. "Excuse me for being concerned with being lost for a few more centuries."

"Estee, what are you talking about?" Isla says, clinging to me. Though I'm not sure if she's holding so tightly to my arm because she needs my presence or because she doesn't want me to unleash my simmering wrath on her sister.

"Declan is just a pawn," she says. "Just like I was. He killed me, but it was as if he wasn't in his right mind. His eyes were black just like you said mine were and he didn't speak a word. He found me at the falls and stabbed me in the chest, then drug me back to the castle."

My eyes narrow, glancing between Estee and Isla. "How do you remember that if Isla doesn't?"

"I fought back." She shrugs. "Well, sort of. I remember seeing the glint of the blade under the sun and trying to dodge out of the way. I went down quickly, and my body felt paralyzed, but my mind was still aware until he dumped me in the basement. More importantly, until we get down there and remove the daggers from our bodies, we're still cursed."

Fucking hell. While this isn't more bad news, we're still no closer to figuring this out. Though at least Isla will be a little safer with this information.

Estee was right. We need to get to the basement now.

CHAPTER THIRTY-SIX

ISLA

As we're racing toward the basement, I try to recall every detail about the day I was killed. I want to know if Declan was there and whether he had black eyes then as well. I still can't see the other person in my room, but I do put more pieces together.

We're running down the stairs, but I don't wait to share. "They used the secret passageways."

"Who?" Dad asks, keeping pace right behind me.

"Whoever was in the room with me," I say, my heart racing. "I was alone in my room when I walked in to call the kitchen about arranging dinner. It also explains why nobody saw me leave or be taken out. I never left the castle that day or any day after if Estee is correct."

Asher looks over at me, a dark look in his eyes, but he doesn't say anything.

"We better still be there," my sister practically growls. "If we don't break this curse, who the hell knows whom we can trust if Noen is screwing with people's will."

"It wasn't Noen," Asher says just as I open my mouth to say the same thing.

"What?" Estee gapes. "When did you figure that out and where is he, then?"

"This morning," I say. Then I add, "It was safer to leave him in the holding room, but maybe we can let him out after this."

I have no idea if that's true, but suddenly, I feel like Asher isn't sharing something.

"What are you thinking?" I ask through our bond link.

"That I'd really like to finally fucking kill someone." He doesn't say anything more and because we get to the basement door, I don't get to press him.

Asher grabs the handle, but it doesn't budge.

"Do we need a key?" I ask, assuming he's at least had access to this space throughout his time as king.

His growl is low and deep. "No, we need a new door."

As I ask for clarification, he lifts his leg and slams his booted foot through the wooden door. It shakes but doesn't even crack. That doesn't deter my mate, though. He repeats the action two more times, and once it finally fractures, he charges forward, crashing through with his shoulder taking the brunt of the impact. Wood splinters fly around us, but that's the least of my worries.

"Asher!" I call out, but he doesn't seem the least bit fazed as he gets up.

"I'm fine." He grabs my hand, ignoring the slivers from the door that protrude from his shoulders as he pulls me forward.

I expect him to let go, but the space is dark and his grip only tightens.

My wolf comes to the surface, helping me to see.

There are stacks of crates, their labels covered in dust and cobwebs, as if this space has remained untouched for decades. The walls are made of brick with crumbling mortar between them, yet nothing has fallen out of place. Old, ceramic vases are stacked past the crates, along with what I can assume are paintings covered by canvases.

Estee steps next to us and points to the left. "Back there, I'm pretty sure."

I expect to feel some sort of pull since it's my body down here, but there's nothing, not even a nudge or a recollection of having ever been in this part of the castle.

We move around the boxes, doing our best not to touch anything, but that's hard when Asher won't let go of my hand.

Dad reaches for my shoulder, causing me to glance back at him. His face is lined with tension and he's trembling.

"What's wrong?" I ask, forcefully removing Asher's hold from me so I can pay attention to my father.

"This is a lot to process and..." He seems to choke on his words. "I don't know why any of this happened and while I'm more grateful than I hope you will ever understand to have the two of you back, I wish your mother were here with us."

Tears burn in my eyes, and I nod. Even with the gift of my memories back, so much has happened since then that I haven't had the time to grieve what I've lost. I've only been thankful for what I've gotten back. There hasn't been time for anything else.

Yet the moment my mother's face comes to my mind, I throw my arms around my dad. "I'm so sorry you had to endure all of this alone, but selfishly, I'm glad you managed to find the strength to hang on. Without you, I don't know that I would have opened my mind to believing I belonged here and that would have been the biggest mistake of my life."

He sniffles against my shoulder. "I almost didn't."

"But you did and we're going to get through this," I promise him as I pull back. "And if there's a way to bring Mom back, we're going to find it, okay? And I know I haven't been around for you these last couple of days, but once all this is sorted, I'm going to be in your life so much, you'll be sick of me."

"Oh, sweet girl. That could never happen."

We hug again and I don't want to let him go, but the need to know if my sister's and my bodies are still here is too big to ignore.

When I turn back around, Asher has only moved about ten feet ahead and has his back to us. Even though I know he can still hear us, I appreciate him attempting to give us a bit of privacy.

"Over here," Estee calls out.

This time, it's me who holds on to Asher. The thought of seeing my corpse suddenly doesn't sound so appealing. Yet there's no chance of backing out now.

We come around another stack of crates and in the far recesses of the basement, there we are. Me and Estee, lying side by side as if we're sleeping, our bodies perfectly preserved. I'm wearing the same blue dress I had on when Asher returned home on my final day and Estee has on a black skirt and white blouse. Neither of us even have a speck of dust on us, as if the dark magic from the daggers sticking out of our chests has repelled everything around us.

"That's fucking creepy," Estee mutters.

"Agreed," I say and I don't step any closer until Asher does. When he bends to pull the blade out, I stop him. "What does breaking the curse entail once that dagger comes out? This is dark magic, right? It can't be that simple, not if we've been kept half alive this whole time."

Estee kneels next to her former self, inspecting her face. "Elyn just said to remove the dagger. I didn't ask any questions after that."

"I can go back and find her," Dad says, his gaze averted.

"No," Asher chimes in. "Look at Isobella's hands, even her face. They're ashy. She was never that pale before."

As much as I don't want to, I step closer to my body. There's no warmth coming from me, yet I can still feel Estee's. "What's different between us?"

"You died two days ago," Asher says. "I think when Elyn stopped your hearts that a part of the curse was already broken. I have no idea what that would mean if you died again, but I don't think you're linked to these bodies any longer, not after seeing how yours is only recently deteriorating."

"I think you're right," Estee says, placing a hand over her body's chest. "I'm still warm, but if we want to be sure, we can wait to see what happens to me in another day."

For someone who was so insistent on getting down here, I'm surprised to hear her provide that option. At least until she adds, "Might be fun to stand guard over myself and see what happens."

She is insufferable sometimes. Still, I wouldn't change a single thing about her.

"I don't think that's a good idea," Dad says, still staying behind me. "We either need to take the daggers out and trust the elder wolf knows what she's talking about, or we need to move the bodies to a safer place."

"We pull the daggers out." Asher's gaze is still locked on my corpse. "Elyn hasn't been wrong yet and I'm not going to chance losing Isla to Earth again, where it might take years to find her again without the use of magic there. It took three centuries for the two of you to find each other again. I can't…"

I place my hand on his shoulder and turn him toward me. "No matter what happens, I'll always find you again. Don't give up hope."

"Never," he murmurs, fear and love passing between the two of us.

"Oh, hell." Estee groans. "Let me do the honors. If I don't die, then we'll know Isla is safe."

When she says it like that, I no longer agree with taking the risk. I move to stop her, but she's grinning at me, hand already wrapped around the hilt. "You deserve happiness, little sister."

"No!" I shout at the same time as Grayson, but it's too late.

She pulls the dagger out of her dead body's chest, then sucks in a breath. I watch in horror as she stiffens, drops the dagger, and falls to the ground, next to her corpse.

"Estee," I cry with a gasp. "No, no, no. This can't be happening."

I shove past Asher, going to my sister, my best friend. I roll her over, inspecting her body. When I don't sense a heartbeat, I start shaking her shoulders. "Damn it, Estee. Why couldn't you have been patient?"

Holding her to my chest, I weep over both her bodies. I equally hate and love her right now. I can't believe she did this for me, yet I shouldn't have been surprised.

Dad and Asher kneel next to us, each placing a hand on her, both shaking with grief that threatens to choke me.

Suddenly, I can't sit here anymore. I have to stand, I need space and air and…vengeance.

No, I need *blood*.

First, from Elyn for telling my sister what to do without warning of what would happen, then from the asshole who started all this, whoever they are.

Pushing to my feet, I step away from the bodies and jerk my hand back when Asher tries to grab me. "Isla, stop," he half-demands and half-pleads.

"No. I'm going to find the elder wolf and then I'm going to kill her." My gaze narrows on my mate. "And if you try to stop me, you're not going to like the consequences of your actions."

"So dramatic," Estee says with a cough from the floor. "I appreciate the willingness to avenge my death, but it's not necessary. At least not this one."

All the air leaves my lungs and I drop to my knees next to my sister. Once again, I'm weeping, except this time, it's with relief. "Don't you ever fucking do that again."

She tries to shake a finger at me. "Language, little sister. That's no way for a queen to speak."

Dad helps her sit up, tears still falling down his face as well. "You're lucky that's all she said for what you just put us through. Consider yourself grounded for the next decade."

She leans her head against his chest. "I think I can be cool with that, but we should probably finish the task at hand first." She nods toward her old self, moving farther back. "I'm turning to ash and that dagger is putting off a lot of heat."

"What happened when you pulled the blade out of yourself?" Asher asks, joining us.

She shrugs. "I don't remember, really. It was like someone shocked me and I was shrouded in darkness for a bit until I heard Isla talking about murder."

He looks at me, pulling me up. "I really fucking hate this, but seeing as how her body is disintegrating right now, I don't think we have a choice."

I glance back to find Estee's old self beginning to crumble as if she's been turned to stone. Cracks form on her skin, growing deeper until pieces of her turn to dust. I shudder and turn away, not needing to see that, regardless of the fact that I know the current her is fine now.

"Don't let me go," I tell him, then I look around at my sister. "Care to do the honors?"

She grins wickedly, a sight I hope to have around for many more centuries. "You know it."

Asher picks me up, cradling me in his arms. "I love you, Issie."

"I love—"

The last thing I hear is Estee saying "oops" and then... fire.

She fucking lied, and I can't blame her.

My entire being feels as though it's being turned inside out, then held over coals. I can't breathe, nor can I move or scream. I'm trapped in a cacophony of suffering that pounds within my mind, branding me with the shadow of a life I never got to live.

Bones begin to break, snapping over and over again,

like I'm trying to shift, but my body's confused, unable to find the form that matches the spirit within me.

My wolf's howls sound in the distance, but they're too far away.

Panic claws at my insides. I can't feel her within my chest or my mind. There's a hollowness that overtakes the torment, proving that things can always get worse.

I open my mouth to scream for help, but no sounds escape me.

I'm trapped and alone and…Asher.

Leaving him again isn't right. I can't hurt him like that. I promised him that everything would be fine. I promised myself that I wasn't going down without a fight this time.

I won't give up so easily. Not again.

Picturing Asher, I search for our bond, for the tether that I know exists within me. He's here somewhere and no amount of stabbing pains are going to stop me from getting back to him.

"I'm coming, Asher."

There's a flicker of light and I reach for it, kicking and screaming as I attempt to swim through the depths of this hell that are relentless in their attempts to break me.

Dying isn't an option. I focus on Asher, my dad, and Estee, knowing that if I don't come back, Estee's life would be the next one snuffed out because Asher would never forgive her. Worse, she could never forgive herself.

The glow of warmth comes closer and as I push forward with all my might, there's a whisper of a voice, taunting me.

"Life was just the way it was supposed to be. You came back and ruined everything, but I can still fix this. I'm going to fix everything."

"I'm going to fix everything."

Tension seeps deep within me, reaching my soul and my mind as a memory comes back to me. I've heard those exact words before. Except the voice wasn't clear before, and I was so weak, but not any longer.

"The hell you are," I reply back, having no clue if he can hear me, but it doesn't matter.

I know who killed me now.

CHAPTER THIRTY-SEVEN

ASHER

Seconds pass as I hold Isla in my arms. I'm trying to remain calm, but as more has been revealed this morning, I've begun to realize that the number of people who could be responsible for all of this is now narrowed down to just a few.

Thanks to my mother telling me about the vault of dark objects and only the king plus at least one of the advisors having access, I've realized that my father is someone I can't ignore as a person who might have orchestrated my mate's death. Then there are his top advisors, one of which is still on my council today, and who has never once mentioned this vault to me. Yet I have no doubt that they know of its existence.

My mother could have been right that nobody told me for fear of me losing myself to the dark magic, but regardless of that reason, one of those three men has something to do with this, even if it was unknowingly so.

At some point, one of them revealed the vault's contents or took it upon themselves to take what they wanted. I'm going to figure out who, then I'm going to kill whoever dared to harm my mate.

Even if that person is my own flesh and blood.

There are a million scenarios in which someone could have thought taking Isla away from me was a good idea, but assuming I know which might be true isn't going to do me any good.

I know what needs to be done next and I won't rest until I have the truth.

Summoning a god isn't done lightly, but I'm going to tempt them with the dark objects and hope that will be enough incentive for them to tell me who killed my mate.

They may not do much with our world that they created any longer, but they somehow always know everything that's happening. They've proven that over the years by randomly appearing, doing as they believe is best when it suits them.

As far as I know, it's been centuries since that's happened, so maybe I'm wrong, but something tells me that our creators want to keep an eye on us. They may have decided we no longer need them, but they're not idiots. They've seen our strength. Pretending wolf shifters don't exist would be ill-minded on their part. Something I've rarely known our gods to be.

"She should be awake by now," Grayson says, concern etched into his face.

I've been so preoccupied with my racing thoughts that I haven't been paying attention to the time that's passed.

Isla is still within my arms and her heart doesn't beat, but her body is still warm and her cheeks are flushed. "How long has it been?"

"Twice as long as Estee was out," he answers, then he looks at her. "What aren't you telling us?"

Estee is staring hard at her sister, fingers twisting in front of her. "She can do this. Just give her another minute."

"*Do* what?" I demand, trying to not get angry so that Isla doesn't have to feel my discontent when she comes to.

"Just wait," Estee says, still without tearing her gaze away from my mate.

My chest begins to rattle with the force of the rumble building there, but before I can rip into her, Isla gasps, gaining my full attention.

Her eyes are wide as she blinks rapidly, confusion seeming to weigh heavily on her. "I'm alive."

"Yes, love." I hold her closer. "No thanks to your sister."

"You wouldn't have let me pull the dagger out if you'd known it would hurt her," Estee says and she's not wrong. I would have found another way, if there had been one.

Isla rubs her fingers over the side of her head. "Everything feels fuzzy in my memory. How long was I out?"

"Maybe five minutes," Estee says, coming closer. "Do you remember the pain?"

She shakes her head, then wiggles out of my arms but starts to sway. I grab on to her again, keeping her tucked into my side. "Let's take things easily. First things first, we need to get out of here and I need to summon a god."

All stares land on me, just as I assumed they would. "Why?" Grayson asks first.

"Because the curse on them might be broken now, but those dark objects still exist," I explain. "I'm going to bring a god here to either destroy them or take them back to their world. We have no use for them here."

"What if we need one to kill whoever did this to us?" Isla asks, and I want to tell her I don't believe we do, but then she'll ask how I might know that. Considering my father is one of the people I think could have taken her from me, I'm not willing to say anything until I know for sure.

Mostly because if I think too hard about this, I might end up killing all three of them just because I can.

"We won't. Now, let's get out of here," I tell her as I reach for the daggers on the ground and tuck them into my back pocket before picking Isla up to carry her out of here.

"You're not telling us something," Grayson says through our mind link.

"There's nothing to say yet," I promise him, which isn't a lie. *"I'm going to do everything I can to keep Isla safe. I assure you that."*

I can feel his eyes burning into the back of my head as we walk and his voice carries through my mind. *"Just remember that keeping Isla safe means keeping you alive as well. Don't put yourself at risk by believing you have to do this alone. Summoning a god is a gamble at best."*

I cut the connection with him because there's nothing else that I can say without revealing too much and he might be family, but I'm still his king. I'm going to do this.

All of my instincts are screaming at me that this is the best path forward and I'm going to trust them, just like I did for all those years that I spent believing my mate was out there somewhere, waiting for me.

She may not have known it, but my soul never let me

forget. Though, my chest constricts, knowing she was literally under my feet all this time. Maybe not her soul, but a piece of her, and I'd never known. I hadn't sensed her the way I should have if we'd been officially bonded. Maybe if I'd pushed harder...

I shake my head. I can't do that now. Not when there's still so much to do and there's no changing the past.

We exit the basement, moving quickly through the castle until we get to my suite. I walk in and set Isla on the couch. She hasn't said much since waking back up, except that things are fuzzy, but she still seems to know who we are. Everything else, we can figure out later.

As I get her some water from the bar cart, I address Grayson and Estee. "The three of you need to stay in this room while I'm gone. Do not open the door for anyone, not even my father or mother. Do you understand?"

Estee shudders. "You don't have to tell me twice. Dying twice in one day is enough for me. We have no clue who else might be being controlled by dark magic."

No, we don't, which is why it's so hard for me to leave Isla when I know Estee was previously one of those people.

Still, I know this is what I must do.

I go back to Isla and hold the ice water to her lips. "Drink this, love."

She only takes a few small sips. "I feel really tired."

Estee slides in next to her and yawns dramatically. "You and me both. If we're going to be trapped in this room, we might as well nap. Who knows what tonight will bring?"

If I have my way, *death*, followed by peace.

"Your sister is right." I kiss Isla's head. "Get some rest. I'll be back as soon as I can be."

She nods, her eyes growing heavier by the moment.

I turn to Grayson, knowing I can count on him, but also hating that I'm leaving right now. "Don't take your eyes off them. Don't even let them use the bathroom with the door closed. I don't care if that curse is broken or not. I won't lose my mate again."

"You know I'll protect my girls with my life." His eyes glance over my shoulder, focusing on his daughters. "Nothing will happen to them if I can help it."

"Use the communications unit on my desk if anything happens," I tell him. "Mali and Cain will be able to reach me while I'm at the portal cave."

"Let's hope you're back before I need to do that."

As I look back at Isla, her eyes are already closed and her chest moves steadily. Still, every step toward the door is physically painful.

Yet I don't stop.

I know what I need to do and I should have done this days ago, maybe then Declan wouldn't be on the run and Noen wouldn't be locked in the holding cell. I'm tempted to let him go, but I don't want anyone to think I've changed my mind about considering him a suspect.

The risk of the real murderer running is too great, which is why I decide I also can't explain to anyone what I'm doing.

Grayson wasn't wrong. Calling for a meeting with a god is a gamble, but I have a feeling fate is on my side, finally. I have to believe that Isla came back for a reason, and this is it. To stop whatever happened to her from happening to anyone else here ever again.

With one more glance at my now-sleeping mate, I head out of the suite, locking the door behind me. It's time for some answers.

As I race through the castle, ignoring the staff, I reach out to Cain. *"I need you to shut down the portal. If we have anyone coming back soon, they either need to get home now or wait."*

"Yes, Your Majesty," he replies. *"May I ask for how long?"*

"For as long as I need it. I'll be there in five minutes."

I can sense his shock. It's not often I use the portal since going to the other worlds has never held an interest for me. Our kind has rarely been welcomed by the other shifters and magic users. Still, I never prevented our people from exploring. We live long lives here. I know being stuck on these islands isn't for everyone.

Cain has been our master gate keeper since before I was alive. He's soon to retire and has been testing replacements. While he only has one role in our world, it's an important job. This portal is the only one in Lunara and all four kingdoms must agree with the new chosen keeper.

Cain's eventual retirement from the job is a day that I'm not looking forward to because getting all four rulers to agree on the same thing hasn't ever been easy, especially when one island benefits most.

In this instance, I have more say because the portal is in Polaris. My people are more at risk and that's not something I take lightly.

Though that's a problem for another day. Once I'm outside, I shift, ignoring the wide-eyed stares of my people as my wolf snarls and races his way through the castle grounds. I'll explain as much as I can later. Right now, I can't worry about being proper. Not when I need answers more than my next breath.

"The portal is shut down, King Asher," Cain says. *"I have Sampson here with me. Shall I send him away?"*

Sampson is one of the potential replacements. Even though Cain seems to trust him, this is too big to have more people present than needed.

"Yes," I reply, then I cut the connection and reach out to Malimorte. *"Are you still with Noen?"*

"I am, Your Majesty," he replies immediately.

"Find someone else to take over, and if you can't, leave him there alone. He's not going anywhere," I say, knowing Isla was right and if she hadn't wanted to speak with him first today... I might have killed one of my best friends.

"Understood, sire," he replies without question.

"Once you've done that, go to the portal with a comm unit, and stand guard with Cain," I add. *"I'm going to be summoning a god and I'm not to be interrupted for any reason or by anyone except Grayson. He's the only one with the authority to demand you interrupt me. Do you understand?"*

"Yes, my king." He pauses, then asks, *"Is there a threat we should be aware of?"*

"Only to my mate, it seems."

I arrive at the portal and Cain stands outside the doorway, dressed in full uniform and holding his staff that powers the portal. He bows as I shift back to human form. "King Asher."

"Malimorte will be here soon to stand guard with you," I tell him. "I'm going inside to summon a god. Unless you sense the foundation of our world at risk, I'm not to be disturbed. The only person who may say otherwise is Grayson Blackwood, and only him. If anyone else shows up to stop me, you have my permission to put them down by any means necessary."

He swallows roughly. "Yes, Your Majesty. Take the second opening on the left and you'll find a room already prepared for such a task on the right."

"Thank you, Cain."

He bows again as I walk by him. As I enter the cavernous space, light begins to diminish, but that's not a problem for me as I pass the stone platform for the portal and take the second path, as Cain suggested.

The rock walls are covered in moisture and the temperature drops the farther I get from the main area. I start to wonder if I took the wrong path and nearly turn around when I finally see the shadow of another room.

Slipping through the narrow entryway, I find myself in a ten-by-ten room with a raised stone basin at the center of it. Next to that is a small table with an unlit candle and a bowl of water, nearly everything I need to summon the gods.

I strike the match against the basin and light the candle. Its soft glow confirms there's nothing else in this room with me besides what's in front of me. Carefully, I pour the water into the shallow stone, then extend one of my claws.

Blessed water and the blood of the reigning monarch. The only two objects needed to summon a god. Now, I just need to hope the right one is listening.

Cutting my wrist, I hold it over the basin and mutter the enchantment to call the powerful soul's presence.

Rogamus superiorem, praesentia postulator, sanguine solucionus.

Seconds tick by and I repeat the words again and again. Still, nothing happens.

I pull the two daggers from the basement from my back pocket and set them on the basin. "I have more of these to offer if you'd quit being so selfish and give me a moment of your time."

"I'd say it's you who's selfish, Asher Josiah Cromwell." A woman's voice echoes around the room. "Let's be honest. You're not here for anyone's benefit other than your own."

"I might be here for my own benefit, but that doesn't mean I don't have something to offer you," I state clearly, unwavering from my position, even though I know I'm no longer alone.

"Yes, the dark objects my brother left behind." She clicks her tongue. "I *might* have a use for them, but I know you need them gone, which confirms what I've always known. Once again, you wolves need me more than I ever needed you."

Aurora.

She chuckles. "Don't seem so shocked that I would answer your call. Remember, you only exist because of me."

While she speaks the truth, I know better. Still, I choose my next words carefully.

"You haven't been in our world for longer than I've been alive, so yes, I didn't expect your presence, but that doesn't mean I'm not grateful for it."

If she's here, I hope that means she's been watching the world that was originally created for her and she'll have the answers I seek.

"Yes, little pup," she says, finally shimmering into

appearance. Sleek, red hair falls over her naked breasts and the only adornment she wears is a diamond-shaped wolf around her neck. "You evolved, stopped begging for belly rubs and returning the sticks. What else might you have been good for?" Her violet eyes rake over me as she licks her ruby-red lips. "Well, I guess now that I'm older, I can think of a few things."

I keep my stare firmly on her face, not wanting to give her any other ideas. Yet before I can say anything else, she steps closer, placing a finger on my shoulder as she twirls around me. "But King Asher, I have so many good ideas."

How did I not know she could read minds? That might have been something passed along then forgotten years ago.

She takes a deep breath next to my cheek. "That's a new development thanks to... Well, we're not talking about me, are we? We're talking about you and your mate and the naughty things your father has been up to."

Her mention of my father fills me with a wrath that leaves me paralyzed. I can't breathe. Hell, I can barely think. My wolf pushes to the surface, a steady growl echoing from me. He's ready for blood and there isn't a part of me that wants to stop him.

"Easy, puppy," Aurora coos. "There is still much to discuss. So, why don't you get comfortable?"

She snaps her fingers and a light flashes within the small space, blinding me. By the time my vision returns, we're no longer in the cave.

Hell, we're not even in Lunara any longer.

"That's right, Asher," Aurora purrs. "You're in my home. Now, be a dear and take your boots off before you dirty my floors." She looks over her shoulder at me as she walks away, the daggers dangling from her fingers. "I won't complain if you decide everything else needs to go as well."

"Not a chance in hell," I mutter.

"Not even for your precious mate?" She cackles, tossing her long tresses over her shoulder. "I'm kidding, Asher. While you're no longer the pets I once desired, I do find your values…interesting. So much so that I'm willing to help you, but there's something you must do for me first."

I tense, not feeling any better than I did a few moments ago as I stand in the doorway of her pristine, white home that I'm pretty sure is floating on a cloud if the bright-blue skies and silvery billows of cloud vapor are as telling as they seem.

"What do you want?" I finally ask, unmoving even as she grabs a sheer robe to somewhat cover herself with.

She grins widely, showing off two rows of perfect teeth. "For you to bite me."

"Why the hell would I do that?"

Her head shakes and she rolls her eyes, as if the answer were so obvious. "So that your entire kingdom doesn't fall, little pup."

CHAPTER THIRTY-EIGHT

ISLA

I don't think I've ever been this groggy and weak in my life. My eyes feel as though there is so much sand in them that they're intent on making a pearl. On top of that, my muscles ache everywhere and the pressure in my head is turning into a fiery roar of pain.

I try to sleep as Asher suggested, but it's not easy. Estee and Dad sit nearby, watching me and whispering, discussing all the things they should and shouldn't do if something is truly wrong with me. Yeah, not helpful.

Throwing the blankets off me, I ever-so-slowly roll over in bed and groan. "I'm taking a shower."

"Oh, not by yourself, you're not," Estee replies, starting to walk toward me from the other side of the room. "I'm going to help…"

I don't hear anything else she says. The pounding in my head drowns out the world and I squeeze my eyes closed, wobbling on the axis of the world.

This isn't good.

My body is falling, yet my arms and legs refuse to do

anything to prevent me from crashing into the hard ground.

With a heavy thud, I not only hit the floor, but my head on the bedframe. I expect another wave of agony to hit me or to even lose consciousness, but instead, the pain begins to recede. At least until I hear Estee's screams and Dad's growls.

"Asher's going to kill us."

"Not if he doesn't find out." Estee's soft hands lift me up. "Is, wake up, damn it."

"I'm trying." My eyelids lift, then immediately close. "It's bright in here."

I hear shuffling, then the movement of the curtains as they're drug across the rail. "That should be better," Dad says.

Chancing the stabbing pain once again, I crack one eye open first. The room is much darker, but still, I don't look for long. "I need to shower."

"That's not happening, little sister," Estee says. "You need to stay in bed until we figure out what's wrong with you."

My skin starts to itch as I shake my head. "I'm telling you, I *need* a shower."

I wince at the growl in my voice, but I can't stay like this. I need to do something, to be clean, to rinse away whatever this is. I have no clue why, but the weight of this pressure and the weariness is too heavy, like a blanket trying to smother me. I have to make it go away any way that I can.

"Just take her before she tries to go by herself again," Dad says.

I try to smile at him, but I'm rather sure it comes out as more of a grimace than anything else.

Estee keeps a tight hold on me, helping me walk toward the bathroom, and I'm forced to keep my eyes closed as a wave of nausea slams into me, making me groan.

My sister stops, but I growl at her and she mercifully keeps moving. I think she's said something, but I can't focus on anything other than keeping the vomit inside me.

The hard tile presses against my back as she sits me down. I hear more murmurs, but nothing is making sense. I don't even have enough strength to keep my body upright and I start to slump to the side, allowing my cheek to rest against the cool floor.

I'm overheated. I need to be free of...everything.

Extending my fingers into claws, I begin to rip my clothes away, not caring when I end up cutting myself in the process. They have to go.

Estee's hands grab on to me, but I kick her away forcefully. "Let me finish."

I don't hear her reply, but within another minute, I'm naked, lying curled into a ball on the floor. My chest heaves as I suck in rapid amounts of air. Maybe this wasn't the right answer.

I can't keep my lungs full. I can barely feel my body. Everything feels like it's on...

"Fire!" Estee's screech finally breaks through as she shoves me into the shower.

Looking back, my clothes are smoking dark black.

Dad bursts into the room, his gaze wide and his face going pale. "That's not a fire. That's dark magic."

He throws a towel over the clothes and picks the pile up, snarling as he takes them away. I don't know where he's going, but I know he's right because the moment I'm free of them and the water is cascading over my naked body, I'm no longer feeling weighed down.

"How the hell did that happen?" Estee asks, but I can't answer her.

Seconds pass and I begin to heal from nearly dying again. I don't know how, but I feel rather confident that my body was slowly shutting down just then. With every new breath I take, my strength and memory return, but with that comes a soul-deep ache, a knowledge I almost wish I didn't know.

Tears fall freely down my cheeks and I shake my head, not wanting to believe what I now remember.

Estee bends down, coming into the shower with me, still fully dressed. "Are you okay?"

"Physically, yes," I manage to say, then I look up at her, my body shivering with the weight of this truth. "I know who's behind our deaths."

She tenses beside me. "How? Who?"

"When you took the dagger out of me, I felt like I was suspended in this weird in-between place," I tell her. "There was pain and the call of death, and I felt so alone, but there was also light. Just as I began fighting harder to reach for it, there was this voice."

She grabs my shoulders, fingers digging into my skin. "Who, Isla?"

The single word feels like razor blades being forced up my throat as I speak it. "Gideon."

"Like Asher's dad, Gideon?" Her eyes widen and her face pales. "You're sure?"

I nod, never more certain of anything before in my life. "He said the same thing to me when he was in the room after you stabbed me. 'I'm going to fix everything.' I don't know what he's trying to *fix* by killing me, but I don't think he's done."

"We have to tell Asher," she says, standing up, but I don't move from the shower floor. "What's wrong?"

"How am I supposed to tell my mate that his own father is responsible for hurting him in the worst way possible?" I shake my head, wishing I never would have pushed to find this information.

Sure, I'd love to fucking strangle Gideon right now, to pluck out his eyes and jab daggers into every inch of his body, but he's not my father.

While he killed me and my sister, he betrayed his son, my mate. The man I care most about in the world is going to have his entire existence rocked.

So more than my fury, my heart is already breaking for what he's going to go through once he finds out.

Asher will kill his father, no matter how fucked up that will be, no matter how much I intend to beg him to let me handle this. He'll need to do this because he'll feel responsible for Gideon's actions.

So, not only will Asher be hurt, but he'll also be branded with guilt, and for those two reasons most, I want to murder Gideon myself.

How could he have done this to his own son? It no longer matters that I lost centuries of my life. The scars this will leave on my mate are all that concern me.

"I need to find Asher." I close my eyes and try to reach him through the bond, but there's no answer there. I can still feel him and he doesn't seem to be in distress, but it's almost like he's nowhere close to me. "Where did he say he was going?"

"He's requesting a meeting with the gods," she says, reaching for me again, but this time, I don't fight her. "Come on. We'll get him back here."

As she pulls me from the shower and grabs a towel for each of us, I almost tell her we should just wait for him to come back on his own. Except that's the part of me that's terrified of hurting the most important person in all the worlds to me.

This truth can't wait to be told. Asher needs to know, not because he deserves to, but because I'm now wondering, who else might Gideon have killed over the years because they didn't fit into his plan?

CHAPTER THIRTY-NINE

ASHER

Aurora pours two drinks, humming joyfully. The pink, bubbly liquid stops just at the edge of the flute before she picks each one up, walking back into the room with the utmost grace.

I expect her to offer one to me, which I would have declined, but instead, she takes both with her to the couch, sipping on the first as she practically floats over the floor.

"So, are you going to take me up on my offer?" she asks once she's settled, ankles crossed and fiery-red hair spread around her shoulders.

I keep my gaze on her violet eyes, considering her robe doesn't cover much, and stay rooted in the same place I arrived at when she brought me here.

"You said before why I should bite you, but you never said *why* you want me to." It's not as if I could turn her into a wolf shifter by doing so. If anything, there's a greater chance of me taking some of her power.

She smirks, peering at me from over her drink. "That's

because the information isn't for you to know, *King Asher*. You'll either do it or you won't. It really doesn't matter to me either way. Just know that if you don't, the dark objects stay in your world and *Father* is going to escape. He's halfway there now. Once that happens, your people will revolt, and it will be the beginning of the end for you. Lunara won't survive another war and that's exactly what this will cost you."

My chest rumbles and I clench my fists. She's a goddess. Easily more powerful than me, even though the energy of her ancestors runs through my veins. I stand a chance of taking her down, but she's not the real enemy here and I need to get back to my mate. Yet I know I can't leave without accomplishing both things I came here for.

"Smart boy," she coos. "You bite me, and I'll take care of your dark magic issue. Hell, I'll even tell you right where your father is currently hiding with his hostage."

Her being in my head is fucking annoying, but I don't bother to express that for long.

"I will bite you and you won't just 'take care of' the dark objects," I tell her, knowing that deals with the gods need to be clear. "I want to hear you say that you'll remove every single one of them from my world and that they'll never find their way back."

Her head shakes as she chuckles over her drink. "You're smart. I'll give you credit for that, but do you really have what it takes? I can do as you've asked, but will you be able to finish the job? Your father betrayed you, stole your *mate*. Do you believe you'll be able to take his life even for that treachery?"

"Without shedding a fucking tear," I say without a single ounce of hesitation coursing through me.

The moment Aurora confirmed what I already suspected, that man was no longer my father. He's nothing to me. Just a problem to be taken care of and there is nothing in all the worlds that will stop me from doing so.

Aurora's eyes grow dark. "So you think, but maybe we're not as much alike as I thought. I guess we'll see." She moves her hair to the side and cocks her head. "Now, we're wasting time. You'll bite me on the back of the neck and in exchange, I will remove every single dark object from *my* world, never allowing them to reappear. Does that deal agree with you, King Asher Cromwell of Polaris?"

The fact that she still considers Lunara hers is a joke, but I let it go. Technically, she isn't wrong.

"We have a deal."

Energy slithers over me, forcing my body forward, beaconing me toward her without my control. I try to halt my movements, but stabbing pains shoot through my entire being every time I resist.

"You made a deal with a goddess," she explains with a haunting laugh. "There's no backing out now unless you want to spend the rest of your life withering away in agony."

Of course there was a magical binding with that verbal exchange.

My feet don't stop moving until I'm standing behind her couch, looking down at the petite goddess. An image of my hands around her neck flickers through my mind, but it's quickly replaced with Isla's bloodied body.

A roar leaves from deep within me and I'm filled with grief that brings me to my knees.

Aurora peeks over the couch, our faces near level. "If you ever threaten me like that again, the death of your mate will be the least of your problems."

Her voice is saccharine, but the sneer on her face is anything but.

She settles back into her seat and pulls her thick hair out of the way again before pointing to the back of her neck. "Right here. If you miss, you'll have broken your end of the deal and I will have no reason to honor mine."

"How will I know when you do?" I ask, considering I don't even know where the vault is.

"Check behind your Great-Great-Grandfather's portrait on the second floor," she replies. "You'll find a hidden door there and inside is the vault. Your blood will unlock it, as does that of any currently living ruler. Now, do your part before you're in too much pain to be of any use to me."

With forced effort, I push myself up and brace for what I'm about to do. Biting another woman when I have no intention of killing her feels like a betrayal to Isla, but I'm doing this to keep her safe. Something I hope she'll forgive me for.

Aurora sighs, shaking her head. "I can't understand the emotions you beasts developed. Now fucking bite me before I change my mind."

My wolf surges to the surface, intent to rip her jugular out, but I rein him in. *Not today.*

Extending my canines, I open my mouth, hating that I have to get so close to her, but also knowing I have no other option.

Before I change my mind, I do as she's asked. The

sharp points of my teeth break through her skin and she sucks in a breath that seems to echo through the room.

I try to pull away, but she reaches back and grabs on to my head, holding me in place. Her fingers massage my scalp and tiny moans escape from her. All while I want to fucking rip her head off.

It's only seconds later, but it feels like minutes before she releases me.

I push away from the couch, sending it five feet in the opposite direction with her still sitting on it. "We're done here."

She stands, hands moving slowly over the curves of her body. "Are we? Don't you feel the power, Asher?"

"I feel fucking furious," I spit out, using the back of my hand to wipe my mouth. "Now, send me home so I can kill my father and make sure you follow through with your end of the deal."

Her face falls. "You really love her."

"Of course I do. Isla is my whole life."

She frowns. "I almost feel bad for not bringing her back sooner. Oh, well." She laughs then appears in front of me, locking my face between her hands. "Use me wisely, King of Polaris."

Her lips crash down onto mine and I lift my hand to slash my claws down the side of her, but my movements are halted. Magic seeps into me, recharging my body to the point I don't know up from down.

Energy courses through me unlike anything ever has before, not even when I finally bonded with Isla. The taste of power fills me, but so does betrayal. This isn't right. Whatever Aurora is doing, I can't do this to Isla.

I start to push the goddess away, knowing this is

exactly why we don't summon them. They're difficult at best and this is far from that.

Except before I can take more than a step backward, my body drops through the floor and in the next second, I'm landing back in the chamber within the cave.

The basin wobbles beside me as I use it to hold myself up and spit out the taste of that woman's blood within my mouth.

My first thought is to go to Isla, but maybe I shouldn't. I can find my father—something Aurora didn't end up revealing, but I don't need her for that—and finish this nightmare, before going to Isla and begging for her forgiveness. If it weren't for her being my mate, I have a feeling her soul would have never been stuck on Earth.

Damn it, why would my father have done this to us? None of this makes sense, yet I feel as if I should have known.

"Asher," Isla's voice calls through our bond. *"My dad won't let me leave this room, but I need to see you."*

"I'm sorry, love," I tell her. *"I need to take care of one more thing and then I'll come for you."*

She's silent for a beat, then adds, *"You know. How?"*

"I'll explain later," I tell her, quickly running toward the cave's exit. *"Just know that I love you and I'm going to make this right."*

"This isn't for you to do on your own, Asher," she pleads with me. *"Don't do this. Let me, or even my father, who is just as eager, finish this."*

I shake my head, even though she can't see me. *"He is my problem, Isla. I'm going to make it right."*

I close off the connection to her, hating that I block her out and knowing it's just another thing I'll need her to forgive me for, but this isn't something she needs to be part of.

I reach out to Grayson as I get to the main section of the portal cave. *"Do not let those two women leave that room for any reason."*

"Her clothes were covered in dark energy, Asher," he replies quickly, wrath in his voice, which I'm not surprised to hear. *"He tried to take her from me again. I won't make any promises to you, but I will do what I think is best for my daughters. Just know, if you're going to end this, you better do it quickly."*

I hear what he's not saying, and I won't hold whatever decision he makes against him. Not when we were all hurt by Gideon's treachery.

Cain is still standing guard, but this time, Malimorte is with him. They both stare at me with wide eyes as I exit the cave.

"What?" I demand, expecting them to have more bad news.

Mali points at me. "You're glowing, Your Majesty."

Looking over myself, I try not to be disgusted by the gift that was given to me. "It's nothing. I need to go. Do not open this portal until I tell you otherwise. I need both of you here keeping guard. If you see anyone approaching, tell me immediately."

They both bow, murmuring their agreements.

I don't give them any other further explanation. My wolf pushes to the surface with a ferocity I haven't sensed in him since Isla was first missing. Our form is taller and wider and more powerful than we've ever been.

As much as I hated Aurora touching me, she did give me a gift. No, more than that. She told me to use her power wisely. I didn't catch that before because she'd also said she could have returned my mate to me sooner, but now, I realize she's given me exactly what I need to finish this.

The unwillingness to give a single fuck about anything other than killing the man responsible for taking my light away.

CHAPTER FORTY

ASHER

I race around the castle, avoiding the main roads in search of my father. With my wolf's nose to the ground and the connection I have to all members of my pack—including Gideon—I know we need to head west, away from home, away from our mate.

Every step becomes heavier until the energy thrumming within our body overtakes even the thoughts of Isla. As much as I know I love her, I can't consider her right now.

I just need to stop this nightmare.

We run, mile after mile, the earth churning beneath our paws with each forceful, lengthening stride. The air, warm against our fur, carries a silence so profound that it seems even the forest creatures sense the shadow of death looming near.

Leaping over the river just before the falls, we pick up Gideon's scent. Though it's changed, become tainted. I might have been able to find him as his Alpha King, but he's barely the man I once knew. This shifter is doused in darkness and backed into a corner.

My wolf surges forward with unwavering resolve, our shared courage unshaken by the dark fate we are about to confront. We race toward Aklo Falls, where the roar of the water does little to mask the sinister presence lurking behind its veil.

My father hides like the coward I now know him to be. He's been the architect behind centuries of problems, yet he's never dirtied his own hands. He used Estee and Declan and who knows who else to harm the people I care about.

This ends today.

My wolf runs forward and leaps through the waterfall at the mountain's base. There's a wall of jagged rocks that we narrowly miss slamming into, but beside that, there's a path leading farther into the mountain.

Before we continue, I demand my wolf to release control. I need my father to know that it's me, his son, who takes his life. Not the animal that lives inside me, not anyone other than his own flesh and blood.

My shift back is seamless, even though I can still sense my restless wolf. He remains close, a vigilant shadow ready to spring forth but respecting my need to do this.

I follow the path and not too much farther forward, I know Gideon isn't alone. My mother is with him.

Gods, if she's known about what he did…

Killing her won't be as easy, but I know there's no stopping with him if so. I can't leave my mate at risk. I can't and won't do that to her.

I continue forward, my gait even and every step sure

of my destination. When I come around the next bend, a sense of peace fills me.

He's here.

Gideon has his back against the side of the mountain and holds a knife to my mother's neck. Yet her expression reveals no fear, only a fierce resolve mirroring my own fury. Something that adds to my relief.

"Son," Gideon says, tightening his arm around my mother's waist.

"You ceased being my father the day you chose to tear my world apart," I reply, my voice steady with cold resolve.

He grinds his teeth together as his head shakes. "You stupid boy. Why can't you see that everything I've done has been to make you a better king?"

A bitter laugh escapes me. "A *better* king? You broke me when you took Isla away!"

He sneers, his disdain palpable. "I tried everything to make you a son I could be proud of. I thought I'd succeeded, I thought that you'd finally become the alpha I made you to be, but you haven't changed one bit. You're still the weak and pathetic boy who could only think of a woman instead of what he was meant to be."

"You never gave him a chance before," my mother says with a snarl. "He was a boy. A boy in love who should have had centuries to prepare to be king, but you stole that from him, just like you stole his mate. I should have known there was nothing—"

The blade against her neck cuts into her skin, drawing a line of blood that disappears beneath the collar of her dress.

An inky smoke forms around the weapon as he roars, "You shut your fucking mouth, woman."

She barely winces from the wound. "I'd rather die than keep your secrets."

"What is it?" I try reaching her through our mental link, but it's as if she were nowhere to be found, even though she's right in front of me.

Gideon must be blocking my ability with one of the dark objects, but that doesn't matter.

"Let her go," I demand, my alpha command amplifying more than normal, likely thanks to Aurora.

He tenses, defiance etched across his aging features. "No. It's too late. I'm not letting her go until you open the portal and let me off this world."

"Not a fucking chance in hell." I growl, taking another step forward.

He just shakes his head at me. "Look at you trying to be the worthy wolf now. It's too late, Son. We both failed and now, you'll either let me go or lose both the women in your life."

"Do you still have Isla?" I ask Grayson, needing to know she's safe.

"Yes, but she's not staying patient and I won't hold her back for long."

At least I know she's not at risk, regardless of what he says. For now, anyway.

"Don't listen to him, Son," my mother says, a tear falling down her cheek. "I failed you for so many years. Don't worry about me any longer."

Easier said than done.

My glare falls on my father again. "I've grown this

kingdom into more than it's ever been, even under your rule. Why couldn't you have left things alone?"

"The moment *she* returned, you were lost," he spats. "You reverted to the boy who couldn't even go a week without getting his dick wet and I couldn't let that stand. I won't watch our kingdom fall because you're too weak to put the crown above your heart."

"Of course I was distracted recently," I snarl, my lip curling. "My mate was gone for five hundred fucking years. I think that taking some time to be with her is more than acceptable. And before, you never even gave me a chance to grow up, to be the man you expected. Something I could have done with Isla by my side. Instead, you stole that from me, set me decades behind, put our home at risk. For what? To prove a fucking point? Well, you lost, Dad. You're the one who failed and now, you're going to lose everything."

He reaches behind his back. "I'd rather lose everything than live with you as a son."

"That's enough!" Isla's voice booms as she joins us.

"I thought you said you had her?" I snarl at Grayson, not removing my stare from Gideon. I don't trust him not to pull some bullshit and try to hurt Isla at the last minute.

"I do. Just not where you assumed," he answers a second after I sense his presence.

Fucking stubborn Blackwoods. I'm sure Estee is somewhere around here as well, but I can't worry about that now.

Gideon chuckles as he grips my mother's hair and tosses her into the side of the mountain. "You're of no use to me any longer."

Her eyes flutter closed and there's a cut on her head

from landing on one of the protruding rocks, but I can still see her chest moving.

"I should have gotten rid of her years ago," he says with disgust, glaring down at her prone form.

My rage increases on my mother's behalf. This has to be the dark objects making him act this way. There's no other possible explanation as to why he would throw her aside as if she means nothing to him, not with them being bonded mates. Still, this is the path he chose and there's no going back. He has to pay for the choices he's made.

"Seems you were too weak to do that yourself, just like you have been with everything else." My chest heaves even as Isla presses her palm to my back.

"Let me help you," she whispers with unrestrained love filtering through our bond.

I start to shake my head, but Gideon speaks before I can move into action.

"Just as I predicted." He holds a shadowy orb within his hands, the dagger now sheathed at his hip. "Your mate is here to finish what you can't. She always outshone you, making you even more pathetic. I couldn't stand to watch that happen. No son of mine would be less than his woman."

Isla steps to stand at my side and takes my hand, the power from Aurora pulsing off her just as I feel it within me, somehow. "That's where you're wrong," Isla says, her voice sure and calm. "You've somehow failed to see your son's worth. Not who he was within your shadow and not as the king, but as the man I know him to be." She lets out a strangled huff. "Even worse, there's probably a part of you that's always known Asher is better than you. You didn't hurt him because he wasn't good enough. You saw his ability to love and be a strong leader at the same time and that terrified you. It was never me that outshone your son. It's your son that outshone you."

His face turns red, darkening with every word my mate has spoken. "You stupid little bitch. I'm going to shut you up for the last time."

He throws the orb toward her and as the sphere travels through the air, the glass encasing the black energy starts to shatter.

"It's a bomb!" Grayson shouts from behind us.

I grab Isla, covering her with my body, knowing that there's no escaping what's about to happen, but I can at least do my best to shield her.

Pinpricks of agony jab into my skin, slicing into me like tiny blades. Tightening my grip on my mate, I draw on every bit of power I hold within me as the Alpha King.

Only that's not all I am right now.

Aurora.

The goddess's energy expands within my chest, spreading through the rest of me until it seeps out of my skin, creating a sort of shield around me. One that extends beyond my body and also shields Isla.

I lift my head, searching for Grayson and Estee, but I don't see them.

"How the…?" Shock colors my father's voice.

I rise once more, standing tall and helping my mate up as well. There's a soft, lavender glow around both of us, somehow absorbing whatever was intent on killing us from that orb.

When I turn around, Gideon is standing there, shrouded in dark energy. His skin is ghostly pale and he trembles with the weight of the power he's chosen over his family.

"You won't win with those," I tell him calmly, a sense of right filling my mind.

His head thrashes back and forth as he reaches for the dagger at his side, one now pulsing the same inky power as the orb. "You're wrong, just as you've always been."

No, *he's* wrong, but more than that, he's no longer anything to me. The man standing before me is a shell of what was once a great king, but at some point, he chose power over love.

It's time to put him out of his misery.

"We're done." The words leave me as I charge forward, intent on ripping his heart from his chest.

Determination and strength ignite deep within me as I leap toward him, claws extended. Except as I swipe out, Isla begins to scream.

Distracted with fear for my mate, I miss my chance to take out Gideon and he dodges me. Before I can register what's happening, he's racing toward Isla, who's on the ground, no longer protected by the goddess's energy.

All it takes is picturing my wolf and his presence takes over, shifting with renewed intensity. We go after Gideon before he can reach our mate, but even with Aurora's power pulsing through our veins, we're going to be too late.

With his blade poised to kill, Gideon aims for Isla, who seems to be overcome with the dark magic and unable to protect herself.

"*No!*" I shout within my own mind, feeling as though my entire being might explode with the force of the gods.

Time feels as if it starts to slow as I watch Grayson

leap in front of his daughter, protecting her from the poisoned blade and taking the hit himself.

"Do as you were always meant to," he says weakly through our pack link. *"Protect my daughter and love her more than your own life."*

"Damn it, Grayson!" My connection to him fades as the veins along his neck turn black. *Fuck!*

Turning my focus back to Gideon, I notice he's not done yet. He's reaching for something in his boot, but I act before he can find whatever he's looking for.

I shift back to my human form and grab the dagger from Grayson's shoulder, doing my best to ignore how Isla is still unmoving on the ground. I can at least still sense her through our bond and that will have to be enough for the moment.

The hilt burns into my palm as I go to Gideon. I grab him by the neck, lifting him from the ground. Black blood trickles from the corner of his mouth and his once-blue eyes are like charcoal as he sneers at me.

"Killing me won't change the fact that you're still pathetic," he says, his voice garbled thanks to the tight hold I have on him.

Instead of wasting my breath, I arch my wrist to carve his heart out, but before I can finish this, I'm distracted with how the dark energy still swarming around us begins to come toward me. My body tenses, waiting for the hit, but it never comes.

The lavender glow still clinging to me expands and it's almost as if the energy from Aurora is drawing the black magic in. I can feel its weight pressing in around me just before the power starts to move down my arm and toward the dagger I still hold.

I can hear Estee's shouts behind me. She must not have been able to come any closer after the orb exploded. She cries for both her father and sister, but I can't do anything for them yet.

Looking into Gideon's dark eyes, I realize the man before me hasn't been my father in centuries. He might have even been lost before I was born, pretending to be a sage king, fooling even his own mate, but it's over now. I don't know why he chose this path and I don't need to, but there is something I need to tell him before I end this nightmare.

"I forgive you, Dad. Whatever brought you to this point, whatever allowed this darkness to take hold of you, I hope you find peace with that, but for taking my mate, there's a price to be paid."

A crease forms between his furrowed brows, and I know he's heard me. That's enough.

With the power of Aurora and the dark energy now pulsing through the dagger, I don't wait for his response. I drive the tip through his chest, straight into his heart.

As the blade burrows deeper, the dark cloud of black magic moves from me to him, consuming his body with a finality that I know he won't come back from.

"Be at peace," are my final words to him and I truly mean them.

As furious as I was before, hearing how bitter and power-driven he was changed everything for me. I don't want to hold on to this hatred. I just want to be with my mate, like I always should have been.

He turns to ash right in front of me and the moment he's gone, so is Aurora's energy along with the dagger.

While I'm thankful for what it did just now, I hope to never feel her essence within me again.

I turn around and my chest constricts at the sight of Grayson's lifeless form lying next to Isla. Estee sits between them, holding on to the only family she has left in this world.

My mate begins to stir and I'm at her side in the next second. She blinks rapidly, her eyes wide with fear. "What happened?" Estee sobs louder, answering the question before I can.

Isla's gaze finds her father's lifeless body. Her shoulders go rigid and when I reach to hold her, she shakes me off. "No."

I'm sorry, love. I'm so fucking sorry," I tell her through the bond as I helplessly watch her shake Grayson's body, begging for him to wake.

Even with Gideon's death, there's no victory here.

"Dad!" Isla cries louder, holding his limp form to her chest.

Estee clings to her as they weep together. I wrap my arms around both of them, attempting to hold all the pieces together, even though I know it's impossible.

Movement catches my attention a moment later and I blink away my own tears until I see my mother beginning to sit up. With everything else, I forgot she'd been tossed aside, but Gideon doing that might have unknowingly saved her life.

She covers the lower half of her face as our stares meet and she sobs along with us.

CHAPTER FORTY-ONE

ISLA

There is only soul-crushing anguish as Estee and I hold our father's unresponsive body in our arms. I only just got him back. I didn't have near enough time with him. I'm not ready to lose him again, not so soon.

Yet I know in that moment the dagger pierced his skin, he was gone. And with the way his veins turned black, this isn't the same as what took the two of us out. No, this was meant to end a life, not to curse one.

Though he can be reborn. We can wait and see him again one day. It might take decades, and this is still heartbreaking, but this isn't the end. I hope.

Maybe I'm wrong and he's cursed to never return, especially since the dagger was meant for me, but I can't think that way. Not when I was so close to having almost everything back.

Asher's fingers wrap around my shoulder. "I'm so sorry, Isla. I don't know how he moved so fast, but your dad, he saved your life when I might have been too late."

"We can't control fate," I tell him, doing my best

not to be consumed with grief and, thanks to our bond, knowing Asher is also battling with guilt, I add, "None of this is our fault. Not mine or yours. At least it's over now." I glance back down at my father. "We'll see him again, one day, and I know this is what he wanted. He knows we're at peace and safe and now he can be too."

Estee holds Dad's hand tighter. "Daddy, please come back. I know Mom is there, but we still need you. Tell the gods you want to come home."

There's a chance he'll stay for Mom, but maybe, considering the power Asher was just wielding, we can get both of them back.

With that hope in mind, I turn to my mate, moving to stand. He helps me and we take a few steps away from Estee. "Why were you glowing—"

My words are cut off as Sosheena limps toward us. She's gasping for breath through her tears and keeps her eyes on the ground. There's blood on her face and thanks to her pale skin, she looks decades older than she did... Gods, was that really just this morning when I last saw her?

She's not speaking even as Asher tries to talk to her. Her feet barely lift from the ground as she walks, hiccupping through the tears. Even though Gideon turned out to be a vicious man, my heart still hurts for her. It breaks for the woman who just lost her mate, who realized her whole life was a lie, and now, needs to find a way forward.

For the years I knew Sosheena while I was growing up here, she was always a strong woman whom I could look up to. She might feel shattered just like the rest of us do right now, but she'll make it through this. We'll make sure of it.

Asher speaks softly to her and I stand quietly by, feeling lost yet at peace all at once. None of this seems real, maybe because I never would have suspected Gideon could hurt his family like this, or because I'm not ready to process that I've just lost my father. Either way, I stand there, numb to the world around me.

Malimorte's auburn wolf arrives just a minute later. The lone shifter transforms to his human form and, without uttering a word, takes Sosheena from Asher and begins to walk from the bloody scene with her safely tucked against his side.

Asher turns to me and wraps me in his arm, muttering his apologies again.

I hug him back, clinging to the love he has for me like a lifeline. "I don't blame you for any of this. Please don't apologize for something that isn't your fault. No matter how much I might grieve for my father in the coming days, I know in my heart that I'll never hold you responsible, so you can't, either."

His head shakes against mine and his chest rumbles. "I forgave him because I didn't want to be bitter like him, but I hate that you're hurting, that none of this would have ever happened if I weren't your mate."

Pulling back enough to see his face, I look sternly into his sapphire eyes. "You have been the best part of my life. Even if our moments have been brief, that's not your fault. You gave your father your forgiveness—now you need to give it to yourself. You've always been better than him and deep down, he knew that. It was his own insecurities that did this, ones that are likely responsible for whatever choices brought us to this day. Not you or me or us."

He presses his forehead against mine and breathes me in. "You might need to keep reminding me of that as I'm forced to clean up the messes he's made." He tenses and holds me tighter. "Declan."

Oh, hell. I forgot he'd gone on the run. What if Gideon already got to him?

"The dark magic lifted from his mind," Asher explains before my thoughts can get too out of control. "He's been hiding under a literal rock ever since he attacked you."

"Tell him to come home," I say, knowing there isn't a single part of me that holds him responsible for the things he was forced to do.

"Already done." Asher crushes me against his chest, the vibrations growing from deep within, moving from him to me. "Fuck, Issie. I almost lost you again."

"Care to explain how you were wielding god energy?" I ask, keeping my head against his chest, listening to his racing heart, in hopes of keeping mine from completely breaking.

I can feel his cringe move through his whole body. "When I summoned the gods for a meeting, Aurora appeared. She might have kissed me before I left and temporarily transferred some of her power to me."

Now, it's my turn for my chest to rumble. My teeth grind together and growl. "I'll fucking kill her for touching you."

Asher's hands smooth over my back as nothing but love flows through our bond. "I thought the same thing, but I don't know that I would have been able to kill my father without her. Let's just be grateful this is over now."

Easier said than done, especially when I know this is far from *over*.

My mate takes my hand and together, we face the biggest loss of the day.

I'm not ready to say goodbye. I'm not ready to admit this is real, that my father is dead, but I know I don't have a choice.

Though as much as I want to break down, I have a feeling that between Asher and Estee, that moment is going to have to wait for me.

I reach for my sister with my free hand. "We need to take him back to the castle."

She shakes her head. "No, he's going to come back."

"Maybe," I tell her softly. "But not in this body. He's gone and we need to release his soul so he can make his choice."

She looks up at me, her eyes swollen and red. "What if he stays with Mom? What if we've lost both our parents?"

Asher releases his hold on me, and I bend down to hug Estee. "Then we get to know how lucky we were to have them for the time we did and be thankful they're at peace, together again. We'll still have each other, no matter what happens next."

She nods against my shoulder, her body shaking. "I don't know how you're being so strong right now, but I'm really glad because I don't think I can be."

"I know," I tell her with a smile she can't see. "You've been the big sister for long enough. It's time I pulled my weight."

"I love you, Is." She sniffles. "We don't say that enough, but I need you to know how grateful I am that I found you again and that we made our way back home together."

"I know, and I love you, too." I kiss the side of her head, then pull her upward. "Come on. Let's go home."

Asher is still right there beside us. He picks up our father without saying a word and we leave Gideon's ashes behind. At least we won't have to burn him ourselves.

His death, while welcome, is a disgrace and when he appears before the gods, they'll know. I just hope they don't give him a choice to come back and make up for the horrible things he's done. Asher deserves to live the rest of his lives without worrying about his bastard of a father trying to interfere in our lives ever again.

RIGHT AFTER SUNSET, ESTEE, ASHER, AND I LEAD A procession of people through the town and toward the beach. My dad's body has been prepared and blessed and now it's time to say goodbye.

Estee hasn't stopped crying since we left the waterfall. Even when she's yelling, there are still tears. Her grief weighs down on me along with Asher's guilt at what's been lost and the mess that still needs to be cleaned up, but I keep reminding him that we have time and we need to be thankful for what did go right.

Aurora followed through on her part of their deal. The dark objects are all gone, the vault empty of anything sinister. Plus, our pack isn't in an uproar over the betrayals from Gideon, and the threat against us is gone. At least for now. Of course, once word gets out about the duplicity within our own kingdom, the others may talk and someone might think we've weakened, but that's the farthest thing from the truth.

Our sadness doesn't show how vulnerable we are—it shows how fiercely we love. And we will fight to the death to protect our family. I hope that's what anyone else sees when they hear about what happened here. If they think otherwise, they're in for the fight of their lives.

We arrive at the shoreline where we will give our father the sendoff he deserves. My hands shake and there is a pain in my chest unlike anything I've ever felt, but there is also peace. I don't know how I know, but everything is going to be okay.

Somehow, we're going to get through this hardship and we're stronger because of it. Maybe it's shock from everything we've been through, or just an overwhelming desire to no longer worry, but I'm choosing to believe this sense of unity is only the beginning of what's to be the best life I've yet to live.

Asher steps in front of the platform that's been created for my father and faces those who have traveled with us. When I turn around, I'm rendered speechless.

Nearly the whole pack is here to honor his life, and they're here for us. That's a kind of loyalty that can't be forced and proves my mate is more of a king than Gideon ever gave him credit for.

Noen and Declan move to stand next to us with Mali and a few of the other council members opposite to Asher as he speaks.

"Today has been a day of tragedy, but we end it in celebration," he says, his voice rough with unshed emotions. "Grayson Blackwood was one of the best of us. He served this pack well, always putting others before himself, even when life wasn't kind to him. This king never lost his way."

Asher pauses and looks at me, tears in both of our eyes as he continues. "Grayson will never be forgotten and, if he chooses not to return, his essence will live on through those he's left behind. Tonight, we honor him, we celebrate him, and we set him free."

Sorrowful cheers erupt through the crowd of our people as Estee and I step forward. Asher hands us the torches before lighting them and I sob uncontrollably for the first time that day. I can't hold in the pain any longer.

I nearly fall, but my sister grabs my hand and holds me up. "I've got you."

I thought earlier that I was going to need to be strong for everyone else, but this loss isn't on any one person. We'll bear the weight of this together, picking up the pieces as needed.

"Are you ready?" Asher asks through our bond.

"As much as I can be."

Only then does he ignite his own torch, signaling for us to say our final goodbyes.

Closing my eyes, I picture Dad's warm eyes. I remember that first day back when it was him who made me feel something for this place. Without that moment, I don't know what may have happened.

I love you more than I ever got to show you, Dad. Give Mom hugs from us every day.

Maybe that's why this is so hard because there's a part of me that doesn't believe he'll choose to return. More so, that part of me doesn't want him to. He deserves to be with his mate, resting, even if that means we're left missing them both.

Together, Estee and I set fire to our father's body, giving him the freedom to be at peace. Noen and Declan move to the end of the platform and begin pushing it into the water as we step back.

Asher steps in to help as the flames get bigger, enveloping the body without hesitation.

When the pyre is officially in the water, I hug Estee tightly and we cry together, mourning more than just the loss of a great man.

Asher is close by, continually reminding me how much he loves me through our bond, while also giving me space to be in this moment. At least that's what I sense until his love turns to fury, and I hear him snarl.

"What are you doing here?" he says, his chest rumbling at a stunning woman with long, red hair and wearing a slinky, blue dress.

"Is that the way to treat the goddess who saved your mate's life?" She clicks her tongue, then turns toward me, her violet eyes bright with delight. "I'm sorry about kissing him, but it was the only way to gift him the power that would save your life. I figured you'd understand."

"I don't think you've ever been sorry a day in your life." My canines beg to extend and I'm tempted to punch her in that smug, perfect face, but Estee's grip remains tight on my wrist, holding me back.

I don't stand a chance against a goddess and we both know that.

"Down, girl. Good puppy," she taunts, then she addresses me and Asher together. "Maybe it's from the bite, or the two of you have managed to catch me on a good day, but I have a present for you."

"We don't need anything from you," Asher says stiffly. "We made our deal and it's finished."

Aurora shakes her finger at him, light-purple energy swirling around her hand. "*You* don't get to decide when things are finished."

"If you hurt him…" I start to say, and her dark chuckle cuts me.

"Here I am trying to give you a gift and I'm being threatened." The power starts to extend up her arm, growing brighter. "Maybe I should just go and the next time your world is at risk, because there will be a next time, your call for help won't be answered."

"Are you offering us a gift, or another deal?" I ask, knowing with the gods, there is rarely anything ever given freely.

"A little of both." She winks at me. "You'll accept this gift and when the time comes, I will expect your cooperation by sharing your beasts with me. You see, that nibble Asher gave me earlier did exactly what I hoped, but it was temporary. When I require it, I will get all the nibbles I want. And if you deny me, I will burn this entire world to a crisp."

She says that last bit with a joy that tells me we have no choice here, and the rumble coming from Asher's chest confirms he understands the same.

Aurora claps her hands together. "Great. Now that we're all on the same page, how about that gift?"

I look around to see what she's talking about, but the only thing I notice is that nobody is moving. It's like time has frozen for everyone other than me, Asher, and this pain-in-the-ass goddess. Even my father's raft has ceased moving, the flames barely flickering.

Aurora's glow increases and the light covers her entire body, blinding me until I'm forced to close my eyes. When I can see again, I don't know how to believe what I'm seeing.

My parents stand on each side of her, both of them in one piece and...*alive*. Or so I think. They're not moving, but I can sense their warmth, even with the distance between us.

My heart soars and I want to run toward them, but my feet won't move. Hell, I can't move any part of my body except my head. One look at Asher and he appears to be in the same position.

"Now, listen," Aurora announces. "You see what I'm offering, and I know I said this was a gift, but we goddesses, we really prefer things to be done cleanly. Do I have your promise that when the time comes, you will lend your pack to me?"

"No," I answer first and while my reply kills me, I can't allow this to happen. "I won't sacrifice the lives of others to reverse what's already been done."

Her lips flatten and she speaks with disgust. "You wolves and your *hearts*. I don't understand, but fine. If I promise that none of them will be at risk, will you make the deal?"

"Yes." Asher answers first this time, then looks at me. "You deserve this, love. Take this second chance and let me worry about the pack." His gaze returns to the goddess. "At any point in the future, while I am still King of the Polaris pack, we are indebted to you for one favor in exchange for the lives of Florence and Grayson Blackwood. In order to repay this debt, none of the wolves will be at risk while they cooperate with your one-time request."

She looks him up and down and licks her lips. "It really is a shame you're spoken for. Your words are almost as good as your body. We have a deal." She blows him a kiss. "I'll be seeing you, Asher, King of Polaris."

As soon as the goddess disappears, Estee's grip releases my hand and I realize she was only holding me back because she was frozen. Before I can say anything, she gasps, her sobs returning tenfold. "How?"

"I'll explain later," I say, pushing her forward as we rush to hug our parents.

Mom's arms wrap around both of us. "Oh, my girls. You have no idea how much I've missed you."

There are too many tears to speak, but there is enough love flowing between the four of us that there isn't any need for words.

I see Asher over my mother's shoulder and his voice whispers through my mind. *Everything is going to be okay.*

"It's going to be more than okay," I tell him. *"It's going to be the way it was always meant to be."*

"Always and forever," he promises, and for the first time in five hundred years, we can finally have that again.

CHAPTER FORTY-TWO

ASHER

I t's only been a week since everything unraveled and then somehow came back together. There have been waves of discord within the pack, as I expected. While they all gathered without hesitation for Grayson, the next day, the whispers began.

At least this time, they're not about my mate.

I know we can handle whatever comes our way and that it will take time for the kingdom to settle, but that's thankfully something we have plenty of now.

Though I do still wonder about Aurora. I'm grateful for Isla to have her parents back—seeing my mate's bright smile again isn't something that can be replaced—but I don't like not knowing when the goddess might be back.

She's up to something and us being part of that in any way puts Lunara as a whole at risk. Whatever god she's plotting to piss off, I know there's a chance we could be collateral.

Still, that was a risk I had to take.

Not only for my mate, but for me as well.

Grayson had been like a father to me growing up. Isla and Estee wouldn't have been the only ones to grieve his loss for years to come. Not only that, but Florence was also my mother's best friend. This was a gift I wanted to give her as well.

Something that has been helpful every day since.

While my mother hasn't left her room since being brought to it after Gideon had been killed, she's at least begun to speak again and that is all thanks to Flo. Isla's mother has spent every minute she's not with her girls with my mother, helping to heal the fragmented pieces of her heart.

I'm not sure she'll ever be whole again, but I do hope that a day will come when she won't blame herself for not seeing what had become of her mate.

I find my mate standing in our closet, wearing a silver gown and adjusting the crown atop her head. The sight makes me grin from ear to ear. "Is my queen ready?"

Her shoulders relax and she turns, smiling back at me. "I believe she is. How about my king?"

Grabbing her hand, I pull her flush against my chest, mindful not let her dress get snagged on my suit. "I've never been more ready for anything in my life."

The pack has accepted Isla as their queen, but today is the ceremony that will officially bind her to them and them to her. She'll be able to communicate with them as I do and will formally become the Queen of Polaris, a crowned member of the Lunara monarchy.

The ceremony typically draws the attention of the other kings and queens of the islands, but only two of the three have shown. King Theo being the only other alpha not to show. A fact that surprises me, given his new role within the monarchy and something that I'll be following up on soon, but not today.

I take Isla's hand in mine and lead her out of our room. Noen and Declan are waiting for us when we exit our suite and bow for their queen as we pass.

"Seriously?" Isla groans. "I thought we talked about this."

"We must follow protocol, Your Majesty," Declan teases, ignoring my mate's earlier wishes.

Isla glares at them, then me. "When I'm officially queen, I'm changing protocol."

Kissing the side of her head, I grin. "Whatever you want, love." My stare meets Noen's, causing me to release Isla. "Will you give me a moment?"

She glances between the two of us and smiles warmly. "Take your time."

Declan offers her a hand, which she easily takes, even though he's been driving her crazy all day with his apologizing, then subsequent jokes about trying to kill her. Something that is much too soon to consider funny, but I also know humor is how Declan copes.

Once they're around the corner, I face Noen. "I received your transfer request today."

He holds my gaze and nods. "I'm sorry I didn't talk to you first, but I didn't want you to talk me out of it."

We've spoken every day since he was set free from the holding cell, and I've apologized each time. Still, I've known he wasn't okay, but Isla insisted that I give him space.

Noen clasps my shoulder. "This has nothing to do with you thinking I might have killed your mate, Asher. You're still one of my closest friends and I hope you'll remain that way, but seeing you and Isla back together... I want that."

I raise a brow, stepping back, but he continues before I can say anything.

"Not Isla." His face pinches. "Gods, definitely not her. I want *my* mate. She's out there somewhere and I'm going to find her. I know there's a chance to do that by staying put, but my wolf is restless. We need this."

That, I can understand.

"I have no intentions of denying the transfer," I tell him sincerely. "I just hope you never forget that you'll always have a home here with us, and if you ever need anything, I better be the first person that you call on."

The smile finally returns to his face. "Thanks, Ash. For everything, even for holding back when I knew you wanted to kill me. There was always a part of me that wondered if you'd ever truly forgiven me, but even if you didn't realize it, the moment you didn't immediately tear me to shreds that night, I knew there was a fighting chance and that I'd been right these five centuries."

I tilt my head. "Right about what?"

"That the gods were right." His eyes get brighter. "You were meant to be king and you're the perfect mate for Isla —you always have been. I'm just sorry I couldn't see that before she was taken from us."

"It's all in the past," I promise him. "Today, we're moving forward, as we should have done years ago."

"I like the sound of that." He glances back down the hallway. "I think your queen is waiting eagerly for you."

My gaze follows his to see a flash of Isla's silver dress. Of course she didn't go far.

"Let's go," I tell Noen as we walk to catch up.

My mate leans against the wall, whistling casually. "Oh. Hi."

I grab her by the waist and growl against her neck, letting my teeth lightly scrape over her skin. "Oh. Hi."

Noen goes on ahead with Declan and I unashamedly pin my queen against the wall. "Eavesdropping is very unqueenly," I tell her, holding her stare.

She keeps her chin up and grins. "Try to take this crown from my head and see what happens."

"I wouldn't dare." I steal a kiss then wink at her. "You're mine first and foremost, but just as I was born to be king, you were born to be my queen. Tonight is just formality."

Isla grips the lapels of my suit coat, bringing me closer. "We're going to do this together, and nothing will ever stand in our way again. It's me and you, forever and always, my love."

"Nothing has ever sounded more perfect."

EPILOGUE
ESTEE

Life is damn near perfect. After too many lifetimes of loneliness, I finally have everything back in my life that I thought I lost.

My sister is the Queen of Polaris, my parents are alive, together, and healthy, and I have my wolf.

While Isla has always been my sister, my inner animal was my first best friend. She's been my constant companion for every day I've been aware of her existence and since getting her back, I've done my best to show her how grateful I am for her presence.

We run at sunset throughout the forest beyond our home and I let her chase all the four-legged creatures her heart desires. The hunt brings her a joy that I hope she never loses and—

"Where are you at?" Isla's voice sounds within my mind, cutting off my thoughts.

"Out. Why?" Something sounds off with her and I don't like it.

It's only been a month since she was crowned queen and if someone is already threatening the kingdom…

"I need you to come to my room."

Shit. Something is wrong.

Sorry, Wolfie, I think. *Fun time is over.*

We circle back toward the castle and run until we get to the back door. When I shift back to my human form, I smooth my hands over my dark jeans and cream blouse, grateful that I'm once again living in the castle. I've not only taken over Isla's room, but half her wardrobe that she didn't want.

"Be right there," I tell her through our connection as I bound up the stairs inside the castle.

When I get to her door, I don't bother to knock. Being the queen's sister means there are few protocols I'm forced to follow, and I may or may not take advantage of that a little too often.

My sister stands from the desk she shares with Asher, holding a folded piece of paper. There's a crease between her brows as she fidgets with the note.

"What is it?" I ask, closing the door behind me.

"You're not going to like it." She gestures to the couch on her right.

I shrug as I take a seat, then hold my hand out. "Let me be the judge of that."

She places the letter in my palm, then stands beside me, shifting her weight from one foot to the other as I read.

King Asher and Queen Isla of Polaris,

First, my apologies for not making an

appearance at the queen's coronation. I do hope you understand the stress I'm under having only just recently taken on my role as king without much notice.

Though that's also the reason for my letter. I'm writing in hopes of having your cooperation in locating my future queen. As is my right as the King of Selaris, I hereby request that every unmated adult female within your kingdom be sent to my home by the end of the current moon cycle so that I may claim my mate.

Your cooperation in this matter will be rewarded with your pick of our next crop.

Please respond in kind at your earliest convenience.

Signed,
King Theo of Selaris

My eyes move from the slip of paper to Isla. "What are you going to do? This seems asinine to me. Why can't he come here instead of forcing dozens of women to travel the seas to him?"

In fact, the longer I consider the request, the more it makes my blood boil.

Isla finally sits next to me and grabs my hand.

"Oh, hell no," I say before she can get a word out. "I'm not going to answer that lazy king's demands."

"Estee."

My head shakes and I pull out of her grip. "Don't *Estee* me. This is crazy and you know it."

"You're the queen's sister," she tells me, as if I don't already know. "Venaris has already sent their women. If we refuse, it won't look good for Asher and me. Worse, I can't ask all the other unmated females in our pack to go, but not my own flesh and blood. I need you to set an example."

So much for being thankful to be the queen's sister.

I cross my arms and lean back on the couch. "I don't like you right now."

"I don't expect you to be happy, but just know I'm grateful." Her grin widens. "Who knows? Maybe you'll actually find your mate."

There's no stopping the gag that gets caught in my throat. "If the gods think pairing me with a king too weak or capable of leaving his own kingdom in the hands of his people is a good idea, the world is doomed already."

Isla's chuckle echoes through the room. "Maybe, but let's hope not. I'd like to live this life longer than a couple decades this time around."

Yeah, her and me both. Still, I shudder at the prospect of King Theo being my mate.

No way in hell is that happening.

Thank you so much for reading A Curse of Shadows! I hope you enjoyed Isla and Asher's story as much as I did writing it. If you did, please consider leaving a review on Amazon and/or Goodreads to let me know!

A Crown of Fates is the next book and is Estee and King Theo's story. Get ready for sparks to fly and tensions to rise with these two!
Their book is now available on Amazon, Audible, and in Kindle Unlimited!

In the meantime, flip the page for ways to stay in touch and talk all things Wolves of Lunara!

STAY IN TOUCH

Find Heather on Facebook:
Reader Group
Want to talk all things books and get updates before anyone else? Come hang with me in my reader group:
Heather Renee's Book Warriors

Author Page
Teaser and big updates are also posted here:
Heather Renee Author

Newsletter:
I send this out sporadically, so don't worry. You won't ever be spammed by me and you get a couple goodies when you sign up!
http://smarturl.it/HeatherReneeNL

ALSO BY HEATHER RENEE

Paranormal Romance Books:

The Mystics and Mayhem World—These series are connected by characters crossovers, but not the plots. You can read them in any order. Though, this is their timeline order.

Broken Court

A complete New Adult Urban Fantasy series featuring an unconventional and anti-heroine leading lady, a broody love interest, and a fae kingdom with a vile king.

Luna Marked

A complete New Adult wolf shifter series (dual POV) featuring a strong-willed leading lady and a patient, yet fierce alpha male.

Scorned by Blood

A complete New Adult Vampire series featuring a supernatural hunter and the sexy vampire bound to protect her no matter the cost.

Fated to the Wolf

A complete New Adult Witch and Wolf series (dual POV) featuring an abandoned witch, a rogue wolf, and their broken bond.

The Hidden Realm

A complete New Adult wolf and dragon shifter series (dual POV) featuring a feisty wolf shifter just looking for her freedom and a broody dragon trying to save his world.

Mystics and Mayhem Novels

This includes *Christmas Mates*, *Fractured Mates*, and *Shattered Mates*. Each book is a standalone and between the three stories, you'll find a holiday gathering with all the shenanigans, vengeance to be had, and risks to be taken.

The Ashmark Series

A new series that will release in 2026 featuring wolf shifters, fated mates, secret prophecies, a talking ferret, and a kooky grandma to keep you turning the pages!

Wolves of Lunara

A New Adult Romantasy trilogy with a murder mystery, fated mates, reincarnations, royalty, and swoon-worthy wolf shifters.

Raven Point Pack Series

A complete Upper Young Adult Paranormal Romance series featuring wolves, witches, vengeance, and fated mates.

Shadow Veil Academy

A complete Upper Young Adult Urban Fantasy Academy series featuring shifters, elves, witches, and more.

Elite Supernatural Trackers

A complete New Adult Urban Fantasy series featuring witches, demons, a smart-mouthed female lead, alpha males, and a snarky fairy sidekick.

Royal Fae Guardians

A complete Young Adult Urban Fantasy series featuring fae, magic users, a sweet romance, along with snark and humor.

Standalone Fantasy Books

Ignite Me - A spicy wolf shifter story featuring a lost heir, the mate who doesn't want her, and the enemies who wish them dead.

Cage Me - A spicy wolf shifter story featuring a shadow cursed wolf and a mate who's on the run.

Marked Paradox - A Young Adult fae story about a realm divided and one fae to bring them back together.

Contemporary Romance Books with Harper Reed:

The Wicked Duet

A mafia romance with enemies-to-lovers, forced proximity, and more than a bit of unaliving before there's a happily-ever-after.

Ruthless Truths

Tangled Deceit

The Unexpected Series

A Spicy RomCom trilogy featuring three best friends and their happily-ever-afters!

A Mutually Beneficial Proposal

A Mutually Beneficial Mistake

A Mutually Beneficial Secret

Standalone

A Royal Oops

A Spicy RomCom with royal antics, an epic second chance romance, and a kingdom that needs their new queen.

ACKNOWLEDGMENTS

This book was a beast, but in all the best ways. She pushed me beyond my limits, helped me grow, and became something so beautiful that I'm beyond of proud of!

While I wrote all the words, it wouldn't have been possible without the support of my people.

A big thank you to Michelle Fritz for always being my biggest cheerleader. I couldn't do this without you!

Another thank you to Malissa, Shannon, and Nat. My super squad who listens to all my crazy ideas and is always lifting me up!

Thank you to Jay Villalobos, my cover designer. You've been such an integral part of my release team with all your beautiful designs throughout the years! Thank you!!

And to all my readers, if you've made it this far, thank you for giving this new world a chance and helping to keep my dreams of writing alive!

Love and hugs,
Heather Renee

ABOUT THE AUTHOR

Heather Renee is a USA Today Bestselling author from Southern Oregon who writes Fantasy and Paranormal Romance packed with romance, humor, and the perfect amount of sass. She's best known for her wolf-shifter worlds, magical chaos, and the addictive escapism her readers have come to crave.

When she's not writing, Heather is exploring waterfalls with her husband and daughter, wrangling her pets, or tucked away with a good book. She loves hearing from her fellow book lovers—find more ways to connect with her at www.HeatherReneeAuthor.com.

www.ingramcontent.com/pod-product-compliance
Lightning Source LLC
Chambersburg PA
CBHW031642200726
48289CB00004BA/1186